NONE SHALL SLEEP

NONE SHALL SHALL SLEEP

ELLIE MARNEY

LITTLE, BROWN AND COMPANY
NEW YORK BOSTON

Copyright © 2020 by Ellie Marney

Cover art copyright © 2020 by Janelle Barone. Cover design by Karina Granda. Cover copyright © 2020 by Hachette Book Group, Inc.

Little, Brown and Company
Hachette Book Group
1290 Avenue of the Americas, New York, NY 10104
Visit us at LBYR.com

First Edition: September 2020

Little, Brown and Company is a division of Hachette Book Group, Inc. The Little, Brown name and logo are trademarks of Hachette Book Group, Inc.

The publisher is not responsible for websites (or their content) that are not owned by the publisher.

Library of Congress Cataloging-in-Publication Data
Names: Marney, Ellie, author.
Title: None shall sleep / Ellie Marney.
Description: First edition. | New York : Little, Brown and Company, 2020. | Audience: Ages 14+. | Summary: Eighteen-year-olds Emma Lewis and Travis Bell, recruited by the FBI to interview juvenile serial killers, must turn to a notorious teenage sociopath to help track down a new murderer.
Identifiers: LCCN 2019056594 | ISBN 9780316497831 (hardcover) | ISBN 9780316497800 (ebook) | ISBN 9780316497824 (ebook other)
Subjects: CYAC: Serial murderers—Fiction. | United States. Federal Bureau of Investigation—Fiction. | Criminal investigation—Fiction.
Classification: LCC PZ7.M34593 Non 2020 | DDC [Fic]—dc23
LC record available at https://lccn.loc.gov/2019056594

ISBNs: 978-0-316-49783-1 (hardcover), 978-0-316-49780-0 (ebook)

Printed in the United States of America

LSC-C

10 9 8 7 6 5 4 3 2 1

For all the scared, stubborn, angry girls

I think of the journey

we will take together

in the oarless boat

across the shoreless river.

Ursula K. Le Guin, "Travelers"

CHAPTER ONE

Edmund Cooper, federal agent, stands at the edge of the training field and looks up. There is flashing movement between the trees in the forested area beside the athletics oval. Ohio State University maintains an obstacle path in the woods there, and students sometimes run drills. Two students emerge from the tree line now. Cooper watches one of them carefully.

She's a very slight figure, her smallness exaggerated by a baggy gray OSU sweatshirt and black training pants cut off at the knees. She looks healthy. That's positive. In the photos from two and a half years ago she looked like a wreck. Now her cheeks are ruddy from exertion, her focus keen. She runs hard, though, the armpits of her sweatshirt stained dark. Her skin is white, but her legs are very tan.

And she's buzzed her hair. It's a regulation-style Number One, like you'd get in the corps, or in jail. Cooper tries not to read too much into that. He doesn't really know this girl, except for what he's seen in the file.

He waits by the edge of the oval as Emma splits from her running partner and talks with the coach. Patience is one of Cooper's particular talents.

She's heading for the locker rooms when he calls out. "Emma Lewis? Miss Lewis?"

It's there in her body language: that jerk, the instant of animal tension. The flat assessment in her eyes, even once she realizes he's wearing a suit, holding up credentials.

He stays exactly where he is. "Miss Lewis, my name is Edmund Cooper. I work for the government. I'd like to speak with you, if I may. Somewhere public, if that is your preference."

It's okay if he sounds rehearsed. Formal and polite is fine. Emma waits a few beats, then takes the business card he's holding out. Cooper is reminded of feeding deer off the back of his mother's porch in New England.

"You work for the government?" She's still perspiring after the run, but her breathing is already back under control. She glances at the card, at him. "You're a federal agent, this says."

"That's correct. I work for the Federal Bureau of Investigation."

She makes a single styptic blink. "I don't have any more information about the Huxton case. I've told the police everything I know—"

"No, no," he says. "Miss Lewis, this meeting is not in regard to that case. This is unrelated. Can we perhaps sit down somewhere to talk?"

Hesitation before she relents. "Sure. Uh—here is fine, I guess."

She directs him to a picnic table in a grassy open area beside the equipment shed. Nice and public, but with enough distance for privacy. It's sunny, though. He's sweating a little in his jacket.

Emma has a towel draped around her neck and a canteen on the table to her right. The dark stubble on her scalp is like a fine down.

It suits her, actually. She looks compact, contained. Fierce. Cooper makes sure to sit across from her at the table, give her space.

"Thank you for speaking with me. It's nice to meet you."

She doesn't respond to that. "Did you fly from Virginia?"

"No, I drove."

"That's a long drive."

"Yes, it is. You study psychology here at OSU, is that right? Hoping to specialize in pediatric psychology? Your professor said you were inspired by a positive experience with an excellent therapist—"

"Yes." She tilts her head, lets the sun fall on her face. "Mr. Cooper, why have you come to see me?"

Time to plunge in. "Miss Lewis, have you heard of the Behavioral Science section of the FBI?"

"Yes." Her gaze is direct. "They do psychological assessments—profiles. They did a profile on Huxton."

"We help in cases like that, yes. Violent crimes. Behavioral Science is a young area—we've been working active cases for less than a decade. But we seem to be one of the sections producing results."

"You catch killers."

She's quick. He knew she was quick. "We look at the evidence and the information we have and try to figure out a pattern of behavior. Once we have a pattern, it allows us to narrow down suspects, even predict what a perpetrator might do next. It helps us find them faster."

"Okay."

He understands the change in her expression straightaway.

"It's not one-hundred-percent accurate, Miss Lewis. Nothing is. We just do our best. But our success rate is generally high." *Not with Huxton. Huxton was a mess.* Cooper buckles that shit down. It's not helpful here. "The reason we're successful is because we do our homework. We go into jails and institutions and interview the perpetrators we incarcerate. It's a lot like a research project. The information we gather is compiled in a database and used to inform our profiling work."

"Great." Emma's posture is very stiff.

There are times Cooper wishes he still smoked. He could light a cigarette, look more normal, relaxed. If you seem to relax, it relaxes the subject.

"Miss Lewis, we've interviewed about thirty-five incarcerated perpetrators from all over the country. But there's a cohort of people we still don't have access to. And it's not because we can't see them. They just . . . won't speak to us." He's been looking at her, but now he really looks. "I'm talking about juvenile offenders."

The OSU Buckeyes cheer squad is rehearsing on the other side of the oval. Cooper hears the rallying calls as a far-off stir of echoes.

"Juvenile killers." Emma rolls the syllables in her mouth. Then she reaches for the canteen and takes a swig, like she's washing away the taste. "There can't be many teenage serial killers, though."

"There's enough." He doesn't want to come in hard, but he's getting the feeling she responds better to that. "Everyone starts somewhere."

"Like it's a career." She looks toward the oval.

"Bundy started at fourteen."

She stares at him. She looks very young. He resists the instinct to be gentle. They need this. Her, or someone like her. There aren't many people like her.

"Miss Lewis, we think the reason these teenage offenders won't talk to us is because they distrust authority figures, including our interviewers. And this is why I've come to speak with you. We need someone to—"

"No." She shifts, ready to rise.

"Five inmates. Five interviews, total."

"Ha. Still no."

"You would have support. A partner. A unit. It would be entirely safe—"

"Is that what you think?" She stands. "Mr. Cooper, you've come a long way, but you're asking the wrong person."

"I don't believe I am. And I'd like you to think about what I'm offering."

Her jaw locks and she breathes out her nose. "Okay. What are you offering?"

He keeps his voice even. "The chance to come in on a kind of scholarship. You'd defer your summer classes and come live on base with us over the break. You'd be paid as a candidate and given some bureau instructional training. If forensic psychology is something you decide to pursue, you could enter our program. Your education after your freshman year would be subsidized. Or if not, you could return here to complete any further units in pediatric psychology."

"That…" She sinks back down. "That sounds very generous. I suppose I don't need to ask why me."

"Mostly, it's because you're the right age. But you're also studying in a field of undergraduates we're already interested in. You have the academic background, you're top of your class—"

"And I have first-hand experience of the subject."

"That is only one of a number of considerations." For the first time, he leans forward. "We're looking for a certain mindset, Miss Lewis. These interviews…Every piece of information we gather helps us. And every time our knowledge increases, we get faster. Save more lives."

The "saving lives" line was heavy-handed. He still thinks that's how he'll win her.

She narrows her eyes. "I've spent two and a half years trying to get out of that mindset, Mr. Cooper."

"Do you think you've succeeded?"

Her expression doesn't change, but he sees it again: that flare of animal panic in her face. But it is sometimes his job to do hateful, necessary things.

She looks away from him, looks around at the grass, at the trees and buildings. Then she gets to her feet, slowly this time, as if the conversation has aged her. "Mr. Cooper, I appreciate what you're doing. But I don't think I can help you. I hope you have a safe drive home."

"You're driving home yourself, is that right? Back to Apple Creek?" He rises to match her. "Would you please think about what we've discussed over the weekend?"

"I'll think about it." She retrieves her canteen.

"You have my card, if you need to call. Thank you for your time."

"Goodbye, Mr. Cooper."

He watches her walk away, dark head bobbing, sun glaring off the white of her running shoes. They're good-quality shoes.

His pager beeps at him. He walks back up the rise, to the bus stop area above the oval, where there's a pay phone, and calls collect. "Cooper."

FBI section chief Donald Raymond sounds pissed even at a distance. "I call down to your office, they tell me you're in Columbus. What the fuck are you doing in Ohio, Ed?"

Cooper's habit is to always respond to Raymond with calm. "Don, we talked about this."

"I thought you were kidding. You're not kidding? You seriously want to send an eighteen-year-old girl into maximum security prisons to interview serial murderers?"

"She won't be going in alone."

"Oh, right, sure. She'll be going in with your other candidate, what's-his-name... Travis Bell, who's—" There's the sound of Raymond flicking through file notes. "Who's not even old enough to buy a beer. That's great, Ed."

"Don, we tried sending agent interviewers in to see these prisoners. You could hear crickets three states away. If we send in teenage interviewers, at least we'll have tried something different. And these aren't green kids, remember. They're veterans."

"This Lewis girl," Raymond says. "She survived the Huxton thing, right? How many did Huxton do? Nine?"

"Nine," Cooper confirms.

"So number ten got lucky."

Through the plexiglass of the phone booth, Cooper tracks Emma's retreating figure. "It had nothing to do with luck. She didn't get rescued. She fought. Escaped."

"Okay, so she's a soldier. Same as this Travis Bell. He's Barton Bell's kid? From the Gutmunsson case? Jesus."

"Yes." Cooper pauses, so they can both give the Gutmunsson incident the moment of somber contemplation it deserves. "Bell went into USMS training soon as they let him. Takes after his dad, the instructors are saying."

"Good for him." Raymond pauses. "This is gonna be a tough gig, Ed. You really want to send these kids back into the nightmare?"

Raymond is not known in the bureau for his insight. This is the first insightful thing he's said since the conversation started and Cooper runs with it, speaks now with the terrible authority of battlefields served. "After a thing like that, Don, I don't think the nightmare ever lets you go. You just get better at dealing with it. These two are dealing with it. Let's give them a chance to help."

Raymond huffs. "All right, then. You want to give it a try, you let it run. But listen to me, Ed. This is a one-time pass. They come in, they do the work, claim their per diem, go home. I find out they've overstepped, or I hear one single whisper about this in the press, and I'll pull the plug so fast you'll hit your chin on the drain hole going down. Are we perfectly clear?"

"Sir, yessir." Cooper finds himself slipping into his old Marine disciplines when something sticks in his craw.

"Now, any updates on Pennsylvania? Carter said there were two bodies this time."

"That's correct. I'm still waiting on forensics—I'll give you a full report when I return to base."

"All right, keep me in the loop. Goddammit, these monsters just keep multiplying like the fucking Hydra." The sound of Raymond's pen clicking. "Did the Lewis girl even agree to come on board?"

"She's getting back to me." Cooper can't be sure Lewis will

8

accept, or that she'll be capable of doing what he needs her to do. She's just a kid. But he remembers the way she looked around at the university buildings and the training fields, like she was memorizing them. He thinks she'll bite.

"I get Bell," Raymond is saying. "Bell makes sense. But I don't know about this girl."

Cooper is aware that whatever he says right now, he has to believe it.

"Emma Lewis has experience with these types of offenders. She understands the way they think and behave. She's not fooled by them—she knows what they are." He thinks of Emma's dark-stained sweatshirt, her twitchy reactions. Her bright, fierce eye. "We can't be sure until she settles in. But I think she'll do just fine."

CHAPTER TWO

In the lonely hours of the morning, Emma jerks awake in the dark, gasping.

It takes her a few moments to remember where she is, to get the outlines of her body solid. She's all right. She's home. Her T-shirt is damp. She's safe. *Breathe.*

She lies there with her eyes open, listening to the sound of katy-dids outside. She hasn't had a bad dream in months. This dream was not Cooper's fault, although it's hard not to feel resentful. Emma allows herself to clutch the resentment tight for the space of a few heartbeats, then deliberately releases. It's okay to acknowledge the emotions, but that sort of thinking is not useful to her.

She flicks the switch on the lamp on the nightstand, throws off the bedclothes, and goes to change her shirt and collect her robe.

Downstairs, the kitchen of her parents' house is lit up like always. Emma fixes herself a glass of milk with one of her mother's choc-chip cookies. She's just sat down at the kitchen island when her older sister, Roberta, shuffles in.

"Don't eat all the cookies."

"It's after midnight," Emma points out. "*Teen* magazine says I can eat as many cookies as I want after midnight."

"*Teen* magazine..." Roberta humphs, opening the fridge for the milk. She's pulled a quilted nylon dressing gown over her men's flannel pajama pants and Blondie T-shirt. "Fine, but you've gotta help me bake replacements tomorrow."

"I can do that."

"I'm bummed you're not staying the whole week."

"Eh, summer classes."

"Eh."

Emma eats her cookie. Robbie pours milk into a glass and returns the carton, careful not to bang the fridge door closed. If the door bangs, it jostles the Boston fern their mother has balanced in a saucer on top of the fridge.

"You're not gonna tell Mom and Dad about the fed guy, are you?" Robbie finally says.

"It's not worth freaking them out." Emma goes to the sink, takes an empty glass from the draining board, and half fills it with water. "He just wanted to ask me something."

"New set of questions?"

"No, weirdly enough." Emma walks to the fridge and balances on tiptoe to pour the water from the glass into the soil around the fern. "It was more like...a job interview."

"No shit." Robbie leans against the counter and sips her milk. "That's different."

"Right?"

"I still wouldn't tell Mom and Dad. They will most definitely freak."

Emma places the glass in the sink. "It was just a conversation. I said no."

"Is that why you're down in the kitchen after midnight, eating cookies?"

"Hey, you're here with me."

Robbie grins. "I'm providing moral support."

Emma knows this is only partially true. Her sister developed insomnia when Emma went missing. Even two and a half years after her return, Robbie's sleep problems have lingered. The toll hasn't just been on Emma. For a while there, it was like the whole family needed therapy.

"I said no," Emma repeats gently.

Robbie nods. She picks up her glass and heads toward the hall. "They flew a fed guy from Virginia to speak with you? Can't fault them for effort."

"He drove." Emma picks at the crumbs from her cookie. "He drove from Virginia, he didn't fly."

"Man, that's a drive." Robbie pushes back her mass of dark hair with one hand. Emma had hair like that once. "He must've really wanted that conversation."

Her sister waves, then wanders back to her room along the hall. Emma sits on her stool, staring at the cookie crumbs, the Boston fern, the pendant light above the kitchen island. Cooper drove from Virginia. Suddenly she knows what it signifies. *I will go the extra mile for you*, it says. *I wouldn't ask a recruit to do anything I wouldn't do myself.*

He expects her to drive back in return. He was telling her the way is open.

On Saturday morning, Emma helps Robbie bake replacement cookies and helps her mother plant seedlings—petunias, mostly—in flower boxes around the house. Then she goes to the barn, where her father is cleaning the air filter on the tractor.

"How's it going, Emma Anne?"

She's careful to reply without hesitation. "All good, Dad."

"The Rabbit's running okay? It's probably due for a new carburetor."

"The carburetor's fine, Dad. The car's holding up."

"Glad to hear it. You wanna pass me that can of Dust-Off on the bench?"

She passes him the Dust-Off, and later, there's a family dinner. Everything about being home is comfortable and safe. Except for the fervency of her mother's mealtime grace blessing, it's like the world never changed.

Hours later, when Emma's wrenched up in bed, choking, she realizes the thin, high tinnitus in her head is not tinnitus. And it's not just going to go away.

She changes her shirt in the dark, pads downstairs. Slips a fresh cookie from the tin and encourages herself to consider the problem from all angles.

Cooper talked about a partner, a unit. The idea of being part of a team is tempting. It's the isolation of the thing that eats away at you: being alone on the island of the mind. The number of people who have brushed up against what she's experienced and are still breathing, still functioning, is almost infinitesimal.

So the concept is appealing: a team of other people to bounce ideas off, to share misgivings, to share the load. But Emma has no sense of what such a team might look like.

And that horseshit about saving lives... Emma used to think she could've saved the others—the other girls—if only she'd run faster, gotten help quicker. But on her therapist's suggestion she read the police report on Huxton, and she doesn't believe that anymore. She's wary of that response in herself now. She's alert to guilt. Guilt doesn't help anybody.

So it's not guilt tugging at her with tiny hooks, she tells herself, but rather the idea of the research. New information is the key. If she could play a part in gathering that information, if they could spot these guys more accurately, find them more quickly... then yes, other potential victims might be spared.

Emma sits under the pendant light for some time. Then she uses the phone in the kitchen, with the long curly cord. The call picks up after two rings.

"Cooper." His voice is raspy but he sounds alert.

"I'm in."

"Miss Lewis?"

"I'm in," she says. "I'll join the project, the unit, whatever it's called. But I won't join the bureau. I want to go back to OSU once the interviews are done."

She hangs up, not waiting for his reply. Immediately, she feels a sensation like her soul is flying out of her chest.

Only when she catches sight of the digital clock on the microwave does she realize it's three thirty in the morning.

CHAPTER THREE

After some initial fretting, Emma wears jeans and a white T-shirt and running shoes for her first visit to Quantico, because that's what she'll feel normal in.

There are lots of oak and maple trees around the parking area on the base. She slows her car for runners, training groups of guys in black gym shorts and regulation gray sweatshirts. It's been three days since she herself ran, and she feels it like a twitch in her thighs and the balls of her feet.

Once she's parked, she sits in the car thinking about Robbie's parting hug, and going through the instruction notes from the second phone call with Cooper. *MPs at checkpoints have your name. Park outside Jefferson. Ask at the desk for Behavioral Science.* Yesterday she drove six and a half hours to reach Virginia, and she's still not sure she really wants to be here. She stares at the buildings until the heat gathering between the windshield and the dash forces her out.

The Jefferson building is much cooler. Lots of people in khakis and dark polo shirts in the foyer. The man at the desk directs her to a bank of elevators, and the basement offices.

The basement, she thinks. Of course it has to be in the goddamn basement.

The elevator door opens onto low ceilings with concrete coffers, pipes for heating, pipes for air-conditioning, cable chases. The corridors are disconcertingly similar and anonymous. Lots of white and gray cinder block, fluorescent lighting, like a nuclear bunker or a morgue.

There are a few people in suits in the corridors, all moving with purpose. At the end of a hallway, behind a glass door, a woman at another desk.

"Please wait. An agent will be with you shortly." The receptionist extends a hand to the other side of the tiny foyer, which is the entry to the suite of offices beyond.

There are no chairs, but the opposite wall is decorated with a board of FBI Most Wanted posters. A guy stands facing them, hands on hips, pushing back the fall of his windbreaker.

Emma stands nearby and checks her watch. Cooper said ten, and it's edging toward ten past. She could've come at ten thirty, slept in an extra half hour.

Last night's motel off Route 1 turned out to be seedier than she would've liked, but the woman in the diner poured her extra coffee. It was probably on account of her hair, Emma thinks. She wears a scarf over it occasionally, which makes her look like a cancer patient. She's found that it's sometimes better to look like a cancer patient than to deal with random strangers sneering at her.

Yesterday she wore her scarf. Now she's here without it, in the foyer of Behavioral Science, as the boy to her right continues his contemplation of the Most Wanted posters. He has pressed cargo pants and his collar is stiff and neat. He checks his watch, and Emma realizes they are both waiting. This is a waiting area, though. There are many offices. She wonders why Cooper didn't have her directed to wait in his.

Emma anchors herself in the solid press of her feet on the concrete floor, her hands in her pockets, shoulders square. She's relieved to find herself steady, holding firm.

Then she rubs a hand across her head and it arrives: She has not seen anyone in this building so far who is younger than their midtwenties. She is young. The guy beside her is young. They could be the only young people in the building, and they are both waiting here.

When she turns, he is already looking at her.

"I'm thinking...I'm thinking maybe we should introduce ourselves," he says.

He has very dark hair and eyes, olive skin. He holds out his hand.

"Bell, Travis J." He doesn't squeeze her fingers out of existence. It's a short, professional handshake. "I'm waiting on Special Agent Cooper and I believe you might be, too."

"I am. I mean, yes. I'm Emma Lewis."

"Pleased to meet you."

"Likewise."

She absorbs his accent: southern, probably Texas with that laconic delivery, and if she had to guess she'd say army brat or law enforcement trainee. After the handshake, they return to standing side by side, like a pair of trout who've somehow found themselves swimming together against the current. Through the glass door, Emma sees a figure approaching. When she straightens, Bell does the same and speaks out of the corner of his mouth.

"Were you told about a unit? I was told there was going to be a unit."

Emma presses her lips. "I think we're the unit."

Cooper has already breached the door.

"Miss Lewis, Mr. Bell." He shifts the folders he's carrying and shakes their hands in turn. Emma finds it easier to take his hand here, in a formal setting. "You've already been introduced? Thank you both for coming. There's a place for us to talk—please follow me."

He leads them, not toward the offices as Emma had anticipated, but back out to the hallway. Cooper's walk is brisk, military; otherwise, he is just a slight, Caucasian man in a regulation suit who looks more like an accountant than an FBI agent. He steers their course farther along and then around a corner into another corridor.

"Why aren't we talking in your office about this?" Emma asks.

Cooper stops at the door to a room. He unlocks it, opens it, gestures for them to enter. "Because my office—like every office in Behavioral Science—is covered in paperwork about active cases, which is something you're not allowed to see."

The room they've entered is large, gray, and dim. There's a wooden desk, four folded metal chairs with cushioned seats, an office lamp on the desk, two large filing cabinets. More than a dozen cardboard file boxes are stacked on the floor and against two walls.

"We can only see information on cold cases," Bell says. It's not a question. Emma notices how straight his posture is and wonders if *upright* translates to *uptight*.

Cooper nods. "This unit is not concerned with active cases. That's a bureau directive, by the way. You're only researching perpetrators who've been convicted and are serving sentences."

"And we're the unit, aren't we?" Emma wants to know for sure.

"Yes," Cooper confirms.

Bell, Travis J., turns his head and looks at Emma, and Emma

finds something she wasn't expecting in that look. *You were right*, his eyes say. Unusual to meet a guy who'll admit that.

"Okay." Cooper points to the groupings of file boxes. "Subject one, Clarence McMurtry. Subject two, Michael Gesak. Subjects three, four, five... I've made up a summary for each subject so you won't need to review all these files, although they're here for extra research. But I think it's better if you relate to the subjects as teenagers. I'd like you to go in with an open mind."

"When do we go in?" Bell asks.

"Your first interview is scheduled for tomorrow."

Fuck, Emma thinks, but what she says is "That's soon."

"Yes." Cooper makes no apology for it, and Emma liked him better when he was pussyfooting around her during his first approach at OSU. "Grab a chair, that's it, any of those chairs is fine. Here's the summary for McMurtry. These folders have the questionnaires— the pink one is for the interviewer, the blue one is for the subject, if he consents to fill it out."

Bell hunkers forward on his chair, lifts the cover on the folder holding the pink pages. "So we go to the facility, follow the admission processes, and we get, what, an interview room?"

Cooper nods. "You'll be provided with identification—the interview times are already set up. You go in, conduct the interview, write up your report, and submit it with your travel receipts. It should be pretty straightforward."

This is all happening very fast. Emma thought there would be more preamble.

"Back up a little," she says. "These interviews... This is the second run at them, is that right?"

"That's correct," Cooper says.

"What went wrong the first time?"

"The subjects . . . I explained this with you. They don't talk to us."

"They refuse to speak? They clam up?"

Cooper grimaces, undoes the button on his suit jacket. "Sometimes it's like that. They withdraw. You can see the shutters roll down. Other times they reply in monosyllables. Swear. Whine. Last time we tried to interview McMurtry, he gave us a long diatribe about his treatment in prison—everything up to and including the quality of the toilet paper."

"But nothing about the murders," Emma says.

"That's right."

"And that's the information you need."

"We need details. What was their state of mind prior to each crime, what were they thinking about. How did they select their victims, what preparations did they make, if any. We don't really expect any useful insight into motive from teenage subjects. Half the time they don't know why they're doing what they're doing. But information about preparation, process, aftermath . . . that's all stuff we can use."

Emma watches Cooper's face as he speaks and notices the cold in her fingertips. The room itself is cold, and in its emptiness she can hear the humming echo of the air-conditioning. Her chest feels tight. She's about to go into prisons and talk to people like Huxton. No—Huxton was forty-two. She'll be talking to teenage versions of Huxton, then.

It occurs to her again that she has almost no understanding of her *own* motive in this situation. Why is she doing this?

Bell fills the silence. "We'll do our best, sir. What time should we—"

A knock on the door before it opens. The woman from Behavioral

Science—the receptionist from the foyer—walks in and hands Cooper a folded note on yellow memo paper.

Cooper scans the note, rises, re-buttoning his jacket. "Excuse me, I've been called away. Tomorrow's interview is at Beckley. That's a four-and-a-half-hour drive, and you'll need to report here at oh eight thirty tomorrow morning and collect materials before you leave. Don't forget to keep your receipts."

"Wait, what?" Emma starts to lift from her chair. "My suitcase is still in the trunk of my car—"

Cooper turns to the receptionist. "Betty, would you mind, with these two?" The woman nods. She is a white woman, about sixty, her hair blue-rinsed and perfectly coiffed. Cooper glances at Emma and Bell again as he walks toward the door. "Talk to Betty about photo IDs and dorm allocations. Unpack, get settled. I'll speak to you again tomorrow, after the interview."

He and Betty leave. Emma stares.

Bell gathers the folders, straightens them carefully. "He's under the gun. There's an active case in Pennsylvania—"

"Are you apologizing for him?" When Bell doesn't reply, Emma sits back in her chair. "How do you know about active cases?"

"It's been in the news. Don't you read the news?"

"No."

"You need to get out more."

She turns to shoot back, before realizing his eyes are amused, his lips twitching. A sense of humor. Maybe this guy isn't a zero-personality FBI cipher after all. "I just drove four hundred miles to interview a bunch of teenage crazy folk. You don't think that qualifies?"

He looks at the folders and smiles. "Sounds like you're just getting warmed up."

He is one of those people whose entire face and demeanor are transformed by smiling, Emma discovers. Then he sobers and taps the folders.

"You thought we'd be eased into this," he says, "but that's not how it works. I've got a law enforcement background, I know the life—they throw you into the deep end. And I'd lay fifty dollars on Cooper wanting to get these interviews done before this Pennsylvania thing blows up, and the manpower and budget are transferred."

She sighs. "So he's not being an asshole on purpose, he's just under pressure."

"In the FBI, always," he says gravely.

She collects the folder with McMurtry's summary off the desk. "Okay, then."

Bell stands. "Okay, then. Now I guess we go see Betty."

Later that night, after she has been photographed, allocated, processed, after she's unpacked her small suitcase in her gray-carpeted dorm room in the Jefferson building, after she's eaten a cafeteria dinner, filled out more paperwork, lain down at last on the polyester comforter on her new single bed, Emma wonders how two men, Cooper and Bell, find their purpose in hunting serial murderers.

Cooper likes the challenge, the puzzle, she decides. With his alert stillness and fastidious manners, he reminds her of a fox.

Bell is different—he relates to her differently. She thinks he might have sisters. Tomorrow she'll find out. Tomorrow she'll see if they can make this "unit" thing work, and that is her last thought before exhaustion claims her.

CHAPTER FOUR

They take Bell's car to Beckley. Emma doesn't trust her Rabbit—she loves it, but she has realistic expectations, and driving to Virginia seems to have overtaxed the engine somehow.

Bell's driving a Dodge pickup; it's in good shape and it has air-conditioning. They've had the radio tuned to some local station, and now Bell has switched to the news. They're fast approaching Lexington, where Emma is hoping for coffee and pie and a clean women's bathroom.

"So you've been in pre-US Marshal training for a year?"

"Ten months." Bell shrugs. "My birthday's in August. I basically started the program the day after I turned eighteen."

Bell has brown-tinted aviator sunglasses on and the driver's side window rolled down. Sunlight dashes itself against the white of his shirt. His suit trousers still look neat after three hours on the road and his jacket is on a hanger behind them. At least he's left off the tie until they get to the prison. Emma thinks he drives like she expected, staying exactly at the speed limit.

A folder of paperwork lies open over her knees. She's been reading Cooper's summary on McMurtry out loud, and she and Bell have talked awhile. Cooper is canny, she realizes. One road trip is a better get-to-know-you than a thousand formal handshakes at Quantico.

"Living away from home is tough," Emma notes.

"It is." Bell takes off his glasses and rubs his eyes with his knuckle, suspends the glasses off the neck of his shirt. "But being away for LEO training is no different than being away for college, I guess."

"I go to college in my home state, though. Wisconsin's a long way from Texas."

"That's true. But Texas won't let you start until you're twenty."

"How did you get recruited for this? If you don't mind me asking," she adds quickly. "Cooper said everyone on this detail had some kind of experience with, uh—"

"My dad was a US Marshal. He was murdered by a serial offender." Bell keeps his face forward, eyes trained out the windshield. "It was during an arrest. There was a situation, and my father was involved, and he got stabbed."

"Oh." She feels a little winded. "Jesus. I'm sorry."

"It's all right. You asked—it's all right to ask. It was two years ago."

"Okay."

"We've gotta know this stuff about each other if we're gonna work together."

"Right. Yeah." She nods at the folder in her lap, closes it, and places it on the bench seat between them. Sweat in her palms at the prospect of talking about this. "Well. I'm the only survivor of the Daniel Huxton case. He was the guy in Ohio who—"

"I know," Bell says. "You don't have to tell me. I know about it."

"You do?" Emma wishes her heart would stop beating so fast. "Ah, of course you do. You read the news." She looks out the window and tries not to think about it. Tries to think of something nice: her mother and the petunias, the soft black loam in the flower boxes.

"I remember," he says. "My dad put the newspaper in front of me at the breakfast table and said, 'This is what real bravery looks like.' I paid attention." When Emma doesn't reply, he continues. "You'd just turned sixteen. You fought off Huxton, escaped, then found help and led the police team back up the mountain to the location."

"It wasn't..." Thinking about petunias isn't working. Emma reaches for her inner gyroscope. "It sounded really straightforward in the media. It wasn't."

"It never is," Bell says. "There was a standoff, right? And Huxton shot himself."

"He..." Her breath is thin, like she's at high altitude. "He was, um..."

"I understand. You don't have to go over it. It's okay." Bell looks at her, looks away. "It was messy, right? Every situation like that is messy."

"Yeah." *He doesn't need me to explain.* The relief of that makes her light-headed, but Emma keeps her eyes on him. She finds the sight of his profile steadying. "You get through it, though."

"That's right. You get through it."

This small agreement between them is calming. Which is good, because at the end of this road there is Beckley, and Emma's nerves are plucking at her. She reminds herself this was her choice. She chose to do this, and she's sure the reason why will come clear in time.

For now, the late May air is rushing by her from the open window, the sun warming her face and shoulders, and they've got the war-wound talk out of the way.

They're coming into the outskirts of the town, so there's more traffic. Emma looks out at the colors in the foliage by the roadside and presses her palms flat onto her knees. "Why do you think Cooper sent us to McMurtry first? I mean, we could've seen Gesak, or Campinelli. Their prisons are both closer to Quantico by about a hundred miles."

Bell reaches to turn down President Reagan's voice on the radio, his focus not straying from the road. "Beckley is only medium security, with a work camp. McMurtry is one of the younger subjects, and he's in a more comfortable environment. He might be less hardened, easier for us to talk to. I mean, Cooper said he spent some time complaining about the toilet paper."

"Mouthy. Great." Emma grimaces. Not that she's expecting any of the subjects to be Mr. Personality.

"If he's talkative, that's better for us. We just need to direct the flow of the conversation." Bell lifts one shoulder. "But hey, I'm just spitballing about Cooper's motivations. Maybe he picked the file closest to his desk."

"I don't think he would do that," Emma says slowly. "He's particular. And I get the impression he's reasonably good at his job."

Bell nods, checks his side mirrors as they come off the interstate. "He knows this assignment is going to be tough. It's in his best interest to ease us in with a softball subject before we get to the hard stuff."

"You said you're a Marshal candidate, but you seem to know a lot about FBI procedure."

"Like I said, I know the life. My dad used to talk about working with other agencies. He admired the bureau. Said they trained hard." Bell shrugs again. "I'm used to law enforcement. I guess it must seem weird to a civilian."

Emma snorts. "My dad is a third-generation farmer and my mom's a grade-school teacher. They watch *The Love Boat*, not *Hill Street Blues*—they're about as far from law enforcement as you can get. The only time I ever dealt with the FBI was after Huxton."

"There's a Waffle House up here on the right," Bell says, indicating with his chin. "I'm gonna pull over. So did the FBI treat you okay after Huxton?"

Bell seems like a true believer so she doesn't want to be too critical of the FBI, but she can't help a certain sharpness of tone. "They were polite. Respectful. But they were still trying to figure out what went wrong. They questioned me pretty thoroughly. And then they kept coming back with more questions when I just wanted to put it all behind me."

As she gets out of the pickup, Emma feels that twitch in her legs again—she's spent too much time in cars over the past three days.

"So did they figure it out, why Huxton wasn't arrested earlier? What went wrong?" Bell locks the truck, shrugs on his jacket as they walk.

"They had some circumstantial evidence but nothing solid."

"The same thing that went wrong with Bundy."

"I haven't read much about Bundy. He was smart, right? Educated? Huxton wasn't smart like that, but he had animal cunning—he covered his tracks. And the FBI didn't know about the mountain house. They were chasing their tails." That sharpness again. But Emma likes her sharpness—it's kept her alive. "Then two more girls went missing. And then he caught me."

"And you brought him down."

"It was a group effort." She pulls open the door to the restaurant.

They order coffee and food, and Emma uses the bathroom. It's clean enough. They eat at the counter. The pie is not as good as she hoped, so she smothers it with cream.

"So, this interview," Bell says, finishing his waffles. "We got a plan for that? Or did you want to play it by ear?"

Emma hesitates. "Not sure."

"Are you going to cope with the interview okay?"

She hasn't wanted to express those doubts to herself, so she's surprised Bell picked up on them. "I don't know. I hope so. Are you?"

He nods. "It'll be uncomfortable. But I usually find I feel better going into an uncomfortable situation if I've got a plan. Then I've got something to fall back on if I need it."

"A plan like what? Good cop, bad cop?"

"Maybe. Do you think that'd work with a guy like McMurtry?"

Why is Bell deferring to her on this? Emma blinks with the realization: It's because he thinks she's an expert. *Three days of horror in a serial killer's basement—that's all it takes to make you an expert.* Jesus. She toughs out the urge to vomit or cry, takes a breath. Chases the last of the cream around with her spoon, considering the question.

"I think McMurtry will have had plenty of adult officers trying to nail him down with questions. I think we should keep it conversational."

"Okay. Sounds good." Bell smiles softly. "I don't know how to run good cop, bad cop anyway. That was more my dad's thing—he and my mom used it on me more times than I can remember."

Emma's voice gentles. "You were close with your dad?"

"Yeah." He looks at his plate. "It's kinda weird, doing this. Wearing his suit, working the job. But it's what I always wanted."

"Is your family okay with you going into training, after what happened to your dad?"

"I guess." Bell leans his forearm on the counter and sips his coffee. Even without the tie, he really couldn't look more like a cop if he tried. "My mom's fine with it. She understands. One of my sisters keeps getting on my case about it, though."

"How many sisters?"

"Two. Both younger."

Gotcha. Emma raises a finger. "One older."

"Your family getting by okay, after what happened?"

She shrugs. "They're okay."

"And how do you get by?" Bell keeps his eyes on his coffee when he asks, as though the question isn't important.

"I run." *On the earth, and sometimes in my dreams.* Emma doesn't voice that thought.

He meets her gaze. "I lift. Hit the weights, hit the bag. It helps."

"Running definitely helps. Sometimes you need to funnel the energy somewhere. When my mind starts looping, I run through it."

He nods. He understands. "It's good to have a strategy."

"I can run through almost anything, I think." Emma sets her spoon down. "It's not just moving your feet—it's a mental discipline. I haven't had a chance to move much since I left Ohio, though," she admits.

"Well, hell, you should go out as soon as we get back to Quantico," Bell says. "I've been to the gym room already—the equipment's real good. And there's a track all around the base."

"I've heard about it."

"You should check it out. Okay, I'm gonna pay." Bell flips his napkin onto his plate.

They get back on I-64, heading deeper into coal country. Soon they're on the Industrial Park Road outside Beaver. They're close; Emma feels a humming in her blood. They arrive at a checkpoint before the parking area, the stone sign carved like a grave marker.

Visiting hours are from eight until three—they need at least an hour for the interview, so they've just made the cut. Signing in, they have to show their flimsy new ID cards and hand the paperwork over for inspection. The guards inspect them, too: a girl with a buzz cut and a boy wearing his father's suit. Bell acts like law enforcement, though, and he seems to know the right way to talk. Emma's already noticed that his social intelligence is far from standard-issue.

There's a bitter taste in her throat, like she's been chewing aspirin. As she initials an entry waiver, the pen shakes in her fingers. She works to tamp it down.

Before the metal detector, they hit a snag when Emma is informed her T-shirt is inappropriate and she can't wear it into the prison.

"It's orange, ma'am," the guard at the station explains. "Same color as the inmates' jumpsuits."

"Oh." The guard's hair is about the same color as her shirt, but Emma's not inclined to point that out.

Bell frowns. "Is there a shirt she can change into?"

"On site?" The guard looks confused. "No, sir."

"Or maybe I can just wear my jacket?" Emma suggests.

"No, ma'am, no hooded jackets of that type allowed. But you can go back into Beaver to the charity shop there. They got supplies for cheap."

Emma and Bell exchange glances. By the time they get back from Beaver, visiting hours will be nearly over and this whole trip will have been for nothing.

"One second," Bell says to the guard. He pulls Emma away a little. "I've got a white T-shirt on under my button-down."

"Are you serious?"

"It's better than going in solo." He lifts his chin at the guard. "You got bathrooms close?"

"I can't wear your undershirt!" Emma hisses.

He's already loosening his cuffs. "It's a T-shirt, not an undershirt. Gimme one minute."

The bathrooms are in an adjacent hallway. Bell comes out tucking his tails in at the back, with the T-shirt under his arm. Emma blushes to high heaven. She grabs the shirt and stalks into the women's room.

Bell's shirt is worn soft from many washings. It smells unfamiliar and is still warm from him. She stuffs her own T-shirt into the pocket of her jacket, which she'll be leaving in the locker, it seems.

"All good now?" The guard appears bemused.

"Peachy," Emma mutters.

"We're good," Bell says.

They're buzzed through.

A series of rolling gates and barred windows, beige-painted cinder block corridors. Emma squeezes her hands into fists.

Another guard unlocks the door to the interview room. The room is not like the general visitation area: It's private, compact, and there's a single chair facing two other chairs across a screwed-down metal table. There's also a one-way mirror on the wall, which Emma doesn't like.

"McMurtry will think they're observing his responses."

"This is all they can give us, I think," Bell says. "But let me ask."

He knocks on the door, steps out to speak to the duty guard. For the moment the door is open, Emma hears the buzz of gate releases, the clang of metal, a faraway yelping that sounds more animal than human.

She rubs the cold out of her biceps and searches for balance. Her armpits are damp and the tinnitus in her head has returned. She tries to block it out, to simply recall everything she read about Clarence McMurtry in Cooper's summary.

Seventeen years old—his birthday was only a month ago. White male, five-six, brown and brown, no identifying marks or tattoos. That might have changed since he entered prison; he's been incarcerated for nearly a year. His aunt, Joanna McMurtry, visits him at 11:00 AM every other Saturday. The aunt, a sixty-one-year-old widow, is the woman who raised McMurtry after his own mother, Joanna's sister, broke parole on a variety of drug and solicitation charges eleven years ago and left the state, current whereabouts unknown.

Bell steps back in. "This is what we've got. And McMurtry's on his way."

"Okay." Emma nods, sits in one of the chairs, stands up again.

Bell frowns at the door, hands on hips. "You still want to keep this conversational, like we talked about?" He glances at her. Looks more closely. "Lewis?"

"Yes. Maybe." Emma is aware that her voice sounds detached. "Maybe not."

Bell angles in front of her. "How're you doing?"

"I don't know."

"Because we can—"

"Just stop talking for a second." The walls suddenly feel very close and the room seems over-warm. "I need to focus."

Bell becomes a kind of stillness, like lake water. "Are you gonna be okay? We don't have to do this."

"Yes, we do." Emma meets his eyes. "We actually do. We've been given a job, and we've come all this way, and...it's important."

He pauses. "Do you need to be angry at me? To let off steam before this happens?"

In that moment, of him offering to be her release valve, Emma realizes she can stabilize on her own. She can do this. She has been in far worse situations and survived.

"No," she says, softening. "No, I don't need to be angry at you."

"Okay. Phew." Bell's lip quirks. "Because we can do that, but I'm betting you've got a mean right hook."

She blows out air, almost surprised into laughter. "The meanest."

"Lewis." He doesn't touch her but it's as if she can feel a steadying hand anyway. "Can you run through this?"

"Yeah." She firms her feet. "Yes. I can run through this."

"Then we're good." He turns at the sound of keys in the door lock. "Okay, we're on."

Now here, the door is opening, and they are in the presence

of their first juvenile serial killer. Clarence McMurtry is accompanied by a guard, a heavyset man who looks bored. McMurtry seems younger than seventeen in the orange prison jumpsuit, and he does not look bored. His bulgy eyes have a gleam. He seems to shiver with contained energy.

This boy is not Daniel Huxton. This boy isn't in his forties; he's barely old enough to drive. Physically, he's a world away from Huxton's paunchy brawn. But there is something about him that resonates in the same way, like a musk that Emma recognizes.

It's a scent that hovers, always, in the back recesses of her mind. She breathes through her mouth. Giving in to it, falling into a memory of Huxton now, in this room, would be the end of everything. She needs instead a symbolic memory, and when she scrabbles inside herself and finds one, she latches on to it hard.

It is a memory of her mother in the barn, wearing rain boots and holding a stainless steel carving knife. Their farm has run dairy cows for longer than Emma has been alive, and it has always been her father's practice to select a few young steers to butcher for the family. The carcasses are hung in a concrete-floored room in the barn for about a week to cure—the room is the perfect temperature and humidity for dry aging.

Her mother checked the carcasses daily, sometimes twice daily if there was a hot spell.

"Smell that," she said to Emma, offering up a strip of backstrap. "That there's done. And this one here is spoiled. Can you tell the difference?"

Emma learned to tell the difference. Now her nostrils flare again as McMurtry is set across from her at the table. She's got it now; she knows what she's dealing with. Confident her instinct still holds, she sits down.

The same instinct gives her a basis of approach: to sympathize, wheedle, compliment. Not too many compliments—McMurtry is a talker, he'll pick up on obvious flattery. She'll need to be direct. And let him brag.

Bell takes the chair to her right. As the guard leaves, Emma squares the manila folder in front of her. "Clarence McMurtry— thanks for meeting with us."

"Who the hell're you?" McMurtry barks out. He has pimples, skinny arms, a snappable neck. His head is too big for his body, like a baby chick.

"My name is Emma Lewis and this is Travis Bell. We're—"

"You're not a G-man."

Emma registers a whole lot of Down in the Holler in McMurtry's accent, which is something she figures she can work with. She allows more Apple Creek to slide into hers. "Actually we're both with the FBI."

"Now that ain't right," McMurtry scoffs.

"Pardon?"

"You're a girl."

"Indeed I am."

"And there ain't no girls in the FBI."

"This girl is." She shows her teeth.

McMurtry leans back in his chair, hands on his thighs. "Well, goddamn. Now I seen everything." He squints at Bell. "That right? There's girls in the FBI now? And Mexicans, too, by the look of it."

Bell's face darkens. "Mr. McMurtry—"

Emma cuts him off. "Clarence, we're here to talk to you about the crimes you're in prison for, if you're willing."

"Well, hell yeah, I'm willing." McMurtry squints. "What's with yer hair? You a dyke or somethin'? Why'd you cut yer hair like that?"

Emma has been made aware that the golden rule of interrogation is never to answer the subject's questions. Now she leans over the table as if she's sharing a confidence. Her expression does not change one iota. "Lice."

"Ohhh," McMurtry says. "Yeah, I get that. Well, I'm happy to talk, but you gotta know, they don't treat me right in here."

"Is that so."

"Those fuckers in Unit Care, they don't give a spit about folks in the cells. Why, last night I said to my bunkmate Roger, I said to Roger they don't treat us right. They ration the food, the smokes—"

"The toilet paper?"

McMurtry slaps his knee. "Hell yes! They ration that, too!"

"Lord almighty."

"I said to Roger, I've about had it up to here with this ration bullshit. It makes me just wanna—ugh. You know? It makes me wanna—"

"It makes you wanna strangle someone?" Emma suggests.

McMurtry's expression turns sly. "Oh. You got all the details about that, do you?"

She cocks her head. "Clarence, you choked three old ladies to death in their beds. Those kinds of details we tend to take note of."

There's a heartbeat pause, then McMurtry's bray of laughter ricochets into the silence. He slaps his knee some more and yucks hard. Bell stares. Emma waits.

McMurtry laughs so much he has to wipe his eyes. "Oh boy. Oh yeah. You're a funny one, ain'tcha? What's yer name again?"

"Emma Lewis."

"You got a smoke on you, Emma Lewis?"

For the first time, Emma's response is delayed. It's Bell who takes a can of Bugler out of his jacket pocket and offers it to McMurtry.

"There's one already rolled in there," Bell says. "You can keep the can, but I need the matchbook back."

"I do thank you." McMurtry's face lights at the sight of the tobacco, his pale tongue flashing out as he licks the paper before putting the end in his mouth. The match is a puff of red. "Now, what was I goin' on about?"

Emma sits back in her chair and smiles. "You were telling us about the murders."

CHAPTER FIVE

The interview takes nearly an hour. By the time they return to the world outside, it's almost three thirty and there's a long drive ahead. Clouds are coming in from the west. Bell looks at her all the way to the car.

"What?"

"Nothing." He grins and scuffs the gravel as he walks. "*Those kinds of details we tend to take note of.* Jesus."

Emma tips her head back. The sky looks very big, and the joy of release is keen. "You should wear that suit when we go to see Gesak. It seems to impress the prison staff."

"McMurtry even filled out the blue subject forms."

"The parts he could write."

"That was a good day's work." Bell unlocks the pickup, looking satisfied.

Emma walks around to climb in the passenger side. The air in the cab is warmer. "You want to split the driving on the way back?"

"If I get tired, yeah." Bell exhales, sets his shoulders. "Okay, let's get the hell out of here."

He drives them back out the way they came in. Emma steadies

herself against the bouncing of the Dodge as she examines the paperwork scrawled with McMurtry's messy handwriting.

"How's it looking?"

Emma flicks the pages. "Like it needs retyping."

"That boy couldn't spell worth a damn."

"Bad at spelling, good at strangling women. He can put that on his résumé if he ever gets out of jail." The adrenaline is wearing off and now her own comment sickens her. She looks away. "Sorry."

"Nothing to be sorry for," Bell says. He waits a beat. "Do you think he feels regret? He never really expressed anything like remorse."

"These guys never do." Emma's surprised at the way her words lash out, but she can't seem to stop herself. "They just keep protesting they've been hard done by. If they regret anything, it's that now they're stuck in a ten-by-ten-foot cell. McMurtry's no different—he doesn't really care about the things he's done, the women he's killed...."

When the delayed reaction hits her, it's as though all the blood leaves her upper body and pools in her feet. A sea of images and sensations rolls over her: the constant slow, circular motion of the vents stirring the air in the interview room; the pulse of her blood in her ears, like listening to the whoosh and rush inside a conch shell; the way McMurtry pinched his cigarette between finger and thumb....

In the basement in Emma's head, other fingers perform the same action: stubby digits with bitten nails, stained at the tips. She sees grease-dark overalls stitched in yellow; smells the scent of tobacco, of body odor and blood; hears the sound of screaming....

She loses herself for a while, finally blinks herself out of it.

Needing air, she fumbles the window crank, makes a gap for the breeze to rush in. The smell of the pines is restorative. They're almost back on the interstate.

"Lewis?" Bell's collar is loosened. He looks forward at the road but still somehow seems to be concentrating on her.

"How can some men hate so hard?" she whispers. But she's not sure if it's Bell she's asking. She swallows against the thickness in the back of her throat. "Let's get coffee. Can we get coffee?"

"Yes, ma'am," Bell says quietly.

He turns the pickup into the parking lot of a truck stop. The outside has been painted an unpleasant Pepto Bismol pink, but the inside of the place is clean-wholesome, and blessedly quiet. Bell orders while Emma finds a booth. She fiddles with the laminated menu until Bell slides in opposite her.

"You okay?"

"Yeah. You?" She's feeling more herself now she's out of the confines of the car. She suddenly remembers that she's still wearing Bell's shirt.

"That's one down, anyway." He shrugs, shucks off his jacket.

"I guess."

"Something bothering you about it?"

Emma bites her lip. "What do you think will happen when we get back to Quantico?"

Bell rolls up his cuffs. "Cooper'll probably want to debrief. He won't expect a report before Sunday, but he'll want to have a look at what we got. See how we managed. McMurtry is one of the easy ones, remember."

"Who are the hard ones?"

"Have you looked at the other summaries?" When Emma shakes her head, Bell's eyes drift in thought. "Rylan, maybe. Gesak, definitely—he's refused all interviews." He pauses as the server delivers two coffees and a grilled tomato-and-cheese sandwich. When the server leaves, he adds sugar to his coffee. "They won't all be antagonistic, but they'll all be hard."

Emma looks at the sandwich—it smells good, but she's not sure her stomach is up to much—and thinks about what she wants to express next. "Bell, why are we doing this?"

"Say again?"

"I don't mean our personal reasons. Why are we doing *this*? Why create this unit? I don't understand what's in it for Cooper. What new things are we learning from these interviews?"

"We're learning how that kind of mentality develops. How young it starts, and what kinds of triggers—"

"The FBI *knows* this stuff already." She puts her coffee down. "They've interviewed thirty-five adult subjects, and most of them have provided extensive histories. They know it starts in childhood. They know the patterns of upbringing. They know the warning signs, like animal cruelty and arson and bed-wetting, and how the early fantasies develop. The psychopathology has been understood for nearly ten years—it's on my damn course curriculum. Come on, Bell. What's *new* about these subjects, except that they got caught early?"

Bell shakes his head. "Look, with these kinds of sex crimes—"

"These crimes are not about sex. The sex is just incidental."

Bell frowns at his sandwich. "Everything I've read—"

"Are you talking about police investigation manuals? They're focused on sexually motivated homicide, and they're all based on

Psychopathia Sexualis, which was written in the goddamn nineteenth century. So everything you've read is wrong, or out-of-date, or both. It's not about sex. At all."

Bell scowls. "So what's it about, then? What would make a teenager like McMurtry kill three elderly women and jerk off over the bodies?"

"It's about exerting power. McMurtry was browbeaten—and physically beaten—by his elderly aunt from early childhood. Instead of focusing his rage on her, he went out and murdered three other women of a similar age. He had no power with his aunt, so he exerted power over three proxies. Feeling that kind of power is thrilling, and he got turned on by it. End of story."

"Every case is different," Bell insists.

"No. Every case is the same." She leans forward, because she wants him to understand. "Power. Domination. Control. Manipulating the people around you, fooling them into thinking you're normal. The smarter ones cover their tracks better, and they're better at the manipulation part, which makes catching them harder. That's it. That's all there is. So why are we doing this? With these interviews?"

"To be thorough? The FBI interviewed all the others. They want to see if there's anything different in the younger ones."

"And do you think there is?"

"Hard to tell from one sample." He looks at her over the top of his cup. "But you don't think there will be."

"I'm expecting to see five guys who are either dumb or unlucky."

"Which category does McMurtry fall into?" Bell snorts, shakes his head. "No, don't answer."

"Eat your sandwich," Emma suggests. "It's getting cold."

Once Bell has finished demolishing his food, he goes out and gases up the truck while Emma pays. The light outside makes blue-gray shadows in the parking lot, and the smell of exhaust off the interstate is strong. Emma feels like she's a thousand years old. She turns, searching out the last rays of the sun, before she climbs back into the cab.

She buckles up. "I signed on to this because I told myself we'd be gathering new information, that we'd be learning something."

"We are," Bell insists.

"I don't know. And I don't understand Cooper's motivation. Why now, when he's so busy with whatever's happening in Pennsylvania? You said that case is a big deal, right?"

Bell's voice is stiff. "They're talking on the news about curfews for teenagers, so yeah, it's a big deal."

"And Cooper is heading up that investigation unit. He's right in the thick of it. So again, I'm wondering why he's suddenly so interested in all of this."

Bell doesn't seem to have an answer. They merge onto the main road before he speaks further. "If you don't think we're doing anything useful with these interviews, why'd you join up?"

Emma hedges. "I didn't say it's not useful. Every piece of information is useful."

"But?"

She picks at the knee of her jeans. "It would be better if there was a specific goal. Beyond just...making a bigger graph."

He eyes her. "You wanna be putting this information into service? That's active cases. You must want to sign on with the bureau, because that's the only way you're getting on active cases."

"No, Jesus. I just…" She keeps returning to the questions, and the questions are *Why this? Why us? Why now?* She doesn't know the answers.

And this focus on the perpetrators sticks in her throat. It's like the victims get forgotten. Why is it always about the killers?

Emma stares out the window. McMurtry's offender behaviors and thought patterns—what is there to take away from that? Is it just anticipating the behaviors and thought patterns of more men coming after him? Is that all they're doing now, shoring up the ramparts?

The atmosphere in the cab of the truck is subdued. But the rumble of the engine is soothing, and after a while Emma finds herself allowing her head to lean back, closing her eyes.

She wakes from her doze with a mild startle—she's slumped across the bench seat, almost drooling on Bell's shoulder.

"Lewis." He nudges her.

She wakes up fully. "How…how long have we been going?"

"About two hours."

It's black outside. She pushes herself more upright, rubs her face. When was the last time she felt easy enough in a new acquaintance's presence that she could fall asleep beside them? She can't remember.

"I was going to give you a break from driving."

"I'm good." Bell's intently focused on the white lines flashing on the road. "You knew, didn't you? When McMurtry came into the interview room, you felt it in him. I saw you, when he came in, and something changed in your face."

Emma frowns. "What are you talking about?"

"It was like…something twigged in you. You knew he was a killer."

"I'd already read McMurtry's file."

He gives her a sidelong glance. "I don't think you believe it was just that."

She rubs her head. "I don't know, what do you want me to say? It's a learned behavior. I recognize stuff now."

"Can we teach that somehow? That recognition?"

Emma looks at him, her face drawn. "You don't want to teach people the kinds of things that are in my head."

"I get that," Bell says quickly. "I understand. But I think maybe *that's* the bigger goal. That's the purpose of these interviews."

"What's that?"

"How to pick these guys out fast." Bell stares off down the road. "McMurtry was caught because *one* guy from the Ripley sheriff's department followed up on him. That cop—he must've noticed something. And that's what the FBI wants. They want people out in the field who can follow their instincts on this."

"Well, they're using the information collected in interviews to teach agents and cops about new profiling techniques. Maybe some of it is rubbing off." Emma watches the oncoming headlights, considering. "Maybe it even feeds into something they need to know about Pennsylvania."

"So...should we be interviewing the arresting officers as well? Finding out what they noticed?"

"It's an idea." A good one. It would make what they're doing make sense. "Would Cooper let us expand the study?"

"I have a feeling Cooper is already dodging low-flying shit just trying to keep this unit running," Bell admits.

"Well, if he's already in the glue, he hasn't got anything to lose, right?"

Bell grins. "I guess you'd have to ask him that."

"Then let's ask."

"Okay. Let's ask." Bell waits a beat. "Cooper will probably be fine with expanding the study, so long as we keep the receipts."

Emma side-eyes him, snorts.

They pull the Dodge into the Quantico parking lot at nine that evening, and Emma feels pummeled after the drive. She and Bell trudge their weary way toward the buildings, splitting off at the doors to Jefferson—Bell's dormitory is in the next wing along. They shake hands before they separate, like they're business partners.

Emma leans against the wall of the elevator as it travels up, only straightening when two male trainees get in on the floor before her own.

Her room is warm inside, the air stagnant. She lurches into the shower, stuffing Bell's T-shirt into her laundry hamper. While she's washing, his idea to interview the cops who arrested kids like McMurtry strikes her again. It's a good idea. After she gets out, towels off, and puts on the terry cloth robe she brought from home, she sits on top of the comforter on her bed with the McMurtry file.

The idea plucks at her. She checks the time—twenty-one thirty—and figures it's worth a shot. She calls Cooper at the office number on his card.

"Agent Cooper? It's Emma Lewis. We just got back from Beckley."

"Was there a problem?"

"No problem." She's not sure how to start, plunges in anyway. "Bell and I were talking in the car on the way back. We were thinking it might be useful to expand the study. We were hoping to talk to the arresting officers for each—"

"Miss Lewis?"

"Yes?"

"You were asked to interview the subject, complete a report, and hand that report in at oh nine hundred on Sunday. I'd like you to do that. Just that, and nothing more."

He hangs up. She stares at the bleating receiver in her hand.

"Well, fuck you very much, Special Agent Cooper," she mutters.

She'll have to tell Bell that she didn't even get to the part about keeping the receipts.

CHAPTER SIX

After leaving Jefferson, Travis Bell is halfway to his room when he realizes he still has the interview questionnaire pages in his satchel.

He doesn't know if they're important. Emma's words come back to him: *Maybe it even feeds into something they need to know about Pennsylvania.* Does he take the McMurtry questionnaire back to his dorm? The question stumps him for a moment and his brain is tired, so he falls back on the most reliable method he knows for figuring out problems, which is to consider what his father would say.

The answer comes quickly.

Think about it like a chain of evidence—the FBI would want the paperwork. And you don't know if it's important; you're not an agent. Better to give it to a superior.

Bell sighs and turns around.

Jefferson has a hollow, echoing quiet at night. Only instinct guides his way from the elevator through the gerbil-run basement corridors to the Behavioral Science offices, where he finds the reception desk unattended. This is another problem. He needs to hand over the questionnaire, but he's not allowed in the offices. Cooper was very specific about it.

Bell chews his lip and looks around, hoping for a solution to arrive from the air. His fatigue is deep in the bone now. Leave the papers on the reception desk? *No, bad idea. Fuck.*

He spends a minute thinking. Half that minute is taken up with thoughts of Emma Lewis. He's never met anyone so guarded. He's not stupid—he knows where her reserve is coming from—but he has to watch her cues all the time: the flare of her nostrils, the changes in her posture. He thinks of the dreamy expression she gets when she's considering something. Then the expression she gets when she's steeling herself, like when they talked to McMurtry.

Bell yanks the questionnaire folder out of his satchel and pushes forward. If Emma Lewis can talk to McMurtry, he can walk through an office door.

The inside of Behavioral Science is all low ceilings, crummy carpet, and cubicle hallways. Not as impressive as he imagined. Bell hears the sound of someone hanging up a phone farther ahead, then a muffled question, answered by an unfamiliar voice.

"We dusted the letter, and the envelope, then we fumed it. The envelope had multiple prints, but if anyone other than the subject touched the letter, they're not showing up. Should we run the other prints?"

"You'd only turn up the staff at the hospital, maybe the external mailman." Cooper's voice, clearer now. *Bingo.* "Plus the mailman here in Jefferson."

"We got one piece of trace in the envelope—a single hair, plucked not cut. The bulb was still attached. Same kind as the ones we have on file."

"He would've put that in there. He knows we look. It's like when a cat leaves you a present of a half-chewed mouse on the doorstep, just reminding you they're still around."

"Linda analyzed the handwriting. Same deal."

"Thanks for coming down to tell me in person, Gerry."

Bell isn't sure why his feet slow as he comes closer. He sees a white man in a plaid shirt and brown trousers standing at the door to what must be Cooper's office. The man—Gerry—is overweight, about midsixties, drooping in the face like a hound.

Cooper asks another question, but it's muffled.

"Eh." Gerry pushes up gold-rimmed glasses with the same hand holding a burning cigarette. The cigarette smoke eddies up in a bobbing ribbon. "Glenn's still going through the trace from the underwear. It's your basic mess. I'm glad the bodies weren't found in a river, but I wish they hadn't been found in a Pennsylvania garbage dump. I'll have a full report by tomorrow afternoon."

Pennsylvania. Bell is suddenly very aware of what he's listening to, where he is. There's a corkboard on the cinder block wall immediately to his left. Four photos shine out from the board. All four faces are smiling, hopeful, young—horrifically young. The crime scene photos tacked beside them are more horrific.

He jerks back, looks down at the folder in his hands. Takes three steps closer to Cooper's office and clears his throat.

Gerry turns. "Hello. Help you with something?"

"I've got, uh..." Bell squeezes the cardboard folder.

Through the door of the office, he sees Cooper stand up from his chair. Cooper's office is compact, brown-walled, covered in newspaper clippings and a drift of notes, like the den of some forest animal. Cooper's holding a piece of paper sandwiched in plastic film. The writing on the paper is an elegant, smooth-flowing script in what appears to be green felt-tipped pen.

Cooper is frowning. "What are you doing here, Mr. Bell?"

"The questionnaire pages." Bell holds the folder up. "From Beckley? I wasn't sure what to do with them, and I figured you might not want me to take them back to my dorm—"

"Keep them." Cooper gives him an assessing look, seems to realize he needs to be more prescriptive. "Hang on to them, complete the report, hand it all in Sunday."

"Okay. I mean, uh, yes, sir."

"And Mr. Bell?"

"Sir?"

The plastic-sealed paper in Cooper's hand is a letter. It's written on butcher paper, delicately frayed at the edges as though it's been torn off a larger piece. Cooper opens a drawer in his desk, slips the letter inside, closes the drawer.

"I believe we had an arrangement," Cooper says, "about you and Miss Lewis not entering Behavioral Science."

"We did, yes, sir. I mean, we do. I'm sorry, I just wasn't sure what to do with the questionnaire."

"Go easy on him, Ed." Gerry is grinning.

Cooper gives him a look, looks back at Bell. "It's fine. Just...go on to your dorm now."

"Yes, sir." Bell bobs his head. "Good night, sir."

As he pivots and heads back down the cubicle hallway, he hears Gerry say, in a quiet tone, "Good Lord, they just seem to get younger and younger." Cooper replies, but Bell is too far away to hear now. He escapes out the office door into reception, then heads straight for the outside of Jefferson. He no longer thinks about Emma's face, but the faces of the kids in the photos on the wall in Behavioral Science.

After Bell and Gerry leave the offices, Cooper gets the letter out of his drawer. Handling it carefully by the corners like it's poisonous, he reads it through again. The letter says:

Dear Agent Cooper,

Well, here we are again after another eventful month. You really need to start answering your correspondence. Or maybe you just didn't have an opportunity to reply to my last letter before our new friend delivered another surprise—he's speeding up a little, isn't he? And I did warn you that one body wouldn't be enough.

What do you think will happen next? It's a bit like Christmas, isn't it? You can shake the pretty boxes, but you just don't know what will be inside.

I have an idea of what comes next, but you probably won't like it. And I don't imagine you'll do anything about it until you're pushed. But I'm right here, Agent Cooper. Ready and waiting.

You're waiting, too, aren't you? Enjoy sitting on your hands before the next bodies pop up. Two more weeks! Or maybe sooner. The time will fly by, I'm sure. It really is like Christmas.

Best,
Simon

P.S. Don't bother to check for fingerprints. The envelope will be dirty but the letter is all me.

Cooper sets the letter away from him on the desk, steeples his fingers in front of his mouth, and stares at the letter for a long time.

CHAPTER SEVEN

O kay," Cooper says. "Change of plan."

With some consideration of the matter, Emma realizes it's Wednesday. She woke just before dawn and chased away the sour aftertaste of her dreams on the running path that Quantico students refer to as the Yellow Brick Road, slapping around obstacles that she didn't want to engage with and generally pissing off people struggling over rope ladders and trudging through mud pits. Now she feels lighter, elevated after her run.

The same could not be said for Cooper. She's prepared to put aside baleful thoughts about his treatment of her on the phone last night—the man looks heavier today, like the world is weighing on him.

Bell's been restacking file boxes in their basement office, getting McMurtry's stuff out of the way. Now he comes, dusting off his hands, to sit at the desk.

"So what's the change?" he asks.

Cooper fidgets with the folder in his hands. "Sounds like the session with McMurtry went well, so I'm adding another subject to the interview roster. And I want you to interview him next."

"Why is he next?" Emma asks. "Is he an easy subject?"

Cooper is blank-faced. "None of them are easy. This one is the hardest."

He tosses the folder on the desktop.

Emma reads the label. "Simon Gutmunsson."

Bell's expression changes fast. He pushes back from the desk, out of his chair. "I can't do that."

Emma stares at him. "What?"

Bell speaks only to Cooper. "You know I can't do that. Why did you even pull that file?"

"He falls within the bounds of the—"

"You said he didn't fit the parameters of the project. You said we wouldn't be dealing with him." Bell's voice is sharp, his face a stone mask. Emma hasn't seen him like this before.

"He started when he was fifteen," Cooper says carefully. "He fits the—"

"*You said he doesn't fit the parameters.* This is *bullshit* and you know it."

"We need him."

"You won't get him," Bell says. "Not from me."

Bell walks out. The door of the gray office room smacks against the wall before slowly swinging back again. The click of the latch closing is a dramatic punctuation. Emma is dumbstruck.

"He'll come back," Cooper says into the silence.

Emma stares. "What is going on? What's wrong with Bell?"

"Gutmunsson is..." Cooper sighs and sits down, loosening his jacket. "Simon Gutmunsson was arrested for a series of murders between 1978 and 1980 in New Hampshire, Massachusetts, and Vermont. During the arrest, there was a standoff, and unfortunately one of the Marshals on the scene was attacked. He died later in the hospital."

Emma feels a great cog turning. "Gutmunsson killed Bell's father."

"Yes."

"He told me it happened, but not how. That's—" She rolls it over in her mind, both the information and what Cooper has done with it. "That's cruel."

"It's necessary." Cooper maintains his stolid calm. "Bell knows we need this interview."

"Well, you clearly didn't tell him that when he came on board." She narrows her eyes at Cooper. "And if it's so necessary, why wasn't Gutmunsson on the list before?"

"He wasn't on the list before because I didn't have the permissions before."

Emma gets up from her chair because the need to move is strong. She wants a little distance from Cooper, too, so she can see him through a wider lens. "Why is Gutmunsson the hardest subject?"

"You don't know anything about the case?"

Emma thinks. If Gutmunsson was arrested in 1980, that was the year after Huxton. She spent most of that year between her parents' house and her therapist's office, in the daily grind of recovery. There are whole months of that year she doesn't even remember.

"Enlighten me."

"I suggest you read the file." For the first time, there's a flicker of disturbance in Cooper's expression. "Gutmunsson is a difficult subject because he's smart. His parents had him IQ-tested at fourteen— he was in the ninety-eighth percentile then. Now...I don't know how you'd measure him now."

"So he's an intelligent, manipulative predator. What else?"

"He communicates with me." Cooper drops that into the conversation like he's uncomfortable with it. "I was the second unit agent on the case. But I can't be the one to go see him—give him what he wants and he just keeps taking. He's incarcerated at St. Elizabeths, in DC. I'll drive you both up there. I can brief you further on the way."

"You can't ask Bell to do this." Why it's really obvious to her and not to Cooper, Emma can't imagine. "That would be like asking me to interview Huxton."

"Huxton is dead." Cooper says it like a full stop. Now he's not expressionless. Now he's showing some intensity. "And we are waging a *war* here, Miss Lewis. These offices are the primary line of defense. Every day I keep fighting."

"I get that, but—"

"So please understand me when I say this. Huxton is dead— we can't learn anything more from him now. But Gutmunsson is alive. Something he might say, something he might allow to slip out, could form the basis of another insight, another piece of the puzzle. Bell knows that. He knows we need that."

Emma uncrosses her arms. Cooper seems more human to her suddenly, but she also knows this is part of the theater of leadership—to rally, to marshal the troops and press on. For a moment, Emma wonders what it is about Simon Gutmunsson, specifically, that's so important. What it is about him that breaks Cooper's diamond-hard control. But then the moment is over, and she has to answer his question.

"Okay, I'll do it. I won't speak for Bell, though. I'll talk with him about it, if you want, but it's his call."

Cooper visibly relaxes. "Thank you."

She starts toward the exit. "I'd better go find him."

"Miss Lewis?" When she looks back, Cooper has pushed to his feet. "I know you think asking Bell to interview Gutmunsson is a bad idea. But at this stage, I'll take every single scrap of evidence and information and understanding that I can. *Everything.* And if Huxton was alive, you'd best believe I'd be asking you to saddle up, no question."

Emma holds his eyes for as long as she can. Then she breaks for the door.

She searches for Bell in all the places she can think of, before remembering the place she should've searched first.

The Quantico training gym is a vast, high-ceilinged space with FIDELITY BRAVERY INTEGRITY stamped large on one wall. Blue mats are rolled up and the sprung wooden floors are buffed to a basketball-court gloss. On the far side, Bell is pummeling one of the heavy bags, the chain suspending it creaking with the strain.

Emma watches at a distance for a moment. Bell's in sweatpants, running shoes, and a white tank that contrasts sharply with his skin. It's a shock, seeing him wearing something other than formal attire. Sweat shakes off his dark hair as he punches. He has excellent muscle development, and Emma waits for that awareness to pass through her before she approaches.

She keeps her voice measured. "That was a shitty thing for Cooper to do, and you have every right to be angry. But I have to complete this interview. And I don't want to do it without you."

Bell lands one last punch that rocks the bag before turning to face her. His eyes are blazing. "He's a snake. You don't know anything about this guy, do you?"

She's not sure, for a moment, whether he's referring to Cooper or Gutmunsson. She shakes her head.

Bell tugs his boxing gloves off with his teeth, breathing hard. He has a small USMS tattoo on his right bicep. "Three different states. Eleven murders, including my dad. Except for my dad, all of them were posed crime scenes—*the Artist*, they used to call him."

The contempt in his sneer is like acid. Emma finds male anger hard to handle, but this from Bell is of a slightly different flavor: inward-looking, and full of grief.

She tries to refocus. "I don't know any of this stuff, Bell. That's why I need your perspective."

He picks at his hand wraps. "Cooper can brief you."

"Cooper only tells me what he wants me to hear."

"Then go through the archives."

"I need more."

"*Goddammit*, Emma!"

He pivots and gives her his back, rests his forehead against the bag, holding the straps up high like a man readying himself to be whipped. The thought makes her wince. She steps closer, puts a hand on his shoulder—hot with fever, damp with sweat.

"Please," she says softly. "*Don't* do the interview with me. But please tell me what you know. And come with me to DC. If Gutmunsson's as bad as you and Cooper say, I'm going to need the support."

Her hand drops as he turns around. She realizes the dampness on his cheeks isn't all perspiration, and it shames her enough that she opens her mouth to take it all back. But he speaks before she does, his voice very quiet.

"Okay." He scrubs a wrapped hand over his face. "Okay."

CHAPTER EIGHT

They're in the car by nine the next day.

Cooper's car, this time—a wide old Plymouth with sagging suspension. Emma sits in the front passenger seat and Bell commandeers the back, too still, gazing out the window. The trip takes less than an hour but seems longer, until Cooper starts going over all the details of the subject she's about to interview.

"Simon Aron Gutmunsson, nineteen years old, white male, six-three. Has a twin sister, Kristin Margret Gutmunsson—"

"I've seen pictures of the sister," Emma says.

They reviewed the information—everything Bell could stomach—last night. Simon Gutmunsson is not like the other subjects on the interview roster. He is a wholly different kind of beast. The file itself was the first clue: inches thick, the cardboard folder grubby from wear after passing through the hands of multiple agents and officers. Inside the beige folder, a set of Grand Guignol crime scene photos that Emma could barely stand to look at.

Simon Gutmunsson began killing people at fifteen. He not only started young, he was prolific, often killing more than one person at a time. Many of his victims were drawn from within his own social circle. The media made hay with the fact that he'd picked off the young darlings of the upper-class New England social set—and the horrifying detail that he had disemboweled his own friends.

The crime scene photos showed the elaborate arrangement of the bodies in meadows and wooded areas. Emma knows from her studies that outside displays mean the perpetrator is showing off. She also knows that victim-posing is not a common feature of serial homicide—that it's a sign of a sophisticated fantasy, unusual in such a young offender.

"The family is of Icelandic, French, and English origin," Cooper says. "That's why they have the screwy names."

"Old money." Bell, from the back seat. His voice still has grit in it, but he looks more like himself now, out of his training gear and back in his suit.

"That's true," Cooper concedes. He seems antsy, his hands shifting away from the ten-two position on the steering wheel, shifting back again. "Gutmunsson's father owned one of the largest manufacturing plants in New Hampshire, but the family originally made its money in textiles and cotton. Simon and his sister were sent to a private European boarding school until they were ten, and then they were schooled at home when Simon's behavior became an issue."

Emma catches the scent. "What kind of behavior?"

"Pretty much what you'd expect, at first. Bullying of younger students, small acts of cruelty. Then the teachers noticed that the school cat had gone missing."

"I don't need to hear the details of that," Emma says quickly.

"Well, you can imagine without me telling you. The final straw was in 1973, when a number of children at the school were hospitalized with food poisoning. Simon turned out to be the culprit. The family hushed it up, but Simon came home after that."

"It's good to know the background," Emma says.

"You read the file?"

"Last night, yes. You don't need to tell me about the murders." She doesn't want to go over that stuff in the car with Bell. Going through it with him last night was disturbing enough.

She particularly recalls a mug shot from the file: Against a stark background, Gutmunsson gazed into the camera with flat affect. One of his eyebrows was raised.

"Is there anything else I need to know before I go in?"

"The hospital superintendent will cover procedures with you before your visit." Cooper glances over. "I don't think I need to remind you that you shouldn't turn your back on this guy. He is not someone you should ever feel relaxed around. He's about your age, and he presents very well, but it's a mask—inside, he's uglier than anyone you've ever met. Do you understand?"

Emma nods. "I get it."

"Here's the turn," Cooper says, and suddenly St. Elizabeths Hospital for the Criminally Insane rises up before them.

The front of the building is like a castle: red-brown brick towers, crenelated in the old style. Emma almost expects to see archer's slits, but instead there are rows of windows, each one covered with bars. East and west wings stretch out to the right and left of the center edifice for a block on either side. The parking area is out front, a grassy lawn nearby, almost pleasant-looking. But this building is not trying to be anything other than what it is: a gothic structure full of bedlam ghosts and old horrors.

Emma gets out of the car and gazes up, wonders if Simon Gutmunsson can see them from a window. Wind whistles through the parking area. Someone touches her shoulder and she startles, but it's only Bell.

"Lewis, if this gets hairy, back off," he says in a low voice. "There's nothing keeping you in there. Cooper can't complain if you don't complete the whole interview—just do what you can do."

"Okay." Emma watches Cooper approach the front door. "Does Cooper seem nervous to you?"

"Damned if I know." Bell's color isn't great, but he's holding on. "Look, Simon Gutmunsson is a step up from McMurtry. A thousand steps up. Stay alert."

She looks again at the asylum, her senses prickling. "There's something off about this."

Bell frowns. "What do you mean?"

"I don't know," she says. "It's everything. Cooper springing it on us, the timing... Gutmunsson seems like he's well above our pay grade. Why is he the next subject? I've got this feeling like... I don't know. Something is off."

"Forget that now. Lewis—*Emma*. Look at me." Bell's eyes are intent. "Remember the rules. Don't answer personal questions. Don't make physical contact. And don't forget what this guy is. You know what he is, don't you?"

She nods, exhaling.

"Fuck." Bell's hair and the tails of his jacket whip in the breeze as he looks away. "I wish I could make myself go in there with you."

She bumps his arm gently. "Don't. I wouldn't wish that on you."

"Okay. Then I'll be waiting for you when you're done." He turns and walks over toward the grass.

Emma watches him go. She wants a moment to calm herself and she knows she's not going to get it. Cooper is gesturing to her from the doorway, so she walks across the gravel and steps over the threshold.

Reception is a large wooden desk plonked in the middle of a capacious entryway with a dark parquet floor and a wide, dramatic staircase. Emma smells dust and Lysol. A woman is coming down the stairs, extending a hand to Cooper.

"Special Agent Cooper, it's nice to see you again."

"Thank you for admitting us, Dr. Scott." Cooper angles to make the introductions. "Emma Lewis, this is Dr. Evelyn Scott. She's been running St. Elizabeths for nearly ten years."

Dr. Evelyn Scott is a black woman of about fifty, with glasses and stylish short hair. Her clothes are in dark, severe colors but with textures that Emma finds interesting.

"Miss Lewis, nice to meet you. Please come this way, we can chat as we walk." Scott leads them to the left and under the stairs, toward a tall wooden door. "Simon doesn't have contact with his family and he's been requesting other visitors for a while, so your arrival is well timed. Are you aware of the nature of Simon's condition, Miss Lewis?"

Emma is confused by the question. Is the compulsion to commit serial murder a condition? "Uh, I've read Mr. Gutmunsson's case file. I'm familiar with the circumstances."

"She knows how to proceed, Dr. Scott," Cooper says. "Miss

Lewis is here to conduct a formal interview and request that Simon complete a questionnaire."

"That's fine. I'm sure he'll be pleased to cooperate." Scott uses a long, ornate iron key to open the door.

"Anything to report?" Cooper asks. "After his last escape attempt, we—"

"Oh no, we haven't had further problems on that front. But we've taken some new safety measures, with alternative arrangements for Simon's accommodation within the unit. We've moved him out of Secure General into the big room. This whole center section is now specially reinforced."

Scott escorts them through the foyer door into a wide hallway with huge turn-of-the-century columns, and this is where the nature of the facility changes. They have left the realm of parquet floors and entered a new kingdom, one of electronic locks and clanging gates. Emma's breaths start to come in short and shallow. She can hear someone crying, far away.

The grand old hall is cut into two sections by a floor-to-ceiling wall of welded steel bars. Cooper grunts approvingly. Scott raises a hand to an unobtrusive CCTV camera before the bars, and the gate unlocks and slides open, then slides closed behind them automatically. They walk the long remaining expanse of dark hall, their footsteps echoing. Finally they come to a stout oak door, reinforced with steel, with a slot cut into it. Dr. Scott taps on the slot. When it opens, she says, "One visitor for Simon Gutmunsson, please," and the slot snaps shut again. Locks are being opened on the other side.

Scott smiles at Cooper. "As you can see, we've created some safeguards."

Emma isn't concentrating on the exchange between Scott and Cooper. She's working to control her breathing. She can do this, she reminds herself. Confronting McMurtry has stiffened her spine.

She finds that Dr. Scott has taken her hand.

"Now," Scott says, "there is an exclusion zone around his cell—under no circumstances should you enter or reach over it. Don't take anything he offers you, and don't step inside the barricade. It's just a precaution, of course."

"Of course." Emma fights hard against the sense that she is falling, rights herself in her mind.

Scott pats her hand. "Go in there with a cheerful outlook. He'll appreciate that. But take everything he says to you with a grain of salt—Simon can be prone to exaggeration."

"I understand."

"I'll be right here when you come out. Remember my instructions."

"I will," Emma says. "Thank you."

Scott smiles at her kindly. Scott is scared of Gutmunsson, Emma realizes with a jolt. She looks to Cooper one last time, but he is looking at the floor. *Coward*, she thinks.

Emma feels the fear in her chest like a raven tapping at a window. It's too late for misgivings, though. The door is open. A large male orderly stands sentry, securing her passage to the place beyond sanity, and Emma steps inside.

CHAPTER NINE

Scott referred to this as "the big room"—Emma discovers that it is, in fact, a former chapel. The space is large, and there are high, buttressed ceilings. Decommissioned pews are stacked together against the walls. Light enters through a set of charming stained-glass windows at the far end of the room, in the apse; their charm is offset to some extent by the high-security steel bars covering them.

Moth-eaten velvet curtains are drawn back on either side to frame the chancel; by some irony, Simon Gutmunsson's cell sits exactly where the altar should be. The cell is a large box made of metal bars, surrounded by wooden police barricade sawhorses, and it stands like an island in the room. The aesthetic clash between the cell and the chapel's old-world solemnity is jarring, like seeing an actor wearing a digital watch in a period film.

The large orderly is a Sikh man with a name tag that reads PRADEEP. At a desk beside the door, he notes Emma's name and checks her manila folder of paperwork for contraband staples and paper clips before she's allowed to proceed to the cell.

"Mr. Gutmunsson is reading, at present." Pradeep's voice is

deep, his vowels rounded. "Dr. Scott told you about the barricade? Then you may go now—you will be all right."

There is no way to approach the cell without its occupant seeing her coming. Emma straightens her shoulders and walks across the burnished wooden floor until she is immediately before the cell. The barricade prohibits her from coming within six feet of the bars. Finally, she looks up.

Simon Gutmunsson has fashioned his cell into something like a salon, with the bed set beside a small desk on the left, both draped with linens, as if awaiting a servant to whip the dustcovers aside upon the lord's return. The pillows have been liberally arranged. Another sheet has been suspended halfway up the bars behind the bed, to create the illusion of a partial wall. A privacy screen cordons off a commode on the far right. Piles of books stand on the desk, on the floor by the bed, by the front wall of bars, by the privacy screen. Also on the desk is a roll of butcher paper, writing implements, and a wooden bowl with a selection of seasonal fruit.

Gutmunsson himself is sitting in a louche posture on the floor, leaning against the end of his bed, legs stretched out and crossed at the ankles, reading an antique volume of poetry. The white sheets and pillows, the jeweled tones of the old books, the colors of the fruit...the whole diorama has the rich, resonant smack of a Renaissance still life.

"Simon Gutmunsson?" Emma's relieved her voice comes out measured rather than hesitant. "Mr. Gutmunsson?"

When Gutmunsson sets his book aside and stands up, Emma can see that he is very tall. She is reminded of a cobra rising, hood spread.

"Well, hello," Gutmunsson says.

He is slender, with wide shoulders and long limbs and fine pianist's hands. His eyes shine arctic blue beneath dark brows. He is wearing white, and his hair is glaringly white. It must be a family trait; Emma remembers the pictures of his sister. On Kristin Gutmunsson, the effect is like a drift of snow; on Simon, it looks like shards off a glacier.

He is an ice angel. If he ripped out your heart and held it up to the light, the colors would bleed together beautifully. Emma blinks the thought back.

His smile is wide as an eel's. "Did you expect me not to answer when you called my name? Or maybe you thought I wouldn't be here."

"I wasn't sure if you were busy," Emma says evenly. "Thank you for agreeing to talk with me."

"I'm never too busy for visitors. Can I ask who you are?"

"My name is Emma Lewis. I'm involved in a study with the FBI. I'm conducting a series of interviews, and I was hoping—"

"We'll get to hopes and dreams later," Gutmunsson says, still smiling. He has a raised twist of pale scar tissue above his right collarbone. "Has my faithful guard dog taken your measure?"

"Pardon?"

"Your name. Has Pradeep recorded your name?"

"Uh, yes. I've been checked off by Dr. Scott and at the door."

"Wonderful. Then we'll add you to the list for further conversations. Would you like an apple?"

He plucks a green apple from the fruit bowl and extends it out through the bars.

"Thank you, no," Emma says.

"It's because you can't reach over the barricade, isn't it? I can throw it to you if you like."

"Thank you, but I've already eaten."

"Have you? You'll excuse me for saying this, but you actually don't look as if you've had a decent meal for years. It's a bit gamine chic, isn't it, with the hair." He tosses the apple once, returns it to the bowl. "Have you left Ohio just to visit me? I'm flattered."

His eyes flash like blue diamonds. It's only when she looks down that Emma realizes she's wearing her college T-shirt, with the small Buckeyes logo over her heart. So he's not psychic—just observant. It's still disconcerting, knowing that her personal details are now part of Simon Gutmunsson's gestalt awareness.

She plants her feet. "Mr. Gutmunsson, I have a questionnaire here about the nature and process of your—"

"*Mr. Gutmunsson, Mr. Gutmunsson*—you don't have to stand on ceremony in a madhouse, you know. Call me Simon. And I'll call you Emma. Emma, have we met before? You seem familiar somehow."

"We haven't met before," Emma says. Too quickly? She can sense him sniffing around the outskirts of her mind, like a truffling pig.

"No, you're right. I think I'd remember." Gutmunsson steeples his hands and taps his forefingers against his bottom lip. "Maybe it's generational simpatico. We're close in age, aren't we? You're what, eighteen, nineteen?"

His guess is accurate. She'll allow it. "I'm eighteen years old."

"That's very young to be working for the FBI. I didn't realize the bureau was recruiting *juveniles* these days—Hoover will be turning in his grave. And how is Special Agent Cooper?"

He communicates with me. She's glad Cooper warned her about that. "He's doing fine."

"I doubt that's true, although I don't imagine he confides in you." Gutmunsson raises one eyebrow, like an echo of his mug shot. "Cooper will be running himself ragged with the business in Pennsylvania. I've been wondering when he'd come to visit me about it, but he's sent you instead. It's a bit lily-livered of him, if you ask me—you should call him on that."

"I will," Emma says without thinking, then stops herself, changes tack. "You know about the Pennsylvania case?"

"I get my news the same way everybody else does. Dr. Scott tried to have my newspapers clipped to prevent me from gaining access to 'stimulating material,' but that just reduced the broadsheets to rags—I had my lawyer obtain an injunction. I suspect Dr. Scott is one of those earnest people who believe that murder is the consequence of too much violent television."

Emma thinks of her own experience with therapists. "Dr. Scott is a behaviorist?"

Gutmunsson grins. "It's convenient you know the terms. Amazing, isn't it, the quack theories some practitioners believe while still calling themselves doctors."

"And you don't subscribe to the theory."

"That environmental influences are the strongest determiner of a person's actions?" He spreads his hands. "People take their motivation where they find it, Emma, and life is full of motivation. But they have to be inclined to begin with, don't you think? You can't just blame it on popular culture. *The Dukes of Hazzard* is horrifying, yes, but come on—it's no more likely to drive a man to murder than any other excruciatingly banal activity, like going to the mall."

Emma snorts, surprising herself. Gutmunsson's face lights.

"See? We're having a real conversation now. I say something amusing, and you laugh." He sits on the bed to face her, propped back on his hands, legs crossed at the knee. "Now tell me, are the details about Pennsylvania accurate in the papers? Or is the FBI not releasing all the information?"

"I'm not...I don't read the newspapers."

"Truly? You're completely oblivious about current events? I'd have thought that's a bit of an oversight for someone in law enforcement."

She keeps her voice level. "I'm not in law enforcement. I'm a psychology student."

"Oh, you're a *psychology* student, well. That explains the questionnaire, and the questionable fashion choices—I know I've been locked up awhile, but surely acid-wash denim has gone out of style by now. Your running shoes are new, though, or at least well maintained. Do you run, Emma?"

"Sometimes."

"Sometimes, mm. Were you bracing to run from *me*? Is that why you wore those shoes today? You're the psychology student— I'm sure you recognize subconscious behaviors." Gutmunsson's eyes are dark whirlpools. He stands again and approaches the bars, as if he's unable to sit still. "I'm significantly taller, though. I'm betting I could catch you, in a running race. Wouldn't it be fun if we could open this cage and find out?"

Emma feels a tremble in her calves, pushes down hard. "Can I ask what you were reading, when I first arrived?"

"Rereading," Gutmunsson corrects. "*Childe Harold's Pilgrimage*. I'm studying the Romantic poets. It's quite enjoyable—the language has a lovely gothic rhythm."

"You're studying?"

"You think I have something better to do? Should I be dribbling and playing with myself, like the other inmates here?"

"Excuse me, I meant are you formally enrolled."

"At Georgetown University, yes. My dissertation is on the disappearance of the God concept correlating to the flowering of representations of the sublime across texts by Shaftesbury, Burke, and so on." He makes an airy wave. "They won't confer my degree until I leave this fine institution, of course, but that day may yet come."

Emma hopes fervently not. "I see."

"*I see*—ouch. And here I thought we were becoming friends. Actually I'm not sure you *do* see, unless you're familiar with Byron."

"I know a little."

"Well, that *is* extraordinary. Most people of the Podunk rural classes remain entirely ignorant of the existence of art."

Emma reaches down inside herself for her credit class in classical literature and recites: "*There is a pleasure in the pathless woods, there is a rapture on the lonely shore, there is society, where none intrudes, by the deep Sea, and music in its roar.*"

The effect is immediate. Rapid movement in the cell as Gutmunsson thrusts himself against the bars. His expression is electric, grotesque with a nameless hunger, and his voice booms like thunder in the long room. *"I LOVE NOT MAN THE LESS, BUT NATURE MORE! FROM THESE OUR INTERVIEWS, IN WHICH I STEAL! FROM ALL I MAY BE, OR HAVE BEEN BEFORE! TO MINGLE WITH THE UNIVERSE, AND FEEL! WHAT I CAN NE'ER EXPRESS, YET CANNOT ALL CONCEAL!"*

In the sudden resounding quiet, Emma realizes she's taken a step back. She forces her breathing to calm. The manila folder is clammy from her grip: Her hands are clenched around the cardboard. She finds it difficult to relax them.

"I'm sorry, did I startle you?" Gutmunsson sinks away from the bars, long fingers still gripping the metal. Composed as before, his lips bloom red as he smiles. "I'm afraid I couldn't help myself—the acoustics in here lend themselves to oration. You surprised me, too, with the Byron."

Emma finds her voice, dust-dry. "We people of the Podunk rural classes have our moments, from time to time."

Gutmunsson bursts into a laugh. The sound is quite musical. His face, so distorted only moments ago, becomes radiant. "Oh, Emma, you're delightful! I could chat with you all day."

"Unfortunately I don't have all day. Will you do this questionnaire for me? Or should I leave it and come back?"

"No, no—don't go." Gutmunsson makes his look an appeal. It's hard to credit, that a boy with a mien like this should have the soul of a hyena. "Ah, you remind me so much of Kristin...." He shoves a hand through his fall of white hair. "But where do I *know* you from? It's positively tearing at me."

"Maybe I have a common-looking face," Emma suggests. She keeps her expression perfectly blank.

"Goodness, no. All right, I'll put it away, I'm sure it'll come to me. Give me your questionnaire now."

She finds her anchor. "I'd like to, but I can't hand it to you."

"Then we'll call for Pradeep, shall we?"

The orderly arrives holding a long-handled instrument with a pincer grip. "Mr. Gutmunsson, we do this in the usual way. Please go behind the privacy screen. If you do not obey the rules, the usual prohibitions on your news dailies will apply."

"Pradeep, may I have a cigarette while I complete the questionnaire?"

Pradeep considers. "You may have a cigarette now, but not after dinner this evening. Is that acceptable?"

"That's perfectly agreeable, thank you."

Gutmunsson retreats, peers over the screen as Pradeep expertly lifts the folder in the pincer and slides it through the bars of the cell. The cigarette is done in the same way, but with one entertaining variation: Pradeep takes a single cigarette from a pack in the pocket of his uniform, lights it and puffs on it once, then swiftly transfers it into the cage.

As soon as Pradeep calls out, Gutmunsson swoops from his naughty corner and falls on the cigarette, puffing furiously to keep the ember alight. Then he selects a felt-tipped pen from his desk and perches on the end of his bed, blue pages in his lap.

"Let me see what we have here," he says, uncapping the pen. With his long limbs, he looks rather like a large white spider hunched over the pages. "Hmm—boring, boring, boring, the usual dull stuff. I can complete this while we talk."

"Thank you for completing it." She can hardly refute his assessment of the questionnaire. A standardized instrument designed for the McMurtrys of the world is unlikely to be incisive enough for an offender like Simon.

"Not at all. Are you comfortable? Would you like to sit? I'd offer you a chair, but Pradeep is sitting on the only one."

Emma decides that this situation could not really get any more bizarre, so after checking the level of dust on the floor, she sits down on it cross-legged.

Gutmunsson is already intent on scribbling on the questionnaire pages. "You said you don't read the papers, but you're connected through Cooper. So how *is* he getting on with Pennsylvania?"

Pennsylvania—again and again, that word keeps returning. And again Emma's senses ping with the feeling of wrongness, of forces moving, pulling her toward something she doesn't fully understand.

"I actually have no idea." Emma registers the cigarette smoke trailing up toward the rafters, the acrid smell. "My unit is only concerned with old cases at this stage."

"*At this stage*, that's an interesting way of putting it. It suggests you'd like to be more involved."

This is not a direct question, Emma concedes. "I'd like to put the information we're gathering to use, yes."

"To stop more people like me, of course." Gutmunsson grins again, ashes his cigarette, and flicks to the next page. "But, Emma, you *must* know *some*thing. Have they given our Pennsylvania friend a name yet? The popular press is always so entertaining with that kind of thing. The Artist, they dubbed me—they weren't far off, actually. Do you think our new friend is an artist like me?"

"Your activities were very…different."

"By that you mean I didn't use my models and then throw them out with the trash."

Models. Emma registers the word, remembers the crime scene photos she viewed last night. She recalls the sun-dappled "tea party" scene, in which wire, fishing hooks, and catgut line were creatively utilized on four victims beneath the trees. There was strong evidence that Gutmunsson went back from time to time to assess his compositions at each scene and tweak them for his own amusement.

"No," she says, working to keep her expression neutral, "you had a little more style."

"Style—yes, the style of the thing is important, isn't it? But our new friend leaves the bodies in garbage dumps."

"I didn't know that," Emma confesses.

"Didn't you? Well, now you do. What does it suggest to you, Emma, that he disposes of his victims in that way?"

"I...I don't know."

"I'm sure you do. Think harder."

"I suppose it suggests that he's done with them? That they've served his purpose and now they're worthless."

Gutmunsson holds his cigarette up and considers the burning tip. "What worth did they have to him before, then?"

"The experience of killing them might be the primary—"

"*Wrong,*" Gutmunsson pronounces with relish. "Consider it from our friend's perspective. He saw something in them that suited him. That *called* to him, if you like. You spoke about his purpose and how it might be served—try again in that direction."

"His purpose is...He sees something in them that he recognizes

77

or wants. He takes them, prepares them, and kills them, which gives him that something, whatever it is—"

"Unpack that a little for me. He prepares them—how does he prepare them?"

"I don't know." Emma spreads her hands. "Honestly, I don't know. I told you, I haven't been allowed to examine any details of—"

"Active cases, yes, right. Well. That's a bit tedious, isn't it? The FBI has brought you all the way from Podunk, Ohio, and they haven't even given you anything useful to *do*. What's the point?"

Emma is uncomfortably aware that she was making a similar argument to Bell in the car two nights ago.

"But that in itself is interesting, Emma. Why *did* they bring you all the way from Podunk, Ohio? Are you special somehow?"

The hair on her arms lifts. "I told you. There's nothing special about me."

Gutmunsson stubs out his cigarette on the bed rail. "Now, don't be coy. I think you *are* special."

She rises from her seat on the floor, trying to make the movement seem natural. Every cell in her body is blaring a warning. "I'd like my questionnaire back now, if you're finished with it."

"A very special girl," Gutmunsson whispers, staring at her, "who works with the FBI. Miss Emma Lewis from Ohio..."

She sees the moment in him when he knows, feels it like a vibration in her spine. Her vertebrae quiver like a radio antenna and she has to brace her legs. Gutmunsson stands, pages slowly tipping from his lap and onto the floor of his cell like a drift of blue leaves.

"Miss Emma Lewis from Ohio—the last bride of Daniel Huxton..." Haloed by light from the stained-glass windows, his face is enraptured. His pupils expand into a maelstrom of blackness. "The girl who got away, the girl who ran. Oh, if only I'd realized this sooner! What fun we might have had!"

"I think we're done talking now." Emma hears how her voice has gone thready, feels as if she is tipping toward some endless, horrific maw.

"Answer one question for me first—you thought you were running away to save the other girls as well as yourself, didn't you? Did it burn, when you realized the truth?"

"That's two questions," she says automatically. "I'm going to leave now."

"Is that why you came to work for the FBI, Emma? To make yourself feel better about it?"

"I came to work for the FBI so I could help them catch people like you." But her lips are numb, and the words feel clunky in her mouth, like an ill-fitting retainer.

"They don't understand, though, do they?" Gutmunsson grips the bars, shivering with excitement. "The FBI isn't known for its lateral thinking. They've got you slaving over old cases, gathering useless information.... They don't understand you at all! A fighter like you! One of their best soldiers, and they're wasting you! They probably think you shaved your hair to scare people off—"

"Will you give me back my pages, please?"

"Did you know he would slit their throats when you ran?"

She feels pressure building up behind her eyes, and in her soft palate.

"It must have cut you to the quick, when you found out. Did it cut you, Emma?"

Her vision goes white and her voice bursts out like an explosion. "*YES*, okay? *It cut me.* Is that what you want to know? Is that what you want to hear?"

The echoes of her shout ring through the chapel, like ripples in deep water. Gutmunsson looks at her, seems to breathe her energy in. A great calm comes over him.

"Pradeep, would you please retrieve these papers for Miss Lewis?"

As the orderly arrives, Emma regains her senses. It takes everything she's got to step back, wait for Gutmunsson to collect the papers, wait for Pradeep to transfer them with his long claw. Once the folder is in her hands, Emma looks up at Gutmunsson, feeling the wasteland in her expression.

"Thank you for seeing me. And for...this." She holds the folder low and away from her body. "Good luck with your dissertation."

She turns to leave, and Gutmunsson speaks again.

"Emma! One last thing!"

She is holding on to her control with thin reins now. *You cannot look back on the path out of the Underworld.* She looks over her shoulder.

Gutmunsson stands by the front of his cell, the shadow of the bars on his face. Every other shadow in the room swarms in his eyes.

"Tell Special Agent Cooper I said hello." Gutmunsson smiles. "Tell him he chose well."

CHAPTER TEN

Emma's not actually sure how she makes the transition from Simon Gutmunsson's chapel room to the outside of the asylum. But Cooper must notice something about her when she emerges, because he deals with Dr. Scott and the sign-out process, and before Emma knows it, she's walking through the foyer.

Cooper takes her elbow, and Emma, dazed, looks at him and thinks, *I should punch you in the face. Right in the face.* But that sounds as if it would involve way more energy than she is capable of right now, and then she's out the main door and the moment has passed.

The sunlight in the parking lot is weak, but it's clean, and the air is clean. She walks away from Cooper, who is caught up talking to Scott, and onto the grass. Her T-shirt slaps against her body with the wind. Some of the things Gutmunsson said have made her angry, and some of the things she herself said have made her angry. Above all, she hates the hot, prickling feeling that she has been rooked. But she knows if she can get a grip on it now, she can use the anger; she can funnel it down into the great storehouse inside herself, draw on it when her funds of energy are low. She thinks of the Byron, and then she thinks of a quote by Mary Shelley: *I have love in me the likes of which you can scarcely imagine and rage the likes of which you would not believe.*

She senses more than sees it when Bell arrives to stand beside her.

"He got inside your head a little, didn't he?"

"Yes, he did." She feels her gut cramp, tries to ease down and realizes her abdominals have been clenched this whole time. "He's perceptive. And he's cruel. He likes poking at people's scars."

"You can't let him in, Emma."

She turns to face Bell then. "Do I look like an easy get?"

"No. But he would like that kind of challenge."

"I'll be okay. It's like going on a fairground ride—you get tipped up and down and rolled around, but when it's over your stomach settles." It's true. Her equilibrium is returning. "At the end of the day, he's still in there and I'm out here. And he completed the questionnaire."

"What?"

"Here." She hands it to him. "Don't give it to Cooper before we've had a look at it."

Bell stares at the folder in his hands, holds it as carefully as she did. She's suddenly, forcefully relieved that he didn't come in with her to the interview. The memory of Gutmunsson's taunts brings up an uneasy vision of Bell, enraged, leaping the sawhorses, putting himself within arm's reach....

"Another thing. Simon Gutmunsson knows something about Pennsylvania. I was right—the whole interview was a sting, and Gutmunsson is a part of it somehow. I need to talk to Cooper about—"

"One second." Bell touches her arm lightly. "We've got the car ride with Cooper. Pitch it to me first."

"Gutmunsson talked about the Pennsylvania killer's purpose," she says. "Suggested it might relate to the way he chooses victims and prepares the bodies. I need to know the details of the case before I can put it together."

"I can fill in the gaps with what I know."

"This might all end up leading toward an active case, Bell, and we were told to steer clear of anything other than our assignments. Are you comfortable with that?"

He glowers at the asylum, returns his gaze to Emma.

"I can't go in there. But I can support you out here. If you want to get involved, I'll back you up." Bell spares another glance toward the asylum's doorway, where their boss is still talking to the super-intendent. "Let's go sit in the car and figure this out before Cooper's done."

They crunch across the gravel together. The interior of the Plymouth is warm, almost stuffy. It's still better than standing outside the asylum, feeling the building loom.

Emma rubs a hand across the bristles at her nape. "Okay, tell me."

Bell dumps the folder on the seat between them like it's heavy. "Everything I've got is from the media. There's four victims in the case so far. The first was in Crozet, three months ago. The second was in Luray in April. The most recent victims were found in Pennsylvania, between Harrisburg and Carlisle—two in one hit. All the victims are under twenty-one. All the bodies were found in garbage dumps."

"What other commonalities?"

"All of them had their throats cut."

Emma tries not to flinch. "Anything else? All women?"

"No—and he's crossing racial lines as well. Two of the victims were white, but the boy in Luray was African American and one of the Carlisle victims was Puerto Rican. The first two were still dressed, but the most recent victims were found in their underwear."

"So they were tied up? What about sexual assault?"

"I don't have information on that. Evidence of ligature use, but they'd been untied before they were dumped. No fingerprints. This guy is very careful."

"And he's on a monthly cycle." When Bell nods, she asks the necessary question. "What do the police think he's doing with them?"

Bell hesitates, checks her face. Tells her anyway. "He abducts them, ties them, holds them for about twenty-four hours. Then he hangs them by the ankles and bleeds them out."

Everything Emma's been doing for the last few days comes in on her suddenly. She has to fight it, leans forward over her knees. When Bell calls her name, she sits back up. "I'm all right. Gimme a minute."

"Cooper's coming, you don't have a minute. And we haven't looked at the questionnaire yet."

"That's okay." Her chin firms. "I've got a few things to say to Cooper that should keep him distracted."

When Cooper slides into the driver's seat and turns to check on them, the first thing he sees is Emma's level expression. "What is it?"

"Gutmunsson knew who I was. He knew it in the space of one conversation and he wasn't even trying."

"Miss Lewis—"

"No." Her voice is cold. "You offered me up to Simon Gutmunsson like a jig on a line, *knowing* he'd take a bite. Someone like me is pure catnip to an offender like Gutmunsson, and you needed something to tempt him."

Cooper has the grace to look abashed. "Miss Lewis, I'm—"

"If you apologize to me right now I swear to god I will get out of this car and *walk* back to Quantico."

Bell shifts awkwardly. "Uh, this conversation might be—"

Emma stops him with a raised hand. "You're a part of this conversation, too. You really think it was an accident that you, of all people, were recruited to help me interview Simon Gutmunsson? Whatever Agent Cooper has to say, he can say it to both of us."

Bell closes his mouth. Looks from Emma to Cooper and back again. His expression turns flinty.

Cooper watches the interplay, settles on Emma. "I told you Gutmunsson was smart."

"You told me he was smart. Right. You didn't tell me he followed the press. He tagged me from the logo on my T-shirt, my name, and the newspaper reports." She wrangles with her anger. "He's got something you want, doesn't he? Something on Pennsylvania."

"That's not—"

"Do you know what Gutmunsson said to me? *Tell Agent Cooper he chose well.* He knew the score on this before I even walked in the building." Emma shakes her head in disgust. "Was the interview unit stuff all just bullshit? Was it all leading up to this?"

There's a silence. Cooper's expression cycles as he considers holding the line, before he gives up with a sigh.

"The interviews aren't bullshit. The interviews are important. But I needed to know you could handle yourselves before—"

Bell swears loudly, looks away.

"Gutmunsson is a special case—"

"And we were the *only* people you could use for this?" Bell demands.

"You're the only people of his age who report to the bureau." Cooper's jaw clenches. "You're the only people we haven't tried."

Bell exhales through his nose. Emma steps up to the plate.

"Mr. Cooper, would you please just be honest? What is going on? What did Simon Gutmunsson send you? You said he communicates with you, and he talked about how he's been asking to see you." Emma chases Cooper's line of sight. "Look, you don't need to play me, I'm already here. I *want* to help. But if you're gonna jerk me around, I'd rather go back to Apple Creek."

Cooper purses his lips, thinking. Finally comes to some kind of decision.

"He's sent me three letters." Cooper's voice is quiet. "One after Crozet, one after Luray. The last one was just after Pennsylvania."

"He gives you details about the murders," Emma prompts.

"Not details. Insights. I guess he'd know better than anybody how this new killer thinks."

"Is any of the information Gutmunsson's offering helpful?"

"I don't know. He's promised to share more if I go see him. But trying to insert themselves into police investigations, or grandstanding for more attention, is something these guys do. So ... I'm wary." Cooper rubs a palm across his face. "On the other hand, we've been going in circles on this new case and I'm trying every lead I can find, no matter how off base."

Bell's arms are folded. "Sir, I know the Pennsylvania case is tough. And I understand you're in a bind with it. But if you'd told me the real purpose of this unit was to interview Simon Gutmunsson—"

"You never would have joined up." Cooper meets his eyes. "I know. And I'm sorry. The thing is, Mr. Bell, I've got four dead teenagers in the morgue and likely more on the way. What would you have done, in my position?"

Bell bites his lip hard enough to leave a mark. "Okay. I get it. But the way you're doing it, it's not gonna work. If you're sending Lewis in to get leads off Gutmunsson, you gotta give us more information. Send her in blind, without any authority, and he'll just toy with her."

"Bell's right," Emma says. "We need more information. Not to mention we deserve more."

Cooper winces. "I can't give you any details about active cases. Donald Raymond, the section chief, was very specific—"

"Fine." Bell is determined. "Then officially, we're not involved. Unofficially, we'll be more use to you if we're better informed."

"We'll play," Emma agrees. "But not if we're being played."

Cooper looks between Bell's solid resolve and Emma's defiant insistence. "Okay. Fine. You want in, I'll tell you what I know. And when we get back to Quantico, I'll get you some access to the Pennsylvania files."

"Good." Emma refuses to show gratitude.

"Give me Gutmunsson's questionnaire first."

"No. First, the files."

Cooper narrows his eyes. "Miss Lewis, I said I'd share information, but I'm not horse-trading with you. You're gonna have to trust me."

Emma hesitates, looks at Bell. A pause, then Bell nods. She passes over the folder.

"Thank you." Cooper glances back at them as he reaches for the key, turns to start the engine. "You kids drive a hard bargain."

CHAPTER ELEVEN

A large bedroom early on a Friday morning, dark inside, plush sound-dampening carpet and the curtains tightly drawn. The family-sized house is on a cul-de-sac. Not even traffic sounds intrude.

The digital clock on the nightstand ticks over to 6:00 AM—there's a single discordant bleat before a hand reaches, touches the button. Anthony Hoyt, white male, six-two, brown and brown, no identifying marks, woke before his alarm and has been lying in bed contemplating the day to come. Now the alarm is his signal that events are starting, that life is moving in the direction of his choosing, so he flings off the sheets and gets up.

He showers and dries in the bathroom and pads back out to the bedroom. The built-in wardrobe opposite the bed has sliding doors on a long runner, and one door is entirely mirrored. Standing in front of it naked, Hoyt does a thorough check: His hair is glossy, his face is good, the skin over his cheekbones firm and tight. His whole body is nicely toned. Overall, the results of the treatments have been outstanding.

He slides open the wardrobe and selects his clothes, gets dressed.

Feeling a tremor, he takes out the bag with the other clothes in it. Then he goes into the kitchen to make breakfast.

At exactly 7:15, Hoyt leaves the house through the garage door, tucks everything in the back seat of his Mustang Ghia—a present from his grandparents—and clicks the switch to open the garage to the outside. It's a two-hour drive, and the weather is fantastic: sunny and becoming warm. Hoyt slips his sunglasses on as he drives out of Annandale, merging with outbound traffic, humming along to Hall & Oates on the radio until news time. He listens to the news with interest, finally reaches Charlottesville by 9:10.

In the bathroom of an underground parking garage, he changes into the clothes from the bag: a white undershirt, loud Hawaiian shirt, jeans, and loafers. The wig is new, and he practiced putting it on a few times at home in his room until he was comfortable with it. He puts a ball cap—GO HURRICANES!—over his now longish blond hair. The blond makes him look even younger. He returns the bag to the car, collects his alternative identification, and walks to the real estate agency, enjoying the sun.

Burt Wagner, the agent, meets him at the door of the office, and banter is exchanged about the weather and how it's almost too nice a day to drive to the site.

"But we'd be a while walking," Wagner admits, "and you're probably keen to see the place, right?"

They take Wagner's Ford. The drive is about forty minutes and Hoyt keeps up inane conversation about the state of the town and the local climate compared to Miami, maintaining the illusion that he actually lives in Miami. State Route 810 winds out of Boonesville, past an old Methodist church, then uphill along Tabletop Mountain

Road, toward the more marginal wilderness area abutting Shenandoah National Park.

Wagner turns the Ford sharply off the tar and onto a dirt road that snakes past the fence of an agistment pasture and into the trees. Finally they pull onto the road to the property. There's a farm gate, and overhanging trees that peel back to reveal a large old house: single story, shaded wooden porch. Nearby, the barn.

"Well, here we are," Wagner says. "You said your grandfolks wanted privacy."

"Yes, for sure," Hoyt agrees. He's careful to keep the accent steady.

"Damn nice of you to come get the place set up for them. Lord knows, I wish my grandkids would do the same for me."

They step high over the long-neglected grass to the porch. Wagner walks Hoyt through the house, noting the difficulties of the proposed renovation and how that will bring the price down. "But a young fella like yourself, you won't have any trouble with the work."

"Mm." Hoyt makes some noises about a generator for power tools. He has no trouble spinning the tale to fill in the detailed edges: He *does* want to improve the house. He wants to fix the guttering, clean the place up. He has plans. Big plans.

At last they walk to the barn. From the moment he stepped out of the car, Hoyt has felt the presence of the barn nearby like a fizz in his blood. Now Wagner pulls open the great door, reveals the extent of it. Hoyt crosses the threshold, feeling like he's entering a church.

"Concrete floor," Wagner points out approvingly. "Lots of natural light. Hayloft. Faucets there hook up to tank water. Just the one stall, over on the left—rest of the space is open. I think they used it mainly for machinery. You got the grease drain in the floor and the big crossbeams there. See the chain? They were lifting John Deere engines here, most likely."

Hoyt finds it hard to keep the excitement out of his voice. "Granddad said it'll be good to have someplace I can lock up tools while I'm working on the place."

"Well, it's secure." Wagner slaps the solid hardwood walls. "Better condition than the house, really. And if you're running a drop saw, a nail gun, and so on, you're far enough away from neighbors that you won't get complaints about the noise."

"Mm."

"You could store lumber here. Base of operations, so to speak."

Hoyt looks around the interior of the barn. He looks at the faucets, the concrete floor with its helpful drain, the high crossbeams, the chains. This is so much more suitable than the disposable locations he's currently using. The extraordinary potential of the space uncoils behind his eyes. The possibilities make him break out in a wide, sincere smile.

"It's perfect," he pronounces. "Just perfect."

CHAPTER TWELVE

The sky is glowering over Quantico early Friday morning and—still buoyed by the success with Cooper—Emma runs in the rain. On the way back she's flagged by Betty, who delivers Simon's questionnaire. Emma holds the folder by the corners as she returns to her room. She showers and dresses, then heads down, carrying her paperwork and two cafeteria mugs in the elevator all the way to basement level.

At the door to their gray office, she discovers a hand-lettered sign that reads THE COOL ROOM Scotch-taped to the wood. Emma tucks her papers in her armpit and detaches the sign with the hand not holding the mugs, pushes open the door with her butt.

"Hey." Bell is distracted as he scrawls on a notepad at the desk. "Grab a chair. I'm finishing off the McMurtry report. It's anyone's guess if Cooper still wants it, but I thought it couldn't hurt."

"I think he still wants it. Want me to read it through?"

"Yep. Check I got your info down."

"I wrote up the Gutmunsson interview last night." She sets her papers and the mugs on the desk, tosses the sign his way. "Did you see this on the door?"

"Thanks." He takes a mug, examines the writing on the sign as he slurps. "Huh. FBI pranking, I guess. We're supposed to be researching cold cases, get it?"

"Wow. They really dug deep for that one."

"And y'know. We're teenagers, so…"

"So that makes us cool? Are we cool, Bell?"

"Last time I checked, no. But that could change any minute." Bell, amused.

"Jesus." She hesitates. "You want to read through my report?"

"Not really." He tosses the sign into a nearby wastebasket.

"You must be sick of talking about Gutmunsson."

"It's fine. It's like hitting yourself in the head with a hammer over and over. After a while you don't feel it."

Emma bites her lip. "I'm sorry."

"Don't apologize." He puts his coffee down and stands. "I mean, really, don't worry about it. I've got the Pennsylvania file. Cooper dropped off a copy a half hour ago."

Emma feels a thrum inside, as if someone has plucked her heart chord. "You've got it? Have you looked at it yet?"

"Nope. I waited for you."

Bell collects a nondescript drab-green folder, the hanging type used in filing cabinets, returns to the desk with it. Emma has already dragged her chair around to sit beside him.

Before she opens the file, she pauses. "We should take notes. Wait, what do we already know from Cooper?"

Bell pulls his notepad closer, detaches the pages with the McMurtry report, and sets them aside. He clicks his pen. "Three garbage dump sites, four murders—Crozet, Luray, Carlisle. All victims were inverted and exsanguinated. No sexual assault."

Bell probably got the cop lingo from his dad. Emma tries to keep up. "Ligature marks, no fingerprints. Teenage victims. Increasing number of victims. One event a month, for the last three months." An awareness has been hovering in the recesses of her mind; now it takes on a solid shape. "It's a new month—already June."

"There's still time." Bell meets her eyes. "There's still time to catch him."

The file sits there like a malignancy. Emma opens it. She's steeled herself for the crime scene photos but they hurt all the same, like a deep, damaging blow to the kidneys. A display of dead teenagers: She's been *in* scenes like these.

The photos are xeroxed copies of the originals, and some of the finer details are blurred. The graininess makes the images just a little more unreal. But what is actually unreal is that there's a person in the world who could do this. And not just do it once, but do it again and again and again—

"Jesus, Mary, and Joseph," Bell whispers.

Emma is reminded that he puts up a good appearance of being in law enforcement already, but Bell has only ever been in training. She herself has viewed this kind of thing before.

It's different, though. Not just in execution but in tone. The girl from Crozet lies abandoned in a puddle of oily-looking gray water, surrounded by garbage: household waste and metal parts, old diapers, smashed bottles. The Luray boy, dumped carelessly, his limbs collapsed at awkward angles, part of him obscured by a ripped tarpaulin. Then, Pennsylvania—two bodies thrown out together, sprawled on top of each other, undignified, their semi-nakedness making a gruesome parody of intimate relations.

I didn't use my models and then throw them out with the trash. Emma bats at the thought.

Her voice comes out low and rough. "He doesn't value them at all, once he's done with them. He's taken their blood and now they're just... empty."

Bell also sounds muted. "Why does he take the blood?"

"It's part of his process, or he's using it for something...." She clears her throat, tries to steady. "Blood has lots of meanings—the color, the way it shines, as essence. It's the red of love hearts, of virgins. It's used in religious rituals."

"The care with the body is kind of ritualized. It says here the bodies have been washed." Bell taps another sheet from the forensic report. "No sexual assault, though. That's unusual, isn't it?"

"Yes. But just because he didn't molest the victims doesn't mean the murders aren't part of a sexualized fantasy. Think of McMurtry."

"He's very careful. I think the washing is about getting rid of trace evidence."

"But he goes to a lot of trouble to invert them, when he could just cut them in any position. That's ritual."

"Does he cut them when they're still conscious?" Bell squints at the page. "Does it say that somewhere?"

"Check the histamine results. Higher levels will indicate they were stressed at the time of death." It sickens Emma that she knows this.

Bell runs a finger down the columns of pathology results. "I can't interpret these numbers. Can you make any sense of this?"

Emma shakes her head, wordless.

"Let's come back to these when we know more." Bell gathers the crime scene photos and puts them aside, goes to the victim profiles. "Okay. None of the victims knew each other. No correlations in terms of places they frequented, activities, hobbies, et cetera. There's no connection between them that we can see, except for the age range."

"They must have something in common. He chose them for a reason."

"Cooper made a note about it here. Killers usually hunt within their own age demographic—he thinks we're looking for a younger suspect."

"How young?"

"Eighteen to twenty-five."

"But he's crossing racial and gender lines. What makes Cooper think he's not crossing age lines as well?"

"He needs real physical strength to commit these murders." Bell points to the bottom lines of notes. "That suggests a younger, more athletic suspect. Cooper thinks this is a young guy with a grudge."

Emma squints. "Like he got bullied in high school or something?"

"Maybe he got beaten on. It would make sense of why he's focused on people his age."

"I can see why Cooper let us in on this." Emma turns another page. "Here's the first victim."

"Carol Lambton." Bell touches a high school graduation photo delicately. "Found in Crozet. But he got her from Staunton. And they're all like that. He takes them from one town and dumps them in another. The two kids found in Pennsylvania both came from Martinsburg."

"So he's on the move. He's got a vehicle. He travels up and down I-81. He could be driving back and forth from college, or to see family."

"Or he could have a job. Musician, delivery guy, junior salesman."

Emma knows what this means. "He can pass for normal. He's smart. Organized. And strategic. He doesn't just do them and dump them in the same town. There's nothing spontaneous about this. He's thought about it a lot." She considers it. "So he's not impulsive—he's got a lot of control. Doesn't that mean older, statistically?"

"Yeah, but I think Cooper's on the right track. A younger perpetrator would find it easy to attract new victims—they wouldn't suspect someone close to their age. He could just hang out with the kids in any town and fit right in. And look how strong he is." Bell turns pages until he finds the second victim profile. "He'd have to overpower them, but look at Lamar Davis—football, athletics, full-ride scholarship at University of Mary Washington. He's fitter than me." He glances at Emma. "He'd be hard to take down in a fight."

Another realization. "So maybe he doesn't fight them. Let me see the toxicology again?" She checks the report, finds the note she needs to confirm. "It says here he etherizes them. All of them."

"But then he's still got to hang them up. Davis has got to be, what, one-sixty? One-seventy? He's a big guy. That's heavy work, and there's no evidence to show the killer used pulleys or anything like that to hang up the victims."

"He learned from that, though, see? Sienna Ramirez in Carlisle—a hundred pounds. And the other Carlisle victim, Brian Barnes. He isn't big either. And Barnes is younger. Younger is easier." Emma is thinking hard. "What does he see in them?"

Bell grimaces. "Different genders, different races, different physical makeup...I don't know. They're all young."

"They're all young, they're more vulnerable, more trusting. He can be more opportunistic."

"Maybe he's someone they think they *can* trust? A teacher's aide, a camp counselor."

"A college tutor. Or a junior cop?"

"Jesus." Bell seems horrified by the mere suggestion.

"Write it all down," Emma says. "We don't know what might be useful."

"So who are we looking for? A male suspect, eighteen to twenty-five, race unknown."

"Statistically, he's probably white." Emma looks away. "Where does he get the ether?"

"They might've checked that already." But Bell makes a note.

Emma chews her lip, feeling restless. "Cooper sent Betty to me this morning with Gutmunsson's questionnaire. I want to look it over."

Bell grunts, mulish. "We haven't pulled all the details from the case file yet."

"I want to see if anything matches up." She takes out the blue pages from the stack of paperwork she arrived with.

"Have you looked at this yet?"

Emma shakes her head. "I haven't had a chance. And I wanted to wait for you."

The first two pages of answers are just repeated, flowery-script versions of Gutmunsson's full name in green felt pen.

"I'm betting this guy really loves the sound of his own voice," Bell grates.

Emma raises her eyebrows. "I won't disagree with you there."

There's the occasional variation, where Gutmunsson's written *Why are the questions on these things always so puerile?* and *Television made me do it*, but on the fourth page, the answers change.

Pennsylvania, Gutmunsson has written. Then a series of dot points.

"Two means he's not getting what he needs with just one. Expect to see more of that." Bell frowns. "That's not telling us anything new. We know the perp has started doing more than one victim per event."

"But this." Emma touches the paper. *"It's a fine, sharp-edged, non-serrated blade, isn't it.* How could Gutmunsson know that? It's not like he's seen the autopsy reports."

"He's just being logical." Bell sees her expression, clarifies. "The victims were slashed. The perp wasn't sawing at them—to slash a jugular, he'd presumably want a clean cut. So, a thin, straight blade."

"Okay. What about this one: *Why do you think he removes the clothes and leaves the underwear?*"

"That's not an answer, that's another question." Bell relents. "Fine. Again I'm guessing the killer is being extra cautious—the clothes might pick up fibers or residue that he doesn't want found."

"Or maybe he gets a charge off making the victims more vulnerable."

Bell's gaze is weighted. "Do you think we're dealing with a sadist?"

"We can tell from toxicology and the ligature abrasions that he killed them after the unconsciousness and analgesia from the ether wore off, so yes…" Emma sits back in her chair and rubs her neck, crooked at a tiring angle. "But I'm not a psychologist, and that's not a diagnosis. I don't know. I don't know what we're dealing with."

"Okay, let's move on. *Cycle will shorten.* I guess that stands to reason."

"I'm sure we'll find out. Next."

Bell hesitates. "It's his last answer."

"And? What is it?" Emma leans forward to see, then wishes she hadn't. She reads the answer aloud. *"Let me know when he starts taking their hair."*

She feels cold again now. There's a strong instinct to raise her hand and rub it over her shorn head, but she refuses to let Gutmunsson influence her even that much.

"Do you wanna talk about it?" Bell's shoulder beside her radiates warmth through his shirt. It's the only warm spot in the whole damn room, so she can't even resent it.

"No. He probably just put that in there to yank my chain. It would be very on point for him." She snorts, annoyed with herself for reacting. "God, what an asshole."

Bell puts the blue pages back into their folder, slaps the folder shut, looking as if he's had about as much as he can stand. He closes the case file, too, stacks everything together, and sets it aside. "Okay, I'm done."

"You're done?"

"Yep. For now. And you are, too."

"We haven't talked about—"

"Lewis, you can sit here until steam comes out your ears, trying to make this mess of information line up, or you can step back and give your brain a chance to work things over. I like to keep busy." Bell gets up and pushes in his chair, everything about him decisive. "I'm gonna go shoot something. Wanna come along?"

Emma wonders if it's a particularly male reaction, the urge to hit or shoot something when you get angry. But then, she's been known to hit things herself on occasion. "Where do you shoot something around here?"

"There's an outside range and an inside range. And it's raining outside, so..."

The idea is intriguing. She stands up, curious to see where it's all going. "You really want me to come shooting with you?"

"Hell yeah. I mean, Cooper said we'd get instructional basics, right? So we're just getting a head start. You got experience with firearms?"

"A rifle, yeah. Or a captive bolt. My parents run dairy cattle."

"Handguns?"

"Never."

"Then now's a great time to learn. Come on."

Bell whips his jacket off the back of his chair, ushers them both out of the office—or the Cool Room, if you like, Emma thinks. They have to take the elevator up one floor and walk past an area where National Academy students are practicing tactical entry drills. Emma hears students yelling, feels the impact of doors slamming open like a series of thuds in the base of her spine.

Bell checks them both in to the range. The range master is a craggy-faced former Marine sergeant named Hagland who helps them sign for weapons and ammunition. Emma opens the air lock door for Bell, who's carrying the equipment, then works the next door into the high-noise area.

Bell hangs his jacket and lays everything on the shelf in the stall. "Okay, this isn't a full field kit. Normally you'd practice with a gun belt and a holster, work out how to manage a speedloader, stuff like that."

"Right." Emma looks at the box of ammunition, the safety glasses and earmuffs. The two snub-nosed revolvers, the metal rubbed to a dull patina. Her father hunts deer during the season, shoots foxes on the farm. This feels different.

Bell rolls his cuffs two turns. "But you're not qualified to carry, and we're not gonna be lugging these things around with us."

"Are you licensed to carry?"

"In Texas, yeah. I'm not licensed in Wisconsin yet." He shrugs. "Mainly I prefer to keep my gun in the truck."

"I'm not really the kind of person who thinks guns are the best solution to a problem," she confesses.

"That's totally fine. Let's just say *I'm* the kind of person who likes to prepare for every eventuality." Bell turns to face her. "Emma, there's someone out there killing kids our age. And as of today, we're involved in the hunt to catch him."

"But we're not putting ourselves in the action. We're just collecting and analyzing data."

"*Every* eventuality," Bell repeats. His voice goes quiet. "Would you have used a gun against Huxton, if you'd had one?"

She doesn't have to think too hard about it. "Yes," she admits.

"Just think of it as a tool, Lewis. It's useful when you need it."

She blows out air. "All right. Show me."

He picks up a revolver to demonstrate. "Okay. Now, I know the bureau is starting to issue thirteens, but this is the original Smith &

Wesson Model 10. It's a basic service piece—six shot, double action, with fixed sights." He passes it to her. "Feel the weight."

"It's heavy." She's not sure why she's surprised.

"Yep. Revolvers need hand and arm strength to be accurate, and it's usually good to be accurate. Now aim it toward the target and dry-fire it a few times to get the feel of it."

He shows her the Weaver stance, how to aim, how to position. The gun is so terribly heavy, and there's a dread in the pit of Emma's stomach with a similar weight. Every time they looked at the pages in the case file, she felt a knot inside herself tighten.

The Gutmunsson link is impossible to avoid thinking about. She wonders what Simon Gutmunsson is doing right now. Probably reading a book full of terrible Byronic poetry.

"Cooper will want you to go back." Bell's leaning his shoulders against the stall as he watches her. And practicing his mind reading, apparently. "Now that he knows Gutmunsson will talk to you, he'll send you back for sure. Especially if the killer's next victims show up with their hair cut off."

Emma keeps her focus on the paper target twenty yards away. "What happened to 'There's still time to catch him'?"

Bell steps closer and corrects her support hand, steps back. "That's what I'd *like* to see happen. But I'm also a realist. And if any of this information Gutmunsson has given you hits the jackpot, Cooper will have you back at St. Elizabeths faster than you can say 'teenage sociopath.'"

Emma braces her knees. "If I need to go back, I'll go back."

"Have you thought about how you'll deal with Gutmunsson?" He pauses. "I could maybe figure out a way to make myself go in there—"

"No. No way." Emma tries to do the rear-sight blurring technique that Bell instructed was best form. "I was thinking about it last night. I want to go see the sister. The twin."

"She lives just outside Richmond, right? In some kind of private clinic?"

"Yep. I'm going to call her lawyer and ask to visit. I have a feeling Kristin Gutmunsson will have some insight on how to manage her brother."

"The police might have already exhausted that option. You know what it was like after Huxton."

"True." She relaxes her stance and puts the gun down. Her right hand is already aching from tension and pulling the trigger. "But I'll bet you ten dollars the police never used a teenage interviewer to talk with her."

Bell squints. "Not just a teenager—a girl. It's worth a try."

"It is. All right, now stop being delicate and give me some ammunition."

He raises his eyebrows. "You ready for it?"

"I'd better be."

Bell shows her how to load. She puts in the last three bullets herself. Now they don their earmuffs, and Emma picks up her weapon again.

She wants to feel powerful, stronger, shooting the gun—and when she squeezes the trigger gently and her arm jolts back with the kick, she does get a sense of elation. But it lasts only as long as the shot's echo. When that's gone, the ever-tightening knot under her ribs is still there.

CHAPTER THIRTEEN

Around midday on Monday, Emma emerges from Petersburg prison after interviewing Michael Gesak. Sunshine has broken through the clouds, making everything seem bright. It's the exact opposite of her internal landscape right now. Back in the truck, Bell's face is stormy as he yanks off his tie and tosses it on the seat.

"Four girls. He didn't even bury them—"

"Let's not go over it again." Emma's limbs feel heavy as she buckles her seat belt.

They handed in the McMurtry report yesterday, on Sunday morning, and received instructions for the Gesak interview last night. When Emma questioned the utility of keeping up with the interviews, Cooper—still wearing a tie at eight in the evening, his jacket in the crook of his arm—just directed them both to the Gesak summary.

"Simon Gutmunsson might have leads on the Pennsylvania case, but he's not the only game in town, Miss Lewis. I meant it when I said the offender interviews were important. Hell, I still want the *results* of the interviews. It's what I'm paying you for."

But Gesak was tough, and now Bell stares out the windshield, looking lost. "Jesus. Why are some guys so fucked up?"

"It's a kind of sickness, I think. Or a defect of the soul." Emma follows the line of his eyes, but there's nothing for them to see out there except a few windblown trees on the perimeter of the Petersburg compound. "Cooper said we're waging a war, and I think to some extent he's right."

Bell scrubs a hand through his hair. "I want to contain it. It's why I'm in training—I want to protect people from it."

"I just want to survive it," Emma confesses. That seems bleak. "Look, we don't have any answers or solutions. Maybe the information we're gathering will help find some—but right now we've got to dig out more information from Kristin Gutmunsson's head. So let's drive."

The only upside to continuing with the interview charade is that both Cooper and the Gutmunssons' lawyer have agreed to allow them to visit Kristin Gutmunsson, and she lives just south of Richmond. They're practically passing right by on the drive home.

The trip is quiet. They're only ten minutes from their destination when Bell suggests a rest stop—he looks like he needs it. While he picks up some lunch for them both, Emma heads to a nearby phone booth.

"Please tell me they're not making you wear those ridiculous G-man suits," Robbie says on the phone.

Emma laughs, instantly calm at the sound of her big sister's voice. "No to the suits. Polyester is really not my thing."

"But are they treating you right? They're not stressing you out? I don't trust the FBI."

"They're treating me good." Emma has to force some of the cheer. She looks out the side of the booth: Clouds above make the air look gray. "You don't have to worry. Tell Mom and Dad I'm fine—"

"Tell Dad yourself," Robbie says.

There's a fumbling exchange on the line, then her father's voice in her ear. "Are you okay there, Emma Anne?"

He sounds old, Emma thinks. She blinks hard before replying. "Dad, I love you and yes, I'm doing fine. Tell Mama I'm hugging her from far away—it's okay, I know she's at work, but just give her my love."

"Will do. You eating right? Looking after yourself? Don't let them push you around, you hear?"

When the phone call is done, Emma walks back to the Dodge, where Bell is waiting with a paper sack of burgers.

"Thanks." Emma takes the bag of burgers and the cardboard drinks holder while Bell opens the tray of the pickup. "I just realized I hadn't called my folks for days."

He lays down a rug, reclaims the drinks. "They get nervous if you don't call?"

"Sometimes still, yeah. But I mainly wanted to hear their voices." Emma hoists herself up. "Nowadays, I get the urge to call, I call."

"You don't know what's gonna happen one day to the next, right?"

"That's it. I remember…" Emma hesitates, continues. "When Huxton had me, I remember thinking I wished I could hear them. Talk to them. Anyway, I don't leave things the way I used to."

"I get that."

They tuck into the food, suck pop through straws. The burgers aren't bad, but there's a lot of ketchup. The calm from her phone conversation hasn't yet dissipated and it makes Emma grin.

"My sister, Robbie, said I should wear a suit like you, to annoy Cooper."

Bell is surprised into a laugh. "Now that I'd like to see." He licks ketchup off his lip. "So...are we still mad at Cooper?"

"He should've been straight with us from the beginning." Emma softens. "But I can understand why he did what he did."

Bell nods. "He wants to stop teenagers from dying."

"His intentions are good. But my mom has a proverb about that." Time to change the subject. "You been in touch with your family since you arrived in Virginia?" She realizes that could be mis-construed as scolding. "Sorry, that's none of my business—"

"I called them yesterday." Bell busies himself wadding up the paper from his burger. "They're doing okay."

"What are your sisters' names?"

"Selena and Connie." He smiles softly. Wipes his mouth and fingers with a napkin, and the smile becomes muted. "Lena's still angry with me. I just gotta let it go. I keep reminding myself she can't stay pissed forever."

"She'll come around."

"I'm hoping." He jumps down off the tray. "I'm just real glad my family's in Texas right now and nowhere near I-81. Let's move, I want to get this visit done."

The urgency is part of her, too, Emma realizes. The goalposts have shifted. The trip to see Simon Gutmunsson and the photos in the Pennsylvania case file have tilted the world. Emma's hoping they can both keep their balance.

She puts the trash in a dumpster at the edge of the parking lot. Bell's revving the engine by the time she climbs back into the cab of the Dodge. Humidity makes Bell's shirt look wilted; Emma hits the air-conditioning. The change in the weather sings *June, June, June*. Time is their enemy. Somewhere—somewhere close, Emma's sure—the Pennsylvania killer is considering his next move.

"Rosanna" is playing softly on the car radio as Emma provides directions from a map they picked up at a Texaco. She's glad they're driving the old West Hundred Road and not the turnpike, because she's tired of staring at traffic.

Bell clears his throat. "Listen, there's something you need to know. I might have trouble with this. With Gutmunsson's sister."

"What sort of trouble?"

"She was there." He stares forward, fingers gripping the steering wheel. "When my dad was killed. She was Gutmunsson's hostage during the arrest."

"She what?" Emma hasn't yet had a chance to read through all the details of Simon Gutmunsson's arrest. She knows nothing about this.

"My dad persuaded Gutmunsson to trade the sister as a hostage. He let my father take her place. But then Gutmunsson knifed him, so Kristin stabbed her brother in the neck. That's how they caught him. My dad still died, though."

All the things that can't be helped, Emma thinks. *All the things that circle back around and find us again*. She wants to put a hand on Bell's arm, stops herself. It won't make him feel better.

"The police told you all this?"

"I read the arrest transcripts and the incident notes."

For a moment, Emma marvels that while the reports and notes from her own case gave her such relief, the reports on Simon Gutmunsson have done the complete opposite for Bell. The Huxton reports were something she could read and absorb—a firm account, to fill in the gaps when the lived experience had been so jumbled and fast.

For Bell it was different. For him, the reports about Simon's arrest were just a horrifying, drawn-out description of his father's death. He knew all the facts, and they'd worn a groove in him, but they didn't bring back what he'd lost.

"Do you want to stay out in the truck for this interview?" Emma's tone is cautious.

"Not this time," Bell says grimly. He takes the turn past the Walgreens to get them where they need to go.

"Travis. Can you run through this?"

He rolls his lips between his teeth. "Let's hope so."

CHAPTER FOURTEEN

Chesterfield Clinic is in an affluent area of sprawling Virginia hillside, with lots of pretty trees. The clinic is more like an expensive health spa, Emma thinks, with chalet-type bungalows, each set in its own garden. The mental health care of the privileged few.

Bell cuts the engine in the parking lot. "Why's Kristin Gutmunsson living in a place like this anyway?"

"I don't know exactly. Her lawyer said she needed peace and quiet, after the court case. God knows if Simon were my brother, I'd want some peace and quiet, too."

They sign in at a genteel reception office and ask for Kristin's location. It's sunny back out on the manicured lawns. At the correct bungalow porch, they smooth their clothes, knock. Emma notes the potted geraniums, the unobtrusive lock on the outside of the door. Chesterfield is another asylum, just a nicer-looking one.

They have permission to visit, and they were told Kristin's expecting them. Yet she still seems surprised when they enter in answer to her call.

She is sitting on a high-sided white couch with too many throw cushions, reading a book in the light-filled, open living room of the bungalow. Her gaze darts over them, settles on Emma.

"Miss Gutmunsson," Emma starts, "my name is Emma Lewis and this is Travis Bell. We're with the FBI. We've come to talk with you about your brother, Simon."

Kristin breaks into a smile and puts her book aside, claps her hands.

"I thought they said *Emmett*." Her smile is wide and artless. "When they explained you were coming, I thought they said Emmett, not Emma. But you're lovely! Oh goodness."

Kristin Gutmunsson's resemblance to her twin is striking. She has the same gifts of good breeding, the poise and length of bone. She's barefoot, in a simple cream linen shift that likely cost about as much as a small car. Her hair is ice-white and hangs down in long tassels that remind Emma of Spanish moss—which makes her think of chiggers. Then she feels bad, as if her thought associations are dishonorable. Better to note the rest of the girl's features without judgment: the bee-stung lips, blue eyes, high cheekbones, aristocratic nose covered with a smattering of pale freckles, the only ordinary thing about her.

Bell shifts on his feet, uneasy. Emma realizes it's more than the connection to his father's case. It's because Kristin is beautiful. Some men find beauty discomforting, and Emma's not sure why.

Kristin sees Bell's movement and transfers her attention. "Hello. Are you all right? You look as if you've had a shock."

"I'm...I'm fine," Bell says, blinking.

"I'm sorry I look so much like my brother," she says. "I can't help it."

"I know." Bell looks awkward all the same.

"Do you know that the word 'twin' comes from the Old Norse word '*tvinnr*'? It means 'double-born.' In Latin, the word is '*gemina*.' They thought twins were two halves of one soul." She looks at Emma, her expression so open it's disconcerting. "Although you probably don't want to think I share any part of my soul with Simon. It's hard, looking so like him. People find it off-putting."

Emma searches for something appropriate to say. "I understand. Thank you for seeing us."

"Oh, I never say no to police asking about my brother. I feel responsible, so I do everything I can to help."

"You feel responsible?" Emma asks.

"They might have caught him faster, if I'd been more cooperative from the start. But there were lots of reasons why that wasn't possible." Kristin's expression is saddened, but she brightens in an instant. "Please do sit down. Would you like coffee? Let's have coffee."

Kristin uses the coral-colored telephone to call down to "the main house" for a tray of coffee. Then she ushers Emma over to sit on the white couch and takes her hand. Emma can't think of an excuse to pull away.

"Have you seen him already?" She leans forward and peers at Emma's face. "Oh, I can tell that you have."

Emma finds it disturbing, the idea that her visit to Simon Gutmunsson is still written on her somehow. "Yes. Yes, I visited your brother late last week."

"Did he insult you?" Kristin's brows lift. "He uses insults like meat tenderizer, to soften people up. Then he's friendly, so they get confused. That's how he slips inside, you see."

"I know what you mean," Emma admits, although privately she thinks Simon Gutmunsson never really got to the "friendly" part of their conversation.

"He would like you, though," Kristin says.

"Why do you say that?"

"Because you look closed-up and spiny, like a crab in a shell. He's so curious about locked boxes. He would like to crack you open."

Emma swallows. "He gave it a good shot."

Kristin smiles craftily, like she's sharing gossip. "He can't handle *me*, because I'm like marshmallow. Soft and amorphous. There's nothing to hold on to and I keep changing shape. It drives him *crazy*." She chuckles, then her smile droops. "And I'm his sister, of course. His blood. He has to love me. Shall we have our coffee in the garden? It's warm inside, isn't it?"

She leads them out a set of French doors on the left, across a small, brick-paved, sunny area, and onto the lawn, where a rattan lounge setting is casually arranged like a bower beneath a spreading oak. The smell of green is so intense it's like a haze. Insects tick in the grass.

Once they're all settled—Emma and Kristin on the couch, Bell standing nearby, acorns crunching under his boots and clearly unsure where to put his hands—Emma decides it's time to press for details.

"Kristin—" She pauses. "Can I call you Kristin?"

"Oh, please do." Kristin smiles eagerly.

"When I visited your brother, he shared some insights he had. Not about his own case—about a current murder investigation."

"Yes, Simon is very clever. And of course that's his particular area of interest." Kristin plucks a stray blade of ryegrass at the base of the couch, brushes the feathery bud against her cheek.

"We think he might know more. So I may have to go see him again. I was hoping you might be able to give me some ideas about getting this information from him, and also about..." Emma opens her hands to complete the sentence.

"How to handle him?"

"Yes."

Kristin almost bounces. "You could ask him about me! That would put him off guard. He's very protective of me."

"Except for that time he held you hostage at knifepoint," Bell grinds out, and Emma wants to kick him.

Kristin seems unaffected, though. "Oh yes—he was really not in his right mind that day. Officers and agents were everywhere, pointing guns at him....I think he felt cornered. He was upset and scared, and even I didn't know what he would do. Simon behaves according to a certain logic most of the time, but that day he wasn't thinking at all." She angles her head and looks right into Bell's eyes. "He hurt you, didn't he?"

Bell's posture and face stiffen in a way Emma's becoming familiar with. "I think I'd better go wait in the truck."

He starts to turn and Kristin stands, tugging at her own fingers.

"Mr. Bell—I'm sorry." Expression fraught, she waits until he's turned back before continuing. "My brother has done a lot of awful things, and I'm always apologizing to people for them."

Bell's throat works but he stands his ground. "It was my dad. He was the one who took your place the day your brother was arrested. He was the one your brother stabbed."

"Oh my *god*." Kristin's hands fly to her mouth.

Bell looks at his feet. "But then you put a letter opener in your brother's neck, so I guess that evens the scales a little."

Emma's surprised he spoke up. She's even more taken aback when Kristin Gutmunsson crosses quickly to Bell—and hugs him.

"Oh my god, I'm *sorry*." Kristin's voice is muffled in Bell's shirt. "I didn't realize—I'm just *so sorry*."

"It's, uh…it's all right." Bell's face suggests he's regretting he spoke, but Kristin's arms are wrapped around him, holding him fast. "Miss Gutmunsson—"

"Kristin." Emma helps peel the girl away. "It's okay. You've done nothing wrong. You tried to help, remember?"

"I tried my best." Kristin's eyes are glistening. "But Simon was so strong…."

This is a girl whose entire life has been defined by what her sibling did. It tempers Emma's queries, but she needs answers.

"Kristin, you still seem loyal to Simon. Can I ask why? He killed almost a dozen people, some of them your friends. But you're still connected to him."

"I can't give up on him." Kristin sinks back onto the couch, wiping her eyes with her sleeve. "I sometimes wish I could. But he's my brother. My twin."

"You still care for him." Emma is shocked into saying it out loud.

"Of course. Simon still needs love. And I have to hold on to the love I have for him, in the hope that he'll see, and remember love still exists." Kristin looks over at Bell. "But I'm so, so sorry for the hurt he caused you. It doesn't mean I'm apologizing for him, or that

117

I excuse him, in any way. That's the difference between Simon and me—*I* know that what he's done is wrong. It's part of my family's history of shame," she says sadly.

Bell takes a step forward. "Then *help us*. What can we say that will make your brother give us the information we need?"

Kristin swipes her face once more, settles her hands in her lap. "Well, you can't *make* Simon do anything. But to be honest, I think your best asset is Emma."

"Me?" The hair on Emma's nape lifts.

"Why yes." Kristin's expression is tear-stained and guileless. "I already told you. He likes locked boxes. He would be curious about you, and I'm sure he would appreciate some stimulating conversation."

Emma catches Bell's quick, fierce look in her direction; she cuts her eyes away. "What exactly would Simon like to talk about?"

Kristin waves a hand. "Oh, lots of things—Simon has broad interests. Art, music, history, literature…"

"We've already touched on literature." Emma's voice is dry.

"Perhaps you'd like to tell him a little about yourself, your background and family…." Kristin falters, as if only just realizing that revealing personal information to Simon may not be altogether wise.

Emma thinks it might be best to redirect the conversation. "Kristin, can I ask what happened the day of Simon's arrest? Why did he take you hostage?"

Kristin blushes. "I told him to."

Bell jerks forward involuntarily. "You what?"

"It was all so fast and muddled…. Simon rushed into the piano room, rambling about police, saying he had to run, and I…" She examines her hands. "I said he couldn't run, he'd never get away. That maybe he should try another strategy. I said maybe he should use me to get to Father's car."

"And that's what you did." Now Bell seems frozen.

"Yes. But then the Marshal—" Kristin corrects herself. "Your father. He offered to take my place. But as soon as we changed places, I knew Simon wouldn't do the right thing, that he wouldn't be able to resist...." She blinks at the grass. "When Simon stabbed your father, I had to do *something*. So I picked up the letter opener, and I..." She swallows. "Well, you know what happened. And now here we are."

Emma can feel that her mouth has dropped open, so she closes it. Looks over at Bell and immediately thinks of a quote: *And thus the heart will break, yet brokenly live on.* The expression on Bell's face is unbearable. But even as she watches, he composes himself, with a gargantuan effort, into impassivity.

"Anyway." Kristin clears her throat, smiles to lift her mood. "I don't know if I'd bring up that subject with my brother. But there are lots of other things you could chat about. You could appeal to his intellect, too—he enjoys puzzles. And he must get *very* bored, sitting around all day long at St. Elizabeths."

Emma recovers enough to speak. "You're saying Simon might help us because he's bored?"

"Oh yes." Kristin nods. "He *hates* being bored. And your mysterious murder investigation is just the sort of thing he would like. He'd make a wonderful detective if he weren't so..." Kristin searches for the right term.

Evil? Emma thinks. Then she looks quickly at Bell, willing him not to say it.

"…him," Kristin concludes, oblivious to the interchange and distracted by something in the middle distance. "Oh, look, here come the puppies!"

It's like something out of a dream: Up the verdant hill, following the path of a white-aproned woman carrying a silver tray with a coffee service, an old golden Labrador bitch comes with tongue lolling. In the adult dog's wake, four puppies try to keep up.

The staff member arrives and sets the tray on the rattan table in front of the couch, dogs milling about her heels. "I told them to shoo, Miss Kristin, but they wouldn't."

"You must *never* apologize for the puppies," Kristin declares. "I love them. Come here, Sheba. Oh, Emma, look at them! Here, you must cuddle a puppy." She scoops up one of the pups and deposits it in Emma's lap, then pets the old mother dog, attracting the whines of the others, all of them wanting attention at once.

Emma's fingers are suddenly full of wriggling-soft puppy. The creamy fur is like old silk. She maneuvers the warm body to see the pup's face. Its eyes are liquid chocolate, and so wet they seem to brim with tears.

Kristin smiles, sits on the ground, and piles puppies on herself as the aproned woman pours the coffee. The sun filters through the oak leaves. A strand of spiderweb drifts in a graceful ballet into shrubs nearby. If she were ever to go insane, Emma reflects, she would like this to be her resting place: a bungalow in a honeysuckle garden, with a gambol of puppies and thoughtful staff.

She sees Bell, his stoic mask softening as he squats to pet the mother dog, who pushes him over and licks his face. Later, in the cab of the Dodge as they drive back to Quantico against the end-of-day commuter traffic, Emma will notice how quiet he is, and that he has grass in his hair.

CHAPTER FIFTEEN

They write up the Gesak interview on Monday night.

Cooper doesn't even have the consideration to collect their report in person but dispatches Betty, who accepts the paperwork and gives them paperwork in return: class assignments. Bell is gratified, Emma appalled at the idea of more wasted time. They've entered the second week of June. Cooper hasn't yet discussed the idea of another visit to Simon Gutmunsson, and Emma sits, tight-lipped, through Tuesday sessions on Legal Search Procedures and Quantico Library Orientation, then a two-hour introductory lecture on Miranda Rights.

She knows that the legwork on the Pennsylvania case is ongoing, just out of her line of sight. Forces are mobilizing. Reports are being typed and submitted. There's more data now than is contained in the slim, static file she and Bell have been allowed, and it frustrates her that they don't have access to any of it. She beats some of her frustration out on the Yellow Brick Road on Wednesday morning, her footfalls thumping on the pine-needled path.

There's only one avenue open to them, one line of inquiry they've been permitted to pursue. As much as it unnerves her, she'd rather plunge in than sit around waiting for the next bodies to surface.

She talks it out with Bell on the firing range. He's not enthused, but he agrees to help her bring it up with Cooper. When they arrive at the office after lunch, the man himself is there, leaning against the desk.

Emma takes her chance. "I want to see Simon Gutmunsson again."

"You're okay to go back?" Cooper's version of surprised is so low-key it's barely discernible. He must be great at parties.

"We already said we'd play—so let's play." Emma looks at him more closely. "Wait. There was something in our report on Gutmunsson, wasn't there? Something important."

Cooper stands. "It was the comment about the hair. The most recent female victim, her hair was trimmed. We figured it out from photos and then we confirmed with the parents."

Emma glances at Bell. His eyebrows are raised, and she remembers: *If the killer's next victims show up with their hair cut off, Cooper will have you back at St. Elizabeths faster than you can say "teenage sociopath."*

Bell was right. But this makes things easier, in a way. She doesn't need to upsell. "Okay, great. Simon obviously has more information and I want to find out what it is. But if we're going to do it, let's do it. I want to go today."

Cooper considers, one elbow cupped and his other hand knuckled under his chin. Even overworked and under pressure, he's still meticulously dressed. Emma wonders for the first time if he's married, if he has a wife at home who presses neat creases into his suits.

"Okay," he says finally, "I've got a meeting at the Scientific Analysis lab in Washington, so I can drive you up. But if the rest of

Gutmunsson's information proves useless or misleading, we cut off communication. And don't give him any personal details. You don't want that stuff floating around in Simon Gutmunsson's head."

"Noted."

"And I want you to wear a wire when you talk to him."

"I disagree," Bell says.

"Pardon?"

"She didn't wear a wire the first time."

Cooper straightens. "We weren't sure if his information had value the first time."

"Right." Bell crosses his arms. "And now Gutmunsson will anticipate it. He knows how the FBI works. If he thinks she's wired, he'll just lie."

Cooper frowns, undecided. "Miss Lewis?"

Emma is thinking of the things Simon Gutmunsson might say now that he knows her identity. The way she might react. She suspects Bell has thought of it, too. The only way she can express her gratitude for his kindness now is to avoid looking at him.

"A wire would be hard to conceal. I wore a T-shirt last time. If I come in wearing a jacket to do a follow-up, Gutmunsson will know. He's aware that we're curious about his Pennsylvania information— we can't afford for him to think we're invested. I can write down everything he says after I come out of the interview. I have a pretty good memory."

She thinks she might have laid it on too thick, but Cooper gives his assent. As he ushers them out of the Cool Room, away from Behavioral Science, Emma controls the urge to high-five with Bell. He may not high-five back.

She speaks quietly as they walk fast behind Cooper, heading for the elevators. "Travis, what's the problem?"

Bell's lips are pursed. "Gutmunsson is the problem. I don't think we should rely on anything he says. He might help us for fun, then turn around and give us false leads, and he would find that equally funny. He doesn't actually care if the Pennsylvania killer is caught. For him, the longer this circus goes on, the better—he gets more attention that way."

"Sure. But I think we can use that self-interest and arrogance against him."

"He's too smart. He'll see you coming around the corner." Bell's eyebrows knit, which means he's about to say something she won't like. "And Gutmunsson isn't only interested in Pennsylvania. You heard Kristin. He's interested in *you.*"

She's saved from replying—they've already reached the elevator. Standing all together, waiting, she has another thought. "Mr. Cooper, does the bureau know we're getting information from Gutmunsson about the Pennsylvania case?"

Cooper watches the numbers above the door. "I'm heading up the unit. I know. If I know, the bureau knows."

Emma looks at Bell. He's watching her. His blank expression speaks volumes.

The elevator dings.

The door opens, and a tall, big-boned man in a dark suit steps out. He's in his late fifties. Emma thinks, *He's carrying too much weight to be a field agent*, and the way Cooper kowtows to him confirms it.

"Sir."

"Special Agent Cooper." A North Carolina accent, broad features, and a beady eye. He might've been military once—now he looks more corporate. "Good timing. You gonna make the budgetary committee meeting?"

"No, sir. Lab in Washington is ready with final reports on Pennsylvania. I've got to be up there."

"Right, right."

"But I'll contact Howard Carter, get him to belly up to Justice and explain the numbers."

"For sure. I guess the case is the priority."

Cooper looks grave. "The case is always the priority, sir."

"You got it." Cooper's superior turns his attention to Emma and Bell, standing like ornaments in the background. "These are your new recruits, I take it."

He shoots his cuffs unnecessarily, and Emma realizes they'll have to watch their step.

Cooper nods as he makes the introductions. "Miss Lewis, Mr. Bell, this is Section Chief Donald Raymond."

Raymond shakes Bell's hand in that bluff "good ole boy" way. "Great to meet you, son. How's the work?"

Bell has been standing straight since the elevator door opened. "The interviews are going well, sir. It's a privilege to be working with the bureau."

"Well, I'm glad to hear that. Your dad was a fine Marshal. And here you are, carrying on his legacy."

"Yes, sir."

Raymond grimaces. "Helluva thing, losing a man like that. I met your dad once, on the job. You look a lot like him. But good for you, son, keep up the good work."

"Thank you, sir."

Raymond turns Emma's way and she wonders if he's even aware of the casual hurt he's just inflicted on Bell. Then she's concentrating on her own responses as Raymond squeezes her fingers.

"Miss Lewis, good to meet you. That's a tough job you're doing—how're you holding up?"

"Thank you, I'm doing fine." Emma extricates her hand.

"Tricky business, yes indeed. Not the kind of thing we'd normally ask of a young lady like yourself, but Agent Cooper says everything's going well."

"It's good to get feedback from Agent Cooper." She tries not to sound too dry. Maybe Raymond thinks he's being courteous.

Cooper's eyes dart. "If you'll excuse us, sir."

"Absolutely, sure," Raymond says. "Well, a pleasure to meet you both. Let me know how it all pans out."

He passes by, they enter the elevator, and Cooper punches the button. His Plymouth is in the shop, and they have to visit the motor pool to requisition a vehicle. When they get there, Cooper goes to hunt up something suitable as Emma and Bell stand near the wall, out of the way.

"Tricky business," Emma says conversationally.

Bell, eyes forward. "My mom is from Oaxaca. My dad had blue eyes and blond hair. I don't look anything like him."

Cooper comes back folding the paperwork. "The gray Diplomat. Let's move."

Starting this late in the day, there's no way they can beat the traffic. Emma contemplates the scene with Raymond for the first part of the drive, lets it go to focus on more pressing concerns.

"Does Dr. Scott know we're coming?"

"I phoned her, yes." Cooper is concentrating on the Diplomat's handling. "Watch yourself with Scott. She's highly professional but maybe a little too invested in 'reforming' Gutmunsson."

"How does she think someone like Gutmunsson can be reformed?" Bell asks.

"In her philosophy, anyone can be reformed." Cooper frowns. "It's a very humanitarian impulse, but misguided in this case, I think."

Or maybe, Emma thinks, Simon Gutmunsson has simply lulled Dr. Scott into *believing* he could be reformed. She wouldn't put it past him.

Cooper eases the car past the Franconia exit. "I'm not going to escort you inside this time. I'll drop you off at the entrance and come back in an hour."

Emma thinks of something else. "Can I ask you about Gutmunsson's arrest? You said you were the second unit agent during his investigation."

"That's correct."

"Did you suspect anything, when he first became a person of interest in the case?"

Cooper shifts uncomfortably. "A few alarm bells rang, yes. It was the way he presented, more than anything. His story was very smooth. Too smooth."

"You weren't there at his arrest?"

"No. I was examining one of the crime scenes when Agent Gilet decided to bring him in for routine questioning. Barton Bell was Joe's backup." Cooper catches Bell's eye in the rearview, a single regretful glance. "Nobody realized how much danger they were in. The profile was way off—we thought we were looking for a much older suspect."

"Is Agent Gilet still with the bureau? If we could talk with him—"

"Joe Gilet killed himself last fall." Cooper's jaw is like a clenched fist, and he doesn't give Emma time to catch her breath. "Look, don't let Simon Gutmunsson intimidate you. People call him a monster. I prefer not to think of him that way—it suggests there's something legendary about him, and I don't buy into that."

"How do you think of him?"

Cooper scans the sky on the other side of National Harbor, the high clouds scudding across with their pristine, sudsy tops and underbellies the color of mourning doves. "I consider him to be a kind of...human black hole. Sucking everything into himself, every scrap of light. Beyond that, now that he's incarcerated, I try to think of him as little as possible."

Fifteen minutes later, Dr. Scott is greeting them at the door to the asylum.

CHAPTER SIXTEEN

The air in the chapel glitters with suspended particles of dust. Someone has swept the floor. Emma wonders if this is Pradeep's job, or if another staff member or inmate completes such chores. On her way through the foyer, she passed a middle-aged man in a white uniform, but he was carrying a first aid kit, not a broom.

The mundane necessity of housework seems at odds with the time-capsule feel of the space. On her first visit she was too afraid to notice, but entering now it occurs to her that Simon Gutmunsson's jail seems to have its own chronology, like a wight's barrow or a knight's tomb from a fairy tale.

She has to banish fanciful thoughts and refocus. Kristin's advice and the experiences with McMurtry and Gesak have given her a better understanding of how to proceed.

Emma breathes deep. She can box up her anxiety about meeting Simon again, put it aside. Bell is in the lobby to support her in the aftermath. They need this. She can do this.

"No papers today?" Pradeep's baritone and dark eyes are calming. He has a folded newspaper and the sign-in ledger on his desk, which is otherwise bare. The pincer tool hangs from a coat hook on the wall. There is nothing else that could be used as a weapon except the chair. Emma remembers Scott's comment about Simon's escape attempts; Pradeep must have instructions on what to do if Simon ever gets loose. Emma hopes neither she nor Pradeep is ever in a position to enact them.

"No papers," she says. "Thank you."

"I am right here, if you require."

Emma nods, appreciative. She understands why Simon and Pradeep maintain a genteel truce. In a situation where true personal connection—say, between an inmate and his jailer—is impossible, the only recourse is the implied respect of professionalism. Pradeep is very good at maintaining an appropriate tone. It's a social skill Emma has never quite mastered.

She's still trying to figure out what tone to take when she finds herself standing in front of Simon's cage.

He is sitting at his desk, consulting one of his books and writing on a piece of butcher paper, which has been neatly torn off the roll. Now he turns sideways in his bolted-down chair to face her.

"Emma." His eyes give off cold sparks. His eyebrows are dark slashes against the paleness of his skin, his white hair. His mouth is slightly open; she thinks of flies buzzing out, has to push the image aside.

"Hello, Simon."

His beauty is like a lightning bolt: shocking and brilliant and terrifyingly wild. The radiance from the stained-glass windows gives him an almost ethereal glow. Emma reminds herself he is not a magical being, he is a boy of flesh and blood. His cheekbones are sharp and high, his skin smooth—how does he shave?

He smiles. "So we're on a first-name basis at last. What a relief. Being called Mr. Gutmunsson makes me feel like an octogenarian."

Emma plunges straight in. "If we're being informal—your questionnaire answers pissed me off."

He throws his hands up, turns back to his books. "And now we've lost civility altogether."

"After our last interview, I figure we can skip the pleasantries."

He adds another note to his paper. "A personal acquaintance is no excuse for abandoning courtesy. *How have you been, Simon? Thank you, Emma, I've been very well.* It's the small details that lubricate our daily interactions."

"But courtesy can be a type of mask as well. Don't you get sick of people being polite to you?"

"If you'd like to witness people in their more natural state, come live in an asylum for a while. Tell me afterward whether you think good manners are a social unguent."

Emma checks herself, realizes she's being aggressive because she's afraid. *He is a human boy*, she reminds herself. *A human boy, whose sister loves him. An isolated boy, who gets bored, and probably lonely. A smart boy, who likes using big words because*...because he's showing off? Is Simon trying to impress her?

And can she use that?

She straightens. "I'm sorry. It's nice to see you, Simon. How have you been?"

He touches his tongue to the tip of his finger and turns a page. "Thank you, Emma, I've been very well."

"As a courtesy, I'll say I think you've had your nose stuck in books all day. That's great for your vocabulary, but you've lost sight of the big picture."

"What big picture is that?"

"Pennsylvania." She wets her lips. "Crozet. Luray. I've seen the file now. I can give you answers to your questions."

"Did Cooper give you the file?" Gutmunsson glances over to check her expression, rolls his eyes. "My god, that man can't help himself, can he? He's almost as single-minded as I am."

"He wants to catch this killer. Don't you want to know about Pennsylvania? Ask me again."

He sets his pen aside and turns, crosses his legs. Emma is struck over by his almost insectoid manner, his calm, precise movements. "Actually…there's more I'd like to know about you."

She's readied herself for this. "That's a shame. I'm not really prepared to answer personal questions."

"Humor me. You're a lot more interesting than anything in an FBI file."

Emma doesn't believe that. "If you want to play that game, it should be a fair exchange. How about I ask you questions about your own case, like how you got that scar on your neck?"

"My sister stabbed me." He shrugs. "People fight. It happens."

"Did she get angry at you?"

"She wanted me to stop doing what I do. Awkwardly enough, it's not something I can simply switch off. I suppose she thought some time incarcerated would help me kick the habit—or maybe she felt I was too dangerous to leave walking around. She's very community-minded, Kristin."

"I met her."

"Did you?" Simon straightens. A flicker of something across his face—a brightness, a yearning. "She's lovely, isn't she?"

"She is." The change in his expression prompts her to dig deeper. "It must be hard, not having contact with her."

"Yes."

His clipped answer is a traffic sign—NO ENTRY. Emma tries another tack. "The place she's living in is very...refined."

"Very expensive, is what you mean."

"Why did you say I reminded you of your sister? We're nothing alike."

"You're both survivors of trauma. You encountered Daniel Huxton and Kristin encountered me. The behaviors don't present in the same way, but you have the same flavor. It's hard to describe." He gazes off into a high corner of the chapel, his voice singsong. "You are dark and she is fair, you no longer have your hair...."

She needs to redirect. "It was your mention of hair in the questionnaire that annoyed me. But it was important, wasn't it?"

Gutmunsson ignores that. "You and Kristin have both placed yourselves in positions where you can indulge your post-traumatic peccadilloes. She's at Chesterfield, where she can relax into fantasy. You're with the FBI, where you can channel your fury."

She tries for a jaunty air. "Well, I don't feel very furious at the moment."

"And yet you smell of gunpowder." He smiles directly at her. "You and Kristin each have a doorway in your mind that you keep firmly closed."

Emma can't help but feel she's botching this conversation, struggling along two steps behind. "Kristin said you enjoy unraveling mysteries."

"There are twenty-five feet of intestines in the human body—did you know that? I enjoy unraveling lots of things."

She grimaces. "Now you're just being disgusting to get a reaction. Are you trying to *make* me furious?"

"Maybe. Would you say you feel angry pretty much all the time?"

"Yes." Her face feels tight. "In your questionnaire answers, you wrote—"

"And what do you feel when you don't feel angry?"

"Tired. When you wrote, *Let me know when he starts taking their hair*, how did you predict that?"

"No." Simon slashes with the blade of his hand. "I answered your questionnaire, Emma. Now I'd like you to tell *me* something."

She tries to stay firm. "There's nothing about me that could possibly be interesting to you."

"Why don't you let me decide?"

"Seriously, come on." Her hold is slipping. "I'm just a . . . a regular, normal, boring girl—"

"Oh, Emma, you're anything but boring." He tilts his head. "And I have a certain professional curiosity. None of my models survived their transformations—I didn't get to talk with them afterward. But here you are. . . ."

"Here I am," Emma says. Suddenly and inexplicably, she feels like crying.

She works to control herself. Is this what it will take to get answers about the Pennsylvania case? What does it matter if she goes over with Simon Gutmunsson the things she's gone over with the authorities a hundred times?

And the photos of the Pennsylvania killer's victims keep coming to her, in her mind's eye: not the grainy xerox horror copies but the identification photos, the smiling, youthful faces....

She inhales, releases. "I don't know what you want me to say. Huxton was deranged. There's a proper medical term for it, but I don't—"

"No, no, no." Simon turns his head askance. "I don't want the litany you've already recited to the police and the papers. Did you think I would pummel you with questions about Huxton? I'm not the FBI." He turns back to screw his eyes into hers. "I don't care about Huxton. Huxtons are a dime a dozen."

"Then *what?*"

Emma can't remember seeing him move, but Simon is now sitting on the floor near the front of his cell, long legs crossed. His arms are lifted, hands suspended from the horizontal crossbar, and his face is visible through the gap between the metal rods that keep him caged. Emma wants to look away from his gaze but finds she can't. The dark motes in his eyes go back and back without end.

His voice is soft. "You're so very prickly, Emma. However did he catch you?"

"I used to be a more trusting person." A great lassitude is sweeping over her, like a narcosis. Fighting it is hard. Simon is sitting down. Maybe she could sit down, too.

"I'm sure you've been told that you're special, that your courage is what set you apart. But it didn't feel like courage at the time, did it?"

"No." The truth of that lives deep in her bones. "It wasn't courage. Just desperation."

"But Huxton's other brides must have been desperate, too. How did you move from desperation into action?"

"I don't know." His use of the word "brides"—the media term for Huxton's victims—scrapes against her nerves. Her self-control feels slippery now, her hold tenuous. "Why do you care?"

"It's interesting to me. There was a moment, wasn't there? When you decided you'd rather die than be Huxton's bride. And then you realized you'd rather fight than die."

"Yes." A gasp of a word. She claws desperately for better memories: *petunias, soft loam, her sister's hug. . . .*

"What was the moment?"

Emma shudders. *Petunias, petunias*—"I don't remember."

"I'm sure you do. Let's go back to it. You were held in a basement, weren't you? Was it dark?"

"Yes. It was. . . ." Her breath fractures, and all remembrance of sweetness falls away. "There was a sliver of light that came through a gap in the boards of the door."

"I can see you've just remembered that. And the light was important?"

"It meant there was an outside."

"Yes, an outside. An escape route." Simon's voice has a cool cunning. "That must have been tantalizing."

Emma is not looking at Simon anymore. She is staring back into memory. "Vicki and Tammy were afraid of the light."

"They were afraid of the door opening."

"A lot of light meant he was on his way down." The terror in her words is barely contained.

"And that would be very bad."

"Yes." She's hoarse now.

"Were the other girls catatonic by that stage? Had they lost their capacity to reason?"

"Tammy was . . . She couldn't walk." Emma closes her eyes.

Simon prods further. "She tried to rebel, didn't she?"

"Yes. And he . . . he . . ."

"He cut off her foot."

"Yes." She has to float through the nausea. "And Vicki . . . Vicki couldn't function so good. He'd already had her two weeks."

"Yes, she would've been completely tattered by then." He smiles softly. "But you were still functioning well."

"I was the last girl he caught. He only had me for three days."

"So it was fortuitous circumstances. You were still fresh. He didn't have a chance to starve you for very long, and you still remembered what it felt like to be free." Simon waves his hand toward her. "Plus you had some skills that the other brides didn't have."

Emma watches his eyes move. "The other girls were all from the city. I grew up in the country."

"You had a certain mental toughness."

"I guess."

"There's no guessing—here you are. You didn't go into shock and shut down." He seems almost proud of her. "And you had something else, too. Do you know what it was?"

"Not really."

His eyes hold her entire as his fine, graceful fingers grip the bars. "It's the same quality that keeps you running, Emma. That keeps you pounding the track every day. It's what will save you, in the end. But go back for me. How did you and Vicki and Tammy learn each other's names?"

"Our cages were..." She swallows. Such bitterness in her throat! "Our cages were pushed together. We could whisper. We could reach out and touch each other's hands."

"I could reach out from my cage and touch your hand right now."

Her eyes flash and her voice firms. "Don't."

"Our friend in Pennsylvania doesn't keep his donors in cages. How does he control them?"

That flash of fire has cleared some of the clouds in her head. "Ether. He knocks them out with ether."

"Hmm. But I don't think he would want them etherized at the end. He would want the drug out of their blood, because the blood is too important."

"How do you know?"

He smiles. "Let's just say I have a fellow feeling with our new friend. I don't think he would want any impurities in the blood. I'm sure he wants his donors clean and sober for the grand finale. Have you checked the histamine levels?"

"Yes. We couldn't make sense of the numbers."

"We?"

She corrects herself without stumbling. "Me. Agent Cooper just gave me the file—he didn't offer to translate it. I have numbers but I don't know what they mean."

"Then allow me to explain. In postmortem biochemistry, if the free histamine reference range is over thirty-five but not less than twenty-two nanograms per milliliter, the subject was in distress."

Sweat on her brow, her own distress. "Why doesn't the killer want impurities like ether in the victims' blood?"

"He's been particular up until now, hasn't he. He's cleaned off prints, removed clothes to avoid fiber contamination, disposed of ropes. He's a very tidy fellow."

"And the blood is too important."

"Oh, Emma—the blood is *everything*." Simon's shoulders straighten as he elaborates. "It's his purpose, his essence, his reason for all this. I imagine he loses himself a little when the red is all around him. It's so easy to get carried away in the moment."

"Does he need a special sort of blood? How does he know he's got the right donor?"

"That's an interesting question. Have you ever selected fruit at the greengrocer? You squeeze a little to see if it's ripe, ask for a slice so you can nibble—taste is very individual."

"Is he taste-testing them?" Urgency in her voice now. "Simon, how is he choosing his victims?"

He grins. "Another good question. Pick at it a little, I'm sure it will come to you."

It does come, like the pulsing scarlet blaze of a ship's flare. "He knows their blood type."

"It's more than just blood type, though. He sees something glowing in them, something he wants to kindle inside himself." Simon's own eyes are glowing. "It's like the gleam of a firefly."

"What is it?"

"Listen. *No man chooses evil because it is evil; he only mistakes it for happiness, the good he seeks*—Mary Shelley, of course. Our Pennsylvania friend seeks his happiness. Every creature on earth has wants and desires, has things they turn toward—flower to sun, snake to warmth, moth to flame. Daniel Huxton saw something in *you*, Emma. He could not resist your shine."

She feels a cool streak of wet on her cheek. "There's nothing shiny about me."

Simon looks at her kindly. "You think your glow is gone. You think that by saving these new lost ones, it will come back, but that's not true. It never left. You're only a little tarnished. Rub off the rust and your beacon is revealed, like a sliver of light in the dark." He sighs and stands, moves to his desk. "Now all these compliments have exhausted me, and I have a paper to write. Goodbye, dear Emma. It's been lovely to see you. I'll look forward to our next conversation."

"That's all?" Emma stands also. "Simon, I need more. How do we find out who he's choosing next? *Simon.*"

When she steps forward involuntarily, too close to the barricade, Pradeep takes her gently by the arm.

CHAPTER SEVENTEEN

Bell thinks he can endure just about anything so long as it's not a woman suffering.

He remembers his uncle Luther—who wasn't really his uncle but had been his father's partner since basic training—coming to the house to tell Rosa Bell that her husband was dead. She made a long, low, ululating moan as she collapsed in the doorway. Travis could hardly comprehend his own pain, and here was his mother's: no high, dramatic screams, just bone-deep groans, pain felt in the dark, hollow well of the body. It chilled and wrenched him by turns.

His sisters shambled around for weeks, blank-eyed and dry-lipped. He was supposed to be there for them, but their suffering made him feel picked clean. It made him want to punch a wall.

He has a similar feeling of helplessness now as he stands outside the door of the women's bathroom in the foyer of St. Elizabeths, listening to Lewis dry-retch following her interview with Gutmunsson.

"Fuck this," he mutters. He turns and knocks twice on the wood in warning. "Lewis, I'm coming in."

Her voice is threadbare. "All right."

The bathroom is full of old-fashioned tile and fixtures, spacious and echoey. They're the only people in there. Emma flushes the toilet she's been leaning over and leaves the stall. She washes her mouth at the handbasin, swilling and spitting out water.

"I'm okay." She looks more wan than he's ever seen her. He reminds himself he's only known her a week. It's battlefield camaraderie, this feeling like they've been friends for years.

"You keep saying you're okay, but every time you say it I believe it less and less."

"No, really." She dries her face with paper towels. "He just . . . He hit me with some questions about Huxton. It caught me by surprise, is all."

"Lewis, you *know* trading in personal information with Gutmunsson is bad strategy. I said that at the beginning."

"Then why did you suggest to Cooper that I go in without a wire?"

There's a beat of acknowledgment. He tongues his back teeth. "I did that to protect your privacy. Cooper wants the information, regardless of the cost. He wants you in there with a goal in mind. But Cooper isn't the one dealing with this guy. You are. Don't commit more than you're willing to."

Emma doesn't seem to hear him. It's like she's listening to some internal music, her gaze abstracted as she stares at herself in the mirror.

"I need to write it down. Some of the things he said . . . the phrasing wasn't an accident. Nothing he ever says is by accident. And I think he does have insight into Pennsylvania." Light bounces off her face and eyes, the skin over her cheekbones stretched and translucent. The fine hair on her head seems darker by contrast. "He said something about blood type—could the victims be blood donors? Is there a registry of some kind? Is that how they're targeted? I think we've been going about this ass-backward. We've been looking for the killer. Maybe we should be looking more closely at the victims themselves, so we can see how he's choosing them."

Bell wants to tell her to ease down, but it would come out wrong. "If you need to write it all down, I'll get a notepad and pencil from the lady at the front desk."

"That would be good. Yeah, I need to write it."

"Okay, do you wanna come out to the foyer? Cooper's due to arrive in fifteen."

The lady at the reception desk wears a beige skirt suit and frosted eye shadow, and she is very accommodating with writing materials. Bell gives Emma a pen, paper, a cup of water, and a place to sit, then leaves her alone to write.

The gray Diplomat isn't in the parking lot. It finally shows up at about quarter past four.

"Don't drive west," Emma says when she slides into the back seat. "We need to see the bodies."

"What?" Cooper looks at her in the rearview, but Emma is already head-down again, scribbling furiously. He glares at Bell instead. "What happened?"

"Nothing happened." Bell buckles up in the back, reminds Lewis with short gestures to do the same. "I mean, Gutmunsson happened. And Lewis thinks we might have something—"

"The blood." Emma glances at Cooper as she writes. "He kept going on about the blood. We need to check if the victims were blood donors, if there's a registry—"

"No registry I'm aware of." Cooper squints. "We can check it back at Quantico—"

"No. We need to examine the bodies for needle marks." Emma finishes a line, looks up to make her point. "The killer is using the blood, okay? He's using it as part of his ritual, for whatever reason—but he needs to know he's got the right *type* of donor. He's drawing blood *before* he kills them and using it for something. Taking a sample, like he's taste-testing somehow. The medical examiner who did the original autopsies... What's his name?"

"It's complicated." Cooper's turned back over the seat now, watching her as the car idles. "We've got four bodies from three counties."

"Ah, crap." Bell realizes what this means. "They all went to their county medical examiner."

"Correct."

Emma looks mystified. "I don't get it."

"The bodies went to different district health departments," Bell explains.

"They went to different coroners?"

"Three coroners," Cooper says. "The Lambton girl and the Davis boy both went to Central District in Richmond, but they were examined by different staff pathologists. The Pennsylvania victims went to Dauphin County."

"So they got bounced all over?" Emma catches Bell's eye. "No wonder the marks were missed."

Cooper seems to be keeping himself on a tight leash. "Miss Lewis, you don't think it's... *unlikely* that three different coroners missed needle marks on the bodies?"

"No, listen. The county coroner probably saw the throat wounds and figured, hell, he's already taken their blood. But remember the photos? The victims had ligature contusions—here, here." She indicates the insides of her own arms, at the elbow joints. "They had severe abrasions, bruising, rope fibers still in the wounds."

"You think the abrasions hid a puncture mark?"

Emma nods. "And after Davis, when you knew the killer was etherizing them, the ME may not have thought to look closely. He knew they weren't being sedated by injection. But what if the killer isn't injecting anything—what if he's *withdrawing*?"

"It's an interesting theory," Cooper says, "but there's one problem—the bodies aren't here. They're in the county morgues. Two of them have been released back to the families."

"Then let us talk to the pathologists at the Washington lab. Someone there can follow up with the county ME's offices."

"We can't exhume bodies that have just—"

"I'm not talking about exhuming anything right now. If we find needle marks on two, we worry about the others later." Emma thrusts the pages she's just completed at Bell, skewers Cooper with her glare. "Look, are you sending me in to see Gutmunsson for nothing, or do you actually want to move on the information I get? Because you're right. He's figured a few things out. But if you're not going to act on it…"

Cooper stares out the right-hand window for a moment, then swivels to the front and puts the car in gear. "Fine. It can't hurt to talk to the lab. We'll go back to the state building."

Emma releases a breath. "Great. Okay, let me finish these last pages, then I'll tell you what else Gutmunsson let slip."

She hunkers back down over her notes as Cooper pulls the car around.

Bell checks his watch. "It's going on four thirty. Will the offices still be open?"

Cooper nods. "Oh, they'll be open."

"Gonna be hell with the traffic."

For a while there's only the rushing of the wind outside the car as Cooper concentrates on the route. Emma doesn't look at the view, Bell notes. She is deep in the weeds of her exchange with Simon Gutmunsson, the way it felt and what was said. She moves her hand across the paper as fast as she's humanly able.

The Anacostia is a glittering blue-gray blur in Bell's peripheral vision. He sees the concrete and raw steel buttresses of the river overpass and thinks Emma looks as if she's had her foundations swept out from under her. He takes the pages as she shoves them his way, watches her for popping rivets. "Can I read through this? Are you comfortable with that?"

Her pause is only a blink's duration. "Read."

Cooper navigates the roads toward the Capitol Building, and Bell's eyes move over the scrawl of Emma's handwriting. She's taken the entire interview down like dictation, and Bell finds the part he's reading disturbing. Mostly because he thinks Gutmunsson isn't lying to her.

"He's really fixated on his sister, isn't he? I mean, he attaches a lot of emotion to the references about her."

Emma looks up. "What makes you say that?"

"He's got..." Bell tries to figure out the right way to express it. "His answers are all long—he's got, like, long passages where he's just going on. But when he talks about Kristin, he gets clipped. His answers are just a few words."

"He talked about her psychological profile."

"Yeah, her psychological profile—not about *her*. That stuff is real short. He didn't want to talk about her."

"He's deflecting for her," Emma says, suddenly comprehending. "He's protecting her."

"He cares about her." Bell feels it in his gut. "Guys shut down sensitive talk. He was blowing you off. She's important to him, and he didn't want you to poke into that."

"I need to make a call," Cooper says.

They're caught in gridlock past the Peace Monument. Cooper takes a Motorola pack out from under the passenger seat and dials a number he knows by heart.

"Gerry, can you folks hold the line there? I'm coming in to you with a couple passengers who might have some info on Pennsylvania.... No, I'm stuck in traffic. We'll get through, but I need...No, no documents. Hair and Fiber. Maybe Trace as well...Sure, but I'll talk about it with you in person. Warn the escort desk, would you? Yeah, they're gonna bust my ass about security tags, but these two have initial clearance. Thanks. Okay, see you in fifteen."

"We're not gonna make it in fifteen," Bell says.

Cooper ghosts a grin. "Watch and learn."

He stashes the phone pack and flicks the emergency lights on, going hot. Traffic edges up onto the sidewalk, parting to make space for the Diplomat. When folks won't move, Cooper gooses them with a blast from the siren. They're on E Street almost before Bell realizes what's happened.

Emma speaks to Cooper again. "Gutmunsson talked about the importance of the blood for the killer, like it's the source of everything. He suggested that the reason he keeps them for a while is to give the majority of the ether time to clear out of their bloodstream so there's no 'impurities' when he kills them."

Cooper works the gearshift. "We can look at the photo documentation, call through to the county. The remaining bodies are still in Harrisburg. They're not going to like the idea they've missed something."

"I'm just suggesting they reexamine based on new information."

"Sure."

"I don't know what the killer's doing with the blood," Emma says, raking her fingernails across her scalp. "Gutmunsson said he might lose control when he's mid-ritual. There's the possibility he's ingesting some of it."

"Ingesting...?" Bell looks over from his reading, makes a face. "Ah, geez."

She lets her hand drop. "Again, I'm just speculating, but it's a possibility. Gutmunsson was hedging about what the killer's doing. He can't know with certainty."

"How could he know at all? He could be stringing you along."

"I'm thinking he's taking a highly informed guess. And he's giving me his ideas in good faith."

"Yeah—after he's helped himself to the contents of your head." Bell glances at Cooper, quiet in front, before holding up the last few pages from her interview transcript. His voice lowers. "You should let me come with you next time. I could be a buffer—"

"No." She shakes her head, emphatic. "You have personal history with Gutmunsson and he would absolutely lean on that. Don't put yourself in that position."

"You're sacrificing too much. To hell with history—if you can handle this, so can I. I want to help—"

"Travis." She reaches out and puts a hand on his forearm. Even through the layers of shirt and suit jacket, he feels her fingers squeeze. "You help. Being there, and listening... You're doing it right."

They've reached FBI headquarters.

CHAPTER EIGHTEEN

Cooper slides the Diplomat into the underground parking lot, hustles them out to the escort desk, where he has a brief argument with security personnel, resolved in his favor. Emma and Bell have to show their lanyard credentials and sign in. They traverse the white corridors to the elevators. Emma stands in the metal box whizzing them skyward, feeling gravity pushing on her.

When they get out, Cooper leads them to a door, leans at an awkward angle to use his ID tag. Beyond the door are the same dropped ceilings and fluorescent tube lights, but unlike conventional offices, the FBI Scientific Analysis section has alarm flashers and air exhaust vents in the case of contamination spills. Examining rooms with large viewing windows are set to the left, and offices and labs to the right, off a central common room cluttered with file boxes and plastic storage containers.

An older man with gold-rimmed glasses and a jowly, stubbled face comes to meet them. He has a smoker's wheeze, and he's wearing a brown checked shirt with braces to hold up his trousers. "Welcome back. Congratulations on beating the peak hour traffic."

"Why I prefer to come by chopper," Cooper says.

"Ugh, don't talk to me about those flying death traps." The man seems to recognize Bell. "Hello again. Do you have another folder to deliver?"

Cooper gestures. "Gerry, you've already met Travis Bell, although you weren't formally introduced, and this is Emma Lewis—they're part of a new interview unit. Gerry leads the team here. He's old, but he's good."

"I'm keeping that one for my epitaph," the man jokes. The backs of his hands look weathered, but his palms and fingers are soft when he shakes Emma's hand. "Gerry Westfall, Latent Prints. Welcome."

"Thank you for seeing us on short notice," Emma says.

"No problem. Ed, you said you didn't need Documents, so I let Linda go. Her kid has some kind of dance recital, I don't know, anyway, she's left her pager on if you need her."

"That's fine," Cooper says. "Can we walk and talk?"

"By all means. Come on through."

Westfall leads them farther into the bowels of the section, skillfully maneuvering around the containers. There are a lot of containers. Bell frowns at one that holds nearly a dozen pairs of women's panties, before realizing why they're here. The lab examines evidence from all over the country. The volume of backlog is discouraging.

Westfall digs a pack of Camels out of his trouser pocket, looks over his shoulder to check that Emma and Bell are following. "You're part of an interview unit? You been doing that long?"

"Not long," Bell answers.

"We're researching juvenile perpetrators," Emma explains.

"Huh." Westfall glances at Cooper. "Young people interviewing young people. That's smart. Is it working?"

Cooper shrugs. "Wouldn't be here otherwise."

"Good point."

"Also, Gerry—Miss Lewis and Mr. Bell are invisible, okay?"

"Really? They look pretty solid to me."

"They're assisting with interviews—cold case operations only. But they happened to turn up some interesting information, which I'm pursuing. If anyone asks, they waited in the lobby."

"Okay, I'm not touching that, but good to know. Come in and see Glenn."

In the office of the Hair and Fiber section, past a labeled door, Glenn Neilsen is sitting at his desk, completing paperwork. He's white, and quite young, Emma thinks, maybe thirty, but he already sports bifocals and a hunch.

When they enter, Neilsen puts his pen down. He has the distracted air of a career research scientist. "Hey, Ed, Gerry said you wanted me to stay. I'm assuming you didn't leave your keys behind."

"Sorry to keep you from your dinner."

Neilsen pushes back his chair. "My dinner is a ham-and-pickle sandwich, and it's in the staff refrigerator. What's going on?"

"We've got some information on Pennsylvania from an unreliable source, but we think it's worth checking out. You said the bodies are due to be released back to the families soon?"

"The Barnes boy is supposed to go to the funeral home tomorrow."

"Then we'd better talk fast. Glenn, this is Miss Lewis and Mr. Bell. They turned up the info."

"Good for you," Neilsen says, swiveling to shake hands in turn.

Westfall lifts his chin. "Miss Lewis and Mr. Bell are ghosting, by the way. If anyone asks, they're in the lobby."

Neilsen's eyebrows lift. "Well, I'm not touching that. But what've you got?" He indicates a wooden stool near the desk for Emma to occupy.

"Um, a theory." Emma settles herself gingerly. "We've been interviewing a subject...." She trails off, gives Cooper a querying look.

Cooper nods at her, turns to Neilsen. "The information is from Simon Gutmunsson."

Neilsen rears back. "Whoa. Okay."

"I'm assuming this part about the connection to Gutmunsson is ghosting, too," Westfall says. He peers over his glasses at Cooper from his position in the doorway.

Cooper inclines his head. "That would be helpful, until we've worked out whether he's saying anything worth hearing."

Westfall waves his cigarette. "Got it. Continue."

"Um," Emma says.

Neilsen smiles. "He means, please go ahead with your theory."

"Okay." She glances at Bell for support, receives a solemn nod. "Gutmunsson talked about how he thinks the killer is operating. His process. He said the blood is the most critical part of the killer's ritual, and he thinks the killer is drawing blood from the victims, to check that he's got suitable donors."

"Like, he's testing their blood type?"

"Yes? I think."

Neilsen exchanges glances with Westfall. "Well, he can't be testing blood type. ABO testing involves mixing blood samples with antibodies in a lab."

"He could be, uh, *tasting* the blood as part of his ritual. Ingesting it."

"Okay." Neilsen is not as grossed out by this as Bell, which is disturbingly suggestive of the idea that he's seen such things before.

"So I was hoping we could check the bodies for needle marks. To confirm whether Gutmunsson's giving us anything solid."

"Well, the bodies are in Harrisburg, but I've got comprehensive autopsy pictures from the most recent victims. Hold on." Neilsen turns toward his desk, hunts through files. His brown hair is very fine and sticks up a little at the back from what Emma assumes is static electricity. He finds the file he wants, turns back.

He hesitates before opening the file. "These are...a little intense."

She's seen the crime scene photos and the ID shots, but these photos were not part of the file Cooper gave them. They are, indeed, intense. But the intensity of the images is in the way the postmortem process gives the viewer a clinical distance from the subjects, separating them into scaled body parts—a head, eyes closed; a torso; a hand; a length of leg. Emma finds this detached sundering vaguely offensive. She doesn't want to think of the victims as body parts on a white background. She wants to keep thinking of them as people. But she supposes this is easier for the pathologists, to maintain scientific objectivity.

Bell steps closer from where he's been taking up wall space near Cooper. Emma angles so he can see the photos in Neilsen's hands from over her shoulder.

"Are we assuming the marks might be at the juncture of the elbow?" Neilsen sorts the images and pulls out the relevant glossies. "I mean, he could be taking the blood from anywhere."

"That's true," Emma says. "But I thought the ligature abrasions might provide cover."

"Doesn't sound unlikely." Neilsen displays a shot of a mottled arm. It's clearly not from Lamar Davis, because the unmottled skin is pale, but aside from that detail Emma can't tell whose arm it might be. "There's some pallor from the exsanguination, but you can see how the abrasions stand out."

Emma takes the photo and holds it close, then farther away. "Did they happen when the subjects were struggling, at the end?"

"That's consistent with the catecholamines—the free histamine results, yes."

"There's a lot of fiber in the wounds."

"Yep. He used a kind of hemp rope—pretty raw stuff. Here, I've got a sample." He gives her the entire photo file to hold, stretches to his desk, and comes back with a short coil of hairy, twisted cord. "Twelve millimeters. We tested the petroleum content to figure out the brand. It's common as dirt, I'm afraid. They sell it in every Ace Hardware in the country."

Emma takes the sample, tests the rough texture, hands it to Bell. She looks between the cord and the photo in her lap. "Would the abrasions be enough to conceal a needle mark?"

Neilsen grimaces. "Maybe. It depends a little on the gauge of the needle—usually you'd look for a bruise. But you can see what a mess the area is. Be damn hard to pinpoint a puncture. I'd have thought at least one of the MEs would have taken a closer look."

Westfall speaks up from the doorway. "Some of those county MEs…" He makes a face that casts aspersions on the average county medical examiner's level of professionalism and training.

"I don't know," Neilsen says, more forgiving. "Clay Simmons, from Central, is no slouch." He retrieves the photo. "But these abrasion sites are really eroded. Ger, what do you think?"

Westfall shambles closer, accepts the photos for a look. There commences a short collegial discussion punctuated with terms like hypostasis, tissue disruption, extravasation. Neilsen argues briefly for the use of spectrophotometry. Westfall rebuts with figures on excised postmortem samples and large variables.

Cooper checks his watch. Emma and Bell exchange glances. Westfall finally scratches his chin stubble and turns their way.

"Miss Lewis, you've presented us with a tough problem. It's hard to distinguish between bruising patterns and tissue damage after death, so while it's possible there might have been a puncture, I wouldn't call this conclusive." He gives her a sympathetic look. "Maybe you thought you could come in and check the bodies and you'd just find the answer, am I right? I'm afraid it doesn't work like that. Even for us old-timers it doesn't work like that."

"I think she's onto something, though," Neilsen says. "I mean, when I saw the cubital fossa abrasions, I thought they were extreme."

Westfall takes a considering drag on his cigarette. "You think the perp might have debrided the area? Maybe postmortem?"

"I don't know. I've never seen that before. Have you seen that before?"

"No, but there are more things in heaven and earth, et cetera."

"Did you ask Carlos?"

"He's been in court all day." Westfall shuffles back past Cooper, leans through the doorway into the hall to call out. "*Carlos.* Carlos, get in here, we've got a question for your files."

The man who arrives in response to this summons is about mid-forties, short and squat. He's wearing a dapper suit with a wide tie; the pale collar of his shirt contrasts with his dark skin and hair. He has a mustache and a matching short beard, and his thick brows meet in the middle. His eyes are expressive, as bright and alert as a falcon's.

"What's up? What you got?"

"This young lady is postulating a theory, and we're checking it out. Folks, this is Carlos Dixon, Comparison Analysis and Trace."

"Hey, Carlos," Cooper says. "How was court?"

"Great." Dixon grins, wolfish. "We finally nailed Gower."

"Good to hear."

Westfall reclaims Dixon's attention. "Carlos, you ever see someone debride tissue to conceal needle marks?"

"Sure. I trained in New York, I've seen everything. I've seen cigarette burns over needle marks. Tattoos, lacerations. One girl, her boyfriend said it was a dog bite."

"This is abrasions at the ligature site," Neilsen explains. "It's Pennsylvania."

"Ah, okay. Well, I'm not gonna say it's outside the realm of possibility. You got the photos?"

"Yeah, you want both victims?"

"Can't hurt." Dixon finds himself a chair. He scans the visitors, smiles at Emma, then nods at Bell. "Hey."

"Hey," Bell replies.

Cooper thinks of something. "Glenn, have you got the matching shots from all four bodies?"

"Yup," Neilsen says. "Lemme dig 'em out."

Nielsen searches through his photo file again. The room is almost at capacity. Bell finds himself a chair near the wall. Emma, trying to take her mind off the pall of Westfall's cigarette smoke, watches Carlos Dixon as he examines the photos.

"This would be easier if you had an internal ME, huh?" she offers.

Dixon nods. "Yeah, but then the case comes to court and the defense attorney nails the ME to the wall for cognitive bias." He smiles. "It's okay for us, we're just lab grunts. But the coroner has to be impartial. So we have this curious little division of church and state."

"I didn't think about that."

"Of course it could also just be because this is the FBI, and you know how government institutions love bureaucracy." He grins at Cooper before turning to Bell. "This is pretty advanced work for a new LEO. You been doing this kind of thing awhile?"

Bell shakes his head. "Less than two weeks. And I don't have my stripes yet, I'm still in training."

"Yeah, I thought you seemed a little young to be this heavy."

"It's more hard-core than school, I'll say that much," Bell admits.

"Welcome to the real world, my friend." Dixon turns to Neilsen. "Pass me the glass?"

Neilsen hands over the large, square-framed magnifying glass on his desk. Dixon spends a little time poring over the shots, then encourages Neilsen to move aside so he can spread the photos out. He turns on the desk lamp. Suddenly there they are, lit in stark relief: eight arms from four victims, all in various shades of gray. The insides of the elbow joints are scored with horizontal red lines, purple bruises, raw areas that bear a strong resemblance to ground beef.

"Hard to distinguish anything from the abrasions," Westfall remarks.

"True. But look at the pattern."

"What pattern?" Westfall cocks his head.

Dixon indicates the photos on the desk. "Left arms are more abraded than right arms."

"What?"

There's a bit of crowding around the desk—Neilsen pushes his chair aside and stands up. Dixon uses the handle of the magnifying glass as a pointer. "Left arm, right arm. That's Ramirez. And here's Barnes—left arm, right arm. You can see the tram-track bruising from the ligatures and some deep abrasions, but you'd expect the depth and severity to be consistent across both arms, right? Not here."

"Shit," Neilsen breathes.

"What is it?" Emma's pulse quickens.

"Could it have been the way they were tied?" Cooper asks quickly.

Westfall answers first. "Nope. Otherwise you'd see angle variation in the bruising. And we got impressions off the posterior torsos—it looks as if all the knots were at the back. So the rope marks should be evenly distributed."

"Shit," Neilsen says again, more loudly this time. "He's right. Here's the shots for Lambton and Davis—same thing. Left cubital fossa is more damaged. Goddammit."

"Hey, man, don't feel bad," Dixon consoles.

Emma frowns. "What does this mean?"

"It means our perp created deeper abrasions," Dixon explains, "knowing that the debridement would disguise something in the elbow joint. Probably a needle mark, like you suggested. That much abrasion, it all bleeds together. It's the old 'forest for the trees' strategy."

"Would he have done it postmortem?" Cooper asks.

"Doesn't matter. Before death, just after—it'd be hard to differentiate either way. He might've used a file or a rasp, or the same rope, maybe, so the abrasions would match with the ligature marks."

"I'll be damned," Westfall says. He looks at Emma. "We'll need to get the county MEs to dissect and confirm, but it seems like your theory might have legs, Miss Lewis."

"So he *is* drawing blood." Emma gets a rush of energy, but it fades when she considers the ramifications. "But why is he drawing blood, then, if it's not to determine blood type?"

"Didn't you say he could be drinking it?" Bell asks.

"That may not fit, I'm afraid," Neilsen says. "Blood is toxic if you ingest more than a teaspoon or two. It can make you vomit, produce hemochromatosis."

"Iron overload," Westfall supplies.

"Maybe he's only ingesting a little bit?" Emma suggests. "Gutmunsson compared it to a taste test."

"You got this lead from Simon Gutmunsson? ¡Ay Santo!" Dixon raises and lowers his monobrow. "I guess blood-drinking is possible. But the Pennsylvania perp doesn't have the disorganization you'd expect to see with that kind of paraphilia. Guys like Richard Chase, who think they're vampires, tend to demonstrate heavy-duty schizophrenia—they're completely chaotic."

"Do the victims all have the same blood type?"

"Nope. Lambton and Ramirez were O-positive, Barnes was A-neg, and Davis was B-positive."

Bell is looking at the photos under the harsh lamplight. "Could he be...I dunno, injecting it into himself? Something like that?"

"Like a transfusion?" Dixon asks.

He sees something glowing in them, something he wants to kindle inside himself.... Emma wants to shake off Simon Gutmunsson's voice in this office, but it seems to follow her everywhere. "That would actually mesh very well with what we understand of the killer. We know he doesn't kill the victims immediately—Gutmunsson suggested he waits for the blood to be largely clear of ether, to be rid of impurities. The killer seems to have a special relationship with the blood from the victims. I can see him wanting to make their blood a part of him somehow."

"He'd have to be AB-positive, then," Dixon remarks. "Or he'd be in a world of hurt."

"AB-positive is the universal receiver, is that right?" Cooper asks.

"Right. Otherwise you're looking at hemolytic transfusion reaction, cascade clotting—"

"He might know that. He always took blood from the left arm." Cooper looks at Emma.

"Is that important?" she asks.

"The heart skews to the left, and the ventricles point left," Westfall says. "It's generally the preferred arm for blood samples." He peers at Cooper. "You're thinking medical training?"

"Maybe, yeah." Cooper has a light in his eyes. "Access to ether, the abrasions to hide a needle mark, the left arms, a possible transfusion..."

"Jesus." Somewhere in another office, a phone rings. Westfall ignores it. "It would actually work well with the analysis of the throat wounds—no hesitation marks, fine sharp blade. This guy is very efficient at cutting a jugular."

Emma turns to Bell, vibrating a little with the energy of the dots connecting in her head. "Someone they think they *can* trust."

His eyebrows bunch. "A doctor?"

"That seems unlikely, given we're looking for a college-aged suspect," Cooper says.

Emma nods. "I get that, and it's rare—but possible. Especially if he was accelerated in high school. It would explain his control, and the idea of a grudge—a smart teenager, maybe socially isolated...."

"Or he could be passing himself off as a doctor," Westfall suggests. "It's been done before."

The phone is still ringing. Dixon looks around. "Anyone gonna get that?"

"I'll take it." Neilsen drags himself away to the door.

"Or he could be a medical intern." Emma throws out more ideas. "An ambulance assistant, a trainee nurse, an army medic—"

Cooper has pulled out a notebook. He checks his watch. "Gerry, it's going on six thirty—we need to call the ME in Harrisburg at home. Don't let them release Barnes's body until we've confirmed. And tell them we want closer shots of the elbow joints, the... What did Glenn call it? The cubital fossa. We want shots of Ramirez, too."

"You thinking of exhuming the other two bodies?" Westfall asks.

"Maybe. Give me the department numbers for county health?"

Dixon smiles broadly at Emma. "You did good." He turns to Bell and speaks in Spanish. Bell coughs a little, replies, and they both chuckle.

Emma frowns at Bell. "What did you say?"

"I just told him you were too smart for him," Dixon says with a smile.

Bell's cheeks flush, but he's grinning. "And I said he's got it wrong—that I'm the brains, and you're the muscle."

Emma snorts, looks left as Neilsen rushes back into the doorway.

"Ed." Neilsen's face is chalky. "That was Gerry's line. Police in Clarke County just called it in. They've found another crime scene in Berryville."

CHAPTER NINETEEN

Cooper is on the phone in Neilsen's office, using a voice of command that Emma hasn't heard from him before.

"...until I arrive. Yes, the entire area. Tell Clarke County PD if anyone enters the building—I mean *anyone*—I will make it my personal mission to get them demoted to parking inspector for the rest of their career. No one touches anything until I get there with the team.... Yes, Gerry Westfall is coming, I'll get him in the chopper somehow...."

The other members of the Scientific Analysis unit are moving around, gathering equipment. Nobody rushes, but there's an air of brisk efficiency. Westfall is in his own office, paging Linda Brown out of her daughter's dance recital.

"What do we do now?" Emma stands with Bell by the wall in Neilsen's office. The abrupt shift in her concentration, after the most recent discussions, has given her a sense of free fall.

Bell opens his mouth to speak, stops. Shakes his head.

Cooper finishes his call, begins dialing another immediately. Emma thinks it's possible he's forgotten they're here.

"Agent Cooper—" she starts.

He holds up a finger, then his attention goes away. "Yes. Yeah, Don, it's Berryville. I'm still in Washington so I'm leading the team. Betty's organized a...No, sir. I don't think that's necessary. The people who've been working this from the start are the best....No, sir. I appreciate the idea, but that is not my recommendation.... Okay. Yes, that would be better. Thanks, Don, I'll keep you updated."

He hangs up, his finger still pressed on the receiver like he's thinking of where to call next. Then he pauses, turns to Emma and Bell. "Okay, it's like this. DCPD is sending us a chopper, it'll be on the roof in the next four minutes. I want you to go back to Quantico—"

"Are you *kidding*?" Emma blurts.

Cooper rounds on her. "Miss Lewis, this is not your fight."

"What are you talking about, we just—"

"Miss Lewis." Cooper composes himself with effort. "I am not taking you to an active crime scene. I applaud you and Mr. Bell for what you've contributed to this case so far, and we've turned up some important information as a result of your efforts, but now is not the time or place for this discussion."

"Agent Cooper—"

"Lewis." Bell touches her shoulder.

"Mr. Bell, take these." Cooper fishes the car keys out of his pants pocket, tosses them into Bell's catch. "Drive back to Quantico. I'll meet up with you there, most likely sometime tomorrow." He narrows his eyes at Emma. "I'll give you all the information I receive. Don't worry, you'll be kept in the loop."

Emma bites her lip hard. She nods.

"Good." Cooper glances at the wall clock. "Time to get upstairs. Do you both understand my instructions?"

"Yes, sir," Bell replies.

"Yes," Emma mutters.

"Thank you. Remember you'll need to be checked off at the escort desk. I already called them to say you're on your way down. I'll see you back at base." Cooper grabs his notebook and heads for the door.

There are no rousing speeches as the unit makes for the roof. Westfall ushers Emma and Bell out of the offices with the rest of the personnel and everyone hustles to the elevators. Neilsen is chewing on a sandwich he's got in one hand, with a hard case that looks like an outsized fishing tackle box in the other. Cooper is focused on something in his own brain and doesn't even look their way. Dixon gives them a rueful smile and a nod as the doors close.

They have to wait for the next elevator. On the way down to the parking garage, Emma chafes her hands together until Bell looks over. Then she puts them in her pockets.

Forewarned by Cooper, the escort security desk staff member ticks their IDs off a list and informs them that they have to take the rear exit onto E Street NW, as the front exit is locked down for the evening.

When she and Bell are finally in the car, Emma can sense the energy of the last few hours circulating in the air around them, trapped in there with them by the windows and the body of the vehicle. She has a fierce awareness of what has happened, what is happening now, the tense stillness of Bell beside her in the driver's seat, the sound of her own breathing.

Bell starts the car. He waits before pulling out of the parking space. Emma feels the shudder of the engine in the fillings of her teeth.

"I know this isn't our job." Her voice ricochets in the car's interior. "I know our job is supposed to be different. To collect information."

"We *are* collecting information." Bell's fingers are firm on the wheel while the car idles, while he stares forward. "Important information."

"Yeah."

He pauses. "Then why does this sting like I've been benched?"

Emma looks at him. "You know why."

"Do you think we should be involved in this?"

"We're already involved. We've been involved since Cooper first sent us to interview Simon Gutmunsson."

"That's right. We have as much connection to this case as anybody. We can't back out now." Bell sucks his teeth. "How far is it to Berryville?"

Something—her heart, she supposes—lurches inside Emma's chest. "About an hour and a half. You basically follow the Potomac to Leesburg." She heard Westfall say it when he and Cooper were arguing over whether Westfall could avoid the helicopter and go by road.

"Then take Route 7?" Bell is easing the car out of the parking space in the dark garage.

"Yep." Emma buckles her seat belt. "Do you know how to get out of Washington?"

"No. I flew in from Wisconsin to Washington National and picked up the truck from there. I'm gonna be following my nose."

"E Street onto Tenth, I think. Head for Constitution Avenue."

Bell raises his eyebrows. "Have you been to DC before? How do you know?"

"My dad drove us to see the Christmas tree about five years ago."

"God help us." Bell puffs out a breath. "This is probably a terrible idea."

"Probably."

"I guess we'll have an hour and a half to think about that."

They side-eye each other. Emma thinks if she tried to high-five with Bell now, he might actually reciprocate. Then it's all focus as she tries to remember ancient directions that will get them out of the city.

It's forty miles to Leesburg, where Emma buys chocolate and coffee—neither of them have eaten since lunch and they're running on fumes—and Bell gases up the Diplomat. Bell has shucked his jacket and tie, opened his collar. The sun is preparing to close down the day by the time they get back on the road.

"Okay." Emma sips from her to-go cup. "God, this coffee is awful. So we get there, stay on the perimeter—"

"Let's try a different approach." Bell opens a packet of peanut butter cups with his teeth while he drives. "We still have FBI credentials, that should get us most of the way in."

"And then...what? You think Cooper will have his hands so full he won't realize we're there?"

"I think we should just, y'know. Front up to him." Bell's expression has an obstinate cast.

Emma shakes her head. "And folks say I'm game."

"Cooper wants this killer caught. He wants Gutmunsson to stop writing to him. And he's got enough smarts to work his advantages. One of those advantages is us, Lewis."

Emma swallows another mouthful of burnt coffee. "So...how pissed do you think Cooper will be?"

"On a scale of one to ten, with one being mild frowning and ten being Mount St. Helens—"

"Right."

Bell has settled back to drive the last twenty-five or so miles. "Man. Check out that sunset."

Emma looks to the left, where a gap between the trees reveals the hump of Mount Weather. The sun is gone, leaving only a thin line of brilliant orange against the black horizon. The sky has turned a shade of cobalt that reminds her of homesickness.

"You shouldn't be doing this," she says quietly. "This is a worse idea for you than it is for me. You actually want a career in law enforcement. Cooper has the clout to screw that up."

"Cooper has clout, yeah. But if we can help, we should help. It's the right thing to do." Bell's face is a composition of blue planes and sharp shadows by the lights from the dashboard. He shrugs. "I'm not scared."

Your dad would be proud of you right now. It's on the tip of her tongue to say it, but she holds back. She has a feeling he already knows.

They cross the Shenandoah in the half dark. Soon enough, Bell's navigating the turn onto East Main Street, past a sign for Berryville Farm Supply.

"Okay, here we go," Bell says. "Which way now?"

Emma sees the flash of a white van with a roof-mounted aerial. "There. Follow the media."

The van turns past the rail line in the middle of town, so they turn, too, onto Lord Fairfax Highway, heading southwest. A state trooper tears past, turns left after Chip's Auto Sales, and Bell follows doggedly. Half a mile farther on, an area on the left is swarmed with police cars, state troopers, floodlights.

Emma touches Bell's forearm. "Don't get too close."

Bell noses the Diplomat onto the road shoulder behind a bunch of vehicles parked near a hurricane fence, kills the engine. He and Emma unbuckle, watch the people converging up ahead.

Emma drags her ID lanyard back over her head. "You ready?"

"Almost." Bell buttons his collar, slings his tie around his neck. His eyes are intent on the scene through the windshield. "I hope this works."

"Me too." Emma cracks her door open. She suddenly feels nervous and sweaty and travel-worn. "I don't look very FBI. At least you're wearing a suit."

"Take my jacket." Bell reaches into the back, hands her his dark suit jacket, pushes his own door open with his foot.

Emma gets out, brushes herself down, and slips the jacket on. Wearing Bell's clothes is becoming a habit. But the jacket functions as a kind of blazer over her pale T-shirt and jeans. It's big through the shoulders and long in the sleeves—she rolls the cuffs three turns.

"Is this better?"

Bell is knotting his tie. "Yeah. It looks fine." He grins. "Kind of a Talking Heads vibe."

Emma presses a hand to her stomach. "Oh my god, what are we doing?"

"Lewis, relax."

They make their way forward. A TV newshound is adjusting her mic, setting up for a live report in the middle of the road. A placard for Berryville Quarry and Asphalt on the fence, more moving bodies. The first uniform they come across is a Clarke County trooper, her hair tied back except for her Farrah Fawcett bangs.

"Ma'am?" Bell walks right up. "We're here to see Special Agent Cooper. We're with the bureau."

He shows his ID. Emma scrambles to do the same, with the same aplomb.

"Heya. Thank you." The woman examines their cards, expressionless. "Agent Cooper is on the far left of the site, at the crime scene. You need an escort?"

"No, thank you, but if you could point me at your sergeant, that would be great."

The woman points helpfully. "Sergeant Donahee is closer in, he's talking to the witness."

Bell's ears prick up. "We've got a witness?"

"Not to the deaths—the discovery. Jud Cleary, he's a local gentleman. Usually goes out on a tear, ends up in a ditch somewhere until we pick him up and drive him back home. Tonight he decided he'd come visit his former place of employment, got a helluva shock. He's with the ambulance over there."

"Thank you, ma'am—can I say who sent us?"

"Senior Trooper Janelle Winshuttle. You just tell 'em Nelly sent you."

Bell thanks her again and steers Emma away, speaking under his breath. "Always get a name."

"Now we go see the sergeant?"

"Now we walk in his direction but avoid him. We just want Cooper. Keep your eyes out for our guys."

A helicopter circles overhead. Farther into the wide quarry area, the rough gravel crunches under Emma's running shoes. The hot mix plant juts up at the right of what is basically a big truck parking area. Above the illumination of the floods, silos and gantry rigging loom like the backstage set of an enormous theater production.

When they hit an orange tape line, Bell finds another trooper and explains that Nelly sent them. They duck under the tape, blood thumping in Emma's face when she bends over. Outbuildings and warehouse structures are straight ahead. She spots a figure in a crime scene hazard suit, tugs on Bell's sleeve.

"There."

Bell narrows his eyes, heads them both in that direction, left of a giant heavy roller and through a gap in a broken wire fence. Other people pass in and out of the area. A corrugated red storehouse, with a newer silver tin door, stands surrounded by yellow barricade tape.

People are moving around it, in suits and uniforms. Through pinhole rust in the walls, Emma can see the lightning flare of flashes going off inside the building.

She swallows hard. The night is clammy on her skin. New-made ghosts live inside those walls, and now she's not sure she wants to know them.

Bell touches her arm—*there.* By the refracted light of the floods, Emma can see the furrows in Cooper's brow as he peels off a set of latex gloves.

"Do we go to him?"

"No." Bell fixes her in place. "We wait. He'll see us."

He's right. Cooper scans the site as he talks to a county officer. When his eyes hit Emma and Bell, they stop.

Emma gets a wash of guilt, talks out of the side of her mouth. "Let me take the blame for this. You can do a set-pick off me, say I made you drive—"

"No way," Bell says. "I initiated this. I *earned* it."

Cooper approaches in his own good time. He does not look happy. "What are you doing here?"

Bell stands straight. "We decided to come, sir."

"You decided to come." Cooper mashes his lips into a zippered line. "I gave you *very specific* instructions—"

"We know," Emma says. Suddenly she understands why this is important. "But we need to see it. And you need us."

"I don't need a pair of unqualified, rule-breaking *teenagers* haring around this crime scene—"

"That's right," Emma says. "We're teenagers. And these victims are *all teenagers.* We can tell you more about them in five minutes than an adult officer would be able to tell you in an hour, just by looking."

Cooper doesn't seem to know how to reply to that. He turns to Bell. "Are you on board with this? Did she make you—"

"She didn't make me do anything," Bell says calmly. "I made my own choice on this, sir. Lewis is right. We're as much a part of this case as anybody else. And we might see things from a different perspective."

Emma finds her voice has gone imploring. "Mr. Cooper, you're hunting a killer of juveniles. All the evidence suggests the perpetrator is a juvenile himself. We're the only juveniles you have. Let us help."

Cooper tongues his back teeth, still frowning. But the frown looks speculative now. Finally he makes a deep exhale. "I am gonna get my ass kicked halfway to Sunday for this...."

"We won't tell," Emma blurts.

"Somebody will," Cooper says darkly. "All right. You can view the scene. Tell me what you see." He stops Emma with an upraised palm as she opens her mouth. "You do exactly what I say. *Exactly*. Can you follow instructions this time, Miss Lewis, or am I going to have to make you wait out here?"

Emma restrains herself, nods. "Yes. I mean, I can follow instructions."

"Stay here," Cooper says. "That's instruction number one."

He looks at them both, shakes his head, and turns away. For a moment, Emma thinks he's fixing to block them and walk. But he's simply retrieving two packages from the open back of a nearby white van. When he returns, he hands them the plastic-wrapped packets.

"Put these on. There should be booties. I'm going to find someone to give you an escort."

He leaves again, heading back toward the doorway of the red storehouse.

Emma turns to Bell, wanting to jump up and down, careful not to. "Holy shit."

Bell lets out an immense breath. "Jesus, I can't believe that worked."

She grabs a handful of plastic packaging and yanks it away. "Hurry up, let's do this before he changes his mind."

Bell moves equally quickly. The hazmat suits inside the wrapping are a kind of durable blue paper, and they're a little awkward to step into—once Emma ditches Bell's jacket on top of a nearby gallon drum, it's easier. They fit their booties over their shoes.

Cooper returns with a young man who's also in Tyvek, his huge camera slung around his neck by a wide strap. "This is Henry Burns, he's the county ME photographer."

"Hi," Henry says, makes a little wave. He's about twenty-five and looks like he'd be friendly under different circumstances. As things stand, he's pale-faced and solemn.

"Mr. Burns is going to take you inside," Cooper says. "People are working in there. Don't disrupt them, and don't talk to them. Don't go more than three feet into the interior of the building. Stick to the wall if you can."

"Yes, sir," Bell says.

"You can't take anything in. No notepads, pencils, nothing. Don't touch anything. I mean it—if you touch anything, Gerry will have you inked up for fingerprints before you can blink, and I don't want any record of you ever having been in there, d'you understand?"

"Yes," Emma says. "No touching. Got it."

"Get under the tape."

Cooper holds the tape up for them. Once they've breached that barrier, Emma feels a chill—they're getting closer. To what, she doesn't want to imagine.

Instead of leading them to the tin door, which is a mess of personnel and tape rolls and piles of equipment, Cooper walks them around to the left. There's no noticeable path, but the way is marked by the pressed-down fronds of ryegrass and devil's tail vine.

Far at the back, out of sight of the main quarry area, a wide piece of water-stained corrugated iron is pulled up like the curling cover of a paperback novel to make a sneak's door.

"This is where Cleary entered?" Bell asks.

"Yes." Cooper turns to them. "And it's where the perpetrator entered. You'll be seeing it as he saw it. This is a disused outbuilding. The owners have this part of the site security-checked, but only once a month and then just the exteriors. If Cleary hadn't walked into it, it might never have been discovered."

"This isn't a garbage dump." It's the first thing Emma can think of to say.

"That's right. And this scene's different in other ways, too. I want your first impressions, including any thoughts you might have about the victims. You can't take notes—you'll just have to record everything behind your eyes. And I want your questions. Questions usually lead to new questions, new ideas. I'll take whatever you've got." Cooper stops, looks at them both. "Okay, tell me now. Are you sure you want to go in? Because this is it. Once you see this stuff, you can't unsee it. It changes you."

Emma realizes her hands are shaking. She squeezes them into fists. "I've seen this stuff before, Mr. Cooper."

Bell just nods, very sober.

Cooper gives them a final up-and-down, as if he's documenting the people they were before entering. For a moment, his face looks very sad and wise. Emma thinks he's going to say something more, but he just closes his mouth and indicates the entry point with his chin.

Burns ushers them over. Before they can go through the sneak's door, a uniformed deputy exits, looking ashen. Emma and Bell stand back. The deputy makes it about five good paces out of the building before he gags and throws up into a patch of gravel.

Emma glances at Bell, sees him swallow. Then Burns is saying, "Excuse me? This way," and time slows down.

Ducking low, into the smell of rust and old brick. And then the rank smell of blood.

They're inside now. Air wafts around her, indicating the size of the space. Neither she nor Bell look at each other. Emma looks at the floor, notices the pulverized remains of mortar under her covered shoes. In the crack where part of the concrete floor has split, a wild strawberry is growing.

Camera flashes go off nearby. Something inside her is starting to coalesce. A familiar feeling. She doesn't want to look up. She hears the hiss and static of handheld radios, the click of shutters, the sizzle of tripod lights, muted conversation. People move in her peripheral vision, all made anonymous in blue Tyvek. She recognizes Glenn Neilsen's fishing tackle box, set to one side.

A stack of bricks occupies a corner near the illegal entryway, and by it, a pile of clothing protected by scene tape and evidence markers. Emma sees a red T-shirt with glitter on it. Faded jeans. A pair of striped shorts with a brown leather belt, flopped open. Beside the pile lies a tumble of shoes—a pair of Keds with the laces untied, a running shoe, a green sandal. *At least three victims, then.* She closes her eyes.

Somewhere far off, in her own head, a thin, high keening sound.

Her heartbeat hammers her ribs. God, she's so tired. But she has to look at this. It's what she came here to see.

She takes a shuddering breath in through her nose, registers the ozone scent of decaying metal. The smell of heat from the lights, and sweat from the people in the space. The low, raw notes of slaughter.

Emma opens her eyes.

The shock of it. Breathless at the scale of it. The hanging bodies. The ropes and chains and hooks. The throat wounds. The blood in pools and puddles underneath. The smell. The quality of the light.

The poignancy of the bodies. The stillness of them. The way they're suspended like slabs of meat in a freezer, the wrongness of it. The way their hands are bound at the front, arms tied again around the waist, faces obscured with blood. No hair—he's shaved them this time.

The keening in her head magnifies. Resolves itself into a piercing, endless scream.

She looks for as long as she can. Records everything behind her eyes, as Cooper instructed. Records it also in her viscera, in the marrow of her bones, in the sinews of her legs, in the mysterious recesses of her mind where no light enters.

Cold sweat pops on her skin, like she felt in Huxton's basement. She sways on the spot.

Finds herself reeled in. Looks down and is surprised to discover that she and Bell are holding hands. Looks up and he is staring at the bodies, too. His expression is one of absolute despair. Then his eyes close with the awareness that nothing will ever be the same.

CHAPTER TWENTY

After working the scene with Cooper and the Scientific Analysis team for two hours, they peel off their paper suits, collect Bell's jacket, walk back to the Diplomat, and begin the long return drive to Quantico.

They should feel hungry, but neither of them wants to eat anything. Near Manassas, the car develops a subtle yaw as Bell starts to shut down. Emma makes him pull over on the side of the parkway so they can switch drivers. In the passenger seat, he complains that he's not tired. Five minutes later, Emma looks over and his head is heavy against the window, his breathing deep and even. He wakes just before Southbridge with a jolting start.

She rolls the car into an exterior parking space near Jefferson at about 01:30.

"The car needs to go back to the motor pool," Bell says dully.

"Doubt the gate will be open yet." Emma unbuckles and rubs her neck.

Neither of them has the energy to get out. They just sit there listening to the engine tick as it cools. Finally, Bell rouses himself.

"We should go to the dorms. Get some sleep."

"You sleepy again?"

"Nope."

"Me either."

"I'm too wired. I shouldn't have napped." Bell sighs deeply, pushes open his door.

"It was nap or become a road fatality." Emma sticks her tongue in her cheek. She shouldn't have mentioned fatalities. "Wait."

"What's up?"

"I know what we need."

She gets out of the Diplomat, stiff-legged. Brushes crumbs off the driver's seat and shoos Bell out, locks up. Then she walks fifteen feet to her own Rabbit. *Keys, keys.* She finds them in the back pocket of her jeans. The trunk has a sticky lock, and it's been nearly a week since she's paid the car any attention. She pats one cold taillight affectionately.

Bell stands in the parking lot, moonlight giving him gravitas and a thin shadow. "Did you leave something?"

"Yes. But I left it on purpose." She hunts through the open trunk by feel. "Okay. Got it." She lifts up her prize.

"Tequila?" Now Bell sounds interested.

"Hey, we drink tequila in Ohio, too."

Emma's not sure where to go, because alcohol is forbidden in the federal buildings and specifically in the dorms. Bell vetoes drinking in the parking lot, but shows how they can cut across the lawn to reach the grove. There's something about the springy texture of the grass underfoot that Emma finds deeply restorative.

The grove is the paved area where agents and staff can take their cafeteria food to eat outside. At this time of night it's lit only by shadow; the café tables all have their blue umbrellas folded.

Emma pulls out a plastic chair and plonks herself down. "Smoke 'em if you got 'em."

"No glasses." Bell, still standing, grimaces and pats down his front as if he'll somehow find them there.

"Oh no, whatever will we do." Emma unscrews the cap from the bottle and takes a sip. Holds it out.

Bell seems to realize he's being ridiculous because he's tired. He takes the bottle, regards it. "You know this is terrible tequila."

"Thousands of college students can't be wrong."

It's the first snort she's gotten out of him for hours. He parks himself in a chair, knocks back a mouthful, and makes a face. "Jesus."

"Lightweight."

"How can you drink this shit?"

"Like this." She retrieves the bottle and takes another slug. "Talk to me, Travis."

He sighs. "It's nearly two in the morning. Too late to talk."

"Are you okay?"

He accepts the bottle, drinks. "No."

"No." She takes the bottle off him, drinks, sets it on the table to stare at. "I won't tell you that you'll get used to it, or it'll get easier. I'm used to it, and it doesn't get easier."

"So you just suck it up."

"Pretty much. It's like every other kind of grief. Give it time, et cetera."

"Yeah." He takes a shot, presses his lips as he swallows. "I know the routine."

She retrieves the bottle for another sip. "My therapist told me it's better to feel it than to be blunted, so...I guess that's good advice?"

"Hard to feel and keep working."

"Yeah. But when your work involves doing what's needed to catch this guy…"

"Then you stay strong." He nods. "This killer's had no outline for me, y'know. I haven't been able to picture him, since this whole thing started. But today I finally felt like I could see an outline. And more than just an edge—a whole silhouette."

"Yeah. Today we got something." *But at what cost?* She can't think like that. She takes a long pull from the bottle.

"Easy, tiger." Bell takes the bottle gently, sets it down.

She looks at her fingers. "I worry about it sometimes."

"I know you do." He sits back in his chair, hands loose. "Every time I look at you I see your eyes moving like you're scanning the case notes—"

"Not the case. That I'm getting blunted."

The pause drags out, and she looks over at him. He's shaking his head slowly, lips upturned.

"What? It's not funny."

"And I'm not laughing. You're not blunted, Emma. That's not you. You're…"

"I'm what?"

Bell opens his mouth, closes it. His eyes skim over her but his gaze is light. His hand lifts, palm open near her shoulder like he's warming himself by a campfire.

"You're all…There's emotion coming off you. All the time. Maybe other people don't see it, or maybe you work hard to control it, but it's there." He grabs the bottle. "You're about the least blunted person I ever met."

The compliment shuts her up for a while. She recovers enough to extract the bottle. "Gimme that. You're drunk."

"Most certainly not."

"One thing bugging me," she confesses. "I told Cooper we'd have a different perspective. That we could give him insight on this guy, on those kids. Maybe help figure out how he's choosing them. But I've got nothing." *Just their faces, all covered in blood, and a high, constant scream in my head.* She doesn't want to say that aloud.

"You're tired. It'll come."

"That sunset was nice, though."

He smiles softly. "Yeah, it was."

"You get nice sunsets like that in Texas?"

"Sunsets in Texas are like a dream you had once, of a sunset in heaven." He looks up past the tree line, to the star-blasted sky. Closes his eyes in a way that reminds her of Berryville. "Come on, Lewis. Time to go to bed or you'll be seeing the sun rise."

He walks her back to her car so she can stash the bottle, then escorts her to Jefferson. She's proud of herself for not swaying at all, considering she's just downed about six shots on an empty stomach. Once Bell leaves, she relaxes her control enough to hold the handrail on the elevator ride to her floor.

Then—sleep.

At 4:00 AM she jerks awake with a cry. *I know what it is,* she thinks. *Gotta tell Cooper.* But her brain is already fogging over, and by the time she wakes again in the morning, the knowledge is gone.

CHAPTER TWENTY-ONE

Bell yawns through an 8:00 AM class on Investigative Protocols. By the time he gets to the Cool Room, it's after ten and Emma is there, in a long-sleeved tee and nonregulation black jogging pants with elastic at the ankles.

"Did you skip class?"

She ignores that, holds up a file. "Betty delivered information on Berryville."

He comes the rest of the way through the office door, finds a chair. "That was quick."

"There's already a result on two of the three bodies."

Cooper must've used the Policefax to transmit wire pictures of the victims' fingerprints on-site—getting the victims identified early is crucial in these cases.

Travis feels heavy in the head, but reading the xeroxed report brings him around fast. "Mark Spiegel. White male, sixteen years old. He was taken from Strasburg on Tuesday afternoon."

"And Kimberley Berger was abducted on Tuesday night." Emma's sitting sideways with her knees up, feet on the chair. She looks worn down, but it was a bad night and cheap tequila is potent.

"Same location?"

"No." Her face is stony. "From Winchester."

"What is it?"

She pushes the pages toward him across the desk. "She was fourteen."

Bell checks the notes to make sure he heard her right. "Fuck. They're getting younger."

"Yes." Emma chews on a fingernail.

He's getting to know her tells now: Sometimes she shows anger when she's scared. Last night they were both too shocked for anything to register, and after that, her responses were blurred by alcohol and exhaustion. But he thinks she's starting to feel afraid of this guy they're tracking. It makes him angry in turn, because he knows she already lives with a debilitating amount of fear.

How can you keep doing this? He understands why *he's* following this through, but Emma has no personal obligation at all. She's walked back into her own personal nightmare, and it's clear she hates every part of it. What's keeping her going? He doesn't know. All he knows is they're in it now, probably too far to back out, and the only way through is to catch the killer fast.

"Okay, d'you wanna go over the scene report?"

Emma sighs, puts her feet down. "Sure."

The entire case file is open on the desk, ID photos of the identified victims lined up in a row. Images of the victims in death floated through Bell's dreams last night—seeing them arrayed like this, as they were in life, is like hearing the percussive toll of a great gong inside his head. He pulls the pages closer, trying to shake it off. "We won't get the postmortem protocols back for a while—lab results take time. But they're on the lookout now for needle marks, or abrasions hiding needle marks. Otherwise it seems like the process, the ritual he's playing out, they think it's largely the same."

"The quantity and spatter pattern of the blood at the scene suggest that this was the scene of death. That means we can see exactly what he was doing with them."

"He made clean jugular cuts. He hosed them down before he cut them, and maybe himself after—Glenn Neilsen is following up on some unidentified hairs they found. There was no hose, though, so the killer must've taken that with him."

Emma rubs the pads of her fingers over her head. "He must always use a place with a faucet."

"The shaved hair is new."

"Yep." She drops her hand.

"Talk to me, Emma."

"I still don't know why he's doing it." She shrugs. "Gutmunsson predicted it. I tried to ask him about it and he deflected."

There's more to dig there. Bell decides to save it.

"Let's look at the scene." He spreads copies of the photos out across the desk. "Okay, here's victim placement at death—hanging from the ceiling beam like that. We know it takes nearly seventeen hours for the effects of the ether to fully wear off. He couldn't have hung them up during that period, or they'd asphyxiate before he could kill them. Which means he's strong enough to handle them un-sedated, haul them up."

"We already knew he was strong."

"Hanging them by the ankles is part of the ritual, though, so it has deeper meaning, apart from just being a convenient position for exsanguination."

"They stay conscious longer upside down," Emma says. "Maintain blood pressure in the head, the victim stays awake."

Does she know this from personal experience? Bell feels oily nausea. "Okay. And we've got the ropes and chains he used."

"Doubt we'll get any fingerprints off them."

"He tied them here, at the ankles, and tied their hands in front. But he also tied their arms against their bodies, which is how we get the elbow joint abrasions. I don't know why he did that."

"Maybe he's just got a thing for rope."

"Lewis." Bell frowns at her gently, then at the photos. "Why did he leave the scene like this? Why didn't he clean up and dump the bodies like normal? Did something change?"

"Maybe he felt confident the scene wouldn't be discovered. He couldn't have anticipated someone like Cleary stumbling onto it. That was just a fluke."

"But he's usually so careful. He's, like, paranoid careful. Why abandon a scene complete like this, knowing he'd leave so much trace evidence for police to find?"

Emma doesn't answer. She's been avoiding looking at the crime scene photos—now she turns her head and really gives them her attention. "This guy . . . He probably follows the media."

"Most of them do." Bell's jaw clamps. "They're calling him the Berryville Butcher now."

"Right. So he must know the authorities are no closer to catching him than they were in March, when he first started."

"You think it's a kind of slap in the face to the cops? Like, 'Here's more evidence, but you still can't find me'?"

"It would track with the 'young arrogant guy' profile." Her eyes glaze a little as she scans the pictures. "But it looks more like..."

"What?"

She closes her eyes, as if vision obstructs her thinking. "He takes them, hangs them, cleans them, dumps them...." Her eyes snap open. "Bell, he's moving on."

"I don't... What?"

"We know he's been using a variety of locations as kill sites—Berryville is another disposable site. He typically kills the victims, then dumps the bodies in the trash once they're worthless, right?" Her hands move, sift through the photos. "He throws his used things out. Once he's done with something, he dumps it. Maybe this is the same—maybe he's 'dumping' this kind of site. Moving on. He's got another situation, another building, somewhere better—"

"Oh fuck." Bell sits back in his chair, dazed by the realization. "He's got another site."

"Yes. Somewhere secure, maybe. Somewhere private. A property, or a place he can go to do all the things he wants to do without fear of discovery." Emma stands and leans on the desk. Her face is a dark reflection in the glossy photos. "*That's* the change. He's had enough of temporary places. He's got a hideout, a permanent site, and now he can abandon this old site to the police...."

"If he sets himself up somewhere comfortable, and he's real careful, he could keep going for a long time. For years. We might never find him. Jesus."

Emma meets his eyes. "We have to tell Cooper."

They both startle when someone knocks on the door.

It's Betty, in a blue peplum skirt suit. Her professional elegance is a jarring clash with what they've just been focused on. "Excuse me. You have a visitor."

Emma looks blank. "Sorry?"

"Upstairs in the atrium foyer. You'll need to go and sign them in and escort them."

"Wait." Bell's still confused. "We're not expecting any—"

He's too late. Betty has left.

"She doesn't hang around, does she?" Emma says. "And since when do we get visitors?"

"Since now, I guess." Bell's first thought runs to his sisters. He pushes out of his chair—the last thing he needs is to have Lena or Connie anywhere in Virginia right now. "Let me go see what's going on."

He takes the elevator, anxious. In the atrium, he scans the usual clusters of trainees in chinos and federal-issue blue or red polos and regulation windbreakers. As he moves toward the sign-in desk, a flock of Academy students walks by in front of him, then they're gone.

And like a full moon exposed by moving clouds, there is Kristin Gutmunsson.

CHAPTER TWENTY-TWO

It's a shock to see her. Kristin's milky skin and long white hair seem to cast their own light. Bell's struck again by her looks, and he's not the only one: He sees a few bureau guys glance twice. She stands there, oblivious, mouth open and hands clasped, staring around the place like a tourist appreciating the architecture in a cathedral.

He walks closer. "Miss Gutmunsson?"

She spins and smiles in such an artlessly genuine way, it makes his heart hurt. "Mr. Bell!"

"Miss Gutmunsson, what are you doing here?"

"I've come to visit you and Emma!" She appears to be incapable of concealing her emotions at all. "Because I have some more information about my brother. And I didn't know if you would be able to visit me again, because you've been so busy with the Berryville Butcher case—I saw it on the television!"

For a moment he's made stupid by the sheer innocence in her face. "Uh, that's, uh—"

"I mean, excuse me, I know you're not really working that case, because you're only trainees. But I remembered what Emma said, about how Simon was sharing insights about an active case, and I thought, well, it makes sense, doesn't it? That *must* be it."

He steps closer to encourage her to lower her voice. "Miss Gutmunsson—"

"Oh, please call me Kristin!" She smiles and smiles. "I have a special day pass from Chesterfield—my driver is outside in the parking lot. It's very exciting, to be out on a field trip to the FBI. Have you been well?" She puts a hand to her mouth. "Goodness, what am I talking about, I just said how you've been busy."

He decides to abandon chivalry and cut to the chase. "How did you get past the MPs and onto the base?"

"I had my lawyer call and request permission. It wasn't easy, but here I am." She looks around again at the atrium interior. "I can't say I like the brutalist décor. There's lots of blond brick, isn't there? Very Marcel Breuer."

It takes some wrangling with the sign-in desk, but in the end Bell gets his way. On the trip back down in the elevator, he stands beside and a little away from Kristin; she is not her brother, but he still finds her profoundly unsettling. The way she presents doesn't help. She's wearing a long charcoal coat over a white linen shirt with a pointed collar, loose white linen pants, and black ballet slippers. It looks like she's thrown a morning coat over her pajamas.

"Are we going all the way down? We are, aren't we, goodness." She scans the numbers above the door, the inside of the elevator car. "I can't believe the FBI put you in the basement, it seems completely bizarre. You should at least have a window...."

She talks at him and over the top of his head. He can't make her out. All things considered, he's not sure he wants to. So he just stands there, pulling his shirt collar away from his neck.

Then he realizes Kristin might be chattering because she's nervous, and that this trip is a big deal for her. And that his mother didn't raise him to be a jerk.

"Uh, how are the puppies?" His words come out gruffer than he'd like.

Kristin responds immediately. "Oh, they're doing so well! Sheba is wonderful with them, and I'll be so sad when they're adopted out."

"They're selling the pups?"

"Yes—Sheba has some pedigree, and a very long name that no one uses. Everyone just calls her Sheba. I'm thinking I might ask to have one of the pups, just the littlest one."

Bell wonders if they'll let her keep it. "The puppies are pretty cute."

"Aren't they? We had dogs when I was a child—Father's hunters—but after Simon shot them, Mother said we couldn't have any more pets."

He feels his expression freeze in place. They've reached the basement floor and when Kristin steps out, he follows. "I'm sorry, did you say your brother shot your dogs?"

"Yes. It was very sad, actually. Simon loved those dogs—borzois and hounds and adorable German pointers....But Father took Simon hunting when he was nine, and one of the dogs was quite old, and it couldn't keep up on the hunt, so Father made Simon shoot it. Then later that evening, after they came home, Simon stole Father's gun and shot them all."

"*All* the dogs?"

Kristin blinks up at him. "I told you it was a sad story."

"Why would he do that?"

"I don't know. I asked him afterward, and he just said, 'Everything dies.' But I think he was angry at Father. At any rate, Mother said no more pets, so we never had another, but truly, I would *love* to have a puppy." She looks around the corridor walls. "Where to now?"

Bell is aware that serial murderers often break down the moral taboo on killing by practicing on animals. He thinks of what it would take, to shoot a pack of dogs you loved, and then he suddenly remembers the story about the school cat and has to work hard to keep his face blank. He points right. "This way, please."

When he opens the door to the Cool Room and Emma sees their guest, she's as dumbstruck as he was. He tries not to take any reassurance from that.

"Emma!" Kristin swoops forward and clasps Emma's hand. "Oh, it's so good to see you! This is very exciting. Have you been well?"

"Uh, I've been..." Emma plays catch-up real quick. "Sure, I've been okay. Hi. Nice to see you again, Kristin."

"It was so wonderful to have visitors the other day! And I was thinking about the questions you asked me, about my brother. Have you seen him again? You have, haven't you?"

"Yes. Yes, I've seen him again."

"Was anything I suggested helpful? Because he can be very difficult. And I've thought of some more things. They're just little bits and pieces, but I wrote them down on a scrap of paper, here...." Kristin lifts her hand and there's a little satin pouch attached to her wrist by a string. She opens it, feels inside, then steps forward and simply upends it on the desk. "I'm afraid they searched it when I came in, and I...Oh, here it is...."

Among the weirdest collection of handbag items Bell has ever seen—an acorn, a handkerchief, three red leaves, a cork from a bottle, dried rose petals, a stub of pencil—is a loosely folded piece of notepaper. Kristin fishes it out and smooths it open. Over her shoulder, Bell catches Emma's glance, her quickly glared *What the hell?* He can only reply with a helpless shrug, which Kristin doesn't see while her eyes are down.

"You've written out more tips about Simon?" Emma says. "That's, um—"

"Because you might have to see him again." Kristin looks up. "If his insights are about the Berryville case, you might need to. Because solving that case is really important."

"It is important," Bell agrees.

"Then you need my help. Or rather, I need to be able to help." Color in her cheeks now. "It makes me feel better, to help."

The idea of Kristin Gutmunsson assuaging her conscience like this rasps on him. But the Christian in him—or maybe it's his mother's voice—is saying let her have her atonement.

Emma is more merciful.

"I understand," she says gently. "And anything you can give us would be great."

Kristin flattens out the paper. "Look, here are the notes."

Bell sees the case file nearby on the desk. Emma has stuffed all the pages together and closed the folder. A couple of the victim identification photos are peeking out, but Kristin is focused on her list—it *is* a list, he can see.

"Simon likes . . . good-quality red wine?" Emma reads down, following her finger. "And I shouldn't talk about your parents?"

"You could bribe him with the wine. Even one glass! He must miss that so much."

"Your brother enjoys refined amusements." Emma's tone is very borderline.

"Yes, he's a bit of a snob like that." Kristin smiles. "I can't criticize really! It's the way we were raised. Our parents had the best of intentions, I'm sure, but I'm afraid they never did much follow-through."

During Simon Gutmunsson's trial, Bell discovered this part of the twins' history: how their parents absconded for Europe to avoid litigation around Simon's victims. How the Gutmunssons Senior had never been very parental to begin with, except in the old-money way of nannies and detached nurseries and expensive boarding schools.

Emma arrows in. "You think Simon's upbringing is a vulnerability in him. A chink in his armor."

Kristin piles objects back into her pouch. "Well, he's always been an outsider. Our circumstances, our education, plus how clever he is, and of course his own particular tendencies . . ." She sighs heavily. "The difficulty with Simon is that he always drew strength from that, from being different. *I* wanted to be normal, but Simon . . . Simon wanted to be special. It was that or hate himself. Do you see how impossible things were?"

"And your parents?"

Kristin's gaze draws inward. "It was always a matter of what they thought of him. Of us both. There were certain expectations—and understandings about how well we lived up to those expectations. It gives you strange ideas of success, you know. And of what being lovable looks like. Does that make sense? That's why I said please don't mention our parents. He'll get angry, and you won't get anything out of him then."

Bell's pretty sure it's a self-soothing habit, the way Kristin plays with strands of her hair as she talks. She has a peculiar fragility, this girl, but she's been through a lot. He knows that Kristin was a suspected accomplice of her brother for some time, that the question was raised in court. That her legal team reminded everyone how Kristin had stabbed Simon in defense of a lawman. It was one of the things that resulted in her exoneration.

Bell knows, too, that she was socially connected with a number of her brother's victims. He knows a lot of things about Kristin Gutmunsson that he would rather *not* know.

Emma is still examining the list, the looping writing. "Kristin, this information could actually be really useful."

"Do you think so?" Kristin claps her hands together. "Oh, that's so good to hear! And I'm sorry to just turn up in person—I was going to mail it, then I thought I wasn't sure if you would get it. And I did so want to visit. But it's very... How do you *work* in here? It's not very cheery, is it?"

Emma snorts. "Yeah, welcome to the bunker."

"But it *is* like a bunker! Goodness. I suppose it's appropriate, given what you're investigating, but still." Kristin scans the room, the chairs and files and the desk. Before either of them can react, she's plucked one of the victim ID photos from the file. "Who's this? He's handsome, isn't he? Don't tell me he's a suspect!"

"Not a suspect." Bell takes the photo from her carefully.

"Oh my god, is he a victim? He is, isn't he? Oh, that's awful. He's so *young*."

Emma nods. "Yeah, I'm afraid so."

"That's appalling. And look at him—are they all like that? How on earth do you manage?"

"Are they all like what?" Emma's attention changes. Bell can see it in her body language, that suspension of breath, the slight narrowing of her eyes.

"Like...I don't know, let me see again."

He's shocked when Emma takes the photo out of his hand and gives it to Kristin. Even more shocked when she starts pulling other victim photos out of the file. She spreads them out on the desk. When he opens his mouth to object, she gives him a quelling look.

"Oh my gosh, they *are*," Kristin breathes. "Look at them!"

"We've *been* looking." There's an intensity, an urgency, in Emma's face. "They're all different. Different genders, different races..."

"But they're all beautiful. Can you see? Their eyes, their skin... Look at this one, the lovely cheekbones. And this one! Oh, they're all glowing!"

Emma lifts her gaze his way, and they don't need words—it's all unspoken. *This is it, this is the connection.* And now that it's been pointed out to him, it's like a lamp suddenly flicking on.

The victims are all beautiful. Some of them unconventionally, but all of them have a luminous quality. It's in their clear cheeks, their glossy hair, white teeth. They smile out of the photos, young and fresh and radiant, bursting with good health, the vigor of adolescence spilling off them like sunshine. Smooth foreheads and wide eyes and clean jawlines—the bone structure of the newly dead.

"Oh, that's so *sad*," Kristin says, her eyes welling up. "Their families must be *devastated*."

"It is sad," Emma agrees. "Kristin, can I show you some other photos? They're upsetting, but I'd really like to hear your opinion."

She doesn't need to catch Bell's eye this time, the communication between them so entirely unified that he doesn't even blink when she opens the file and starts spreading out the Berryville crime scene photos.

He watches Kristin. What they're doing, this is not allowed. The crime scene pictures are confidential, not intended to be shared, nothing released to the media or the public. But he can feel the buzz from Emma, and he wants to know, too. What does Kristin Gutmunsson see? This girl, who lived alongside a killer all those years... How did that alter her perception? And what does she perceive now?

"Oh my *god*." Kristin gasps, claps a hand over her mouth, closes her eyes—but only for a moment. Something in the photos is as compelling for her as the answer is for Bell.

Emma leans closer. "What is it, Kristin?"

"They're...Oh goodness. Oh, that makes me feel ill." Kristin reaches out tentatively to poke with one finger. Her voice is a bare whisper. "Does he hang them all upside down like that?"

"Yes. He's strong."

"And he cuts them like that....Oh my god."

"He follows the same pattern. We don't know why. We don't know why he bleeds them, we don't know why he cuts their hair."

"It's like he's field dressing them...." Kristin's horror is being replaced by a strange, detached curiosity. "But you said he only takes their blood?"

"Yes." Bell finds he's caught some of Emma's intensity. "You mean he hangs them like game?"

"She's right," Emma says immediately. "That's what I thought when I first saw the scene. Like meat in a freezer." She turns back to Kristin. "But he doesn't gut them."

"How strange…" Kristin tilts her head. "And how high up he's suspended them! Is this photo from eye level? Ooh, yes. Here's one that shows you."

"What does it show?"

"They're a bit more than six feet above the ground, aren't they?" Kristin points. "This lady in the background with the gloves, she gives you a sense of scale. Why on earth would he put them up so high?"

"That's a good point." Bell squints at Emma. "He hangs them to bleed them, but he doesn't have to pull them up six feet to do that. I don't know much anatomy, but I know gravity."

"Why so high?" Emma looks away, thinking. "Everything he does serves a purpose. So what's the purpose of…" She looks back, scrabbles through the photos. "How would he be standing, in relation to the victims?"

Bell finds the pictures she needs. "There. They found plantar prints on the floor beneath the victims. He took off his shoes."

"I don't think that's all he took off," Emma says grimly.

"Ooh," Kristin says. "Yes! He would be underneath, wouldn't he? To get the spray."

Bell frowns. "The what?"

"The spray. There'd be a big gush, wouldn't there? That's what happens when you bleed a deer, at any rate. Have you never been hunting?"

"Turkeys and coyotes, yeah."

Emma looks at him, her face pale. "Bell, he cut them from high up, while he was underneath."

"Maintain blood pressure in the head." *Oh my god.* He presses a hand against the desk. "The neck, the carotid artery—"

"Yes, so it would spray out like a shower." Kristin's fingers splay open with the gesture. "I imagine that's why he cut their hair."

"Explain that for me," Emma says immediately.

"He wouldn't want hair or arms in the way.... Their arms are tied up, see?" Kristin lifts a photo, angles it. "I mean, he probably, I don't know, dances around underneath or something. You can't dance around and enjoy it when there's arms and hair in the way, can you?"

She looks up, her eyebrows raised, as if the answer is obvious. And it *is* obvious, so obvious to someone who has the capacity to imagine it. Bell just didn't have the ability before, to plumb those depths.

But he can see it now. The killer naked—would he be naked? Emma seems to think so—capering beneath the writhing bodies, knife in hand...the waterfall of red, a hot shower, slippery under-foot...that first gush of vitality pouring over your skin, thick and refreshing, so addictive that you'd want to do it again and again: one victim, two at a time, *three* at a time, and oh *Jesus*—

Bell rears back, needing air.

"Kristin, thank you," Emma says, somewhere beyond the ring-ing in his ears. "I know these pictures are disturbing, but you've given us something very important."

"Really? That makes me so..." Kristin casts around for the right word. "*Relieved*, I suppose you'd say. I want to help, more than anything."

"And you have." Emma catches sight of him, and whatever she sees makes her take control. She packs up the photos, closes the file. "Everything you've given us today is going to add to this investigation. Which I guess is a way for me to segue into goodbye—we need to take this information and present it to our supervisor. So I might have to ask you to excuse us now."

"Oh, of course!" Kristin is all cooperation. "I'm so glad that something I said will be useful! That is quite amazing."

Bell sways toward the door. "I need a drink of water."

He thought he knew all this; he thought he was educated, jaded. But Kristin Gutmunsson has torn the veil from his eyes. He wants it back, but he's a better investigator without it. There are no limits, he sees now. There are no monsters. Only people.

He glances over his shoulder. Kristin is smiling at Emma. "I'll have to follow the reports even *more* closely, now that I'm connected to it. So next time I read an article in the newspaper, or see you on the television—"

"You saw us on the television?" Emma blanches.

When Bell opens the door, Cooper has his hand raised, preparing to knock. Bell takes one look at his face and knows they're in trouble.

"I was just…" Cooper peers around him, sees Kristin. "What's going on?"

"It doesn't matter," Bell says. "What is it?"

Cooper's eyes are dull with tiredness, grave with inevitability. "Somebody told."

CHAPTER TWENTY-THREE

R emember," Cooper says. He looks at Bell and Emma in turn.
"Don't go off script."

When Travis was fourteen, his sister Lena got into trouble at
school for busting the lip of a boy who'd called her a derogatory
name. He remembers retreating from the house to the swing chair
on the front porch while his mother called the school principal to
give the man a piece of her mind. Her voice grew strident on the
phone, until it was audible outside. His mother always used a lot of
Spanish cuss words when her temper was high.

As the tirade continued, Travis's father came out on the porch to
join him. "You taking cover?"

"Yep." Travis glanced through the front window. "She's going
off again."

"She certainly is. Your momma is a sight to behold when she's
in full blow."

It was a good opportunity, so Travis asked the question he'd had
on his mind for some time. "How do you handle that?"

His father eased back, elbows on the porch rail, one boot on the
boards.

"Well, you don't 'handle' your momma. That's how she is—that's why I married her. I mean, look at her. The sparks coming off her." He gazed through the glass, his face full of pride. "You don't try to tame the lightning, son. You just give it the respect it deserves."

Bell didn't realize he still had that memory of his dad in the bank, but he thinks about it while watching Emma Lewis square up outside Donald Raymond's office. Cooper's already given them both instructions on how to behave in this meeting: to speak little, let him handle it, nod and agree, and hopefully they'll all get out of it unscathed. But Bell can see how Emma wants to bare her teeth, and how Cooper doesn't know what to do with that.

"Miss Lewis," Cooper says quietly. "Keep it on a leash."

Her eyes flash at him. Cooper retreats a step.

"Jesus. Take it easy." He glances over at Travis. "A little help here? Miss Lewis wants to burn down the world."

It surprises Bell that he understands Emma because of that old conversation with his father. Until now, he just assumed it was because he's a reasonable judge of character.

He modulates his voice to a lower register, touches her arm lightly. "Emma. Let's keep our eyes on the prize."

It works. She doesn't relax her hair-trigger watchfulness, but she stops bristling and settles. Cooper gives him a curious look, but Travis doesn't have time for that bullshit now.

"Come," Raymond calls from his office.

Raymond has a walnut desk so huge it throws the room proportions out of balance. It confirms Bell's understanding that the boss is a power man. Raymond regards them from his position of advantage, leaning forward in his chair on the other side of the desk. The bunching of his shoulders sends another signal: Raymond is the kind of guy who likes to scrap.

Bell feels himself making a number of fast calculations. He's very aware of the hot charge of Emma's body to his right. On her other side, Cooper stands firm.

"So, here we are." Raymond's brow furrows. "Now, you two young people were brought on board to do some research into offenders the bureau has already taken care of, is that right?"

"That's correct," Cooper says. "Their perspective has been helpful with—"

Raymond's glance is a swift cut. "I'd like them to answer the question."

Bell makes sure to echo Cooper's language. "Yessir, that's correct."

Emma says nothing.

Raymond doesn't seem to care to hear her response anyway as he plows on. "And these cases you're looking at are all old cases—prosecuted and put away."

"Yes, sir," Bell says. "We just—"

"Your brief was to steer clear of active investigations." Raymond toys with his pen. "In fact, I had words with Special Agent Cooper about this, and we were both in agreement that active cases are not your area. Does my memory serve me correctly on this, Agent Cooper?"

When Raymond looks his way, Cooper is ready to play his part. "Yes, it does, sir."

"Yes, it does." Raymond waits a full four seconds of pause. "So can you please explain to me, in language I can understand, how

I happened to turn on the television at oh six hundred hours this morning to see *you*, Mr. Bell, and *you*, Miss Lewis, in the background of television footage of officers attending a crime scene in Berryville, which I'm sure you're aware is the latest development in a very *active* homicide investigation."

"Yes, sir," Bell says. "We heard about that, sir—"

"Heard about it? You were goddamn *there*." Raymond puts one fist on the desk. "Do you know what I like to see in officers of this organization, son? Fidelity, bravery, integrity. *Those* things I like to see. The ability to accept and follow instructions—*that* I like to see. You know what it pains me to see? It pains me to see officers of the FBI, and support staff associated with those officers, *on national television without my express permission.*"

"Yes, sir." Bell's neck gets hot.

Cooper quietly clears his throat. At Bell's side, Emma is silent, but he can feel her vibrating.

Raymond's voice becomes terse. "Your role has been made very clear to you, Mr. Bell. You are to adhere to your instructions. You are to assist with inquiries as they have been set out to you. And you are to maintain a *low profile*. Miss Lewis, I'm including you in all these comments. It is not your job to—"

"Do you know the young man you're hunting, Mr. Raymond?" Emma says suddenly.

"Lewis." The way Cooper says her name makes it sound like a swear word.

Raymond swivels to look at her. "Miss Lewis, I am explaining—"

"Do you know what kind of man he is? Because we do."

Raymond's face goes dark at Emma's tone. "Miss Lewis—"

She steps forward. Her eyes are vivid, but Bell sees not the faintest hint of fear in her anywhere.

"He's young," she says. "He's physically strong and fit. He's five and a half to six feet tall, and his blood type is AB-positive. He's probably white—he hunts across race lines, but we see a preponderance of white males in this category. He has medical training, and he holds down a job. He has a psychological disorder that means he finds his enjoyment in standing underneath his victims and bathing in their blood as he cuts their throats. And his prey is getting younger, because the last girl he took and used this way was fourteen years old."

Cooper tries to rein her in. "Miss Lewis—"

"Do you understand this man, Mr. Raymond? Because this is who you're trying to catch. He only hunts *teenagers*. He's likely a teenager himself. And you're telling us to stay out of it? How can we do that, in good conscience, when we've turned up more leads in a week than the police have in three months, and we're the only people in this *whole damn building* who fall within both the offender *and* the victim demographic profile? Are you fucking *kidding*?"

"*Miss Lewis.*" Raymond stands, smooths down his tie. His face is dangerously mottled. "Miss Lewis, I am going to forget you said that last, and assume you have enough intelligence to *get* this. You are eighteen years old. You are untrained, unqualified, inexperienced—"

"Don't you tell me I'm inexperienced." She takes another step.

Bell takes her arm. "*Emma.*"

The blood in Raymond's cheeks and forehead looks like a health hazard. "If you want to continue working with this organization, Miss Lewis, you will *shut your mouth and listen.*"

Emma's bicep flutters under Bell's palm, but her self-control holds. He knows she can stick up for herself, but he would very much like to sock Raymond in the jaw right now.

Raymond's jowls quiver as he leans across the desk. "I could close your unit down with the stroke of a goddamn pen. I've got half a mind to do it anyway, after the disrespect you've shown me and this office. I could bust you back home in a hot second, and Mr. Bell, too."

Please don't do that, Bell thinks. *All those victims.* He sees Cooper bite his bottom lip.

"But I respect Ed Cooper, and I can see what he's trying to do with this." Raymond narrows his piggy little eyes at Emma directly. "You've had some good results so far. But don't *test* me, Miss Lewis. *Stay out of the Berryville case.* If I hear you've been dipping your toe in current investigations again, I won't just break up the unit—I'll lay obstruction charges against you. Do you understand me?"

Emma's lips purse tight.

"Do you understand me?"

"Yes."

"Do you understand me, Mr. Bell?"

Bell knows his face is ruddy. He buckles it down. Sticks to the script. "Yessir."

Raymond stands to his full height, looking like someone tried to spit in his mouth. "Cooper, this was your idea. Get these teenagers under control or get them off my base. Are we clear?"

"Sir, yessir."

"Now get the hell out of my office."

In the descending elevator with Bell and Cooper, Emma's head is aching.

"Well," Bell says. "That . . . could've gone worse."

"Miss Lewis—" Cooper starts.

Emma whirls on him. "What? You want to give me a big lecture about keeping my mouth shut?"

"Actually, I wanted to tell you what happened with Berryville. And I want you to tell me what happened with Kristin Gutmunsson, because that one I did *not* see coming." Cooper loosens his collar by one button, at the neck. "And I wanted to say you managed okay. Don Raymond can be aggravating as hell."

Emma is surprised into an honest answer. "He's an asshole."

"He's easy to read." Cooper regards her steadily. "Also easy to anticipate, and if you want to swim in this pond, you'd better figure out how to deal with people. I *do* want your insights on this case, Miss Lewis—I think you and Mr. Bell have proven you can make a contribution. But we could've used Raymond. Agreed with him, got on his good side. He would've made things easier for us. Now we have to dodge interference."

Emma squeezes the back of her neck as the throb in her temples builds. "I need to go to my dorm. I have a headache, I need some Advil—"

"Don't go running off just yet. Listen."

Being asked to listen by Cooper bothers her less than being told to by Raymond. And Cooper looks exhausted. His eyes are red from rubbing. He's been up most of the night between Berryville and

Washington, but he's here, wearing yesterday's suit and defending them to Raymond and being straight with her.

"You need to remember something." Cooper looks between her and Bell. "It's something I suspect Mr. Bell already knows. And it's this—whether you're in the FBI or in college or out in the world, you're going to meet people like Raymond every step of the way. Sometimes it'll infuriate you, because petty bullshit and stupidity are infuriating, but you have to figure out a way to work with it."

Petty bullshit and stupidity—Emma's had it up to here with both. Her head is pounding like a drum and her control is shaking loose. "But I'm not good at that!"

"Then you'd better learn. Like I said, I'd like to have your input. But the standoff with Raymond was a misstep, and we're gonna pay for it later. You've got real sand, Miss Lewis, but you need to learn to pick your battles, or you'll end up dashing yourself to pieces."

"So you're telling me that I lived through Huxton but I've got to put up with assholes like Raymond? Someone who doesn't even understand why we were recruited in the first place?" Emma can hear the misery in her own voice. "It's *garbage*. And I don't know what I'm doing, I don't know why I'm still here—"

"You're here because you want to spare the next victims. Because you want to put this killer away. Because you know what it's like to survive someone like the Butcher, and that perspective can be a weapon against him." Cooper relaxes his stare, leans back against the wall of the elevator. "Now go to your dorm and get something for your headache. Forget about Raymond. I'm going to stop at the atrium for coffee, then I'll meet you both back at the office and we can think about what to do next."

CHAPTER TWENTY-FOUR

Two hours later, Emma's starting to feel better. Part of it was the Advil, part of it was what Cooper said in the elevator. The rest of it is this time she's spent with him and Bell, pooling the information on the Butcher case.

"Next steps?" Bell taps his pen against the notepad in front of him at the desk. "We've got an outline, and we're getting a clearer picture of his process now."

"Thanks to Miss Gutmunsson," Cooper says. Both he and Bell are down to shirtsleeves.

"But we've still got gaps to fill," Emma says.

"Yes, we do." Cooper looks like he needs to sleep for about a thousand years. "And if he's preparing to take his activities underground, we need to fill those gaps fast. We need information on his vehicle and we need to narrow down his range. At the moment his hunting ground looks like most of Virginia. I've asked Wes Chamberlain, our tech guy, to keep plugging data into the computer banks—possible routes, on- and off-ramps, times of day—to see if we can get some ideas. Do we have anything more on the connections between the victims? Have you got any insights?"

"I'm . . . working on it." Emma doesn't know why the knowledge won't come. Maybe she needs to sleep for a thousand years, too.

"Okay, then the next step for you two is digging into victim backgrounds, especially the three new ones, to see if there's any points of commonality. We got the identification on Donna Williams, the third victim from Berryville, so we can add those details now. I've got other agents looking at this information, but it can never hurt to have a few extra pairs of eyes. Look at their medical histories, see if they gave blood, or got shots, or had a recent checkup. See if they share a doctor's clinic. I don't imagine it'll be that simple, but we should look at everything."

"You want us to visit the victims' residences?" Bell asks, making a note.

"Not yet. I've got other people working that, let's see what they pull up." Cooper tears off a sheet from the notepad and scribbles. "I'm going back to Berryville tomorrow to do a press conference and see if we can drum up any witnesses. Here's a list of some of the other team members—my second, Howard Carter, plus Pete Anderson, Jack Kirby, Mike Martino. Don't contact them directly, but if their names come up, you know you're dealing with my people. If you get really stuck, ask Betty to put you in touch with Carter, he'll steer you straight."

Bell nods. "So the victims are our focus now?"

"Yes. And you need to look like you're still doing interviews. Raymond will be watching to see what you're up to, and I want you looking busy." Cooper drops his pen and leans back. "Work up an interview strategy for Campinelli—you can visit him at Butner sometime in the next few days."

Emma knows that progress is being made on the case, although the pace of it is slow—walking pace. She wants to be sprinting.

It doesn't help that they're still supposed to be going to classes. Bell bullies her into attending a 3:00 PM lecture on Search and Seizure, where she shifts in her chair and the faces of the Berryville victims float behind her eyeballs. She tries switching the images out, tries conjuring the face of the Butcher himself, but that only produces a choking feeling. Once the class is over, she goes to the training lockers and pulls on her track gear, hits the Yellow Brick Road while everyone else is eating dinner.

She runs for longer than she intends, the trees around her gathering shadows. It's cool beneath their branches, the pine needles slippery underfoot. There is no complexity here, no politics, just the burn in her legs and the sharp saw of her breath. Emma thinks of nothing at first, then she thinks of baking cookies with her sister at home, Robbie grinning as she nibbled the raw cookie dough when their mother wasn't looking. Sweat soaks into the waistband at the small of Emma's back, the fabric of her collar.

The hum of insects in the forest is a kind of tinnitus, and the air against her face reminds her of the Gutmunssons' cool beauty, the pallor in Bell's cheeks at Berryville, where a fourteen-year-old girl, Kimberley Berger, struggled to the last because there was nothing left but to struggle. Emma shakes out her arms and steadies her pace. The insight into that girl won't come, and it won't come, and the tinnitus in her ears is insects and heartbeat and breath, not screaming, and she runs harder.

When she finally runs herself out, all her clothes are sticking to her, and her legs are wobbling. Everyone else has deserted the course. The light is starting to go. She drinks her entire canteen and limps back in the gloom.

In the shower, she turns her face into the spray until she thinks of the Butcher standing under his victims with the knife, then she turns the faucet decisively off. She towels herself dry, applies Band-Aids to her blisters, pulls on cotton shorts and a tank. Lays out the victim identification photos on her comforter. Stares and stares, and scrunches up one page after another from the yellow legal pad in her lap until she realizes this is just the way the day is going, finally concedes defeat, and takes half a Valium. Tucks herself into bed, throws the covers off and pulls them back up until the drug takes hold and she sleeps, with no dreams.

At 07:40 she's woken by a knock on the door, and she thinks it's probably the floor supervisor checking on her, knowing her routine is to be out early. Groggy, she pulls her robe on and opens the door halfway to find Bell, in dark pants and a black T-shirt, with a bad case of bed head. His expression is very awake, though.

"Lewis, get dressed." He grips the lintel of the door. "Looks like Simon Gutmunsson just got a letter from the Butcher."

CHAPTER TWENTY-FIVE

Emma dresses quickly while Bell waits outside the door. She winces as she toes her shoes on, grabs a jacket, it's Bell's jacket. Grabs another one, holds them both as she scoops up the ID photos off her nightstand.

Bell, impatient, takes the jacket she proffers, looks at it, tosses it back into her room, and closes the door behind her. Moves quickly with her to the elevator. "It came with the morning mail. The guy who supervises Gutmunsson—"

"Pradeep," Emma says, handing Bell the bundle of ID photos, tying her own jacket around her waist. "His name is Pradeep."

"Okay, so he checks Gutmunsson's mail. Apparently the guy receives a *lot* of mail."

"He's studying—he gets coursework sent from Georgetown University."

"And he sometimes gets fan mail."

"And interview requests from the media. I know."

Bell has that lip curl, signifying disgust. They get in the elevator and Emma has a chance to tie her shoelaces.

"Anyway, Pradeep usually checks the obvious fan mail and leaves the formal correspondence, but he found a Georgetown letter that had arrived open." Bell holds the handrail like it's keeping him tethered. "He decided to show Dr. Scott. She thought it was weird enough to call Cooper. That was about ten minutes ago. Cooper thought the language in the first part of the letter suggested a Butcher link, so he told Scott to put the letter in a ziplock bag and asked her to give us a minute to get you to the phone. Why weren't you up? I looked for you on the track."

"I overslept," Emma says. "Bad night."

"Are you okay to do this?"

"I'm okay." Emma hopes that's not a lie.

The elevator spills them out onto the atrium floor; they move at a fast clip. Her stomach rumbles as they pass the cafeteria, and she remembers she missed dinner last night. A sniff of brewing coffee is all she has time for as Bell herds her toward the basement.

The Cool Room is disconcertingly crowded. Cooper is plugging in a phone provided by Betty. Bell tucks the ID photos back into the Butcher file on the desk as another agent—tall, stocky, mustached—moves closer. He's wearing a tan suit and his dark hair is slightly longer than regulation. Emma thinks she recognizes his cologne: *Savage*, the same one her uncle uses. It may as well be called *Macho*.

"Mike Martino, hi." He shakes their hands. "We're sorting out a phone line here, because you're—"

"—not allowed in the offices of Behavioral Science," Bell finishes. "Yessir, we know. Good to meet you. Has Dr. Scott called back?"

The phone rings as he says it. Betty excuses herself as Cooper picks up and hits Conference.

"...there, Agent Cooper?"

"Yes, Dr. Scott, thanks for waiting. I've got you on speaker, everyone's here." Cooper looks better: Still in shirtsleeves, but it's a new shirt and he seems more rested. "Can you describe the letter for us?"

Scott's voice has a canned echo. "It's typewritten, on some kind of thin paper. Onionskin, maybe. There's a signature at the bottom that looks handwritten. The envelope is official letterhead from Georgetown University."

Emma thrums a little inside.

Cooper's posture is attentive. "Can you read the entire letter aloud, please?"

"There's no date," Scott says. "Here's the content—

> "Dear Artist,
>
> "It's been an eventful month. I've found a place to settle, away from prying eyes, which will make a big improvement, and the most recent donor treatments have been incredibly effective—"

"That's him," Bell says.

"Gutmunsson keeps referring to donors," Emma confirms.

When she looks over at Cooper, he's nodding gravely. His gaze holds hers as Scott continues.

"—much better than I'd hoped.
Finally, real results after the long
process of trial and error! I feel
myself getting stronger, faster, with
each treatment. My friends comment
on the change, and I confess I have
trouble keeping in a small secret
smile. I'm sure you understand. The
minor refinements you suggested were
wonderful, thank you—"

"That son of a bitch," Bell breathes.

"Goddammit." Emma sits down abruptly. "Simon Gutmunsson hasn't been sharing 'insights' about the case. He's been corresponding with the Butcher this whole time."

The shock of understanding is like an evisceration. But in the hollow place left behind, she finds a supple coil of fury. The question isn't *How could Simon* do *this?* This is a boy who disemboweled his friends for entertainment. Why *wouldn't* he do this?

Beside her, Bell is swearing fervently under his breath. Cooper's face is grim, and Emma can tell he's thinking up new and dreadful punishments for Simon Gutmunsson.

"Do you want to hear the rest of the letter?" Scott seems to be getting testy about the frequent interruptions.

Cooper finds his equilibrium first. "Yes, Dr. Scott, please continue."

"We come at things from very
different perspectives—you with your
creative sensibility, and me with my
scientific bent—but I believe we're

alike in so many ways. It would
be exciting to meet at some point.
Perhaps there's something I can do
to lighten your burden—you only
need ask. You know my offer still
stands, and I would be delighted if
you would consider donating. Not a
complete donation of course, haha,
but a professional exchange between
friends.

"I hope your studies are going well,
and the FBI isn't bothering you
too much. Your recent subject seems
fascinating. Perhaps when you've
tired of her, you might point me in
the right direction—"

Emma turns away.

"I do enjoy a challenge." Scott's voice is sharp. "That's it."

Cooper watches Emma as he speaks in reply. "Can you tell me about the signature, please?"

"Your friend, Siegfried. It's signed in blue pen."

"Does Gutmunsson know you have the letter?"

"His mail typically arrives early—he'll know if we're holding it. But he isn't aware of what arrives when. Pradeep sorts the mail before he enters the big room with Simon's breakfast and correspondence, so we could pull this letter for at least twenty-four hours before Simon would be any the wiser."

Cooper focuses now on the softly blinking red Conference light on the phone housing, then he makes a decision. "Dr. Scott, I'm going to give you some instructions. I'd like you to keep the letter and envelope in the bag and hold it in your office. No one should be allowed to touch it. I'm sending someone from Washington to collect it. Does Gutmunsson's paper trash go out with the garbage? I'd also like you to cancel the garbage collection for this morning."

"I think the garbage has already gone."

Cooper grimaces briefly. "Okay, then I need to find out where it's delivered and disposed of. Otherwise, let Pradeep arrive on shift with Gutmunsson's breakfast and the rest of his mail as normal. Don't interrupt his usual routine at all and don't mention the letter. I might need to interview him at some point. I'll call you in advance of our arrival."

"Certainly."

"Thank you for contacting me about this so quickly, Dr. Scott, I appreciate it. Please thank Pradeep as well. I'll be in touch again shortly."

Cooper ends the call, presses more buttons, speaks over his shoulder to Martino.

"Mike, I'm taking this one, and I'll need you with me on the ground. Call Howard Carter and tell him to hold the fort at Berryville today. Talk to him about the press conference—" His call is answered and he changes tack. "Gerry, it's Ed. I need Carlos Dixon to suit up and collect a letter from St. Elizabeths asylum that was sent to Simon Gutmunsson. It sounds like the Butcher.... No, he'll need to delay the court appearance, this takes priority. Tell him he'll need a partial kit. Prints and trace from the asylum's superintendent, the mail delivery guy, and Gutmunsson's attendant... No, Gutmunsson hasn't touched it, but we have him on file anyway. Organize a team to do a trash hunt—the hospital has already released the garbage, they're finding out where it went. . . . We'll need Documents, so tell Linda to get set up. Also Hair and Fiber, and you'll want to see if you can get anything off it. . . . Yeah, I'll be there in an hour."

As Cooper calls Dr. Scott again to confirm arrangements around Dixon's arrival, Emma turns back and looks at him. "Are we coming with you to Washington?"

Cooper nods at her over the handset as he speaks. Bell frowns, leaves the room. Martino has already flipped a notebook open and started scribbling.

". . . be there in about twenty-five minutes. Thank you, Dr. Scott, you've been really helpful." Cooper disconnects, starts gathering his jacket and his own notebook as he turns to Martino. "Carter needs to cooperate with the chief in Berryville, guy by the name of Donahee. I'd prefer to delay the press call, but if Donahee can't do that, if he's under too much pressure, tell them to go ahead. Carter will want to stand at the back and be a presence, but don't make it official. No statement at this time, no immediate threat to Berryville residents, out of respect for the families we're waiting to hear back on investigative analysis—you know the drill. If he's forced to say something, he should refer to Donahee's operation, keep the local force on-side. And tell Carter I want the whole damn town door-knocked if they have to—somebody must've seen this bastard."

Cooper and Martino open the door and head out, and Emma realizes she's supposed to follow. "Where are we going?"

"Motor pool." Cooper's pace is brisk. "Where the hell is Bell?"

"I don't know, he just took off."

Martino lifts his notebook. "I'm gonna make those calls, Ed."

"Stay near a phone," Cooper says. "Use Jack Kirby's office if you need it. I'll call as soon as I have word."

"Good luck and good hunting." Martino gives an almost-salute, splits off toward Behavioral Science.

Emma matches Cooper's strides. "This is Butcher-related—won't Raymond be pissed if we come along?"

"This is Gutmunsson-related, and nothing is confirmed yet. That letter could have come from anyone. Raymond can suck on that for a while." Cooper smacks the elevator button. "I want you to see the letter and give me your thoughts. That mention of '*your recent subject*' spooked you, didn't it?"

Emma tries to shrug. The idea that she's now been a topic of interest for three different multiple murderers fills her head with a shriek of white noise.

"I might need you to go see Gutmunsson again, and soon."

"Damn right you do." Anger firms her knees. "I can handle it."

The motor pool guy is disorganized; a number of vehicles have not yet been returned. While Cooper goes off to raise hell, Emma stands in the corner. The workshop smells of machine oil and solder and that synthetic air freshener they seem to use in the vents of every government car she's ever ridden in. Cooper stops shouting and points at her, points at a dark blue Ford Fairmont. Bell arrives back in a rush with a brown paper bag in one hand. They all make for the car from different directions.

She and Bell arrive first, and she wrenches the car door open. "We're walking the letter through Scientific Analysis."

"I should've grabbed that jacket," Bell muses. "Won't Raymond be—"

"No. Nothing's confirmed about it being the Butcher yet."

"Lord, teach me to split hairs like an FBI agent."

The car has front and rear bench seats. Emma holds the panic bar when Cooper guns it out of the bay doors and into the light. Bell protects his head as Cooper takes the last traffic hump at speed.

"Buckle up." Cooper speaks over his shoulder. "Mr. Bell, I hope that's coffee I'm smelling."

"Watch out, it's hot." Bell unloads three polystyrene cups with lids from the bag he's been balancing so carefully.

"I knew I did the right thing, taking you on."

"Eat," Bell commands as he presses a packaged sandwich into Emma's hands.

It's cream cheese, but she's still grateful. She leans forward in her seat. "We need to find out where the letter was mailed. And how Simon's supposed to reply."

"That's something you'll need to ask him when you speak with him," Cooper says.

"He'll say he was never lying," Emma points out. "That we just never asked the right questions."

"No, I don't expect the incarcerated sociopathic narcissist to actually admit that he lied." Cooper's glance in the rearview is dry. "Think of a strategy to use with him."

Cooper switches on the flashers and the siren on occasion, so the ride to Washington goes fast. Emma has a stressful moment at FBI headquarters security check-in, when she thinks she's left her ID lanyard in her room at Jefferson. She tastes Cooper's irritation for a shameful moment before she finds the lanyard in the pocket of the jacket she still has tied around her waist.

The feeling in the elevator, on the way to the lab, is different from the last time they visited: She and Bell aren't out-in-the-cold trainees anymore, they're part of the team. Emma reminds herself that Cooper has exacting standards. She sincerely hopes she's able to meet them.

When they breach the doors, Carlos Dixon is in his court trousers and shirt and tie, with a lab coat thrown over the top. "I got back ten minutes ago. Gerry has it, but you'll be damn lucky. And that onionskin paper is bad news."

"Is he in the examining room?"

"Yeah, he's got the laser on it. The garbage got dumped at the solid waste place off Capitol Street Southeast—the team's there now. But if there are other letters, they might have already been incinerated."

Cooper swerves quickly through the common room and its stacks of containers, Emma and Bell chasing after. Gerry Westfall is in the Latent Prints examining room, looking unhappy.

"The envelope is dirty as hell, and this letter paper is almost as bad as Kleenex." Westfall settles the letter into the document case next to its envelope and strips off his gloves. "I got perspiration smudges, maybe off a wrist. Nothing else but smooth prints from the surgical gloves he's using, like off the chains and the other surfaces in Berryville. I'd like to fume it, but I'd better give it to Linda first before I stain it. Glenn's already taken a few bits."

Nerves pinging, Emma has to step backward suddenly as Cooper reverses course to find Glenn Neilsen.

"He's in here, on the scope," Dixon calls out.

Neilsen's hair sticks up at the back in that peculiar way as he angles over a microscope eyepiece in the lab. When Cooper arrives, Neilsen just waves briefly with one hand, his attention still on the slide.

"Glenn?"

"I've got, um—" Neilsen raises his head and blinks owlishly. "A curly hair from the attendant, and what looks like a piece of a whisker. There's a stain, which I think is from the superintendent's hand cream. Carlos is doing a comparison."

"Gerry wants to send it to Linda, you okay with that?"

"Go for it. I'm still working these up."

Cooper nods, and then they're backtracking again, this time to an office where a woman in her early forties is waiting patiently, knees crossed. Linda Brown is wearing a necklace of mahogany beads that glow against her umber skin, and she is as neat and put-together as her office space.

"Good morning, Ed. Gerry said it's on its way."

"Linda, this is Emma Lewis and Travis Bell. They've been working the detail on Gutmunsson."

"Nice to meet you—I won't shake while I'm wearing gloves. Find a seat." Her chin lifts as Westfall arrives with the document case. "Here we are."

Westfall is puffing a little. "I'd like to fume it when you're done, Linda."

She nods. "I'll look after it. Gerry, you need to quit smoking if that walk was enough to make you blow."

"May as well ask me to quit breathing."

"Get out of my office, then, if you want to smoke."

Brown takes the case and opens it, carefully transfers the letter onto her dark work blotter with forceps, leaving the envelope. She switches on a strong lamp. The office air goes quiet as she reads the letter's contents. Emma feels heat climb up her neck, then remembers that Brown doesn't know what the final lines mean. Once Brown is finished with the content, she photographs the entire letter in sections.

"I'm going to need some additional time with the phrasing and grammar, to be thorough. But the use of contractions like 'there's' and 'you've' already suggests a younger subject. There's no coded language I can make out."

"That's fine," Cooper says.

She switches on another lamp at a sharply oblique angle to examine for indented writing. She tries again with a filter.

"No impressions." A different filter. "Just the press here, on the left and right edges from the typewriter bail rolls. A bit of tracking—could be a crumb or a bit of trace stuck on the cylinder. This typewriter has seen some action."

"What makes you say that?" Cooper asks.

"Some of the keys are sticky—do you see where the lowercase *a* drops sometimes? Most of the capitals are quite strong, which makes me think we're dealing with someone who's not a comfortable touch typist. But the machine itself is old. It's using a fabric ribbon, and the type design is very cute—I think this was written on an older model Olivetti, maybe even a Valentine. I'll need to examine more, but I'm pretty sure."

"Are they common, those machines?"

"Not anymore. They were first released in 1969." She glances up at Cooper and her eyes have an unsettlingly predatory glint. "Find me his typewriter and I can use the TYPE classification system to nail him with this."

Cooper makes a thin smile. "Talk to me about the paper."

"I can see why Gerry's sighing. I don't think he's going to get anything off it, even with the iodine. The cotton fibers in the onion-skin are at least as old as the machine, and they're just going to leach. There's a little tear here, on the end of the fold—I think the attendant might have snagged it getting it out of the envelope. Now let me look at the signature."

Brown completes photography on the letter from above and all angles, flips it with her forceps to photograph the reverse. Then she flips it back, switches off the bigger lamps, and darkens the room to use a handheld ultraviolet light, scanning minutely. Emma hears Bell's soft breathing close by. She gets a sense of Brown's office as some kind of outer space bubble, airless and quiet. When the ordinary office lights come back on, it's a shock.

"It's a blue ballpoint," Brown says, "and it's contemporary, but I won't be able to narrow down the specific pen. I'll need to use solvent to tell you which ink—are you okay for me to cut away a little section for the liquid chromatography?"

"This letter isn't going to its receiver," Cooper confirms.

"The handwriting is undisguised—he hasn't used any embellishment, or written with his nondominant hand. He's right-handed, by the way, but you already knew that. You don't think that's his name, Siegfried, do you?"

"He used Gutmunsson's nom de plume in the salutation, so no. I think he's using a moniker. I'm not sure what 'Siegfried' means."

"Don't you? Ed, you need to do more reading." Brown takes the envelope out of the case with her steady forceps, deposits it into another clean case for continued examination, closes up the case with the letter to send back to Westfall for fuming. "Siegfried was the hero from Norse mythology. He slew the dragon Fafnir and married the Valkyrie Brynhild."

"How do you know all this stuff?"

She grins. "Benefits of homeschooling." Her grin fades. "The legend goes that Siegfried bathed in the dragon's blood, and it made him invincible."

Emma stares at the letter and feels a chill.

CHAPTER TWENTY-SIX

The front of the envelope is addressed to Gutmunsson, care of Evelyn Scott, St. Elizabeths Hospital, 1100 Alabama Avenue Southeast."

Westfall has crowded them into his office, which looks like someone exploded an illegal ordnance inside it, and Bell is trying not to stare. How does the guy get any work done in here? The office is darkened and everyone looks at a section of the pale wall as Westfall displays stills from the video camera he used to record images of the front and back of the envelope.

"Zip code is correct. The letterhead is for real—that's a genuine faculty envelope from Georgetown U."

"So either the Butcher figured out that Gutmunsson's studying there," Bell says, "or Gutmunsson tipped him off somehow so they could correspond without alerting the St. Elizabeths staff."

"Georgetown has a medical school," Emma says immediately. "The Butcher is young—he could be college-aged. A student maybe?"

Bell looks up. "He could be getting the ether through the med school."

"But this letter wasn't sent through the med school," Westfall says. "It's care of the English department. Sender is a Dr. Gordon Lord."

Emma groans. When Cooper looks over, she makes a face. "George Gordon Lord Byron. Simon's obsessed with the Romantic poets. It's the subject of his dissertation."

"We need to check the Georgetown mail service." Cooper is propped on the edge of Westfall's paperwork-covered desk, arms crossed. "They'll have both an internal and a USPS system, so it might involve some digging."

Emma cocks her head, leaves the room as Westfall adjusts the display to show another image of the envelope.

"Everything seems legitimate. The postmark tag is some kind of departmental code."

"How is Gutmunsson supposed to reply?" Cooper asks.

Everyone spends a little time thinking about that.

"To avoid suspicion, he'd have to send his reply back to the English department, surely," Westfall says.

Cooper squints at the display. "Is the Butcher collecting his mail from the college in person?"

"If he's going to school there, maybe yeah," Bell says. "Or it might be forwarded on to his parents' house, or something."

"Unless you think someone in the English faculty at Georgetown is the Butcher," Westfall adds.

Bell turns to Cooper. "We've been tracking this idea that the Butcher is young. Could we have the age range wrong? Could he be a professor or a teacher at Georgetown?"

Cooper frowns. "I don't think so. The young victims, his physical strength, even the tone of this letter... everything we have about this guy feels young to me."

Emma walks back into the room. "If the envelope is mailed on campus and shows a departmental sender, it'll be tagged with that department's postmark so the postage cost can be credited back." When Cooper looks at her, she shrugs. "I just called the central mail service office at Georgetown University and asked."

"So the Butcher mailed the letter on campus. He used the faculty envelope and the departmental-sender line to make sure it was tagged as coming from Georgetown U."

"Mailing on campus doesn't mean he has to be a student *or* a professor," Westfall points out as he flicks the lights back on. "He could've ridden the bus to campus and used a postbox there."

"Yeah, we shouldn't rule that out." Cooper rubs his face. "Okay, so how are Gutmunsson's replies forwarded? We need to go talk to the faculty mail handler in the English department at Georgetown."

Emma's chin juts. "And I need to talk to Gutmunsson."

"You want to shake him up with this?"

"Hell yes."

Cooper stands to face her. "You need to persuade Simon to write back to the Butcher—today. I want to find out where his reply letter is going, and see who shows up to collect it."

"Then I'm going to need a copy of that letter, to take to the hospital."

"Will a photocopy be okay?" Westfall has packed up his camera.

"That would be great, thank you." Emma turns back to Cooper, bites her bottom lip. "And... you need to take this to Raymond. This really is part of the Butcher case and Raymond needs to find out from us, or things will get complicated. More complicated than they are already," she amends.

Cooper thinks for a moment, nods, then leaves to use the phone in Neilsen's office. Bell walks beside Emma out to the common room, tracking Cooper's exit.

"D'you think Raymond will raise objections to this? To us?"

"Absolutely. But I'm the one Simon Gutmunsson is talking to, so..."

"Fun job."

"Tell me about it."

Bell steps in closer, his voice quiet. "You gonna be okay with him, after last time?"

Emma swallows, straightens. "I guess we'll find out."

Cooper arrives back from his phone call. "Okay, Raymond has an ultimatum for you to pass onto Gutmunsson. He said if Simon isn't cooperative, he'll make sure the bureau pursues a new litigation attempt."

Emma frowns. "Simon's already in for the term of his natural life and then some. What does he care about new litigation?"

"You said he cares about his sister. Raymond said he'll have the old evidence against Kristin reexamined."

"He wants to prosecute *Kristin* Gutmunsson?" Bell is appalled. "For *what*? She was cleared during her brother's court case and she's assisting the bureau now."

"When it comes to Simon Gutmunsson, Raymond prefers to use a stick than a carrot."

"Raymond wants to dangle Kristin's freedom over Simon's head." Emma's lip curls. "Nice. Real classy."

Cooper's expression is cold. "If you're trying to get something out of Simon Gutmunsson, you use every bit of leverage you've got. Raymond might not follow through, but he might not need to. Hopefully the threat is enough. Otherwise Simon has no real incentive to help us." He checks his watch. "Okay, I'm putting you both in a bureau car to St. Elizabeths. I've arranged to have an agent accompany you—like you said, Miss Lewis, this really is part of the Butcher case. We need a qualified agent to—"

"Stand in the asylum foyer while I talk to Simon?" Emma's tone is bullish. "He won't cooperate if there's an agent there, you know that. And he won't tell me the truth if I wear a wire."

"Miss Lewis, you're an untrained civilian." Cooper's tone is placating. "This is an FBI investigation into a person of interest in an active homicide case—"

"Hasn't that been the situation with Simon all along?" Emma's hands go to her hips. "He's been a person of interest since the first interview."

Cooper's expression becomes adamant. "I understand the circumstances, but there should still be some supervision. The local agent will drive you and we can say he supervised, even if he stays in the foyer. I'll catch up with you at St. Elizabeths—I have to speak to whoever sorts the mail in the Georgetown English department."

Emma gives him a bland look. "That'll be fun. University English departments aren't generally very welcoming toward the FBI."

Cooper straightens. "I'm not wearing a sign that says 'FBI Agent.'"

Emma does a visual tour of his brown suit. "Uh...actually, yeah, you are." She lifts her chin at Bell. "Why don't you take Travis and send a real live college-aged person in to see them?"

Bell's head turns. "Maybe you haven't noticed, Lewis, but I don't look like I'm going to college."

"Sure you do." She steps in and ruffles his hair. Snags a tweed jacket with leather elbow patches hanging off the back of a nearby chair, pushes it into his hands. "Put that on. Then find yourself a pair of sunglasses and you're all set. You're much more likely to get something out of the university staff than a government agent would."

Cooper pinches his bottom lip between his finger and thumb. "She's got a point. Okay, Mr. Bell, you can come along. And bring the jacket."

Emma steps forward as they both start to turn. "Wait. Are you going to the School of Medicine as well?"

Cooper nods. "We'll get a list of current students and recent graduates. And ask the staff to check their stocks of ether."

"You don't know if the Butcher's still on campus. Be careful."

"We will," Bell says gravely. "Be careful with Gutmunsson."

"You know it," Emma says, but she smiles with a closed mouth.

Emma asks the bureau agent to make one pit stop before they reach St. Elizabeths. On the last leg of the drive, her attention shifts long enough to notice that the view outside the cab window is bright with sun. It's a lovely day, the long cirrus clouds like pulled taffy, high and white. And here she is, beneath those clouds, being driven to a mental asylum by an FBI agent, with a xeroxed copy of a murderer's letter in her pocket.

The agent doesn't even make it to the foyer—he waits in the car. Dr. Scott meets her personally at the door to the asylum.

"Thank you for meeting me," Emma says as they begin the sign-in procedure. "I know it's been a hectic morning."

"It's fine, Miss Lewis. It's very nice to see you—Simon's behaviors have shown a marked improvement since you started visiting. Until this morning's unpleasantness." Scott looks well, color in her face, her lipstick glossy and perfect. She's clearly perturbed, though. "Can I ask what your intention is with this interview? Are you hoping to get more information from Simon about the letter?"

Emma signs the visitor ledger, avoiding Scott's eyes. "There's been more than one letter."

"It bothers me a great deal, this correspondence. That I wasn't alert to it, that Simon participated in it... You must be angry, that he's been lying to you."

"He never lied," Emma corrects as they walk on. "He simply omitted information that would have given the authorities a better understanding of what was going on."

"You sound a little like him, when you say it that way."

Emma's posture stiffens. "I've had to learn how they think."

"They?"

"People like Simon. Serial offenders." Emma wants the conversation to move past her own experiences. "Does it make you question whether Simon can be rehabilitated, knowing he's been helping another killer?"

Scott seems surprised. "No. Not at all."

"Lots of folks would say he's going straight to hell for the things he's done."

"Simon's deranged," Scott points out as they reach the oak door. "He's already in hell. Whether he's punished further in some speculative afterlife is largely immaterial." She knocks. "Hello, Pradeep. One to see Simon Gutmunsson, please."

Pradeep, glancing through the slot, sees what Emma has brought with her. "That is not, strictly speaking, allowable."

"I'll allow it," Scott says. She turns to Emma. "I'd like you to let me know what you find out from Simon. The more I know, the better equipped I am to treat him. And it's easier for me to cooperate with the FBI if I'm kept in the loop."

Emma weighs this up and decides that Scott has been nothing but helpful. "All right."

"Thank you." Scott turns away, turns back. "Oh, and Miss Lewis?"

"Yes?"

"Simon has told me that he enjoys his conversations with you," Scott says gently. "You seem to be a good influence on him, and I can't help but think of you as an ally in Simon's treatment. I believe he considers you a friend. I know you're trying to get information from him, and quickly, but it would be a shame if you damaged that budding friendship by using an adversarial approach, don't you think?"

Emma blinks, nods. "Understood."

The door opens and Pradeep stands aside to allow her entrance. *Simon enjoys his conversations with you. He considers you a friend.* Emma finds that whole concept more horrifying than she has time to contemplate right now. She has to steady her heartbeat and step inside.

The cage seems farther away today, but Emma knows this is a trick of the light. At this time of day, the sun comes through the windows at just the right angle. Every detail in the chapel room is sparkling sharp.

Simon is standing barefoot on his bed, putting up a small figure he has made out of butcher paper. When Emma gets closer, she realizes the figure is a butterfly. There are a number of paper butterflies, attached with string to the bars of the cell above the level of the suspended sheet. Simon has pierced small holes in the corners of the butcher paper, so it looks as if the butterflies are all hanging helplessly by their wings.

He's wearing a sweater over his institutional whites: a cream-colored knit with a line of blue around the V-neck. Emma thinks it might be a tennis sweater but that's not really her area. The sweater is moth-eaten, with ragged holes at the elbows and hem. It looks like a relic from Simon's past life, and serves to humanize him somehow.

He doesn't turn to face her when she arrives, but Emma knows it doesn't matter: Simon sees everything. She settles herself on the floor with her props, waiting for the harsh floodlight of his full attention.

He ties another piece of string in place. "You seem a little haphazardly groomed today, Emma. Have you been imbibing?"

He's noticed the bottle on the floor beside her. "Hello, Simon. No, I haven't. But I have been talking to your sister."

"Naturally. How is she?"

"She's fine, but I don't know for how long." Emma hates to use Raymond's play, but then she thinks of the Berryville victims, Simon's part in that. Her anger about it is something she has to manage. "The FBI has mentioned reexamining her details from your old case."

He pauses over the final knot. "That would be unfortunate."

"That would be your fault," Emma points out. "You were the one who put everyone in such an awkward position in the first place."

237

He gives her a shark grin over his shoulder. "Putting people in awkward positions is rather my specialty."

Emma recollects the tea party scene again, pushes the memory away. "You can stop pretending now, Simon. We know about the letters."

Another, longer pause. His back is to her and she can't see his expression. He completes his task, steps down off the bed, and sits on the mattress, his face composed.

"Ah."

"Yes. Ah."

Emma opens the bottle, knowing he can smell it, and pours herself a drink. The wine doesn't really qualify as "high quality," but neither did the corner store where she bought it: The age-verification process involved the proprietor asking, "How old are you?" and Emma looking him straight in the eye and replying, "Twenty-one." But it was the most expensive red wine they had, and she suspects that after two years of incarceration, Simon's tastes may have become more catholic.

She takes a cautious sip. "Mm. This really isn't bad."

His eyes are narrowed. "Were you hoping to surprise me about the letters, then soften me up with the wine?"

"Maybe." She shrugs.

"I do have standards."

"Really? But standards and principles are for people who give a shit about the social contract, aren't they?"

Simon's brows lift. "That's a bit harsh."

Emma's having none of it. "Your standards and principles apply to wine, but they don't extend to valuing the lives of other people."

"Are you surprised?"

"Not really. You did once poison a dormitory full of ten-year-olds."

"I was only a ten-year-old myself. Don't I get points for effort?"

She's perilously close to losing patience. "Simon, you've been advising the Butcher on how to perfect his technique. And you've withheld information we could've used to *save* some of those kids in Berryville."

"Teenagers die all the time." He waves a hand. He's drawn thin decorative bands around his wrist in black felt pen. "I couldn't see the point in telling you. Then you'd catch the Butcher and there'd be no more visits, no more scintillating conversations, no bottles of wine...."

"So now you're happy to sacrifice Kristin for the pleasure of my company?"

"I would never do anything to deliberately hurt my sister. She's the one who inspired me in the first place, you know."

Emma rolls her eyes. "She's got nothing to do with it. You just like killing people."

"Nobody's perfect."

"Tell that to Kristin. She's the one who's going to be affected. You say she's important to you, but actions speak louder than words, Simon." Emma sees his blue eyes flash, and gets the feeling she's struck a nerve. "Do you ever consider other people before you do a thing?"

His voice is cold. "Do you ever consider not worrying about what other people think?"

Emma's savoring her drink now. "You know, I'm disappointed. Here I was, thinking you were clever. That you had special insight into the Butcher case, like some kind of homicidal savant—"

He stands. "I believe my credentials as a homicidal savant have already been established."

"But your insight was all from the letters. You're not clever at all. You've just been...faking it."

There's a significant pause, then Simon lifts his chin. "Give me a glass of wine."

"Ask nicely."

"Emma, may I have a glass of wine?"

"Let's consult Pradeep."

Emma is aware that she needs to tamp down this feeling or risk having control of the conversation wrested away from her. She busies herself helping Pradeep as the man attempts to figure out how to pass Simon a drink.

"He cannot have a glass. But there are paper cups in my desk drawer. One moment."

He returns with a cup and the pincer tool. Emma pours three fingers of wine into the cup. Simon retreats to his waiting area behind the screen as Pradeep manipulates the pincer to slip the cup through the bars and onto the floor of the cell. As Pradeep returns to his desk, Simon saunters out from behind the screen to collect his wine and settle himself back on the bed.

He sniffs above the cup, rolls a sip in his mouth, and swallows. "This could at best be described as alcohol. I don't know if I'd stretch so far as to call it wine."

"You're changing the subject."

"Yes." He takes another slow sip. "You don't understand about that dormitory business, you know. They were bullying Kristin. Terrorizing her. Which is something I don't tolerate."

You only tolerate it if you're the one doing the terrorizing? Emma doesn't say that. What she says instead is "You must've been really angry about that."

"I made it stop." He gazes into his paper cup, at the red liquid swirling there. "You don't know what it's like, being two. Before I was jailed, Kristin and I hadn't been separated ever, not for longer than a week—we were together in the womb."

"Then show her that you care," Emma insists. "Stop jeopardizing her well-being now. You can prevent the new FBI litigation attempt—just cooperate with me. Tell me what you know about the Butcher."

"If I'm honest with you, there needs to be some honesty in return." His eyes are not on her, but his posture leans forward.

She thinks the alcohol has made him a little greedy. "I always try to be honest in our conversations, Simon."

"Your voice has a lovely musicality, did you know that? I do miss music so...." His gaze returns from elsewhere. "Last time we talked about how you survived in the basement. That was very interesting, but this time I want to know why you joined the bureau."

"Plenty of times when I don't know myself."

"That's an interesting choice of words—'I don't know myself.' Do you think you're self-aware, Emma?"

She deliberately relaxes her posture. "Sometimes. It depends on the day."

"Please remember that all the little lost ones are waiting, standing by the Butcher's block."

"I try to be self-aware. I'm not always very good at it."

Simon wipes at the corner of his mouth with his pinky finger.

"Did you think joining the FBI would give you a better understanding of yourself? Of why you feel the way you do?"

"I don't think you can tell with any accuracy how I feel."

"Actually I think I can." His eyes are like a laser now. "You still run in your sleep, don't you? You feel guilt that you couldn't save them, and despair at the guilt. You wonder if it will ever go away, and you wonder if you really saved yourself after all. Maybe it would have been better to stay with Vicki and Tammy and all the other sad brides, if living means you'll be slowly eaten away from the inside like this."

"Well. That's very astute. And that's what therapy's for, I guess." Emma puts her glass down before the shake in her hand betrays her. "I haven't joined the FBI, by the way. It was part of their initial offer, but I never agreed to sign up."

"I would hope not—although you could always change your mind. There's no accounting for self-delusion." His lips have been reddened by the wine. "You won't save yourself through good works, Emma. If the FBI says that, they're lying. And if you believe it, you're lying to yourself."

"Simon, I could drink Lambrusco and chat with you all day, but I'm afraid we don't have that kind of time."

"They want me to reply."

"Of course they want you to reply. They want you to reply today. Now."

He makes a put-upon sigh. "Do they need an entire missive, or will a properly addressed envelope suffice?"

Emma had not thought of this. She has to turn it over quickly. "An envelope and a short note. Something congratulatory."

Simon rolls his eyes but moves to his desk and seats himself on the bolted chair like a concert pianist before a baby grand. He selects a scrap of butcher paper and a felt pen.

"This would sound more natural if I had actually read the contents of the letter."

"Oh, I have a copy—here."

Emma fishes the folded photocopy out of the pocket of her jacket. They have to go through the tiresome process of calling Pradeep and transferring the paper into Simon's cell. Once it's in his possession, Simon scans the paper, even sniffs it.

"That last line is quite something," he notes.

Emma bears down on her reaction. "Remember, I'll be reading your reply. It'll be really tedious if I have to make you reword it." She thinks of something else. "And say that you're considering his offer, about donating."

The look Simon gives her is withering.

"What did he call it? *A professional exchange between friends.*"

"Do you know how the reply will be collected?" He writes while he speaks.

"We're about to find out."

"How lovely for you." Letter completed, Simon lifts the edge of his papers to find an envelope. "Will you stake out the collection point? Will you shoot the Butcher with your gun? Or is that Agent Cooper's prerogative?"

Emma ignores that. "Don't stick down the flap on the envelope. I want to read it."

He makes a production out of folding and inserting the letter, addressing the envelope, then turns in his chair. "Catch."

The envelope spins along its narrow edge as he tosses it through the bars. Emma surprises herself by snatching the envelope out of the air before it hits her in the chest. It is direct contact: the first time something has passed between Simon and herself without any intermediary. The spark in his eyes tells her the significance isn't lost on him. *Do not take anything he offers you.* She imagines she can still feel the warmth of his hand on the paper in hers.

She opens the flap and reads the letter. Refolds it and tucks it back into the envelope.

"Satisfied?"

"Yes. Thank you."

"You're welcome." He makes a little sneer when he says it. "Does this mean you'll bring a celebratory picnic lunch next time you visit? I request croissants. I do remember croissants very fondly."

Emma stands, gathering the bottle and the envelope, feeling almost formal. "If we catch the Butcher, then this might be my last visit, Simon. But thank you for your help. I'll do everything in my power to make sure Kristin is taken care of."

"You don't *have* any power. You're not even an agent."

She straightens. "Then I'll do everything I can, as a human being."

"You've been a fascinating subject, Emma." He cocks his head. "You hate the feeling that Huxton might have been integral to your development as a person, don't you?"

Emma senses the truth of that knocking around hollowly inside her ribs. "Yes."

"A girl created by a serial killer who hunts serial killers." Simon's lips curve in a quiet smile. "Farewell, dear Emma. Thou wert lovely to the last."

He turns back to his desk then, picks up a felt pen, and begins writing, suddenly as distant to her as some far-off mountain peak, all covered in ice.

Emma's knees are wooden from being held at tension. She walks toward Pradeep, where he stands waiting, and sets the bottle on his desk.

"This is for Simon, if he wants it. Thank you for everything."

Pradeep gives her a solemn nod. He opens the door, and she exits, feeling oddly incomplete. She doesn't look back, keeps moving forward, clutching the letter. Part of her realizes she should feel triumphant, but she gets a sense as if she is aging decades with each step away.

By the time she emerges into the light outside, she feels ancient. The sun is a shock. When she puts her shading hand down, she sees that the Washington bureau car has gone, and Bell and Cooper are standing by the Fairmont in the parking area. Their figures resolve from dark shapes in the glare, to defined outlines, and then to real people as she walks toward them.

"You got it," Cooper says simply.

"Yes." She attempts to smile.

"We got an address," Bell says, looking as victorious as she should feel. "Jump in, I'll tell you what's happening on the way. We're going to Annandale."

He opens the car door for her. She's been trying to remember the origin of Simon's parting line—*Thou wert lovely to the last.* As she slides into the back seat of the Fairmont, the source finally comes.

It's by Byron, of course. Composed in 1812, and taken from one of the great examples of elegiac poetry, entitled "And Thou Art Dead, As Young and Fair."

CHAPTER TWENTY-SEVEN

The Butcher's collecting his mail from a dead man's address," Bell says.

"What?" Emma is in the rear seat, with Bell turned sideways in the front to conduct a three-way conversation, and Cooper behind the wheel. It feels strange being in the back seat on her own. "Sorry, what does that mean?"

"It means we got lucky at Georgetown." Cooper's driving at faster-than-normal speed, watching his handling. "Bell asked about finding 'Dr. Lord' and they dug up the staff rep who handles the mail. She gave him an address."

"Dr. Lord is listed as an associate emeritus professor," Bell explains. "Like he's retired. Mail that comes in for him is forwarded to a postal address in Annandale. That address turned out to be the residence of a Frederick John Delaney, an old-age pensioner who lived near the Fairfax hospital. Delaney died about eight months ago."

"Fairfax hospital," Emma says.

"That's what we're thinking." Bell's excitement is pressed down firmly, but she can still see it burning behind his eyes.

Cooper continues. "Delaney's estate is tied up in probate, so his apartment can't be rented or sold."

"The Butcher must live or work somewhere nearby," Bell says. "He can just stroll up and check the mail whenever he pleases."

Cooper looks at her in the rearview. "This is it, Lewis. We've got SWAT scrambling—they're meeting us at the Fairfax County sheriff's office. The sheriff's emergency response team is assisting. DEA is providing undercover vehicle support. And you're holding the letter that this whole operation is focused on."

She *is* still holding the letter, and suddenly she doesn't want to be. She hands it across the seat to Bell, who passes it to Cooper. Cooper puts it into his inside jacket pocket without glancing at it.

"So where do me and Bell fit into all this?"

"You'll be in the sheriff's office in Annandale during the stakeout."

"But can't we—"

"Lewis, I can't take you—there's gonna be a lot of guys with guns on-site, and you're both civilians. Don't go getting all sore on me, this might just turn into a long wait. The Butcher might not expect a reply from Gutmunsson within forty-eight hours of having sent the original letter."

"Okay." Emma chews a thumbnail.

"Nothing might happen today. But we've got to assume that if the Butcher's waiting on a reply, he'll drop by every day until Gutmunsson's letter arrives. There's a good chance we might scoop him up today or tomorrow."

Cooper's energy crackles in the car interior. When he steers around a corner, Emma notices that his gun holster prints against his jacket—he's wearing his sidearm. While she was in the timeless zone with Simon Gutmunsson, Cooper and Bell have been out in the world tracking prey. It seems as if the prey might finally be turning in their direction.

Cooper looks up. "One last thing, for both of you. Operations like this, we're talking lots of officers from multiple departments, lots of competing egos. Keep your eyes open and your questions for a suitable time. If you're confused, wait for direction and I'll give it."

Trees whip by on the Beltway before the river, and now the car is over the water. The cirrus clouds Emma noticed earlier have lowered and thickened. It's dizzying to realize it's not even ten in the morning.

Saplings along the side of the 236, then the tidy main street and the tough red brick of the old Fairfax courthouse building. Cooper turns left onto West Street, finds a parking space near a sixties-style high-rise. They enter the sheriff's office through a service door, and when Emma sees the typical dropped ceilings and tile light fixtures, she knows where she is.

A bustle of people inside the hallways, uniforms in various shades of fawn and brown and SWAT black. Cooper goes through the processes of check-in and introductions with a rapidity that reminds everyone they're short on time.

A man in a postal uniform is waiting for them in a deputy's office. Emma assumes he's an undercover cop before realizing he's an actual mail carrier. Cooper shakes the guy's hand while Simon's reply—the envelope and the letter itself—is being photocopied, then the original is folded back up. A stamp is applied, and also a redirect label that Bell got from Georgetown U. The mail carrier won't add an official postmark, though. Cooper chews his lip, then borrows an ink pad at the station's duty desk to add a blue smudge that makes the letter look more official while satisfying USPS propriety. The mail carrier nods and departs.

They go down a hall to the base of operations, which is in some kind of teaching area. More officers in various groupings around the room, drinking coffee and hanging tough. A planning table in the center of the room is strewn with maps and paperwork—the men around it part to allow Cooper access. Emma and Bell find a place nearer the wall.

The room is too warm and smells strongly of carpet cleaner and gun oil. Emma is not the only female in the room: A female junior officer is setting up coffee mugs on a table at the rear. Emma is, however, the only one dressed like a teenage girl, in blue jeans and a pale pink T-shirt. Of all the days to wear pink. The weight of many pairs of male eyes skimming over her makes her feel heavy. She hasn't brought her scarf. She stands awkwardly beside Bell, not wanting to touch her head, avoiding drawing attention to herself.

Cooper is in discussion with a short, barrel-chested man in black combat gear, other men pointing to areas on the big location map. Before the buzz of talk gets too loud, Cooper shucks his jacket and glances around.

"It's real hot in here. Officer, can we get the air-conditioning turned up a little? Thank you." He looks over to Emma and Bell. "Do you want to hear this?"

Cooper waves them closer, indicates a place to stand, near but a little behind him. Now the eyes are assessing them by a different scale. She arrived with Cooper; she has a soldier's haircut. These people are paramilitary—they know what a buzz cut means. Bell is standing feet planted, arms crossed, dressed in black; he already looks half Marshal.

She's aware that Cooper has included them in order to make a point. He understands politics, and she knows he was once military. She sees it in him now: this team-building, the gathering of assets, the focus and clipped professionalism.

He indicates areas on the map. "This apartment block here is the location, yes? Lieutenant Paziewski, this is a little confusing with the road names."

"Yeah, you got Woodburn Road proper, then this whole stretch is also Woodburn Road." Paziewski is tall, thick-necked, big hands on his duty belt. He indicates an upside-down U shape on the map. "Suggest we call Woodburn One, Woodburn Two, Woodburn Three, for clarity on comms."

"Agreed," Cooper says.

"Woodburn Two is the focus." Paziewski pokes a spot on the right side of the U. "It's low, semi-connected apartment buildings. Sidewalk through to the hospital grounds here. Lots of foliage cover, shrubs and tree trunks all over."

Cooper points. "Here's the target building. We've got Agent Martino in a surveillance van here—that's our command post. SWAT has a second van here. What did the drive-by show?"

"Not much action yet, but the nursing shift change is due about now, so you'll have pedestrians soon."

"Mail area is in the front foyer. But you can enter from the back of the building, yes? Sergeant, what are our options with that?"

The barrel-chested man has no name identification and a windburned face. Emma thinks he's probably SWAT. He has a midwestern drawl and farmer's hands, square-nailed and callused with work.

"We're sending out a point man to the back." He touches the map with the blunt tip of a finger. "We need guys here and here in front, but I don't think we can position them before we make contact. The buildings are real spread out, the trees aren't bunched, and it's just too risky."

"Not enough cover?"

"Correct. My guys are gonna stick out like the proverbial, and you don't want to scare off your target."

Cooper nods. "No use baiting him out if we give the game away by leaving your guys exposed. Send one man out jogging or something to reconnoiter, then deploy with first contact."

"I've got a long-range man I can put on the roof."

"Do that. Have we got someone in the building yet? We need to see when the target collects the letter."

Paziewski nods. "We can get someone dressed in civvies, high up on the internal steps."

"Civilian dress, okay, but I want that officer kitted out underneath," Cooper says. "This guy has killed seven people we know of and I don't want to get into a hostage rescue situation."

"Copy that."

Cooper straightens, checks his watch. "All right, let's see how it plays. Mail delivery is scheduled in twenty-five minutes. Mr. Paziewski, Mr. Dewey, move your people out."

Nods all around, men milling in the background head for the exit. Cooper looks like he's making to leave as well, and Emma still has no idea what she and Bell are supposed to be doing.

"Agent Cooper—"

"Communications station." Cooper shrugs back into his jacket, already moving. "Officer Medhurst is on comms—ask someone to show you both the way. Take the map with you so you can decipher locations, we've got spares."

"Stay with Medhurst?" Bell asks.

"Yes, and you'll hear everything that's going on." Cooper accepts a radio handset from an agent. "I'll broadcast when it's over. Like I said, this could be a waiting game—be patient."

"Good luck," Bell says.

"I like to say 'good hunting.'" Cooper gives them an almost-grin.

"Catch him," Emma blurts.

Cooper's eyes are solemn. "I will."

He nods before walking out.

CHAPTER TWENTY-EIGHT

S he knows she should fight it, but Emma has a hopeful feeling.

She and Bell are set up in a dark cupboard of a room with Medhurst, a young, corn-fed-looking guy who handles the switches and dials fluidly. He's been a good sport about them cramming in here, so long as they stay quiet and don't touch anything.

There's a speaker on the desk that relays all the comms traffic. Listening to comms has been like following a radio play. A piece of paper in front of her lists all the actors in this drama: Cooper as CP1, Martino as CP2, all the S-tags for Dewey's SWAT group, the P-tags for police. She's paying particular attention to P2, a young guy named Closse on the inside stairwell of the target building, as well as S2, the SWAT jogger wearing a headset that looks like a Walkman. She heard the tension in the officers' voices when the mail carrier dropped off the letter in Delaney's old mailbox, felt the same tension.

Since then they've had nearly three hours of pedestrian logs and the occasional report when SWAT changes their jogging guy over, or when somebody needs a bathroom break or notes they're bugging for a cigarette. Bell holds the fort while Emma dashes to the bathroom herself, then she keeps an ear out while Bell fetches water and coffee and cookies. Medhurst is appreciative. The cookies don't look as good as her mother's and Emma ignores them.

Now Bell is sitting on a swivel chair beside her, his arms crossed and his chin low as he concentrates. He tilts a fraction, until their warm shoulders meet. "It's going okay."

Emma has the edge of a fingernail between her teeth. "I want this to work."

"I know."

"More than anything."

"I know."

Bell's eyes hold hers, and Emma feels her own wants rising inside. She wants the Butcher to fall into the net. To see him dangle the way he made his victims dangle. She wants this constant fizz of dread and anxiety inside herself gone.

But she's been on hunts with her dad and she knows what it's like to wait in the blind, to sight and fire and still miss.

This time, she doesn't want to miss.

Just after 1400 hours, Cooper rubs his eyes. The body is a funny thing kept under tension, and he knows to stretch and hydrate and give himself a minute every now and then. He's familiar with surveillance's weird combination of boredom and strain, and he's spent plenty of hours in Dodge Ram surveillance vans just like this one, learning patience.

There are swivel chairs in the cramped interior of the van, plus a tiny desk and low-wattage lamps. Mike Martino has turned on the little internal fan, and the oscillating breeze lifts papers at the desk.

"P4 says we've got pedestrian traffic coming through from the hospital." Martino adjusts his headset to speak to Cooper. "The kids are okay back at the Fairfax County office?"

"Yeah, they're set up on comms."

"The girl really kept her cool about that stuff in the letter." Martino keeps a steady log, watching through the tripod camera and the small Betamax video camera.

"She's good." Cooper has worked with Martino a number of times before, shared some war stories. "They're both good. They're pretty much the reason we're all here right now with a solid lead, instead of chasing our tails in Berryville."

"Glad to hear that."

"Mike, do me a favor. If I'm caught up elsewhere and Raymond starts pitching curveballs at the kids, you and Carter follow up with them, okay? I don't want them to get rolled."

"No problem." Martino squints. "They're really that good?"

"I think they've got a lot of potential. They're young as hell, but weren't we all?"

"True enough. I'll keep an eye out." Martino adjusts the camera focus. "Two nurses moving south from our twelve o'clock and a jogger turning in from Woodburn One. And a vehicle coming through from Woodburn Three."

"Have we got a visual on the vehicle?"

S2, their jogger, comes through with a visual. "Solo driver occupant. Coming around the corner now."

"This is S1, has CP got a make on arriving vehicle?" Dewey, ever alert.

"This is S5, I have a brown Valiant pulling up at the target building, over." Trust the sniper on the roof to get a make.

"Acknowledged, S5, stand by."

Bell has been watching everything, listening to everything. He knows he'll never get such insight on field undercover work again, unless he goes in that direction after his training. He's impressed and reassured by the level of professionalism among the men on the ground. It makes him feel like they have a real chance today, but he can tell from Emma's face that she doesn't want to believe it.

He indicates with his chin and rolls his swivel chair away, so they can talk in low whispers without disturbing Medhurst.

"Question."

"What?" Emma's standing, like her legs are restless.

"What will you do to celebrate, when this is over?"

He kind of expected the glare from her, flaring hot. He's not expecting her to press her fingers to his lips to shut him up.

"Don't say it," she hisses.

He moves her hand aside. "Are we not allowed to hope now?"

"Hope. But be sensible."

Then he realizes he's still holding her hand, and it's trembling. This case has taken its toll on them both, but he hates the effect it's had on her. "What do you think will happen? If they nail him?"

When he releases her, she leans back against the wall. "I don't know. Cooper will probably get a promotion. Every teenager in Virginia will let out a big goddamn sigh of relief."

"And then we go back to our regular lives," he muses.

"Yep. Just our regular old teen serial killer interviews." She closes her eyes, opens them. "And I'll feel happy."

"You will, huh?" His lips are still tingling from her fingers.

"Yeah, I think so."

"You *think* so? Hard girl to please."

That coaxes a smile out. "You know it."

And for a moment, it's perfect, just the two of them. Just a guy who wants to go into law enforcement, and a smart girl with a beautiful smile. Emma looks down and kicks her heel against the base of the wall, opens her mouth to say something else.

"Break, break, this is CP1, all teams, we have a party exiting a brown Valiant and approaching the target building, possible sighting of suspect, over."

"Listen up, guys," Medhurst calls. "We might have something."

———————————

Surveillance is like this, too: a sudden rush of adrenaline and the promise of action.

Cooper leans over the tiny desk. "CP1 to S5, what is the status of the party, over."

"S5 to CP, I have a visual on a white male, five and a half feet, beige trousers and white shirt, walking toward the building entrance, break—"

"Go ahead."

"He's wearing a dark hat, no visual on hair color, carrying a grocery bag. Getting out his keys now, over."

"Stay alert, people." Cooper switches focus. "CP1 to P2, we have a possible target coming your way, do you copy?"

"Roger that, I have a visual on target." Closse on the stairs, watching through the glass front door and talking quiet.

A voice out of nowhere. *"This is S4, I have a jogger passing my position, white male, ball cap—"*

"S2 to S4, have you checked my position? I'm jogging in your area, over."

"It ain't you, Farnsworth. Jogger is a white male, black training pants—"

"I'm wearing black, you fucken Barney."

"Cut the chatter," Cooper barks. "P2, go ahead."

"This is P2, target's key is in the door. I'm taking up position, over."

Silence. Cooper watches the monitor. Martino squints through the viewfinder. Cooper hears the imagined sound of a dozen men breathing soft.

Closse's voice breaks through. "That's a *negative*, CP, repeat, negative. The party has bypassed the mail area and entered Apartment Two. Looks like a resident."

"Fuck." Cooper says it off radio, then clicks back on. "Copy that, P2, stand down—"

"Break, break, this is S4, I have a white male jogger approaching target building from rear—"

"S4, are you yanking my chain?"

"Nossir! Jogger approaching the target building fast, sir!"

"What's happening?" Emma whispers.

Bell's face is intent as he listens. "Is he seeing the SWAT guy? Sounds like they're both wearing black—"

A sharp burst of static from the comms and Medhurst winces, holds one headphone away from his ear.

———————— ‐ ‐

"Target is coming up fast, CP, he's wearing black training gear, green-and-orange ball cap, break—"

Cooper swivels toward the monitor. "P2, find your position *now*. S4, go ahead."

"—blond ponytail, white shoes—"

"P2 in position," Closse says in a whisper. "Target is in the building."

"Give me that visual, P2."

"Target has the letter! Repeat, target has the letter—oh *shit*—"

———————— ‐ ‐

Cooper doesn't know exactly what goes wrong in what order, but it feels like everything fucks up at once.

Closse is young. When the target grabs the letter—from what they will later realize is an unlocked mailbox carefully propped to look shut tight—Closse starts down the stairs and gets the fright of his life when the target charges in his direction. Jumping back, all training forgotten, Closse trips over the step behind his feet and nearly knocks himself out on the banister. His headset flies free. By then the target has bolted.

The lack of clarity about which door the target is exiting from acts like a flashbang burst: Men positioned to cover the rear grounds converge at the back of the building, police at each end of Woodburn 2 sprint closer. Paziewski's cruiser team turns onto Woodburn 2 with a disorienting whoop of sirens.

The SWAT group bursts from the back of the van, one man

deploying south and another north, a third heading for the rear of the building. Dewey revs the engine to reverse the van: a squeal of rubber. The movement of the vehicle, the rapid motion of men on the ground, tree trunks obscuring lines of sight—it's like a street tornado. When a black-clad jogger vaults a low fence in front of the building, the newly arrived cops draw their weapons fast.

"*Hold your fire!* Hold your fire, it's *me!*" The SWAT jogger's hands are raised, his face pale.

"*This is S5, I do not have a visual on target, say again, I do not have a visual—*"

"Where's the goddamn target?" Dewey roars over comms. "CP, we do not have eyes on the target!"

Far left of the throng, a black-dressed figure breaks away from the side of the building, weaving through trees and sprinting for the road.

"*S5 has the visual! Target heading east—*"

"What the fuck is going on out there?" Cooper yells into his mic. "Somebody grab this guy!"

"Get the fuck out of the way!" Dewey's going ballistic.

"*CP, no clear shot, too many bodies—*"

The target flies past the Dodge Ram, close enough to skim the paintwork. He jumps through the bushes in front, dodging tree trunks, and disappears onto the pedestrian pathway on the near side of the hospital's front parking lot.

"*Fuck!*" Martino yells. "He ran right by us!"

"We're *losing* him," Cooper says. In that moment, his instinct overwhelms all his higher intelligence. He snatches up a handset, flings open the van door, and for the first time in nearly thirty years of distinguished military and law enforcement service, Ed Cooper breaks cover.

Taking the same route as the target, bolting through underbrush and past trees, swapping the handset to his left hand, and drawing his weapon, Cooper spills onto the hospital's concrete pathway. The Butcher has a lead of twenty yards, running left, Cooper's ten o'clock, heading for the shaded side of the hospital wall, the secondary delivery area and a service door.

"Stop right there!" Cooper aims, realizes he can't guarantee an accurate shot with the target weaving like that. He runs and yells into the handset at the same time. "CP1, I have the visual. Target on hospital grounds, hospital grounds west service side, CP1 in pursuit."

There's a squawk in reply and Cooper sees the Butcher wrench open the service door, thrust straight through.

Not wasting his breath in curses, Cooper sprints harder for the door. He shoves his left hand with the handset into the shrinking gap, his fingers almost crushed against the doorframe but not quite—he's caught it.

The brick that had kept the door cracked open for lunchtime smokers has been kicked aside—if he hadn't caught the door, it would've been all over—and Cooper realizes that the Butcher knows the hospital. That awareness flicks his training synapses back on. He yanks the door open. Diagonal entry, check the corners, one-two, gun forward and aimed, left hand with the handset supporting from beneath.

No Butcher in the cement stairwell foyer. Noise from the stairs above—Cooper flattens himself against the wall. Running footsteps ascending, ascending, and the sound of the fire escape door bouncing open and closed—the third floor. Cooper starts up. The handset squawks again.

He thumbs the button, brings the radio to his face as he takes the stairs two at a time, exertion making his breathing messy. "CP1, inside the hospital, repeat, inside the hospital. No visual, target is running loose and he knows the location. S1, secure area, P1—"

"S1 to CP1, you've got people coming your way." Dewey's voice crackles from the radio interference inside the building.

"Copy that—P1, deploy into the hospital. Eyes out for a WM, six feet, black jogging suit, blond hair in a ponytail, green-and-orange ball cap. He's gone up to the third floor—"

"P1 to CP1, support is nearly at the building, I say again, men will be going floor to floor—"

"CP1 to P1, tell your men to watch themselves inside, there'll be civilians everywhere."

"Roger that. Hang tight, CP1."

Cooper reaches the third-floor door, flings it open, another corner check. He's in a hallway. His breaths are heaving. Shiny linoleum and white walls, too many doors—a service area, no foot traffic. Sweat stings in his eyes. Which way? Right, left—he sees a flash of black, cornering far down on the left. He sprints in that direction, keeping his weapon free.

Corner check at the T-junction—which way? His memory replays the flash of black motion. *Left.* He turns left again into the empty corridor. Doors on either side. Stay in the middle, weapon extended. Farther down, a set of blue flap doors. Rear check shows nothing. Gun close to his chest, he thrusts through the doors.

An empty corridor. Big, light-filled windows at the end, showing views onto the service-side grounds of the hospital. No movement, no swinging doors. Zero. Like the target has disappeared into thin air. *Fuck.*

He raises the handset. "This is CP1, I'm in a west-side corridor, third floor. No visual. No visual on the target. I got—"

Sound behind has him spinning fast.

A surgeon has just come out of one of the service areas, bumping the door open with his butt. A blue paper surgical cap, blue gown over his clothes, no mask yet. The guy's hands are high, fingers open, blue latex gloves, newly gloved for surgery. Brown hair, older, too old—Cooper clocked those details immediately—and a look of horror that the barrel of Cooper's Model 13 is pointed right in his face.

"Heyyy…" The surgeon blinks, swallows hard. "Uh, look. I got—"

"You're a doctor here?" Cooper doesn't lower his weapon yet.

"Yes." The surgeon answers and nods at the same time. His breath comes out shaky. "Dr. Clive Ross. Sir, I'd appreciate if you could put that gun down. I can help you. I'll do everything I can—"

Cooper releases his breath slowly, lowers his weapon. "Dr. Ross. My apologies. I'm Special Agent Cooper, with the FBI. We're pursuing a suspect here in the hospital, and when I saw you…"

"Oh. Oh shit." Ross's exhale is explosive as he drops his hands to half-mast. "Oh *man*." The release of tension as he laughs.

"I'm really sorry. Are you okay?"

"Am I…" Ross is still laughing a little. "Oh *man*. No, I'm fine. It's okay. Oh wow."

"Again, I apologize."

"Geez, no! It's all…it's all okay." Ross looks sheepish. "I mean, I nearly wet my pants, but it's fine."

"Ah hell—"

"No, no, it's fine. You're chasing a suspect, I get it.... You mean there's someone in the hospital? Should I be warning the—"

"Uh, no, not yet." Cooper scans the hall behind Ross. "Can you tell me where exactly I am?"

"You're on the third floor, west wing. Oncology department."

"Okay." Cooper's radio buzzes.

"I mean, this is an older part of the wing. It's mostly just equipment storage and surgery prep now."

"Got it, thank you. Excuse me a minute." Cooper angles toward the windows, lifting the handset. "This is CP1, can I get a—"

"Which made it easy to find all the things I needed," Ross says, and he steps forward and thumps his gloved fist against the right side of Cooper's neck.

Cooper feels it like a punch, and the force and angle of the strike send him off balance, stumbling against the wall when he should be lifting his weapon. The radio handset spills out of his grasp and bounces once, twice, exploding into parts that skitter away. Cooper swivels to face Ross, knowing he should be angry, but mainly angry at himself for being taken by surprise.

"You're not—" Distracted by the feeling of wet on his shirt, Cooper falls to his knees.

"No," Anthony Hoyt says. He tosses the concealed scalpel blade onto the linoleum, so Cooper understands fully.

"Fuck," Cooper says, but the word sounds fuzzy. His vision, too, is fuzzy. He claps a hand against his neck, knowing it's pointless.

"It's a shame to waste all this," Hoyt says, gesturing at the widening red pool, "but you're no good to me. Too old. Already decaying from all those years of memory and regret. I'm right, aren't I? I'm sure you can feel it."

Cooper has memories, and he does feel regret. But he's always made his own choices, and they play before him now like a beautiful, unspooling thread of gold.

"I've spared you, you know," Hoyt says. "Aging is an indignity and mortality is a prison. Think of this as a liberation."

"We'll catch you," Cooper whispers, remembering his promise.

"No, you won't." Hoyt is stripping off his gloves, removing the surgical cap. "The venerable FBI—grizzled old men doddering along the same predictable paths of investigation. You don't stand a chance against someone like me."

Cooper finds gravity bearing him down, until the cool linoleum rests against his cheek. The man before him steps in. *That's right, come closer*, Cooper thinks, before realizing he doesn't have the strength to do anything about it.

Hoyt kicks Cooper's gun aside and hunkers down. "Don't feel bad. It's really not your fault. Not everyone can be what I'm becoming. I have the advantage of medical training, I know, but it's not just about longevity and being well—it's about being *whole*. I'm still in transition, but I can feel it. I'm getting younger all the time. And I'm so fast now. It's like...a burning inside, you know? There's no one who can keep up."

The mention of burning stirs behind Cooper's eyes. *Miss Lewis wants to burn down the world.*

"There's one," Cooper whispers as his murderer stands up.

But his vision is going dark, and Hoyt is already walking away.

CHAPTER TWENTY-NINE

Emma stares out the window of the Fairmont and the world seems to be glazed over, moving very slowly. She's stopped crying. The sense of being in a tailspin is dissipating; now she just feels dazed. Mike Martino is driving, and she and Bell sit in the back seat, and nobody talks on the hour-long trip back to Quantico. It's five thirty in the afternoon, the sun outside making everything look sepia-toned. The car radio is playing "More Than This" down low, and Emma will forever associate the song with this moment.

It's hard to fathom, as Martino slows the car to get the nod from MPs at the gate, that it's still Friday. It's the same day as it was this morning, when she and Bell and Cooper screeched out of the base. Bell hit his head when they went over a speed hump, she remembers. She looks over and he's gazing out the window now, fist against his lips. While she feels like she's been anesthetized, Bell's whole body is shimmering with distress and controlled fury.

Martino takes the car down to the motor pool, and they come to a stop in the cool, dark garage. Bell supports himself with the car door as he exits, like an old man. Emma's reluctant to leave the car. She's not sure where they're supposed to go, what they're supposed to do. She's going to reach the Cool Room and expect to see Cooper waiting for them there. She's not sure if she can handle the feelings she knows will come when she opens the door and finds only empty space.

People stare at them as they move out of the motor pool and head for the elevator.

"Where are we going?" Emma's shocked to realize her voice comes out as a whisper.

Martino presses the button in slow motion. "I've been ordered to take you up to see the Section Chief."

"Do we have to do that now?" Bell's voice is rough, and more curt than Emma has ever heard it before.

"I'm sorry, but yeah."

"Don't you think—"

"Travis." Emma touches his arm. "Let's just get it over with."

His jaw grinds, but after a pause he nods. His face is so tight that the skin over his cheekbones is shiny. This must've been the way he looked when his father died, Emma thinks, and it feels wrong to be staring at him. She drops her gaze and it makes her wonder, how does *she* look?

They enter the elevator. Martino leans back against the wall as the doors close and the car rises.

"Cooper said…" He pauses after invoking the man's name, shakes it off. "He asked me to look out for you. I'll be with you when you see Raymond. It'll be okay."

Emma reflects that people always say things will be okay when everything is completely fucked. She has no confidence that Martino's presence can unfuck this situation. She barely knows the man.

They get out of the elevator, walk to Raymond's office, tap to enter.

Raymond is sitting at his stupid desk. His expression is glum and his face does seem a little more gray than usual, she'll give him that.

"Thank you for coming in." Raymond touches near items—his pen, a letter opener, a stapler—to straighten them. He doesn't meet their eyes after the initial greeting. "This is a sad day. A terrible day. It's unfortunate that you were involved in the circumstances around Special Agent Cooper's death."

It still feels surreal to hear those words connected in a sentence. *Special Agent Cooper's death.* Emma tries to find balance.

"Ed Cooper was a fine man, and a fine agent," Raymond goes on. "His family has been contacted, and they're making the arrangements. The funeral will be held as soon as the body is released by the medical examiner."

And now, with reeling intensity, it comes to her. Westfall and his crew are—maybe right this minute—collecting evidence from Cooper's body, adding it to the file about the Butcher. Photos are being taken, like those stark pictures of disconnected body parts that Emma saw in Glenn Neilsen's office. The idea blindsides her. She hopes Raymond can hurry this along before she succumbs to the urge to be sick.

After straightening his desk, Raymond now straightens his shoulders, steeples his fingers in front. "I am taking full operational control of the Berryville Butcher case. Agent Martino, I've spoken on the phone to Agent Carter about how this is to be handled. He'll be briefing you shortly. If you have any queries, you can address them to Agent Carter or myself."

"Yessir," Martino says.

"Now. As to the matter of you young people…"

Here it comes, Emma thinks.

"I've determined that, at this time, the juvenile offender interview project that Agent Cooper initiated is to be closed down. It's
been two weeks since your arrival, and until the Butcher case can
be successfully resolved, the interviews are simply added workload
for the staff—"

"Excuse me, sir?" Bell steps forward, face haggard. "Lewis and
I have been working independently on the interviews, so it's not—"

"Mr. Bell, I'll thank you to be quiet and listen. While the interviews have been…a very interesting and informative side project,
they're not priority one, and as such—"

"You got the lead on the Butcher case because of Simon Gutmunsson," Emma says dully. "If we hadn't interviewed Gutmunsson—"

"If you hadn't interviewed Gutmunsson, Ed Cooper might still
be *alive* right now," Raymond snaps.

Emma feels like she's been slapped across the face.

"I have a plan for Gutmunsson." Raymond's brows come together.
"But I'm not going to pander to a teenage homicidal maniac."

Martino perks up. "Sir? We can keep pursuing the connection
between Gutmunsson and the Butcher, if you think that might be
useful."

"I do," Raymond says. "I do want to pursue that connection,
and I plan to hold Simon Gutmunsson's feet to the fire to do it. But
I don't want these young people involved in it."

"He won't talk to you." It's like Emma can't help herself. "Simon
won't talk to you. You can hold his feet to the fire—you can stand

269

him in the middle of the goddamn fire, if it amuses you. It won't make any difference."

Raymond's eyes narrow. "Young lady, do you think you have a *special relationship* with this boy? Because I'd be looking very carefully at yourself if you think that to be the case."

All the blood that left Emma's face rushes back into her cheeks. Her forehead feels hot.

"Simon Gutmunsson is just another teenage pervert whose mommy didn't raise him right." Raymond's expression has a malicious cast. "If he talks to you, it's because something about you is pulling his chain, don't you agree, Agent Martino?"

Bell takes a step. *"Sir—"*

"Travis." Emma has to hold his arm tightly.

Martino seems confused, looking back and forth between Raymond and Emma. "I . . . I couldn't say, sir. It's a little out of my lane."

"It's a little out of your lane. Well, yes, I imagine it is." Raymond's sneer takes on a more acceptable professional aspect. "Now, I'm sorry if you're disappointed about the outcome of the interview project, Miss Lewis. You and Mr. Bell will be paid for an extra week, since the project was concluded early, and you'll be provided with a reference for your work. I think the bureau has been very generous in this matter."

Emma doesn't ask about the offer to join the program, the prospective scholarship, the credits toward her college course. . . . None of that applies now that Cooper is dead. She wonders briefly if Cooper was even authorized to make those initial promises, then dismisses that thought. If Cooper were alive, he would've kept those promises come hell or high water. He would've made a point of it.

"I expect you'll both need to make arrangements for packing up your accommodations and organizing transport back to your respective homes," Raymond continues. "But your identification will no longer be valid on base after the weekend, so remember to hand in your lanyards at Behavioral Science. The United States government thanks you for your service. Now, Mr. Martino, could you escort these young people down to the offices? Then get your briefing on the phone with Agent Carter, and I'll expect to see you back here at nineteen hundred hours. Dismissed."

And that's it. No more or less than what she was expecting. Emma finds she is still holding on to Bell's arm. He shakes her off, turns around, and walks out. She follows, with Martino on her heels.

As they approach the elevators, the man comes level with her. "Miss Lewis—"

"Leave it," Emma says.

"No, wait." Martino gets between her and Bell, hits the elevator button. "Let's talk."

Martino waits until they're all in the elevator car before rubbing a hand across his mustache. "Okay, I didn't know the score with Raymond, but now I do. He's obviously got some kind of beef with you two."

"You think?" Bell steps closer.

"Settle down, son." Martino puts a palm up. "Ed Cooper said you've both been contributing to the Butcher case. And he told me to look out for you, so I'm doing it. I have to sell the candy to Raymond, so I won't be able to share any information officially. But you have a phone in your office now. I'll keep in touch."

Bell blinks. "It won't matter after this weekend. We'll be off the base."

"Then we'll have to work fast," Martino says grimly. "Raymond seems like he's gonna go off on his high horse, and that'll keep him distracted. Either way, if you've got input on the case, I want it. If I'm out of the office, get my contact off Betty and call me. I want to catch this bastard. Now more than ever."

"Okay," Bell says stiffly. "Thank you."

"Cooper said you were worth it." Martino looks at them, then looks away. Emma remembers Cooper was his colleague, maybe even his friend.

When they get to basement level and emerge into the bunker corridor, Martino splits off for Behavioral Science. Bell walks to the door of the Cool Room, Emma following. Bell's hand closes on the doorknob. He can't seem to turn it, though.

Emma watches his back, feeling the energy pulsing out of him. "You're going to have to open the door eventually."

"Cooper—" Bell starts.

"I know."

Bell's shoulders tense under his black T-shirt, then he twists the knob and pushes inside. He walks slowly to the desk. Emma closes the door, resting back on it. She straightens up again when Bell makes a muffled noise. He sweeps the papers on the desk onto the floor, where they fall in a tented, fluttering arch.

"Bell."

Another sweep of his hand, and a box of pens splits and scatters. He kicks over one of the stacks of file boxes close to the desk—a waterfall of paper spills out—and shoves the desk chair aside. When he grips the desk itself, like he wants to tip it over, she crosses her arms and raises her voice.

"Travis, *stop*. Stop this *right now*."

He turns and throws his hands up, everything about him harsh and bleak. "Well, what the fuck d'you *expect* me to do?"

Emma plants her feet, buries her own anger deep. "I expect you to act like a professional. If you want to beat the shit out of something, go take it out on the punching bag. Don't wreck the office— we did good work here. All of us."

Bell covers his face with his hands. "It doesn't matter anymore. We're off the case."

"No, we're not. Didn't you hear Martino? He's going to share information."

"What good will that do against the goddamn *section chief*?"

"I don't know, but it's *something*. And do you really think Raymond's going to waltz into St. Elizabeths and get Simon to play ball? That's not how Simon works. But regardless of what Raymond does with Simon Gutmunsson, something will happen. It might happen soon. The bureau is angry about Cooper's murder—they're not going to put the Butcher on the back burner now."

Bell's next word comes out like a groan. "*Cooper—*"

"I know it hurts. I feel it, too." A tearing pain. She swallows hard, controls the urge to break down, to just sit here and collapse. Cooper would not approve. "Listen—you're wasting your energy, and we might need that energy. Cooper would be telling us to use our advantages. He'd be telling us to get ahold of ourselves."

"He was good at that." Bell shakes his head at the floor. "Fuck."

"Yeah." Emma sighs, walks to where the two spare foldout chairs are propped.

"I just can't...I can't get my mind around it."

She takes one of the chairs and opens it out, sinks down on it, her legs watery. "I know."

Bell lets out a deep exhale, like he's exhausted, and slumps back with his butt on the desk. "What Raymond said to you—"

"I don't want to talk about it." Emma drops her gaze. "And I don't trust him. At all. But I think we can rely on Martino, and there's Howard Carter, and the other names Cooper gave us. And I think we could talk to Westfall and his people if we needed to."

In the quiet of the gray office, Bell steadies himself with his hands on the desk. "Question?"

"Sure."

He hesitates before launching in. "Emma, why are you still here? I get why you joined the unit, but why are you hanging on, after everything? I swear to god, I've been trying to figure it out, but I just..."

Emma knows this question is important. For the longest time she didn't know the answer, and even now, she's still parsing it out.

"Travis..." She closes her eyes. "Travis, why do you think I cut my hair?"

"You used to have long hair?"

Emma nods.

"I bet it was real pretty," Bell says gently. "Did you cut it after Huxton?"

She nods again. She's opened her eyes, but she's looking at her hands.

"You fought him, didn't you? A physical fight."

"Yes," she says. Her throat feels thick, her tongue wooden.

Bell pauses. "Did your hair get...tangled up?"

She takes a breath. "Yes. He grabbed it, and I nearly didn't...I nearly didn't get away." She exhales slowly and completely, pulling her sanity back on a fine string. "You think this stuff is over, and eventually you'll forget. But for a year after, every time my hair caught on something, I'd get...I'd have a reaction. Then I buzzed it off and I felt better."

Bell nods steadily. "If you do something, you feel better."

"Yeah. So I think I joined this unit to save prospective victims, but also to save myself."

"Emma—"

"I think a part of me is still in Daniel Huxton's basement. I don't know how to get out of it, and I thought if I..." She presses her lips. "I don't know if it's worked out quite the way I imagined." She snorts, but it comes out more like a sob, quickly swallowed. "What about you? Why did you join this unit?"

"I guess..." Bell looks as if he's had all his pillars of faith stripped away. "I guess I'm trying to be like my dad. But he ended up dead. Just like Cooper."

"Then you have to be smarter than both of them," Emma says softly.

"Cooper said we'd have to deal with people like Raymond. He said we'd have to deal with petty bullshit and stupidity, right?"

"Yeah. But he said we'd have to learn to manage it."

A long silence as they both just sit there, trying to work out how the hell they're going to do that.

CHAPTER THIRTY

Donald Raymond has always considered himself an intelligent man.

Right now, he's sitting at his desk with all the paperwork from Ed Cooper's death in front of him, plus the file from the Butcher case. He had to go into his study last night at home so he could read through it and look at the pictures—his wife won't have this kind of stuff in the house. But he's examined it all, and he's got the photocopies and document analysis from the correspondence between Simon Gutmunsson and the Butcher. He thinks he's found a thread in there that he can build on.

He's signing the message of condolence for Ed Cooper's brother when the call comes through from Mike Martino. "Hey, Mike. How're things working out?"

"It's going well." Martino's voice sounds thin through the phone connection. "But I'm using the phone in Scott's office, so I don't have much time."

Raymond's expression is long-suffering, knowing, as he does, that it's an FBI agent's prerogative to boss people around. "Fine. Out with it."

"Okay, seems like Gutmunsson first communicated with the Butcher via the personal ads in the *Washington Post*—Gutmunsson has pretty much unfettered access to newspapers. He says the Butcher was the one who made initial contact, using the 'Artist' and 'Siegfried' thing. They arranged the Georgetown U system through the personals, so they could communicate privately. About four letter exchanges in all, including the most recent one, I gather."

Raymond finds this information exciting. "That's good, Mike. Great work. Okay, here's what I want you to do for me. You're gonna get Gutmunsson to write a personal ad."

"Today?"

"Right now. Obviously the Butcher is wise to the fact that we've tapped the mail, so it'll make sense for Gutmunsson to go back to personals. Get a pen, I'm gonna dictate a couple of things I want Gutmunsson to include in the ad."

Once Raymond gives him the details, Martino's voice takes on a different tone. "Uh, he may not want to do that, sir. I mean, Gutmunsson's crazy, but he's got a sense of self-preservation—"

"Mike, I really don't give a shit if Simon Gutmunsson is worried about his own hide. He wasn't worried when Ed Cooper was bleeding out on the linoleum at the Fairfax hospital. Gutmunsson needs to learn to do as he's told. He's tender about the sister, right?"

"Uh, right."

"So come down hard on that. Hell, if you think it'll work, start soft and tell him I can get visitor access for his sister at St. Elizabeths." Raymond eases back in his chair, swaps the phone receiver to his other hand. "Arrange to get the ad in the *Post* by this afternoon. I want it on the newsstands by Sunday morning."

"Yessir." No more complaints from Martino now.

"And when you're done on the phone, tell Dr. Scott to call me direct. She and I are gonna have words."

"If you try to organize a sting here in the asylum, she'll fight you," Martino warns. "She's pretty tough."

"I'm tougher," Raymond reminds him. "You let me handle Scott. Just get me that personal ad and get it out by tomorrow."

"Copy that, sir."

"Outstanding. Keep up the good work, Mike. Call me when it's done."

CHAPTER THIRTY-ONE

Emma sweated out her grief hangover on the Saturday morning run, and with every thump of her feet, it felt as if she was running farther away from Quantico. Now, showered and dressed and back in the Cool Room, she pulls out the case files again. There must be a link between the victims somewhere. How is the killer choosing them? How is he finding them?

She can't stare at the photos and expect a miracle anymore. If miracles were real, Cooper would still be here.

By the time Bell arrives, ragged and smelling of gun smoke, Emma has been poring through victim histories for three hours, and the names of the dead are echoing through her skull: Kimberley Berger, Carol Lambton, Lamar Davis, Mark Spiegel, Sienna Ramirez, Brian Barnes, Donna Williams....Each of them was beautiful, each of them special. And Emma can see *herself* reflected in their personal histories. The intensity of being a teenager, the quest for self-direction, the need for individual control—she sees it all there in the files, bouncing back at her like she's standing in some ghastly fun-house hall of mirrors.

Maybe the need for control is the key? Her own desire for

control is exaggerated, she knows, but that kernel of desire is in every teen. In what ways did the Butcher's victims seek to control their own worlds?

She goes back to their families, their hangouts, and finally their medical histories. Bell is packing file papers into the boxes he knocked over yesterday. For a while, the only sound is Bell sighing over the paper mess, with a brief interruption when Emma asks him to pass her the phone.

After a few calls, Emma makes a noise.

On his knees on the floor, Bell squints up at her. "You got something there?"

Her own scribbled notes are starting to blur in front of her. "Maybe. A few crumbs, I don't know."

"Crumbs can leave a mark." They know that now, from Linda Brown.

Emma spreads out her pages. "Seven teenage victims. They all had different doctors. But at least five of the seven consulted another clinic, and saw someone different from their primary doctor, in the last six months. Lamar Davis went to the University of Mary Washington student clinic. Sienna Ramirez had an appointment last February at an upstate medical center. They each saw alternative doctors on occasion."

"For emergency treatment?" Bell clambers up and dusts off his chinos.

"I'm thinking for something personal—sexual health tests or birth control, maybe. Something they didn't want to get back to their parents through a family doctor."

Bell props his hand on the back of her chair as he examines her notes. "Can we narrow down which practitioners they saw?"

"We only have access to partial records. But of the alternative clinics we know about, I found one other detail—they all used the same MT service." She looks up at him. "Medical technicians take *blood samples*, Bell."

"What?" He seems less tousled now, more directed. "Lewis, that's no crumb, that's big. That's the first real point of commonality we've found. Which medical technicians are on the service register?"

"It's a long list. Sixty-two med techs, who were all rotated around half of Virginia."

Bell chews his lip. "The stakeout yesterday…I don't have a transcript, but Cooper said something. He said the Butcher knew the hospital."

"Fairfax?"

"Yeah." Bell's mind is working, his eyes moving across her notes. "Try something for me. Cross-check the medical technicians on the service register against records from Fairfax. How many of them worked or still work at the hospital?"

Another series of phone calls, to dig up the information that the FBI has already gathered from Fairfax, but it gets results. When Emma taps her pen to get his attention, Bell's just finished hauling the last file box back into place.

"Did that help?"

She nods slowly.

"How many also worked at the hospital?"

"Twelve."

"*Twelve.*" He comes forward fast. "Show me."

Emma's written out the names she circled from her original list on a fresh sheet of paper. Bell's hand shakes a little as he holds it up.

"I already crossed out the female names," Emma says. "With them, it was fourteen."

Bell reads aloud. "Robert Fortescue, Raffaele Carozza, Anthony Hoyt, John Frankel...Lewis, the Butcher could be on this list."

"Maybe." She takes a steadying breath—she doesn't want to give in to excitement yet.

"So who do we hand this to? Do we trust Martino?"

"Martino, or maybe Cooper's second-in-command, Howard Carter." Every agent they contact is a question mark, though. How far does Raymond's influence extend? "Whoever we tell, we'll have to hope they'll do something useful with it."

"We need to go see Betty to find out if Martino's around, or at least get his phone contact," Bell says. "You return your lanyard yet?"

"No."

"Then come on."

They leave the Cool Room and walk back through the gerbil run. Even though Bell is taller, they keep step with each other. It's one of the things about being around him that Emma's going to miss.

"Are you flying out tomorrow?"

Bell shakes his head. "Ticket's booked for Monday morning, I'll have to stay off base tomorrow night, but I'll find someplace near Washington National. How about you?"

"Long drive ahead." She bites her lip. "I was going to leave after lunch tomorrow."

"Don't leave without saying goodbye."

"I won't."

Bell chuckles. "I know you want to. Don't bullshit me." When

Emma glances over, he peers at her. "Seriously—don't just disappear. I'll be here or in my dorm."

"Okay, I'll find you." The look between them feels like a promise. Emma tears her eyes away as they go through the door into the Behavioral Science foyer and up to the reception desk. "Hi, Betty."

"Good…" Betty checks her watch. "…afternoon. How can I help you?"

Bell allows his lanyard and Emma's to pool together on the desk. "The Section Chief said we'd be delisted after tomorrow, so we've been instructed to return our lanyards and IDs to Behavioral Science. Is there anything we need to sign?"

"There's nothing you need to sign, and the Section Chief is incorrect," Betty pronounces. She looks radiant today, in emerald-green wool boucle. "Identification invalidation can only be completed during a standard business day. Your identification will remain valid until midnight on Monday evening."

"So we have another forty-eight hours?" Emma asks.

Betty checks her watch again. "Technically, you have fifty-nine hours."

"That's…that's great." It means Bell can stay on base tomorrow night. It also means they're still technically FBI until Monday. Emma exchanges a glance with Bell at the implications. "Betty, can I ask one last favor? We'd like to say goodbye to Agent Martino, but we don't have his contact number."

Betty picks through her Rolodex, writes Martino's contact down on a card. "There you are. And Agent Carter has been engaged with work in Berryville, but he's due to arrive back Monday morning. I took the liberty of suggesting that you would like to speak with him, when he arrives."

"Betty, thank you." Bell leans to shake Betty's hand. After a startled moment, she allows it. "We really appreciate everything you've done while we've been here."

Betty straightens. "It's been a pleasure working with you. And I wanted to say that Agent Cooper..." Her eyes get a little bright and she swallows. "Agent Cooper was a good man, and he put a lot of store in you. In both of you. I just thought you should know."

Emma finds her throat suddenly has a frog in it. "Thank you, Betty. That means a lot."

She and Bell walk out of Behavioral Science together, and Emma's not sure whose face is more surprised.

"Now what?" Bell asks.

"We have extra time." Emma's confused about what to do with it, but they have it, and strangely enough, she's grateful. "And we need to call Martino."

"I'll do that." He steers them toward the elevators. "You've gotta do something else."

"What's that?"

"Eat." He hits the button. "You have breakfast?"

"No, but I—"

"And I know you didn't have lunch, because I've been in the office with you for the last three hours."

"That's not—"

"Lewis, you've lost about ten pounds since you arrived on base, and there wasn't that much of you to begin with." He holds the elevator door for her. "Go up to the cafeteria and get something. Get me a coffee while you're at it. You've done all the legwork, now let me do the phone schmoozing."

Emma knows she should feel indignant, but she can't hold on to it. As the elevator arrows upward, she thinks about the MT list. Then she mentally plans her trip back to Apple Creek, which roads to take. Thinking about both these things hurts less than thinking about saying goodbye to Bell.

She grabs a sandwich and two coffees and returns the way she came. Her brain won't let her be, though.

She's going to miss Bell. Beyond being partners for the interviews, they've got something. They've made a connection. She and Bell look out for each other—she knows he's got her back.

Tucking the plastic-covered sandwich under her arm and juggling the coffees, she opens the door to the office. Bell is occupying the chair she vacated, sitting sideways at the desk, legs stretched out. He has one hand still on the phone receiver, like he just put it down. She closes the door with her foot and he looks over—somehow she knows instantly that something is wrong.

"What is it?"

"I just spoke to Martino, explained about the MT list. He said he'll chase it. But he also told me that Raymond's putting an operation together." He holds out a hand. "Give me the coffee first, because you might drop it on the floor when I tell you about this."

CHAPTER THIRTY-TWO

You got it?"

Bell nods, chafes his fingers. "Wouldn't be here otherwise. Walk back with me."

It's Sunday morning, and Emma can hear the sound of birds nearby. She and Bell move briskly through the big pines, cutting off the main track and heading for the sunny place where the trees change. Oaks signal that the Quantico buildings are close.

Bell is in sweats—Emma guesses he was working the bag until Betty sent word. He's interrupted what might be her last chance to run the Yellow Brick Road so they can both find out how much shit they're in with Raymond's ham-fisted "operation."

"Did Martino call again with more information?"

"Nope. But he sent a message through Betty. Apparently, Raymond served Dr. Scott with an injunction to make sure she complies with the operation at the asylum."

"So this whole thing is really happening."

"Yep. It's crazy, but it's happening."

"Is Raymond planning to booby-trap the entire asylum?"

"That was probably his original idea, but no." Bell ushers her toward the path that leads to the entry to the bunker-style building substructure. "Just Gutmunsson's part of it."

"What the actual fuck."

"That's pretty much what I said to Martino on the phone yesterday. Come on." He opens the door for her.

They can take the stairs to the basement from here. The corridor is like a refrigerator and the inside of the Cool Room is worse. Emma hunches to keep warm.

Bell opens out his copy of this morning's *Washington Post*. "There it is."

Emma still barely believes it. But Bell has the relevant item circled in ballpoint, so there's no denying it. It's a personal ad from Simon Gutmunsson, the key component of Raymond's plan to trap the Butcher.

She reads the ad aloud:

> "Dearest Siegfried,
>
> "Are you safe? Forces swirl around me and, I suspect, my correspondence. I fear for your liberty. If you are yet unconfined, I will rejoice. Reply here to reassure me. . . ."

"Jesus." Bell makes a face. "Does Gutmunsson really talk like that?"

"No." Emma backpedals. "Kind of. It doesn't matter, it's the persona he uses when writing to this guy. He's being pretty smart about it—he wants the Butcher to know he didn't cooperate willingly with the Annandale stakeout. Wait, let me read the rest—

> "Or if your offer still stands, we
> might have a professional exchange
> this evening. A visit from you
> would calm my heart and assuage my
> concerns. But time is fleeting—I've
> been informed my tenure here is at an
> end. Whatever may divide us, I will
> always look back on our connection
> fondly. Please remember I am your
> most sincere,
>
> Artist."

She looks up at Bell. "Simon's inviting the Butcher to St. Elizabeths and offering to make a donation. That's the 'something he can't refuse' that Martino mentioned to you on the phone. What the *hell*, Bell?"

"I hear you." Bell, still frowning at the ad, wipes newsprint off his fingers onto his T-shirt without seeming to realize.

She checks the ad again. "Another thing—the wording makes it sound like Simon's being transferred out of St. Elizabeths. Is this true?"

"Maybe. Can Raymond authorize that?"

"I guess so." Emma tucks her fingers in her armpits. "But how did Raymond get Simon to agree to this? To offer himself as bait?"

"Cooper said Raymond prefers to use a stick than a carrot. He must've explicitly threatened Kristin."

"I can't believe Simon would do this. Let himself be used like this."

"I don't get it either. But he cares about his sister. She might be the only person he's *ever* cared about."

"And having the FBI inside St. Elizabeths is a change in the asylum's routine." Emma stares, unseeing, at the newsprint stain on Bell's T-shirt. "Simon's motivated by boredom, remember? So maybe..."

"What?"

"I don't know." She slides a hand free to rub her forehead. "All I know is that, because of his nature and his previous escape attempts, there are really specific procedures around how Simon is handled at St. Elizabeths. If the FBI comes in and takes over, those procedures might be altered. Weakened."

Bell is suddenly very serious. "You think Gutmunsson's planning another escape attempt?"

"Simon never does anything without thinking about his own self-interest. If he's agreed to cooperate with Raymond, to act as bait, it's because he thinks he can work it to his own advantage."

"That's scary."

"Yes."

"Then we should *say* something. We could ask Martino to contact Howard Carter—the guy flies in tomorrow morning."

"That doesn't help us. Simon's ad says this evening. Whatever's happening at St. Elizabeths is happening tonight."

Emma is starting to shiver, and she's not sure if it's just because of the cold. Bell is warm beside her; his gaze is back on the newspaper, his bottom lip indented between his teeth. He smells of sweat and the vinyl of the gym mats and, underneath that, of soap. Emma pulls her awareness away. They have to figure this out and they're running out of time.

"What the hell do we do now?" Bell asks.

First steps, Emma thinks. They can only start with first steps. What would Cooper do in this situation? "Okay, let's contact Linda Brown about the ad. I don't trust Simon not to include something in there we're not seeing, and she could give us advice."

"It's Sunday—but I've got Gerry Westfall's number, I can call to find her."

"That would be great." She backs toward the door. "I'm going to hit the shower before I freeze to death. And you should go change, too. Back here in twenty?"

"Got it." Bell reaches for the phone.

Emma dashes to the elevators, her mind racing fast. She and Bell tried to reason out Raymond's thinking last night, to little effect. Does Raymond just not realize the bigger threat? Yes, catching the Butcher is critical, but he's a pale shadow of what Simon Gutmunsson could become if he somehow got loose during the Butcher's arrest....

After a hot shower, she pulls on a jacket over her clean T-shirt and jeans. Then she packs up her room; by digging further into the details of Raymond's asylum operation, she and Bell could end up being kicked off the base, "standard business day" or not. She sets her suitcase near the door and goes back to the office.

"Okay," Bell says as she enters. "Linda Brown is at home, but Westfall's calling her there. Take this."

Bell is back in his dark suit, his hair damp. He offers her a hot mug and a pastry, and Emma accepts them both.

"I think we should contact Kristin at Chesterfield," he says. "We owe it to her to warn her about this."

"Yep." Emma speaks around a mouthful, swallows. "But Raymond has already set things in motion."

Bell throws a hand up. "Then we should call Howard Carter in Berryville!"

"And say what?" Emma swipes crumbs off her front. "It's all going to sound like alarmism over the phone. I'm sure Raymond's plan looks solid on the surface. It's only because we know Raymond, know the case, know Simon, that we can see the flaws."

Bell's expression is glum. "Maybe the Butcher won't show."

"He'll show."

"But he *has* to know this is a trap. The letter stakeout, now the personal ad and the asylum...Why the hell would he bite?"

"Don't underestimate his drives. For him, the blood is everything. Simon's offer to donate would be a huge incentive. And if Simon is being transferred..." Emma sets down her mug and pastry. "The Butcher outsmarted the FBI in Annandale. He might think he can do it again. He'll be wary, but he'll have his own plan."

"How the hell is Raymond even going to stake out the asylum?" Bell, lost in thought.

"The center building is a kind of isolation area....Look, it doesn't really matter. What matters is that instead of Scott and Pradeep, there'll be FBI agents taking care of Simon. Let's contact Scott, try to find out more details." Emma peers up at Bell. "Have you packed yet?"

"What? No, not yet."

"Maybe go do that. If this all goes south, you might want to have everything ready for a quick exit."

A knock comes on the door. It's Betty, holding a small black envelope.

"These are the details for Agent Cooper's funeral." She hands Bell the envelope. "It's tomorrow, at one PM. While only family and close acquaintances will be at the burial and the wake, the memorial service is open to everybody. I thought you might like to attend."

Betty inclines her head, departs. Emma walks over to take the envelope, as Bell seems reluctant to do more than just stare at it. Inside, a stiff card provides details of the service; instead of flowers, Edmund Cooper's brother has requested people donate to the FBI Financial Need Scholarships Fund.

"Now I guess we know why Carter's flying back." Bell frowns at the card. "Goddammit. How many more people have to die before we catch this bastard?"

Emma puts a hand on his shoulder. She remembers the first time she did that, in the gymnasium after Cooper gave them Simon Gutmunsson's file. Bell was grieving then and he's grieving now. She wishes more than anything that things hadn't come full circle.

"Go to your dorm and pack," she says. "I'll keep the fire burning."

Emma tries to keep busy. She's anxious and she's angry, and she knows the only thing that stops her from falling off that cliff is to stay occupied, so she sets herself tasks—calling home, leaving messages for Kristin Gutmunsson at Chesterfield, leaving messages for Dr. Scott at St. Elizabeths. Bell changes his flight so he can attend the service tomorrow, then breaks into Spanish on the phone with his mother. The language has a cadence Emma finds soothing, until she remembers what Simon said about the musicality of her own voice. She stops eavesdropping, concentrates instead on cutting down the list of medical technicians by factoring in the date range.

They break for lunch and pick at their food at a table in the grove while watching a busload of National Academy students pull out on their way to the Lincoln Memorial. When Emma and Bell get back to the Cool Room, the phone is ringing and Emma has to run for it.

"Lewis." She remembers she's not officially FBI. "I mean, it's Emma Lewis here. Hi."

"Miss Lewis, I'm glad I caught you." Linda Brown sounds warm and amused on the other end of the line.

There's another noise at the door. Bell is talking to someone, and Emma has to tune it out while she and Linda Brown discuss the phrasing of Simon's advertisement. At the end of the conversation, Emma thanks her for getting back in touch on a Sunday.

"No problem." A hesitation from Brown. "Ed Cooper would've called me on a Sunday. He would've done what he had to do. Call again anytime, Miss Lewis."

Emma replaces the receiver in its cradle. When she turns around, Bell is standing with his arms crossed.

"What is it?" she asks.

"You first."

"That was Brown. No code. The message is flowery but accurate, which means the Butcher has a standing invite to visit St. Elizabeths tonight. Your turn."

"That was Martino. Raymond sent a message—he wants to see us."

"Right now?"

"Right now. Grab your jacket."

He closes the door behind them. Emma wants to ask what it was in Raymond's message that got Bell so angry. Then she decides that overall, she doesn't want to know.

The trip to Raymond's office is short and fast, too fast.

"Remember," Bell says, "we didn't hear about the asylum operation through official channels. Martino's information is all on the down-low. If Raymond asks, we're still in the dark about it."

Emma nods and faces forward, knocks.

"Come," Raymond calls.

They enter together. Raymond sits at his desk as if it's a god-like throne. Martino, aggressively neutral, stands at attention to the right. Raymond's facial expression is puckered and Emma has to take a deep breath to hold on to her anger.

"You two," Raymond says. "I understand your ID badges are still active until tomorrow, and while you're on this base you answer to me—so I'm sending you on an errand."

"What's the errand," Bell asks tonelessly. Emma suspects he is at the end of his patience with Raymond.

"Simon Gutmunsson's twin, Kristin, has been allowed visitation access to see her brother. Whatever kind of weird relationship they might have, I've allowed it because Gutmunsson agreed to cooperate with the bureau on official business."

There it is. Emma exchanges a glance with Bell. Now they know how Raymond got Simon to agree to his terms.

Raymond plucks at his tie. "Unfortunately, Kristin Gutmunsson has only agreed to meet the conditions of visitation if you two are the ones who escort her to her brother's facility."

Emma bites her lip. *Leverage, thy name is Kristin.* "And what if, considering the circumstances, we don't wish to perform escort duty?"

Raymond makes an unpleasant-looking smile. "Then, Miss Lewis, I will have you charged with obstruction of justice. Your IDs will be confiscated and you will be physically removed from this base by serving Marines. Mr. Bell can kiss his police academy spot goodbye…"

He cuts his eyes to Bell, whose jaw clenches so tight Emma can practically see his teeth through his cheek.

"…and needless to say, your per diem for time served will be null and void. So do I have an agreement on this?"

For a moment, the flames of Emma's fury burn so high it leaves her airless.

"What official business is Simon Gutmunsson assisting with?" Bell asks.

"Not your concern," Raymond says. "Just get me the girl. Bring her to St. Elizabeths before the end of the day, let her see her brother, take her home. It's a simple job. So simple even you two can't screw it up."

"We'll do it," Bell says, just as Emma is opening her mouth to fire back at Raymond. She whips her eyes in Bell's direction.

"Good." Raymond waves them away. "Well, go on then, time's a-wasting."

Bell practically hauls her out of the room, closes the door behind them both.

"What the—let go of my arm!" As Bell steers her toward the elevators, she tugs her elbow back. "Why the hell did you say yes? We could've asked for more information, delayed things somehow—"

Bell steps into the elevator car, forcing her to match him. When the door closes, he turns. "Anticipate, accept, agree—remember what Cooper said? Lewis, we can use this. We can't stop Raymond from mounting this operation—the man's set in his own mind. But this gives us a chance to talk to Kristin again, talk to Scott, get more information from Martino. More importantly, we'll be at the asylum when the operation is supposed to go down."

"You want to be at St. Elizabeths for the operation?" Emma's eyes go wide.

"Don't you?" He steps back a pace. His cheeks are pink, almost feverish-looking. "The Butcher could slip through the FBI's fingers just like he did in Annandale. Simon Gutmunsson could be planning to use the upheaval at the asylum to escape, and we know Raymond is going to underestimate him. Don't we have a responsibility to *do* something?"

"Yes, sure, but do *what*? You want to go to the asylum and—"

"I don't know yet." Bell shoves a hand through his hair. "I don't know. But I want to take this chance and run with it." He straightens, looks at her. "I want to see the Butcher go down. I want to make sure Simon Gutmunsson never gets free. If the only way we'll be allowed access is through the back door, I'll take it."

Emma calms her breathing and her mind. Does she want to treat this as an opportunity? Yes. Yes, she does. "Okay. So we do what Raymond wants and escort Kristin, which gets us inside. And from there we can keep an eye on Simon?"

"Now you're catching on." Bell makes an almost-grin that reminds her of Cooper.

Emma realizes he hasn't hit the button for Lower Ground. "We're not going to motor pool."

"Nope. We're going straight out front."

"You're taking the pickup?"

He nods. "It's got my gun in it."

Emma swallows. *This is it.*

Bell checks his watch. "It's going on fourteen hundred now, and I'll be at least two hours on the road with Kristin."

"More like three," Emma says as they reach the ground floor. "Wait—*you're* going to get Kristin? What am *I* gonna do?"

Bell exits the elevator, walking backward. "Research, groundwork—go to St. Elizabeths and talk to Gutmunsson, find out what's going on in his brain. See if you can figure out what he's planning. Talk to Scott, get an idea of how the operation is supposed to play out tonight."

Emma's striding to keep up. "Don't be late."

"Don't let Gutmunsson screw with your head," Bell counters.

"Good luck," Emma says.

"I don't say that anymore." Before he disappears out the atrium door, he meets her eyes. "Let's say 'good hunting.'"

CHAPTER THIRTY-THREE

The Rabbit has a flat.

Emma swears the parking area blue, stops to gather herself. She could ease the car down to the motor pool, but if her father knew she'd done that he'd be mortified, so she rolls up her sleeves and changes the tire herself. It slows her down for more than thirty minutes, which means she hits heavy traffic on the way to Washington.

Sitting in a jam past the Jefferson Memorial, she tries again to find that emotional connection to the Butcher's victims. She had a flash of it, enough to figure out the medical technicians list. She knows she needs that connection now more than ever, but her grasp on it is slippery. She's dangerously distracted by the knowledge of what's happening, of forces moving in the distance like thunderclouds, and also the awareness that they don't have any more time.

When she finally makes it to the asylum, the high redbrick ramparts look ominous, and a stiff breeze pushes at her in the parking area. She pushes against it as she walks for the door, pushes against the low, pulsing pressure in her mind.

In the cool of the foyer, a white-uniformed employee with a first aid kit, who is already speaking to the receptionist, makes way for

Emma to ask for Dr. Scott to be paged. She's kept waiting in the foyer for nearly twenty-five minutes. At last the woman arrives, announced by the clipped enunciation of her heels on the parquet floor.

"Miss Lewis." Scott is wearing black, as if she's in mourning, but Emma finds her calming to look at. "I'm so glad to see you. I was told you went with Mr. Bell to escort Kristin Gutmunsson."

"No." Emma feels a stab of anger toward Raymond. "Bell went alone, and I came here. I'm sorry for the confusion. Things have been...complicated over the last few days."

"I know." Scott shakes her head in disbelief. "The news about Ed Cooper's death was just awful. I'd like to attend his service, if my duties here permit."

"It's tomorrow. But I haven't...I mean, I haven't come just to tell you about that. I'd like to see Simon, if you'll allow it." Emma feels that honesty might work best with Scott today. "I don't have official permission. I'm not even really supposed to be here—"

"Miss Lewis, I've been told to restrict visitors, but if you'd like to visit Simon, you're more than welcome. It might help to settle him, given the current situation." Scott leads her to the wooden foyer door under the stairs, opens it with the long black key. They walk together through the great hall. "I received your message, that you wanted to speak to me—did you want to discuss the FBI operation here in the asylum? What do you know about it?"

"Not much. Only that Simon is part of it." Welded steel clangs shut behind Emma's back. She has to stop herself from jumping.

Scott's heels now sound brusque. "I've been ordered to empty this central section of staff and arrange an area in the old kitchen to the right of this hall for FBI personnel. Oh, and of course, I'm to surrender access to Simon's room and I don't get a say in how they'll manage his care this evening."

Scott's tone is bitter, and Emma immediately knows she needs to use that. "Letting the FBI manage Simon's procedures sounds like a bad idea."

"I'm not entirely confident that Raymond knows what he's doing. Pradeep has some concerns as well. I'm worried they won't know how to manage Simon, and...costly mistakes will be made."

Emma has to walk fast to keep up. "Is it true Simon is being transferred to another facility?"

"Paperwork has been set in motion, yes." Scott looks bitter about that, too. "The FBI wants to transfer Simon to Byberry, in Pennsylvania. I'm contesting the transfer, and I believe the Gutmunssons' lawyer is also contesting."

"How long does Simon have?"

"This may be his last night at St. Elizabeths."

"Is he aware of all this?"

"Yes."

Emma factors that in. "So what's his state of mind right now?"

"Tense," Scott admits. "Overstimulated, because Raymond has provided him with some concessions I don't usually allow. He's also nervous, I think, that the chance to see his sister might be snatched away. He hasn't seen his twin in nearly two years, reinforced by court order, and I know they were close. Here we are."

Scott raps. Emma can hear a hum beyond the oak door. As the locks rattle, she sees pale motes floating in filtered light from the barred clerestory windows high above. She has a sense that time is slowing, fracturing.

"Talk to him," Scott urges. "Be a friend. I know he can seem haughty, but it's largely a defense mechanism. He might open up a little more, and it would be a good opportunity to calm his fears."

"I'll do my best," Emma says. She wipes her palms against her jeans.

He might open up. Emma thinks that Scott means well, but Kristin has the better sense of it—*He would like to crack you open.*

The door goes wide.

The first thing she notices is the music. On the floor, just before the police barriers around Simon's cage, an old record player sits connected to a single speaker. The light in the chapel is golden, and the air is full of violins and the rich, round tones of a male voice.

Pradeep has resumed his post at the desk. He doesn't speak, just bows with his chin and extends a hand to the cell.

Simon Gutmunsson stands barefoot in his cage, one fist pressed against his chest, his face uplifted and blown with rapture. All the color is leached from his skin and hair under a shaft of afternoon sunlight. His eyes are closed, seemingly rolled back behind the lids, but when Emma opens her mouth to speak, he lifts a finger to order pause.

The music swells, crescendoes, amplified by the excellent acoustics of the room. Emma knows nothing about opera, but the tenor's voice creates a vibration in her heart that encourages tears.

When it's over, she's left blinking. The arm of the record player, with its sharp needle, has lifted automatically. Simon is already watching her.

"None shall sleep, indeed. Certainly not tonight." The finger he employed to make her wait is now lifted to his bottom lip. "Are you excited, Emma? There's going to be quite a gala here this evening—I hope you've been invited."

"My invitation seems to have been neglected," she says, still surfacing after the music. "But I've brought myself along anyway."

"And all dressed up, too. Your running shoes are looking a little worn down, though—the path to self-forgiveness is a stony one, it seems. Or maybe you've been running an honor lap for the fallen dead. Poor Agent Cooper."

The quip about Cooper stings, even though she braced for it. "Dr. Scott said you might be leaving St. Elizabeths."

"For new adventures, yes." Simon grins, moves to his desk, and settles himself on top of it. He picks through the fruit in his bowl.

"There are worse places to be than here."

"It doesn't really matter, does it, if they're all jails?" His eyes gleam, a cold flare on a vast tundra.

Emma forces herself not to recoil. "You must be looking forward to seeing Kristin."

"I'm reserving judgment. It never pays to get too excited about FBI promises." He takes an apple from the bowl, tosses it. "Did you enjoy the Puccini? It's the most hackneyed aria, but I was restricted by Dr. Scott's execrable taste."

"It's beautiful. But you know that."

"Perhaps we might attend the Kennedy Center together one day and hear something good. Consider it an open invitation." He tilts his head, clearly tickled by the idea, before returning the apple to the bowl. "But you have to catch the Butcher first, of course. Do you think he'll fall into the FBI's trap this evening? Are you here to keep watch over me, so I'm not exsanguinated in my sleep? That would be fun, like a slumber party. We can wear our pajamas—oh, look, I'm already wearing mine."

She takes a measured step closer. "I'm here to see how you are. And…to make sure you don't take advantage of the situation. I know you've got something planned, Simon."

"Do you?" He crosses his legs, resting his lower foot on the chair. "Then perhaps you're not keeping up. I'm the *bait*, you know. When the Butcher arrives to harvest my 'donation,' will the FBI rush to my rescue? I'm sure they'd be perfectly happy just to nab their target and leave me a bloodless husk."

"I'm going to make sure that doesn't happen," she says evenly. Nobody deserves a death like the Butcher's victims suffered—not even Simon.

"And ensure that I stay in my cell, yes, naturally. But it would be nice to catch the Butcher yourself. Why give all the credit to the FBI?"

"I don't care who catches him, so long as he gets caught."

"But think about it, Emma. You'd be securing your reputation with the bureau. And aside from all the professional kudos, think of the personal relief. No more anxiety about the deaths of other people hanging over your head—you'll save a fortune in therapy bills."

Simon steps down off the chair to approach the bars. The sun haloing him now turns his red lips dark and his white hair into fire. He looks like a figure in a Russian icon, bestowing blessings with the same harsh mercy.

"Do you think you understand your emotions enough to be a worthy opponent for the Butcher?" he asks. "He's not just going to walk into your arms, you know."

Emma straightens. "I don't know if I 'understand my emotions.' It shouldn't be about that. It's about following the evidence, being methodical—"

"Oh, come on, Emma—you're no plodding FBI sleuth. You're a teenager! Teenagers *feel* things. If you'd just let go of guilt, you could feel things, too. If nothing else, you'd have a proper awareness of what it was about *these* teenagers that made them so appealing to our Butcher friend....Ah, you've been trying to figure that out, haven't you?"

"Yes. It's...difficult to hold on to."

"Do you know why you can't see through the eyes of the victims, Emma? I mean, you should have total understanding. You've *been* a victim—it makes no sense at all that you're blocked."

Emma wets her lips. "Why am I blocked, then?"

"It's obvious, really. It's because you can't stand to look at yourself."

She startles. "No. I'm recovering from—"

"You're not *recovering* from Huxton, Emma." Simon waves a hand. "Oh, you tell yourself you're making progress, returning to normal, but you know in your heart it's not true. You're still that scared, wretched girl in the basement—the one you don't like very much. The one you hate to see in the mirror."

"That's not—"

"The one who *ran*." His blue eyes arrow to their target, unerring. "Ran away from all the horror and the fear, and left Huxton and the other girls behind. Ran to the police and became a hero *by accident*."

Her throat is thick. "I'm not a hero. I never said—"

"You've tried to bury her with drugs, and therapy, but it doesn't work. *That's* why you can't see the victims. Because you refuse to see yourself. To acknowledge who you've become."

"I haven't..." Her breath stutters. "I know I've changed, parts of me have—"

"Parts of you?" Simon grips the bars of his cell. "Emma, it's *all of you*. You've been inextricably altered by what you experienced in Huxton's basement. Like a chemical reaction, from the inside out. The sooner you accept it, the more free you'll feel."

She doesn't feel free. She feels like she's choking on bile. "That's a lie."

Simon's expression is kindly. "I've never lied to you, Emma. Not like the FBI. I've only ever told you the truth. If you want to catch the Butcher, you'll have to embrace your past. That scared little girl who you keep pushing away."

Her eyes are hot with shameful tears. "I'm not...I can't..."

"Of course you can—you can embrace anything, if you're desperate enough. I've embraced my own darkness. Don't you think I know what I am? But I'm one with the darkness now, not apart from it. Only Kristin is my light." His voice has changed, no longer mocking but serious. "Emma, listen to me. The girl you were is dead."

"*No.*"

"*Yes.* But you can dig into her grave and draw strength from her still. She gave you a lot of things you're going to need. The anger, for one, and the instinctual fear, and the ruthlessness you used to escape. You're going to rely on all those things when he comes."

"The Butcher?" Emma latches on to his meaning. "You're sure he's coming?"

"Of course. I've been sure for months. I've just been waiting for the day to arrive."

And suddenly the insight is there before her, glittering like a diamond. "You know who he is, don't you?"

There's a knock on the oak door. Pradeep moves from his chair to attend to it.

Simon holds her eyes. "I believe we have another visitor."

"Simon. *Tell me.*"

He angles himself away. "Do you know the story of *Turandot* at all? She has to discover the prince's name before dawn. The lyrics of the aria are particularly apt. *Il nome suo nessun saprà, e noi dovrem, ahimè, morir, morir....* I think we should listen to Pavarotti sing one more time."

"Simon?" Into the beat of silence, Kristin Gutmunsson's voice quavers out.

CHAPTER THIRTY-FOUR

Simon's sister is standing near the desk, with Bell standing close behind.

Emma catches the movement as Simon looks up. In the same moment, she realizes that he never expected Raymond to keep his promise, to allow his twin to come.

"*Kristin.*" Simon's whisper travels the length of the room. His surprise leaves him almost tenderly vulnerable.

Emma sees Kristin gasp and press her midriff. Dressed in the same costume she wore to Quantico, she looks like a glowing star in the chapel: complexion radiant with two high dots of color, white hair flowing loose. Then Simon's sister moves, faster than Bell or Pradeep can catch her, bolting forward and slipping between the sawhorses, reaching for the bars.

Emma jerks forward. "Kristin!"

But Kristin is pressing herself against the metal, clasping her brother's hands, touching his face, as Simon strains forward to kiss her cheek, press his forehead to hers. Kristin is crying. Simon's eyes are glistening. Their matched coloring makes them hard to distinguish from each other.

They really are one flesh, Emma thinks numbly. Two people connected at the most basic level, through blood and breath shared in the womb, skin and muscle and hair and nails formed from the same material.

But the division was imperfect: Instead of two mirror images, they are one being split apart—Kristin the repository of the single soul, and Simon the beneficiary of pure mind. Between them, one beating heart.

Kristin laughs through tears and Simon wipes them away, kissing her. They can't embrace but their arms are tangled through the bars.

Only Kristin is my light. After a shocked few moments of noting Simon's expression, how different it looks from normal, watching the couple feels voyeuristic. Emma ducks her head, turns to see a chagrined Pradeep, and beside him, Travis Bell.

Bell is by the desk, his face drawn tight with tension. In his black suit in the golden room, he seems as out of place as a crow in a field of daisies. His eyes are glued to Kristin and Simon, but primarily to Simon. Emma doesn't know if Bell has seen Simon Gutmunsson in person before.

Emma walks to him, her legs unsteady. "Bell."

"Yeah." Replying but not replying, utterly distracted.

"Travis, look at me." She squeezes his arm and he drags his gaze to hers. There's nothing she can say to make this better, but she can offer him relief. "You don't have to stay in the room. I can keep an eye out for Kristin."

"I...I wanted..." Bell's gaze drifts back to the Gutmunssons like his eyes are magnetized. "I should be here." His voice is husky, though, and pain vibrates from him in waves.

"No," Emma says. "Not if it hurts this much."

"Do you think he knows what he's done?" Bell whispers. "How many people he's destroyed?"

Emma's first reaction is to say, *Yes—he just doesn't care.* But that would probably be too much for Bell right now.

He wrenches himself sideways. "I think you're right—I should step out."

Which, of course, is the perfect time for Simon to call through the bars. "Excuse me? Are you Mr. Bell? My sister has instructed me to thank you."

Bell stops but doesn't turn around. Standing near enough to touch, Emma feels his body shudder as he speaks over his shoulder. "No thanks necessary."

"On the contrary," Simon says brightly. "You've reunited me with my twin—that surely deserves some acknowledgment." His voice changes. "Do we know each other?"

"Get out," Emma whispers sharply to Bell. "Now."

"Mr. Bell..." Simon draws the syllables out. "I remember the names that were included on my charge sheet when I was prosecuted. You're his son, aren't you."

Bell turns slowly to face his father's murderer. "Yes."

"Simon." Kristin pulls on her brother's arm.

Simon makes a grimace. "Well, this *is* a pickle. I was preparing to be effusive, which I'm sure would be unwelcome *now*. You don't look anything like him, you know."

"I know." Bell's voice is a rasp.

"Ah," Simon says, "you hate me. That's understandable. But you've done me a great service by bringing me my sister, so let's call it water under the bridge." He cocks his head. "It's disappointing, isn't it, when you realize that the terms of judicial punishment don't adequately align with one's need for personal retribution. What should I have gotten from the court, do you think? Firing squad? Hanging?"

Bell wets his lips. "Death by torture."

Emma's head turns fast. Bell's face is completely impassive.

Simon only smiles. "And you'd be the first to carry the hot pincers from the fire." He releases a short laugh. "I like you, Mr. Bell. Let's not make a habit of meeting like this—it's socially awkward."

"Simon, *stop*," Kristin whispers. Even from this distance, Emma can hear her perfectly because of the room's excellent acoustics.

Her brother's gaze is indulgent. "How many times have you said that to me, do you think? You know it's impossible."

Kristin shakes the bars between them. "I wish you weren't in this cage."

"The last time I saw a tree was more than a year ago." He cups her cheek. "You're a balm to the soul, you know."

"I miss you so much." Kristin's voice is breaking.

"Listen to opera with me? We can imagine we're curled up on the lawn at home." Simon's eyes are bright and his hand on Kristin's face trembles. Before Emma has a chance to reconcile this softer side of him with the side she knows, he shakes it off and lifts his head. "Pradeep can work the record player. He'll succumb to apoplexy if we don't give him something to do—look at him there, wringing his hands. It's already a huge distress to him that you're inside the barricade."

"It's too late for me to step back now."

"And you never would." He kisses Kristin's soft cheek. "It's one of the reasons I love you."

Emma feels compelled to look away, and the nearest diversion is Bell. "What's happening outside?"

Bell seems relieved for the chance to focus on something else. "Raymond's arrived with the SWAT team. Martino's here, too." He lifts his chin at the Gutmunssons. "I don't think they have much time."

Emma remembers what's more important. "Listen. There's something else you need to know—"

But now another knock on the door interrupts, this time a booming pound. Pradeep is looking increasingly irritated. When the door is opened, Dr. Scott stands beside Agent Martino in the entryway.

"Uh, I've been told it's time to clear the room," Martino says, speaking loudly for everyone's benefit. "Miss Lewis, Mr. Bell, Miss Gutmunsson, time to go."

"Let the twins say goodbye, at least," Dr. Scott admonishes. She lifts her eyes to Emma's. "Miss Lewis, walk with me?"

Emma's torn: reluctant to leave Simon and his tantalizing information, reluctant to leave Bell alone. But Scott is wearing an urgent look, and Pradeep and Martino should have enough combined muscle to hold Bell back if anything happens. She steps out of the room, keeps pace with Scott's clicking strides in the great hall.

"I have a SWAT team in my courtyard, Miss Lewis, and I don't like it. How did Simon seem to you?"

Emma considers saying, *He's as much of an asshole as always*, but it probably wouldn't go down well. "He's angry that the FBI is using him."

"I know how he feels." Scott's lips purse as they walk through the rolling steel gate. "Raymond is being argumentative. I had to draw a hard line about keeping essential staff in the building, and as my presence is not considered essential, he refuses to let me supervise."

Two black-clad personnel—Emma recognizes the SWAT markings and gear—have been deployed to supervise exiting staff near the foyer door beneath the stairs. Through that door, Emma can see straight out to the main entrance, where the sunlight is starting to weaken and ebb.

As Scott stares at the SWAT men, her mouth gets tighter. "Miss Lewis, I have the impression that no one is actually looking out for *Simon*. That he's expendable. I have a duty of care, and I'm worried that the entire focus of this stakeout is on catching the Butcher, and if Simon's personal safety is compromised, then that's just too bad."

It's the break Emma's been waiting for.

"I can help you." She allows the words she's been holding in to spill out. "Let me back into the building—me and Bell. We can take up a concealed position nearby, somewhere out of the action, and keep an eye on Simon."

Scott blinks in response. "That's...Do you know what you're suggesting?"

"Yes." Emma holds the line doggedly. "You trusted Cooper, now I'm asking you to trust me. Let me be your ally—if Raymond won't let you stay, *I* can look out for Simon. Put me somewhere out of sight, put me in a side room, I don't care. But someone needs to be here. It's the only way to hold Raymond accountable." *And to get the information about the Butcher's identity out of Simon.*

There's a pause. Scott presses her lips. "You'd stay out of sight?"

"Yes." Emma keeps her voice firm.

"How are you going to get past FBI personnel? They're closing off the side entrances to everybody. You can't just walk in the front door."

"This is a big facility, Dr. Scott. And you know it better than anyone."

Emma leaves the comment hanging and Scott bites. After a quick perusal of eyes in the hall, she turns sideways to retrieve a heavy lanyard from inside the vee of her jacket. She unhooks two small keys from the ring on the lanyard, tucks the rest away.

"Take these." Scott slips the keys into Emma's nearest hand. "On the far west side of the complex is an outside alley that leads to the superintendent's residence—my residence. Go through the house and the back gate, and you'll be inside the walls. The rear door of the wing adjacent to this center building is painted brown. I'll arrange for someone to meet you there."

Emma grips Scott's free hand. "Thank you."

"You care for Simon, don't you? As a friend?" Scott's gaze is searching.

Emma fights her immediate reaction, which is to jerk back in horror. Yes, Scott has a duty of care. But she seems so *invested* in Simon...too invested, in Emma's opinion.

The way Simon has influenced even someone as intelligent as Scott makes Emma doubt the wisdom of her plan for a moment—until she remembers it's their only option.

"Simon's . . . complicated," she says finally. "But I don't like the way the FBI is running this operation." *And I want to make sure Simon stays in his cage, where he belongs.*

"There are a lot of damaged people within these walls, Miss Lewis, and it's my job to look after every one of them—even the complicated ones." Scott gives her a nod. "Good luck."

Scott walks off, and the SWAT team waves Emma forward, toward sundown.

CHAPTER THIRTY-FIVE

Mike Martino finds Donald Raymond unpleasant to be around. He thinks the man looks like a bulldog walking on its hind legs, and Raymond's manner does nothing but exacerbate that impression. Martino doesn't mind taking orders—he's used to taking orders—but the way Raymond has steamrolled through this operation, his treatment of Scott and of Cooper's students, doesn't fill Martino with confidence.

Raymond is currently strong-arming Scott over personnel access. "Dr. Scott, forget the keys business—you've got no reason to worry about your patients. This center building is like a goddamn fortress. We have SWAT—all trained in emergency first aid—stationed inside, in the old kitchen, and more outside the building. Our agent in the front foyer is protected with Kevlar. Your man in the control booth is locked down in his room. Gutmunsson is locked in his cage. The way I see it, the Butcher comes in, SWAT takes him down, problem solved."

"I may not be considered essential supervisory staff, but I'm *legally required* to have medical and control systems staff on-site in order to operate—and they need keys." Scott appeals to Martino. "Even if they have no cause to use them, there are some things my remaining staff needs just to be able to function, and that's one of them."

Martino hesitates. The fact that he doesn't actually like Raymond makes his decision easier. "Sir, I think we should just give the paramedic a set of keys. He's gonna be stuck in the control booth with the technician most of the night anyway. And if there's an issue and he needs to attend to someone, it might come in useful if he doesn't need to be escorted—"

"Oh goddammit. Fine, then." Raymond expands like an air bladder. "But this is my last concession, Dr. Scott."

"It's the last concession I'll ask for," she replies coolly. She unhooks a large keychain from the lanyard around her neck, detaches a set of keys on a ring, and hands them to Martino. "Contact me if there are any problems—you have my phone number. I'll be monitoring the situation from the east wing. I sincerely hope you know what you're doing."

She walks off. Raymond grinds his teeth as he turns Martino's way. "Where's the paramedic? I want him locked into the control booth."

"I'll find him, sir."

"And are those damn kids off the site?"

"Yes, sir." Martino consults his clipboard. "They should be taking Kristin Gutmunsson back to her facility right now."

"Thank fuck. That's three less inconveniences I have to deal with."

"Yes, sir. Ah, the paramedic is right over there, sir. I'll go speak to him."

Martino pats the lapel of his jacket as he walks toward the

building entrance. The list of MTs that Travis Bell faxed over is sitting in his inside pocket. He gave a copy to Jack Kirby in Behavioral Science, for follow-up, and he's been waiting for a spare moment to examine it himself, but no spare moments have come: He's been bustling after Raymond for nearly thirty straight hours. It might prove unnecessary anyway, if everything goes well tonight.

"Gentlemen," he says when he reaches the two remaining asylum staff members, "we're all set. Mr. Hannity, is there anything else you need?"

"Nope, I'm all good." Doug Hannity, a stocky man of about sixty-five, doesn't look like a smooth-hand "technician" but more like what he is, an old jail screw who knows how to press the right buttons.

"Okay, SWAT has wired up the control booth so they can share vision with the facility's monitors," Martino explains. "They'll give commands to you by radio handset."

"I tell you, I've been working at this facility goin' on fifteen years—I ain't never seen a brouhaha like this before."

"Hopefully it'll all be taken care of quick, Mr. Hannity. You're ready to take up your spot? That's great. Now, Mr. Ashton, I've been informed that you need keys, so here they are." Martino hands over Scott's keys on the ring, makes a check mark on his clipboard notes.

"That's incredibly helpful, thank you." Ashton is a lean, tanned guy, probably in his forties but so fit it's hard to tell. He must get plenty of exercise running around after patients here at the asylum. Ashton attaches the keys to a lanyard around his neck. "I'm just going to take a pit stop, then I'll go straight to the control booth. Doug can let me in."

"Good idea," Martino says. "But I won't check you off my list until I hear from you both that you're locked in. Get on the handset and inform us when you're present and accounted for."

"Will do. Oh, and Agent Martino, you've got it switched around on your clipboard there. Ashton is my middle name."

"Really? Ah crap, sorry about that." Martino points. "So this is you?"

"Yeah, that's me." The man smiles. "Hoyt. Anthony Hoyt."

CHAPTER THIRTY-SIX

They meet up at a community ballpark off Savannah Street SE as the sun is disappearing.

Emma arrives first. She's been trying to stay calm, but her throat is very dry. She doesn't get out of her car until she sees the headlights from the pickup. When she reaches Bell's truck, she hears the sounds of argument.

"...no way we can go back in there with you, you know that, right?" Bell winds down his window, so Emma can see and hear the ruckus.

"No, I *don't* know that, and I don't agree," Kristin says. "He's *my* brother, and you're telling me that I have to just sit here and wait?"

"Yes, that's exactly what I'm telling you. Me and Emma know what we're doing." Bell glances out with a *Help me* expression.

Kristin has her arms crossed and a very uncharacteristic scowl. "You *don't* know what you're doing. You literally *just* said to me that you're going behind the FBI's back on this. There's no valid reason why I can't come along."

"Except you're not FBI, you don't know how to defend yourself, you're emotionally compromised because Simon is your brother, and I swear to god, I don't understand why you think this is such a great idea!"

"What if there's a problem? What if you two get arrested for interfering and I'm sitting here, useless, when I could be inside helping? What if Simon's being disagreeable—"

"Simon's pretty much always disagreeable," Emma points out.

"But that's something I can help with!" Kristin's scowl becomes stubborn. "If you're not going to take me with you, I'll...I'll follow behind you anyway! You'll have to tie me up to make me stay in the car!"

Emma sighs. This is wasting time they don't have. "Bell, let her come. We might need help with Simon, she's right."

"Lewis—"

"Talk with me."

Emma walks toward the ballpark. She hears Bell exit the car, then his heavier tread as he catches up to her near home plate.

"Having Kristin come with us is a bad idea," he grumbles.

"What do you want to do, Bell, lock her in the trunk?" Emma folds her arms, holding herself together. "It's less dangerous to have her with us than chasing along behind."

"Shit. Fine. Scott gave you the keys? Okay, so what are we waiting for?"

"Night." Emma breathes in deep, looks around. A poisonous orange tints the sky, and the air is still and heavy. "Travis, are you okay? You just met your dad's murderer."

Bell focuses off toward second base. "I'm okay."

"Is that the first time you've met him in person?"

"Yes."

She can see in his face that this is all he's going to say. Better to stop tapping this vein. "Okay. There's something else I need to tell you, and it's the most important thing."

"What's more important than—"

"Simon Gutmunsson knows who the Butcher is."

Bell's head turns so fast she fears whiplash. "He what? How is that possible?"

"I don't know. He wouldn't tell me more than that."

"He could be bluffing. He could be goading you—"

"To what purpose? Bell, I'm starting to think we've read this situation all wrong. Simon and the Butcher have been communicating, maybe for longer than we realized. I think they've been playing a kind of game, and we've let ourselves get caught in the cat-and-mouse between two sociopaths."

"Fuck." Bell's hands are hooked on his hips, his jacket pushed back in the same way as the day they first met. "That's great."

"Tonight is the endgame, and whoever makes it out alive is the winner." Emma lets her arms drop. "But Simon's in a cell—that's an obvious handicap. And Raymond using him as bait like this is wrong."

"You feel *sorry* for Gutmunsson?"

"In a way." She concedes it reluctantly. "But what matters is that Simon knows the Butcher's identity. Simon is being transferred tomorrow—when he goes, his information goes with him. And if this operation goes bad, like Annandale, and the Butcher escapes again, goes to ground..." She pauses to give the idea the weight it demands. "We *need* Simon's information, Bell. Now more than ever. And Raymond has no idea what Simon's capable of. If he gets free, we'll be wishing like hell we only had the Butcher to worry about."

A moment of quiet, into which they both breathe.

Emma stops gnawing her lip, walks back toward the truck, knowing Bell will follow. In the pickup, Kristin Gutmunsson's hands are splayed on the bench seat as if she's trying to glue herself down.

"I'm coming with you. I won't let you—"

"Kristin, it's fine." Emma leans on the rolled-down passenger window. "We talked about it, we decided you can come."

"You'll really let me come?" Kristin's big eyes glisten. "Simon is...I know he can be awful, but I want to help my brother. I want to be there for him."

"It's okay, but listen, Kristin—you have to follow our lead. This will be dangerous." *So dangerous.* Emma swallows, presses on. "If you can't follow instructions, we really can't bring you along. We just can't."

"I can follow instructions!" Kristin clasps her hands together. "Oh, thank you! And there's something else I have to tell you. Not about Simon—about the Butcher."

"What's that?" Emma exchanges a glance with Bell through the other window of the car.

"It's just impressions. From the photos you showed me, and the reports I've been following...Like, I know the Butcher wants to be in control of things. And I think he likes knives over guns."

Emma frowns. "Why do you say that?"

"He didn't kidnap the teenagers at gunpoint, did he? He knocked them out with some drug—"

"Ether," Bell supplies. "That's right."

"So I think he's less comfortable with guns. And he's very particular. He has the victims arranged just so, the way he likes them.... I think he'll know what the inside of the asylum looks like."

Emma pauses. "Again—why?"

"He's a very careful, meticulous person who makes precise plans. If you're planning something, you have to know the location it will all happen." Kristin nods, confirming to herself. "He'll know the inside of St. Elizabeths. He'll have a schematic, or a map of the fire exits or something." Her fingers twine together. "You may not need any of that information, but if it helps you, or if it helps Simon..."

"Okay," Emma says. "Thank you for sharing that. Now I need to ask one more time—are you sure you want to come with us? You don't want to stay in my car, where it's safe?"

"No," Kristin says, resolute. "If I wanted safe, I would have stayed at Chesterfield. I don't want safe. I want my brother."

Emma catches Bell's eye. They meet again near the front grille of the truck.

Bell seems unsure. "What do you make of all that?"

"I don't know." Emma keeps her voice low. "But she had good insight about the Berryville scene, and she lived with a killer almost her entire life. She's got an instinct for it—better than mine. Her information may not be useful, but you never know."

"Okay." Bell gazes back toward the ballpark's outfield. "So we need to sneak into an asylum and grill a sociopathic liar for information while making sure he doesn't engineer a jailbreak. And we also have to avoid another multiple murderer, who—according to Kristin—might know the asylum better than we do."

"That's right."

"And we'll already be watching out for SWAT, who might shoot us by accident if they run into us. . . . Lewis, are we crazy to be doing this?"

"It's starting to look that way." She makes an uncontrolled huff of laughter, although nothing about this is funny.

Bell's face is shadowed in the twilight. "Emma, are you okay going back into the asylum? I mean, it kinda makes sense for me to go in, but you don't—"

"Have you ever dodged a serial killer, Travis?" Emma feels a tide rising inside her, a wave of tension and fear that washes higher as each minute passes. "Because I have. And you need me in there if you want to get out of St. Elizabeths tonight."

He nods, glances down. "Are you scared?"

"Yes." Her voice trembles. "Are you?"

He holds up his hands. They're shaking. "Real tough guy, huh?"

She makes a tiny smile as she puts her hands over his, as he curls his fingers into fists. "Travis," she says. "You're doing it right."

CHAPTER THIRTY-SEVEN

Hoyt has studied the literature on surveillance psychology, researched perception, attention deficits, and team effectiveness under stress. He's determined that there are a few key moments in the timeline of a stakeout. He employed this information to useful effect in Annandale, and now he is in the quick of it once again.

The moments immediately after a stakeout is established are good, because everyone is still settling into their positions and nobody expects an immediate threat. People are alert, though, not fuzzy with boredom and the wear of held tension, so he has to be careful.

There is no longer direct entry into Gutmunsson's room via the old sacristy; that doorway was bricked up in 1962. Visitors must now cross through the foyer, then the great hall and its steel barricade to the oak door to see Simon. During Hoyt's time working here, it's been a great inconvenience that Gutmunsson's room has only one entry, and that the man employed to guard it is never lax.

The very helpful Agent Martino informed him that there are six SWAT officers stationed in the courtyard to the east of the center building. An additional four SWAT officers are stationed inside, in the former kitchen on the east side of the great hall. Their job is to watch the camera footage beamed from the asylum's control booth monitors.

SWAT personnel will hold their positions until they catch sight of the target. At that point, they will instruct the control booth technician to close the barred gate, then they'll call in their courtyard reinforcements and execute a dynamic entry through the kitchen and into the great hall.

Including the command agent in the surveillance van out front, the female agent in the foyer, and Martino, the number of active personnel is blown out to thirteen. If Hoyt thinks in terms of numbers of combatants, their positioning, the kinds of weaponry they're wielding, and the strategies they're inclined to use, he would be put off. It looks like a complicated problem. But the beauty of his own plan is in its simplicity.

Using the asylum's own special high-security internal system, he's going to lock them all out.

The front foyer has no CCTV cameras; the FBI is relying on the female agent impersonating the receptionist to keep them informed. The foyer is not as warmly illuminated as usual, but the agent at the desk has a small lamp positioned to allow her to "work." A phone sits on the desk as well, plus a box of Kleenex and the ledger that Hannah Lempki—the real receptionist—uses when she herself sits in that chair.

Hoyt walks toward the desk from the left-hand side of the foyer, on his return from the men's bathroom in the west-wing corridor, where he washed and dried his hands thoroughly.

"Ma'am." He bobs his head at the agent on the desk as he approaches.

"You're heading to the control booth now?" The woman is the

same age as Hannah—midthirties—but her dowdy tweed skirt suit does nothing to disguise her physical fitness and musculature, and she does not look like a receptionist. "Will you contact Agent Martino to let him know, so he can check you off? Or should I call him?"

The control booth door is behind and to the far right of the sign-in desk. He is passing behind the receptionist's chair now. "Thanks, I can do it."

"Great."

He times it so he is only one step past her. "Uh, excuse me, ma'am?"

His position means she's forced to swivel awkwardly to face him. "Yes?"

When she turns, his hand darts out with the scalpel. The No. 22 scalpel blade is the largest on the market and is customarily used for bronchus resection; he uses it to open up her windpipe and carotid artery in one quick slash. He's very good at this now. Before she has a chance to scramble for her weapon, she is already bleeding out.

Once she's gone, he positions her so she's slumped on the desk. Using a Kleenex, he removes her gun and tucks it into the desk drawer, making a grimace of distaste while handling the gun. Then he checks himself: a little blood spatter on his shirt cuff and the back of his hand. He rolls his cuffs, wipes his hand with another Kleenex, puts both tissues in the wastebasket, and plucks another to take with him.

He steps smartly over to the front entrance door of the asylum, closes it, and locks it with the two heavy bolts at the top and bottom that are relics of another age. Then he resumes his progress.

It's time to call Martino and deal with Hannity in the control booth.

CHAPTER THIRTY-EIGHT

Now, here is Evelyn Scott's home in the moonlight. A big pecan tree grows nearby; Scott's late-model Volvo is parked by the white-railed porch and portico. It's an old house, the roof slightly sagging.

"Are we breaking and entering?" Kristin's bright hair is covered by Emma's scarf.

"Just entering," Emma says. "No breaking."

She and Kristin exit the truck. Bell leans over and unlocks the glove compartment, retrieves his gun belt and revolver. The gun is a stainless steel, double-action Colt Python with a six-inch barrel and rubber combat grips. It's significantly heavier than what he's been shooting with Emma, and he's had a lot of practice with it. He gets out and secures the truck, buckles the belt around his hips. Looks up to see Emma watching from the portico.

"Come on," she calls softly. "Door's open."

The house is dim inside. A standing lamp illuminates the downstairs living room, and the curtains are closed. They move through to the kitchen and the back door. The outside air in the rear yard is cooler, and the back garden is overgrown. A path through tall bushes; Bell winces at the sound of three pairs of shoes on gravel. Then a large wrought-iron gate with a modern lock, set into high redbrick walls. Emma works the gate open and they file through to a lawn area.

There's a short disagreement over which way to go.

"SWAT could be patrolling nearby," Bell says quietly. "Keep the volume down."

Being on the lawn of the asylum from a different side is disorienting, and the buildings loom larger than he remembers. Bell struggles to get a concrete sense of where they are. He's not as familiar with the asylum as Emma, and he hopes this won't disadvantage them further.

Emma jogs forward to scout, then back to lead the way. The long, flat expanse of the west-wing wall stretches out to the right, dotted by barred windows. They're looking for a brown door and they find it at the top of a set of wooden service stairs, deep in shadow.

"Do we just knock?" Kristin whispers.

Emma taps gently and in under a minute, the door opens. It's the Sikh man who stood at attention in Gutmunsson's room. *Pradeep.* Bell's glad he remembers the name.

"There are only supposed to be two," Pradeep says, scanning them.

"I know." Kristin, sotto voce. "It's my fault, I made them bring me along."

"She was going to follow us. We had no choice." Bell hears how his voice sounds heavy. He wishes more than anything that Kristin had stayed in Emma's Rabbit.

Pradeep ushers them inside an antebellum-style hallway. High ceilings and a gloomy interior that looks like every horror-movie-asylum nightmare Bell has ever had.

"You must be very quiet." Pradeep's voice is low, rumbling. "Residents are sleeping. Come this way, please."

They walk down the dark hallway in the asylum, closed doors on each side. Somebody behind one of the doors is moaning in their sleep. Bell feels goose bumps pop on his skin, lengthens his stride.

Pradeep escorts them to a small wooden door. "This leads to a room off the great hall. Once I lock this door behind you, I must return to my duties here in this wing. I cannot give you the key to open the door—it does not open from the other side."

"That's fine," Emma says. Bell's not convinced it's fine. "Thank you, Pradeep."

"You have always been considerate of Mr. Gutmunsson. I wish you well." The man's bearing is upright, stately. He unlocks the door, then notices Bell's gun belt. "Ah. That may not go through."

"Excuse me?"

"The weapon. It is expressly forbidden in the facility."

"SWAT has guns," Bell points out.

"You are not SWAT personnel. I am sorry, but I cannot allow it."

Bell holds himself carefully. Patience and low voices. "You want us to go into a situation like this with no weapons?"

"Sir." Pradeep's dark beard and mustache are the background against which his eyes glitter. "You are here only to observe, correct? And Mr. Gutmunsson cannot think there is an opportunity to gain access to a weapon. The result could be very bad. Very bad. You cannot go through the door with the weapon."

Bell's frustration gnashes at him. Surrendering the Colt seems about as good an idea as cutting off his hands. Then Emma gives him a look that seems to say, *I need you more than I need the gun.* Bell sighs.

He unbuckles the gun belt. "This was my father's."

"I will be careful with it," Pradeep promises. He holds the gun belt correctly, a man familiar with weapons. This reassures Bell a little.

They file through the open gap—Bell goes last. There is a significant moment of transition: The room they enter is much colder than the one they've just left. The girls stick to the wall. Bell turns to thank Pradeep.

"Sat Sri Akaal," the man says. "I wish you good fortune."

The door closing behind them feels very final.

CHAPTER THIRTY-NINE

It was a shame about Hannity.

Hoyt arranges the man's head off to the side of the control desk, so the blood doesn't foul the switches, and tries not to feel bad. He hasn't ever killed someone he's worked with before, and sometimes Hannity spoke about his grandchildren.

But then Hoyt reminds himself that he's about to visit Simon Gutmunsson in his cell, and the concerns go away.

For a moment, his anticipation of the evening's upcoming events blots out even the chirps and buzzes of the radio handset on the floor. Awareness returns and he collects the handset, switches it off. He turns off the cameras and monitors, too. Now the FBI has no vision inside the asylum.

He felt stymied, at first, when he heard about the FBI operation, but then he realized: Why not use this? He's comfortable with all the nooks and crannies in the asylum, he knows the back-end processes of security, and he's had plenty of opportunity to familiarize himself with the workings of the control desk during his last four months' employment here. He's perfectly placed to take advantage of the FBI-created change in routine.

Now he's about to enact the final step in his arrangements. He stands over the desk, surveying the dials and switches, then leans forward and—with his finger covered by a tissue—presses a single red button. It's marked CENTRAL EXTERNAL: ALL CLOSE.

He's just locked all the external doors for the center building, including the doors from either wing.

His Kleenex-covered finger dances over other buttons, to a button that locks the door from the old asylum kitchen into the great hall. He presses that. Now those four SWAT officers are locked behind the massive kitchen door. Another switch opens the metal gate in the hall—he flicks that, too. He imagines the steel-barred rollers sliding open, smiles in delight.

Is there anything he's missed? The old-fashioned doors to some of the small internal rooms off the great hall are still unlocked, as well as the foyer door under the stairs, but he will remedy this manually.

He looks around at the blinking lights and the dead monitors, the dead man on the padded swivel chair, the quiet radio handset. The FBI will be wondering what the hell is going on. Time to move.

He turns and leaves the control room.

CHAPTER FORTY

Pradeep has sent them into an old lobotomy and autopsy theater.

There is a stink of mildew in the small room. Emma sees a tile floor, stainless steel shelving, peeling paint on the walls. Wire-covered windows let in moonlight that glints off a steel surgery table bolted to the floor's center.

Kristin has a hand pressed over her mouth.

"It's okay," Emma whispers. "We'll be out of here soon. Bell?"

Bell steps carefully around old surgical lights, past the horrifying table to a set of skinny double doors on the right. He tries one of the doorknobs for give, nods.

Kristin points, whimpering. "There's . . . there's . . ."

At the opposite side of the room, the square hatches of the steel body lockers—six in a row—are set into the wall. Emma wishes fervently that Kristin hadn't noticed that. She wishes she herself hadn't noticed that.

Emma screws her nerve in place. "Come on, let's move."

But when they pick their way over to Bell, he's frowning. "Hear that?"

"What?"

He cracks the door a scant half inch, closes it again. "The big jail gate in the great hall just slid open."

"Let's get out of here," Kristin whispers. She's tense as a plucked wire.

"Wait." Emma turns back to Bell. "Maybe they're setting up a direct access path for the Butcher?"

Bell's frown deepens. "I thought they were gonna open the gate later."

"Maybe they changed strategy."

"Maybe." Bell's expression says he finds this doubtful.

"Let's just worry about one thing at a time," Emma says. "First, we get the Butcher's identity from Simon."

She lifts her chin and Bell opens the door properly, wide enough for them to slip through. The great hall is dark and echoing. She and Kristin huddle by one of the giant columns while Bell closes their point of exit. Emma can see the line of steel bars behind them; over Kristin's shoulder, the chapel entrance. Even from here, it's very obvious that the reinforced oak door has been left open by the FBI.

Simon's room is always guarded and always locked. That it is no longer either of those things feels so fundamentally wrong that it kicks off a warning siren in Emma's brain, starting low and getting more strident with each passing second.

Kristin sees the line of Emma's eyes, turns. Her gaze fixes on the oak door, and her face is yearning. She tugs in that direction; Emma holds her fast.

"Wait for Bell."

"I'm here." His face is dim in the dark hall, only the whites of his eyes showing clear. "Let's go."

They step out of the shadow of the column, and when Emma turns her head to peek behind them she sees—

A man in a white uniform shirt and maroon trousers standing in the center of the hall.

Her gasp is like a gunshot, and she jumps back so fast she nearly knocks Kristin over.

"*What the*—" Bell jerks sideways, in front of Emma and Kristin. His hand goes straight to his hip, clenches on nothing.

The man's hands are raised—one of them is palm out; the other clutches a small gray pouch marked with a red first aid cross. He is in his forties, tanned, lean, and utterly shocked to see them there. "Who the hell are you?"

"Who the hell are *you*?" Bell retorts.

The man looks scandalized, then laughs. "Holy shit, I'm—" He laughs again, presses his free palm to his chest, then collects himself. "Jesus. Okay, I'm Clive Ross, I'm the rostered paramedic on staff. Did you know this section of the facility is on lockdown? What the hell are you kids doing here?"

Emma is still getting her heartbeat under control. But she recalls Scott's mention of essential staff. "We . . . we came in from the other wing. We—"

"I just want to see my brother," Kristin says plaintively.

Ross looks flabbergasted. "I'm sorry, Miss . . . ?"

"Gutmunsson. My name is Kristin Gutmunsson, I'm Simon's sister."

Emma would like to quietly strangle her.

Ross grimaces. "Miss Gutmunsson, I'm really sorry. But visiting hours are over, and there's some kind of police operation happening tonight, and I can't…Look, you folks will have to leave. I could get into a lot of trouble with Dr. Scott if you're here, and the police seem really serious."

Kristin's eyes are imploring. "*Please.* I've come such a long way, and I just want to see him for a moment."

"This isn't…" Ross scratches his head. "No. Again, I wish I could let you stay. But I'm gonna have to contact the law enforcement people about getting you escorted out."

Oh shit. Emma's panic of a moment before is now replaced by the greasy feeling of disappointment and frustration.

"Do you have to contact the LEOs?" Bell looks frustrated, too. "You can't just walk us through to the east wing and—"

"I'm afraid not." Ross shakes his head sadly. "I'm really sorry, but it's my job. Where did you come in from? The old lobotomy room?"

"Yes." Emma feels sick. They were so damn *close* to getting the information they needed out of Simon!

"Okay, look," Ross says. "I have to go talk to the police—they might need to send someone in for you. How about you go back into the lobotomy room, and I'll—"

"I'm not going back in there!" Kristin shudders. "I'm not staying in that room. If you put me in there, I'll just go down to my brother's room as soon as you leave." There's steel in her spine, and she looks uniquely determined, and for the first time Emma's grateful Kristin came along.

Ross narrows his eyes. "Well, if you won't stay put…Look, how about this. I can walk you down to Mr. Gutmunsson's room. I'll have to lock you in, because of security concerns, but if you wait there for me to get back, then at least you'll have a few minutes with him, okay?"

"Oh, that would be wonderful," Kristin says, her eyes brimming.

That will have to be long enough, Emma thinks. She and Bell exchange glances. She's still shocked that Kristin has been the key to getting them all the way in to see her brother.

"No problem." Ross steps closer, tucking his medical pouch under one arm. He pulls a lanyard with an attached set of keys over his head. "Uh, come on this way."

There's only another twenty feet before the oak door. Emma's already considering how she's going to wrangle the information they need out of Simon before they're escorted out of the building—but at least they'll be out before the Butcher's anticipated arrival.

She can hardly believe they got caught and they're *still* getting a chance to do this. It puts the idea of dealing with Raymond outside into perspective. She can just ignore Raymond, she decides. She can make herself do that. Getting the Butcher's name is more important than her pride.

"Again, I'm real sorry about all this." Ross's sleeves are rolled to the elbow; he has the tight, hard muscle of a gym junkie. "It's a bit crazy here tonight. Man, when I saw you, I really jumped. That took years off my life, no kidding. Okay, here we go."

He stands at the open entry to Simon's room, ushers them in. They mill near Pradeep's desk. There are subtle differences in the room. The record player and speaker are both gone. The pincer tool is still suspended on the wall, but the desk, bare of objects, has its chair pushed in tidily. The lights inside have been darkened; before Emma can locate Simon in the dimness of his cage, Ross speaks again.

"Uh, would you mind just…" Ross lifts his chin toward the door.

Bell pushes the heavy oak until Ross can grab the handle.

"Thanks." Ross fits the key in the outside lock, gives them a sheepish smile. "Thanks again for being so cooperative. I'm gonna lock this door now, but I'll be back with the police in a few minutes. Remember to follow the rules in here—don't go past the barrier. Okay. One sec."

The door fits into its jamb and they lose Ross's face. Emma hears him turn the key, tumblers clanking into place. As soon as they're locked in, a noise starts up—a series of slow, mocking claps.

Emma turns around.

"Oh, well done. Nicely played." Simon is reclining on his bed, barefoot in his usual way. A single dull spotlight on the far side of the cell casts shadows into the loose folds of his white T-shirt and white asylum pants. He looks as if he's applauding a particularly terrible fault stroke in a game of croquet. "Emma, you never cease to amuse."

Emma goes up to the barricade sawhorses. She still hasn't forgiven him for psychoanalyzing her earlier. "Sure. Creeping around a mental asylum in the dark—I can't imagine a more entertaining way to spend my Sunday night."

"It's keeping *me* entertained, at least. I see you've brought the bloodthirsty Mr. Bell along. And—" He sits himself up. "*Emma.* Why did you bring my sister with you?"

"Don't blame Emma. I lobbied to come." Kristin walks around Bell, who seems reluctant to get closer than Pradeep's desk, and strolls up to the barricade, pushing back Emma's scarf. "Goodness, Simon, look at you—you're so skinny. Don't they feed you properly?"

"If I told you about the food here, you'd cry."

"Poor Simon."

It's still jarring to see Kristin slip under the barricade and go straight up to the bars of the cell. Even more jarring to see Simon meet her there, to see them hold hands and press foreheads.

"You shouldn't have come," Simon whispers. "Go out again right now."

"I can't. The man locked the door behind us. You're stuck with me."

"Tonight will get scary. You know how you hate scary."

"They're taking us out in a minute." Kristin cups his jaw. "And I can be brave if I get to see you again."

Emma glances away to Bell, whose hand slides automatically to his hip as he stares at Simon and Kristin, until he remembers again that the gun isn't there.

Simon chucks his sister under the chin. "Kristin, be a dear and have a look in that big desk over there for my pack of cigarettes? I haven't been allowed any for days and I'm *gasping*."

"Sure." She makes an indulgent smile and meanders off toward the desk.

Emma waits until Kristin has begun her search for the cigarettes before turning back to face Simon. "Okay, let's make this easy for everybody. Tell us who the Butcher is and we'll get Kristin out of here as soon as possible."

Simon's eyes are still following Kristin. "Do you have a favorite fairy tale, Emma? I've always loved the old German one 'Brother and Sister.' Two children run away from their evil stepmother and wander lost in the woods. But the stepmother bewitches all the streams, so when the brother drinks from one, he turns into a beast...." He tears his eyes away from his sister. "Well. It doesn't look as if you and I will be having that slumber party after all, Emma. Such a shame. You should have walked more quietly in the hall."

Emma isn't here for repartee. "Simon, you said you know who the Butcher is."

"Indeed." Simon stretches, elbows out, a picture of indolence. "But I can't just *give* you the information. You don't need to be spoon-fed, surely. Why don't you take a guess?"

"Simon, I could stand here all night taking guesses, but we don't have time, your sister doesn't—"

He looks up at the ceiling, his attention becoming an absence.

Emma digs her nails into her palms against the need to hurry. "All right—I can tell you that this...arrangement with the Butcher, it's a game you're playing. You've been playing it awhile. Tonight is the finale. But now Kristin is caught up in it."

Simon's gaze returns. "Yes. It was foolish of you to bring her."

"Then you have extra incentive to win." Emma takes a step closer. "If you tell me the answer, I can help you."

"I thought you'd have figured it out yourself by now. I mean, you're reasonably intelligent.... Yes, I'm sure you can manage."

A prickle of awareness on her skin. "You think I can work it out from the information I already have?"

"Why not." He smiles in anticipation.

"Simon, we're running out of *time*. We're not in a fairy tale now, this isn't Rumpelstiltskin...." She stops when she sees it's no use. In Simon's kingdom, he gets to make the rules.

Emma presses down hard on this strangling sense of urgency, tries to think. There's something wrong here. Something is disturbing her, like hearing a familiar piece of music played slightly off-key. Simon's presence obliterates her concentration, but she has to ignore that—she needs to narrow this down.

To find the right questions, she returns to basics.

"Simon, why is the Butcher focused on teenagers? You said the Butcher is trying to kindle a light inside himself, using young people's blood."

His head turns back. "I did, didn't I."

"So he doesn't have that light already? Is he unwell, or impaired in some way?"

"In a manner of speaking." Simon examines his nails.

"He's trying to kindle youth, is he—" The natural trajectory of this makes her pause. "Simon, is he *older*?"

He cocks an eyebrow, and for a moment she can't breathe. This whole time, they've been tracking a young man—eighteen to twenty-five. That's what Cooper said; that's what all the evidence pointed to....

"Is the fog clearing, Emma?"

She realizes she's been staring at Simon without seeing him. Now her eyes focus as she thinks of a new question. "Simon, how did the Butcher know to communicate with you through the *Washington Post*?"

"What an interesting question. Perhaps he assumed I read the papers."

"But how would he know that?" She tracks the dark motes spinning in his eyes. "And how would he know *which* papers you receive? You and Kristin are from New Hampshire—you could've been reading your local paper for all anyone knew."

"Perhaps it was mentioned in an article or something, around the time of my trial."

She knows he's lying. "I don't think so."

She squints, looks across to Bell. When she gestures for him to approach, he's reluctant. She glares. He grimaces, starts walking over.

"Ahhh." Amusement in Simon's voice. "*We couldn't make sense of the numbers....* I *knew* you said 'we.' So Mr. Bell is part of the 'we'? How interesting."

Emma doesn't respond to that. Bell finally arrives, standing a good three feet farther back from the barricade, pointedly ignoring Simon.

"What do you need?" he asks Emma.

"An answer to a question."

"Now?"

"Now is all we have. During Simon's trial, was there anything mentioned in the press coverage about how he reads the *Washington Post*? Do you remember anything?"

Bell considers, shakes his head slowly. "Not that I can recall. Is that important?"

"I'm not sure." She bites her lip, looks back through the bars. "If it wasn't public knowledge that you read the *Washington Post*, who else would know?"

Simon shrugs carelessly. "I can't imagine."

Over by the desk, Kristin calls out. "Simon, I can't find the cigarettes *anywhere!*"

Bell steps closer to the barricade. "Cooper," he suggests. "Cooper knew."

"Cooper was the second agent on Simon's case—he had a special interest." Emma feels the weight of time. Ross could return with the FBI escort at any second. Probably right this moment, footsteps are tapping, coming toward them down the hall. She forces herself to hold firm. "Simon, no one else knew you read the *Washington Post*."

"Well," he says, "not exactly *no one*."

"Pradeep knew."

"That's true," he concedes. "Wonderful Pradeep."

"And Dr. Scott. But there's no one else, except..."

Simon smiles encouragingly. "Come on, you're almost there."

Emma hears it: the sound of a key in the door. The mnemonic unlocks a recess within her own brain. She looks at Bell wildly. "Kristin said the Butcher would know the inside of the asylum. A schematic, a floor plan—"

"He knows the inside...because he's *been* inside?" Bell has turned to face her now.

"A *staff member*." Emma clutches his jacket. "Bell, I think the Butcher is an employee of the asylum. And he's *not* young, he's not a student, he's—"

The door is opening.

"An older employee." Bell's eyes are very wide. "With medical training—"

"Oh *god*," Emma says, and when she looks over Bell's shoulder, she sees Clive Ross stepping into the room holding the lanyard of keys, with his other arm raised and an FBI-issue Smith & Wesson Model 13 pointing directly at them.

"Surprise!" Simon exclaims.

And the gates of hell swing wide.

The first shot is aimed at Bell. He has turned toward the door, half shielding Emma. His left arm lifts, an instinctive blocking movement, hand open in the universal sign for *Halt*.

The bullet—unsilenced, an explosion of sound in the echoing room—rips through the fabric of Bell's jacket and shirt, spinning him around. He hits the floor before he has a chance to cry out.

Emma doesn't hear herself scream.

Ross keeps advancing.

A great wailing cry, and Kristin Gutmunsson launches herself forward from the corner of Pradeep's desk, wielding nothing more than the pincer tool off the wall.

She manages to hit Ross once, and hard. Not expecting an attack, he lurches sideways to his knees, the keys falling from his hand.

This is their only chance—Emma sprints forward, hunkered low. She skids across the floor and overshoots, ends up sprawling. Arm stretched back, she snatches up the keys. The lanyard slides into her hand as if it wants to be there.

Ross staggers up, turns and aims at Kristin. She gasps, backs up, not fast enough to avoid Ross—he wrenches the pincer out of her hands, throws it aside, grabs her by the hair, and drives her down against the wooden surface of the desk so violently that her head and body rebound. She slithers to the floor in a heap of linen and white tresses.

"*KRISTIN!*" Simon bellows.

Emma slips, stumbles, gets up, takes two strides for the exit. Her consciousness is ablaze with a kaleidoscope of images: Ross, the gun, Bell on the floor, Simon in his cage, Kristin's bright hair falling, the awareness of the FBI forces just beyond the walls. If she can get to the door, if she can tell them—

"Run out that door and I will shoot him in the head."

Emma stops.

Time comes to a standstill. She's facing the open doorway. In her peripheral vision, Kristin is a puddle of white. Behind her, Bell groans. Ross's voice has come from the same direction. If she turns her head, she knows what she'll see: Ross standing over Bell, the Model 13 aimed and ready.

Every muscle in Emma's body is shaking on the precipice.

"I'll say it one more time. If you run, I'll shoot."

Not you. The voice in her mind sounds like Simon's. *He won't shoot* you.

It doesn't matter. She's been to this country before. She knows what's at stake. She'll run and she'll be safe, and the FBI will catch the Butcher. She'll run and Bell will die. She'll run and Kristin will be defenseless, and Simon will be alone, and her world will reverberate endlessly to the sound of the shot, just like it trembled to the sound of a knife parting flesh—first Vicki's neck, then Tammy's.

Her whole body shudders, ripped with the force of irreconcilable instincts.

"Turn around," Ross says quietly, "and bring me the keys."

The keys are in her right hand. Clutched in the bundle, the thin black key for the foyer door. She brings right and left hands together, brings the keys in, presses them to her stomach. Hardly able to think with the shaking. Screaming in her mind and tears in her eyes.

The *click* of the hammer being cocked.

Emma sobs once.

She turns around.

CHAPTER FORTY-ONE

"Good choice," Ross says.

Ross is in front of the cell, his hand tugging Bell's hair, lifting his head, the gun pressed into Bell's temple. The cords in Bell's neck stand out. Red stains his shirt. When he sees Emma, he groans.

Emma's chin and bottom lip are wobbling. Her body shudders. It's all she can do to stand there, silent.

"Come here and give me the keys," Ross says. He is utterly expressionless. His previously warm brown eyes are now dark and hard with cold.

The Butcher.

Seven steps back into the room, away from the open doorway. Each step feels like a death sentence. When Emma gets close enough, Ross releases his grip on Bell and aims the gun at her forehead. The tears tracking down her cheeks don't move him at all.

He holds out his free hand, palm up. "The keys."

Emma's hand is shaking so much it's hard to release her fingers. She gives him the keys. Her grip on the metal has scored white marks into her skin.

"Thank you." Ross smiles. He slips the lanyard over his head. "It's nice to finally meet you in person, Miss Lewis."

The Butcher knows her name. She might have passed him in the asylum's halls, and Simon has shared her name, and they are trapped here, *trapped* here, and Emma wants to throw up.

"Now," Ross says, "you're going to help me. Drag the boy over to the desk, beside Miss Gutmunsson."

Emma feels herself shifting into an altered state of perception: her breaths hard and fast and deep, her skin acutely sensitive to the temperature of the air and the fabric on her skin. The taste of copper is in her mouth. Sounds seem to mute and narrow their focus. She can smell the musk of testosterone from the three males in the room.

The black mouth of the gun looms large in front of her eyes.

Ross tilts his head. "Do I have to repeat myself?"

"No," Emma says.

"Move slowly. Take him under the armpits."

She sinks to her knees. She has to turn Bell over. The fabric under his left armpit is wet. When she tightens her grip on him, he makes a tortured noise.

"I'm sorry," she whispers. "I'm so sorry."

"Emma." His eyes are rolling with pain. "Why didn't you run?"

She can't look at him and do this. She grabs handfuls of his shirt, has to tuck her chin into the side of his neck to get purchase. He's shaking. His skin smells warm and raw as she pulls him backward awkwardly, stumbling over her own feet, pulling again until her backside bumps the desk. She settles him against one thick wooden desk leg.

"Here, it's okay now," she whispers, uncertain whether she's reassuring Bell or herself.

"Pull down his jacket and tie it around his wrists at the back," Ross says from behind her.

"He can't move. He's just—"

The hard metal of the gun barrel presses at her nape. "Just do as I say."

Emma shuffles on her knees to face Bell, uses her shoulder to prop him up as she sits him forward. When she tugs his jacket down his arms, he mashes his lips against her T-shirt, pants heavily through the thin cotton. She has to reach around his body to tie the sleeves of the jacket together. By the time she eases him back against the desk leg, his face is like wax.

"What if he bleeds out?" Her voice is quavering.

Ross presses the gun against her temple as he leans forward to inspect Bell's wound. He pokes his fingers into the sodden red fabric under Bell's armpit. Bell turns his head aside and bites his bottom lip, eyes squeezed up tight.

"Clean through the edge of the latissimus dorsi," Ross pronounces. "Might've just grazed a rib. Don't worry about him now. You have something else to do. Drag Miss Gutmunsson closer to the desk."

Emma makes herself move. Compliance goes against all her natural instincts.

Dragging Bell has left a blood trail across the floor—Ross tuts disapprovingly. Emma has to step over the blood to reach Kristin. A large dark bruise is starting to form on the side of the girl's forehead. Emma checks her pulse at the neck: It's slow, but strong.

"She's all right." Emma pitches her voice a fraction louder. "She's just knocked out."

Far across the room, Emma glimpses Simon—braced against the bars—as he lowers his head.

"Fine," Ross says. "Now move her."

Kristin is lighter than Bell, but there's somehow more of her: long, boneless limbs moving out of concert, strands of white hair getting in Emma's mouth. During her attempts to prop Kristin against the desk, Emma has a chance to slip the long iron key out of the front waistband of her jeans and into the pocket of Kristin's coat.

"Hurry," Ross says.

"I can't prop her up."

"Then leave her on the floor."

She sets Kristin on her side on the wooden floor, a little away from Bell. The exertion and the subterfuge have made Emma sweat in a horrifyingly familiar way.

"Very good," Ross says. "Now go to the door. Just outside it, on the left, you'll find a coil of rope and my medical pouch. Bring them both inside. If you run away, you know what will happen."

Emma faces him directly. "I know what will happen if I stay here, too."

"Do you want me to shoot them both? You can choose which one will go first."

Emma grits her teeth and goes to the door. Cool air from the dark hall floats against her face. The urge to take flight exerts its pull on her once again. She fights against it, collects the rope and the pouch. *Where the hell is the FBI?*

"Put the pouch on the desk. Bring the rope here."

Emma does as she's told. The rope is a heavy, coarse bundle. Ross takes the coil and slings it over his shoulder, indicates for her to move forward, to take up position beside him in front of Simon's cage.

Simon is standing in the glow of light inside the cell, a tall ice sculpture. His posture is loose but his eyes are like hard sapphires, unblinking.

When he speaks, his voice is dangerously silky. "Siegfried."

"Artist," Ross replies. "At last."

Ross smiles. Emma's not sure how he can smile, the way Simon looks at this moment.

"You'll excuse my delay," Ross goes on. "I had to collect my equipment, and the weapon."

Simon doesn't acknowledge Ross's aside. "That wasn't very polite, the way you treated my sister."

"I'm afraid I don't react well when attacked by surprise."

Simon's lips turn up. "Kristin can be a handful, no doubt. Did you know she stabbed me once? It's an old story, never mind. Suffice to say I sympathize."

"Miss Lewis here is much more cooperative."

"Oh, she can be unruly when the mood takes her." Simon's eyes light on Emma, flit away.

"I wasn't very happy when I found out the FBI was staking out the building." Ross's tone is quietly reproachful.

Simon spreads his hands. "What can I say—I was put in a difficult position. You seem to have made it work for you. I do hope you'll forgive me."

"What's to forgive? Here we are, and you're about to give me everything I've ever wanted." Ross steps toward the cage. The light catches the hollows in his face, and he suddenly looks ravenous.

Emma clenches her fingers. The feeling that she's standing too close to a pair of jackals is overwhelming.

Simon prowls forward. "I don't suppose you'd be satisfied with a small donation? I could stretch an arm outside the bars.... No, I don't imagine. It's been a long road to get here."

"Long enough. But not without its pleasures along the way."

"The letters were the most fun."

"I would have to disagree. The treatments have been...extraordinary. I can't tell you. The physical benefits are satisfying, but I wasn't expecting the mental benefits—that's been a real delight."

"How fortunate." A hint of dryness in Simon's reply. "So what happens now? I imagine we need to move things along with the FBI banging around outside."

"It's fine. I locked them out via the control booth. The asylum's old wiring is complicated—I think it'll take them at least thirty minutes to find the circuit breakers. I've already dealt with the booth technician and the agent on the front desk, so we have some time. You know I don't like to rush."

Emma suspected the FBI had been held up somehow—they surely would have heard the gunshot—and the confirmation of it ping-pongs around inside her head. *No FBI. No cavalry. Not yet.*

Simon presses his hands together. "Of course. So you'll bleed me, and then the others? Or maybe it should happen in reverse order."

"I'll take samples from the others, of course. That won't take very long, and I wouldn't want to waste them. You, I think I'll...savor."

Simon seems unfazed by the prospect of his imminent demise. "Excellent. Although before we start, I'd like some assurances about what will happen to my twin."

"I'll let her go once we're done," Ross says. "She's seen my face, but she doesn't know my real name. And I'll be disappearing soon anyway—as you know, I have a place to stay where nobody will find me. Your sister poses no threat."

In normal circumstances, Emma would roll her eyes.

"Well. That's very kind." Clearly, Simon doesn't believe a word of it either. "My life for Kristin's. That seems appropriate."

"I like everything to be balanced."

"Naturally." Simon cants his head. "So how would you like to proceed?"

"I was thinking you could take the sheet off your bed and secure your ankles together with it."

Simon grins in reply. To Emma's shock, he begins to do exactly what Ross has suggested, whipping one of the sheets back and separating it from the plain ticking of his bed. He twists the sheet like he's doing laundry. Then he sits on the bed with his bare feet together.

"Like this?" He winds the sheet carefully. "Or in a figure eight?"

"That's fine."

"Now what happens?" Simon's level of enthusiasm for the process is entirely inappropriate.

"Now Miss Lewis assists me again with the rope."

Ross dumps the coil on the floor. Emma's eyes feel dry trying to track the movements: Simon in the cell, Ross with his paramedic costume, the black hole of the gun's muzzle as Ross nudges her with it.

"Unwind a length. Toss one end over the top of the bars, to go through the roof of the cell."

The rope is rough, the coil unspooling against her legs. Having something to do helps control the shaking in her hands. She has no idea what Simon is planning, but she feels it inside the room like a whispered promise of chaos.

The cell is about twelve feet high. After two attempts to throw the end of the rope into position, she realizes it's not going to work.

"I'm not... It's too high."

"You're standing too far away," Ross says. "Go inside the barricade. He won't bite."

Simon grins again at this.

Emma pushes one of the sawhorses aside and steps into the forbidden zone.

"Come on, Emma," Simon exhorts. "Best efforts now."

She takes a deep breath. Swings the rope end for a lasso effect, throws—the rope flops onto the bars of the cell's ceiling. A few judicious flicks and it snakes into the cell from above. She pays out rope until the end curls into Simon's lap.

"Oh, well done!" He applauds her.

This can't be happening. This is too surreal, too dangerous, too wrong.

Simon ties the rope firmly around the twisted sheet between his ankles. "Ready to go. Haul away!"

Ross waves the gun at her. "You heard."

Emma stares. "I'm never going to be able to pull him up. He's a foot taller and about fifty pounds heavier."

"Then you'll have to pull hard."

"You can do it, Emma!" Simon is smiling ear to ear. "Don't be defeated by a little thing like physics!"

This is amusing him, she realizes. Simon is pandering to Ross because it amuses him.

It makes her angry enough that she picks up the slack rope and pulls.

The first eight feet are easy: Simon is already sitting on his bed, and he even uses his hands to push himself up higher once his legs are in the air. Then he is off the bed, and she is bearing his entire weight. She has to brace her feet against the slipperiness of the wooden floor, bend at the waist. Then, crawl on her knees.

Sweat stings in her eyes. The rope is taut at her shoulder. It slides twice, and she cries out from the burn of the coarse hemp. When she reaches some appropriate point, Ross says, "Stop," and she forces herself to hold, and hold, and hold, while he ties the rope off.

"It's done," Ross says behind her. "You can let go."

She collapses to the boards, utterly spent. Her hands are throbbing like she thrust them in a fire. When she rolls over, she sees everything laid out like a tableau. Kristin lies unconscious by the desk. Bell is tied up and shivering nearby. Ross stands by the barricade, smiling as he surveys his domain.

Simon is hanging upside down in his cell, swinging gently and laughing. Did she expect Simon to do something? To save them all? What was she thinking? Simon is deranged, and this is over.

She's escaped one sociopath, only to be enslaved and murdered by another. She should have run.

And Emma knows in her heart that she is going to die here.

CHAPTER FORTY-TWO

Ross walks over to the desk and begins unpacking his medical pouch. Emma sees latex tourniquet tubing, syringes, plastic-wrapped needles, a large-bladed scalpel.

"Oh, this is *fun!*" Simon exclaims. He opens his arms wide as he swings, suspended. "All the blood is rushing to my head. Emma, you should try this, it gives you a whole different perspective on things."

Emma pushes herself up. "I want to check on Bell," she rasps. "Mr. Ross—"

"Did he tell you his name is Ross?" Simon wriggles in the air to steady his swinging as he faces her. "Goodness, I thought we'd already dealt with introductions."

Clive Ross, the Pennsylvania killer, the Berryville Butcher, Siegfried, Gordon Lord—she honestly doesn't care about true names or aliases anymore. The man in the paramedic uniform has multiple identities, but they all mean the same thing.

"His name is Anthony Hoyt!" Upside down, Simon's grin looks demonic. "I'd say *Anthony Hoyt, MD*, but I'm fairly sure he faked his medical credentials so Dr. Scott would employ him."

"Be quiet now, Simon," Ross says.

She remembers the name Anthony Hoyt. He was one of the technicians on the MT list. The list that Bell gave Martino, in a yesterday that feels like a million years ago. She wonders if Martino ever followed up on those names, and the thought reminds her that there's still a SWAT team outside this building.

She has no idea how long they've already been here; time has become elastic. But if they can survive the Butcher for thirty minutes...

"Come over and check on your friend, Miss Lewis." Ross, or Hoyt, or whatever he's called, is feeling magnanimous. "I need you over here anyway."

"Yes, go on over, Emma! I can keep chatting to you both from this position," Simon declares.

It's quite possible that Simon Gutmunsson would talk underwater. Emma clambers to her feet, trying not to use her hands. Her palms are red and swollen, and some of her fingers have small white blisters on them. The blisters pulse with the beat of her heart. She wipes her hands carefully against her T-shirt as she staggers closer to the desk.

Bell's head is turned, his eyes closed. His left side, from armpit to waist, is dark crimson and his lips are almost white. Emma drops to her knees in front of him.

"Travis." She shakes his shoulder. "Travis."

"Hmm, he's not looking very good, is he?" Simon, ever helpful.

When Bell doesn't respond, she slaps him, which sets her fingers alight.

"*Bell.* Bell, wake up."

His eyes blur open. *"Emma."*

"I'm here."

They can't do anything more than stare at each other. There's a lot she wants to say, but the Butcher is watching.

"Anthony Hoyt," she whispers finally.

Bell blinks, then he stabilizes and it registers. "The list."

"Miss Lewis," Hoyt says, "untie Mr. Bell's jacket sleeves and pull out his left arm. Tie his right arm back onto the desk. And then get the needle—"

"No," Emma says. "I won't take *donations* for you."

Hoyt hits her with the gun. It knocks her sideways and onto Bell's sprawled-out legs. The force of the blow explodes inside her head, hammers her skull as she pulls herself back up.

Bell's sweating with the pain of the bullet wound, but now he's about as far from passed out as he could possibly get. "Emma. *Emma.*"

"Well, that was uncalled for." Simon, from his unique viewpoint in the cell.

"Do I need to repeat myself?" Hoyt asks.

"Emma, do it," Bell says. "Just do what he says."

"He's going to bleed you," Emma whispers. The red line now leaking down her cheek from her eyebrow feels like a tear.

"I don't give a fuck. Untie me. Come on."

She has to clamber closer to untie Bell. When his left arm comes loose, Bell makes a soft gasp. He keeps that arm tucked against his body as she secures his right arm. She leaves some wiggle room in the jacket, and she doesn't think Hoyt notices.

Simon is talking again. "Why do you think he uses the blood, Emma? Do you know?"

"Simon, now isn't the time." Hoyt is starting to sound exasperated.

"But I feel so inspired! It's because of his *vanity*, Emma. His fear of mortality and death. Everyone ages and everyone dies. Even me. Even our friend Mr. Hoyt. But he wants to slow the aging process."

"Shut up now, Simon."

"Oh, Anthony! Come on! It's textbook Byron, the 'mortal coldness of the soul' from 'Youth and Age.' Can you really not see that? Or did you pull all those lovely quotes in your letters out of *Reader's Digest*?"

Hoyt seems to find the whole turn of the conversation irritating, and it makes him aggressive. He reaches down and grabs Emma's arm, hauls her up.

"I only brought three needles, so I suppose we'll have to share." He selects the scalpel, tests it on the hair on her forearm. The scalpel has dried blood on it. "You're going to take blood from Mr. Bell, and I'm going to hold this scalpel to his throat. If you don't behave nicely, I'll slice his carotid. Now take this."

He thrusts tubing and plastic packets into her hands.

"Kneel down—that's right. Roll up his sleeve and tie the tourniquet above his elbow."

"Yes, Emma." Simon's voice is sardonic. "Make sure you get a good sample."

Bell watches her the whole time. He doesn't seem to care about the sharp steel Hoyt has poised under his jaw. When Emma falters—opening the packet with the needle, fitting the needle to the syringe, inserting the syringe into his arm—he says, "Come on, Lewis," and she recovers enough to keep going.

Bell's blood has a viscosity, moving slowly into the syringe cylinder. Hoyt seems to find it fascinating.

"That's good," he mutters. "Yes."

The cylinder goes up to ten milliliters, and Hoyt prods her, so that is how much she draws. When she's done, Bell looks paler than before. He's already lost a lot of blood.

"Now Miss Gutmunsson," Hoyt says.

He lets her go over to Kristin alone. The plastic packets feel heavy in Emma's hands. Kristin is lying on her left side, facing away from the desk, and Emma decides to leave her that way and just tug her arm carefully into position, so it's stretched out on the floor.

She fumbles with the packets. Every second she delays, the FBI has more time to find the circuit breakers and unlock the doors—

"Miss Lewis," Hoyt says. Light glints off the scalpel he has poised near Bell's right eye. "Shall I blind him first?"

She wets her lips. "No."

"Then don't *dawdle*, Miss Lewis."

She ties the tourniquet.

Simon is suspiciously quiet, but she can't glance over her shoulder right now. She looks again at Hoyt. He's set the scalpel down; with the gun in his right hand, he's injecting himself with Bell's blood. His gaze loses focus for a moment, becomes narcotically glassy as he pushes the plunger in.

Emma wants to retch. She looks down at Kristin Gutmunsson's arm.

Kristin is awake.

It seems she's been awake for some time. Her eyes aren't fluttering. They're peeking behind her lids.

"Make sure you do a good job on my sister," Simon calls. "Don't leave her with a scar!"

There's a subtle change of timbre there. Attenuated darkness. Emma suddenly knows in her gut that Simon has realized his twin is conscious.

Kristin does an outstanding job of pretending to be still passed out. Her body is lax as a dancer's in repose, and there's no giveaway flinching when Emma inserts the needle, begins to draw blood. Emma feels the presence of the foyer key—lying hidden in Kristin's pocket—like a hot secret coal, glowing warm through the fabric. She snaps the tourniquet off.

"Bring the sample here," Hoyt says.

As soon as he has Kristin's syringe, Hoyt walks over to the cell. He puts the scalpel in his pocket and the gun in his waistband as he stands in front of Simon with his inner elbow exposed.

"I thought you'd like to watch while I inject your sister's blood." His expression is much less civilized now. He inserts the needle smoothly, presses the plunger. "Oh, yes. That's nice—very nice."

"I will kill you, you know," Simon remarks conversationally.

Hoyt removes the needle, bunches his arm, and grins, a forty-something man taunting a boy less than half his age. Simon's a psychopath, but the power differential is disturbing.

Hoyt turns. "Now you, Miss Lewis."

"I wouldn't bother taking any from Emma." Simon is spinning and unspinning himself. He looks like a long white grub trying to emerge from his cocoon. "She hates you so much her blood would probably poison you."

Emma winds the tourniquet around her own arm below the sleeve of her T-shirt. Heightened senses make everything more visceral: the grime on her skin, the smell of her sweat, the vein popping in her arm, the blood rushing there. The blood Hoyt's so desperate for, the blood that is everything to him...

The blood that is everything.

There's only one clean needle left, and suddenly Emma knows what to do with it. She's going to take control of Hoyt's ritual, sully it. She's going to hit him where it hurts.

She unwraps the needle and slides it—without attaching the plastic barrel of the syringe cylinder—straight into her vein. The sting is mild. She takes a deep breath. *Please let this work.*

Then she turns around to face Hoyt and releases the tourniquet.

The effect is dramatic. Blood—*her* blood—gushes down her inner arm in a thick scarlet runnel that bifurcates halfway to her wrist. She watches it drip onto the floor. If nothing else, letting part of herself out like this feels like a release.

"Emma, *no*!" Bell cries.

"What are you—" Hoyt still has Kristin's syringe in his hand as he rushes over. "Stop that! Don't *do* that! For god's sake, you're *wasting* it!"

He's so intent on stopping the flow of Emma's blood he doesn't realize when Kristin Gutmunsson pushes up off the floor and flies at him.

CHAPTER FORTY-THREE

Kristin slams into Anthony Hoyt with an earsplitting scream, shoving his own right hand violently toward his face. The used syringe he's holding buries itself deep into his cheek.

"TAKE MY BLOOD, YOU MISERABLE FUCKING SHIT!" Kristin's face is twisted in a snarl, like she's been possessed by her brother.

Hoyt makes a garbled cry.

In a single smooth motion, Kristin yanks the revolver out of Hoyt's waistband and aims straight at him. Hoyt dives to the floor, and the gun goes off like a deafening crack of thunder inside the chapel room. The shot goes wide. Hoyt rolls, scuttles. Still screaming, Kristin fires once more. But her aim is wild, and a fourth bullet plows into a floorboard. It doesn't look as if she's handled a gun in her life.

"Kristin, give me the gun." Emma jerks the needle out of her arm, snatches the weapon out of Kristin's hands. "Untie Bell. We're getting the fuck out of here."

"Simon—"

"Kristin, *NOW*!"

In less than five seconds, they're falling out the door of Simon's room and into the great hall.

Cool air slaps Emma in the face and if she weren't running, she'd be crying with relief. She's holding Bell's arm, Kristin is on his other side, they're running, Bell's stumbling, half bent over, Emma's checking over her shoulder as they sprint for the barred gate.

"The key," Emma pants. "If we can get to the foyer door—Bell, *move!*"

The great hall is an echo chamber of their thumping feet and struggling breaths. Bell's sweating, it's a cold sweat, Kristin looks green in the face. Emma hustles them past the steel bars, spins to check their path of retreat, holding the gun in a two-handed grip, muttering, "Come on, *come on.*"

Another sprint, and the dark wood of the foyer entrance is just up ahead. Emma slams into the door like she's trying to break it down.

"*The key,*" she cries, makes a beckoning gesture.

Kristin looks baffled. "I don't know what you're—"

"Coat pocket," Bell wheezes.

Emma gives up, grabs for Kristin's pocket, the hard, thin object inside. She pulls it out, sound of metal scratching metal as she struggles to get it into the keyhole with her hands shaking like this and one hand holding the revolver.

"Gimme the gun," Bell says. He takes the weapon and braces his back against the wooden wall, right arm out and aiming down the hall, all color stripped from his face.

Emma gets the door open, it swings wide, they tumble through, slam it shut.

Calm dark under the stairs of the foyer.

Emma locks the door. Bell staggers forward, drops to his knees, bent over, propping himself up with the muzzle of the gun, breathing like he's about to pass out or die. Kristin holds the wall as she edges away to give herself space.

Emma closes her eyes for the briefest moment, opens them.

Kristin is clutching an arm about her ribs. "My brother is still back there in that room, and he's back there with *him*, and he's—"

"Kristin," Emma says. "*Kristin.* We'll get your brother."

Emma sees to Bell first, tugs him up gently, turns him around. His hand, placing the gun flat on the floor, is palsied with tremors.

"You need to lie down." Emma yanks his shirt free, tears it down the front, ties it hard around his midsection over his undershirt. "You need to lie down, and Kristin's going to open the front entrance, and SWAT will come in—"

Kristin is vomiting in a corner. Emma sees to her next.

"Kristin, look at me." The girl's eyes are glassy, and one pupil is slightly larger than the other. "Kristin, you have to help Travis. You need to get the front door open—"

"*Simon!*" Kristin shrieks. She clutches Emma's arm. "We can't leave him there, *tell me you're not going to leave him*—"

"Nobody's leaving anyone," Emma says, and she feels very old in years as she picks up the gun.

"No," Bell gasps.

"Yes." Emma tries to get her heartbeat to slow. "He helped us, Travis. He helped *me*. I don't want to go back—look at me, okay? But I'm not leaving him there to get his throat slashed. And he could still get loose—Hoyt has the keys to the cell."

"It doesn't matter."

"Of course it matters, Travis. You *know* it matters."

"Emma—" He just breathes for a second. Then he gives her his tie to wrap around her arm, which is still bleeding. "Listen to me. You've only got two bullets left. That's it."

"Got it."

"Check your corners. Remember what we practiced."

"I will."

"Don't go."

"Have to." She checks the chamber like he taught her, confirms the two bullets. "I know what it feels like to be in a cage."

Emma Lewis, fitting the key back into the lock, unlocking the door, peeking, slipping out.

Back into the ominous quiet of the great hall.

The first corners she checks are the ones nearest the door. Weaver stance adapted, double grip, watch ahead and watch the sight. Her breath has a burr from the recent sprint, but she's in better condition than she's ever been. She jogs in her soundless running shoes down to the barred gate, checks her firing line, head moving with the gun.

By the time she scoots behind a column to come up on the oak door at an angle, her knees are starting to shake. She's not sure how to hold the gun while she's moving—tucked between her breasts, okay. Her feet get slower as she approaches the door. The door is still wide open; she can see the edge of the desk.

The doorway, not the doorway, tactical suicide but she's got to go through, Emma Lewis with her heart in her throat as she plunges forward, ducks inside Simon's room.

Movement to her right—before she can swing, a sharp, hot

feeling slicing her right shoulder blade—but Hoyt has mistimed his attack.

Emma spins and fires; all she can see is muzzle flash, but she hears a grunt, the pattering sound of footsteps. Her vision clears. She's inside Simon's room, the room is lit dimly, Hoyt is hiding.

Simon is still swinging gently in his cell, his cheeks ruddy from being upside down. "Hello again, Emma."

She detaches a hand from the gun and presses a finger to her lips. Hoyt could be behind the side curtains. She only has one bullet left and she wants to make it count.

"It means a great deal to me, you know, that you came back."

"Be quiet, Simon, I'm trying to hear."

She edges forward. Too dark in here, too many shadows. So many miles to reach the cage, and she's worried about hitting Simon with her next shot.

"And you got my sister out—that was *marvelous*, wasn't she a banshee?"

"Simon, shut *up*."

Emma Lewis panting, with the thin, high screaming in her head, eyes wide and edging carefully past the desk. It's a big room and the Butcher could be anywhere. Step. Step. Closer to Simon's cell, she can get a view of the whole room there, or maybe she just doesn't want to feel alone. Two hands on the gun, turning as she steps, swinging to cover too many angles. Maybe not the curtains, maybe the old pews at the sides of the room—

"*Emma!*"

Swinging back and Hoyt's on her, slamming into her—she

sprawls to the floor near Simon's cage, knocks her head on one of the legs of the pushed-over sawhorse.

Emma on her back, dazzled by stars, and Hoyt above her, looming over her, his face contorted, ugly with rage, the bloody gouge in it from Kristin's needle. Hoyt's hot breath on her, his arm lifted with the scalpel, keys dangling low off the lanyard in front.

She slings her arm up with the gun, and her other hand lifts to grab the keys, to pull him down to her.

He drives the scalpel into the meat of her left bicep.

She *shrieks*, finger jerking on the trigger—the gun goes off.

Wide.

Emma could cry because that's it, that's the end, an empty gun and a ringing in her ears—she wails in fury and despair, energy deserting her, it takes everything she's got to throw the weapon at him.

Hoyt bats it aside.

She scrabbles away on her back, one arm with the blade handle protruding obscenely, she can't feel it. Hoyt's face victorious, his slow advance, like a man relishing what's to come. Emma sobs, clenches her last fist, the crunch of metal as she clutches the keys.

The keys on the lanyard that slipped off Hoyt's neck.

And now Emma Lewis with a terrible choice, and the sudden awareness that the thin, high screaming inside her head isn't the screaming of Vicki or Tammy, it has never been their screaming, it is her *own* screaming, her own screaming—

She rolls sideways and throws the keys through the bars of Simon's cage.

The lights go out.

Beyond the door of the chapel, a clanking sound as the steel gate in the great hall slides ponderously and automatically shut.

FBI found the circuit breakers, Emma thinks. It is her final thought, perhaps.

Scrambling forward on her stomach and knees, trapped and going nowhere in the dark, her breath gasping, the Butcher behind her, he might slice her Achilles tendons before he kills her, oh god please no—she rolls back over. Hoyt is staring down, smiling, he must believe he's smiling, he's slavering.

"Miss Lewis," he says. Lips pulled back from his teeth, showing his gums.

Sprawled back, slippery elbows hurting, blood beneath her, blood thumping in her palms and fingertips, blood thumping in her head. She can only stare up at Hoyt's expression. Her finger squeezes, spasming on an absent trigger.

Movement from the left.

And the most terrifying thing Emma has ever seen emerges from the shadows.

Simon Gutmunsson, free and unrestrained, walking closer, sauntering really. In the darkness of the asylum he resolves like smoke poured onto glass, gleaming like a phantasm when the moonlight hits him. White skin, red lips, his hair a beacon. Eyes glittering, fathoms deep.

Emma has time to think, *He is out, he is out and you can't stop him now,* before the clamor in her mind takes over, older instincts kicking in.

She freezes, a prey animal trapped between two apex predators.

"Artist—" Hoyt starts.

"*Surprise*," Simon whispers. He drives the edge of his hand into Hoyt's throat.

While the man chokes, Simon puts a gentle palm over Hoyt's mouth, backs Hoyt to the cage wall. Hoyt's eyes bulge.

"Hello, Anthony." Simon pins him tight. "I think you've been under the impression that I didn't understand the game we've been playing."

Hoyt struggles. Simon leans in, his eyes incandescent.

"The years sneak up on you, don't they? Wrinkles, and forgetfulness, and liver spots on the backs of your hands... But it doesn't have to be that way. You have the skills, the training to do something about it, and you can be *transformed....*"

Simon's beauty in the dark room, Hoyt mewing beneath his hand.

"And then you see me from afar, and you wonder if you dare. Do you dare, Anthony? Of course you do. You are transformed, and Simon Gutmunsson is just a boy like any other boy, an exaggerated myth.... So you make your plans and place your ads and send your letters, and you're thinking about it *the whole time*, aren't you? What it would be like to dance beneath me in the warm-rushing shower of red..."

Hoyt whimpers, his body restricted by Simon's entire length, his head pressed hard against the bars of the cage.

"I understand, Anthony, truly I do." Simon brings his lips close to Hoyt's ear, sharing the secret. "You've been searching out the glow, the spark, the lamp against the night, hoping to rekindle it in your own breast. The young have it, don't they? Look at our lovely Emma—how she shines!"

He forces the man's head around. When Hoyt's panicked gaze falls on her, Emma lets out a sob.

"But Anthony, Anthony...all that gold is wasted on you. If you're going to commit *murder*, Anthony, at least make it *worth* something. Something more than a *midlife crisis*."

Hoyt recoils from Simon's snarl, but Simon's arms are iron.

"*I* killed for transcendence. But I don't think you know what transcendence means. You probably don't even know how to *spell* it. Look at me, Anthony. Do you think my mythology is undeserved? Did you really believe I didn't understand the game? That I didn't know who you were *right from the start*?"

Simon's expression changes, and Emma cries out with the change. He removes his hand. Hoyt takes a gasping breath, opens his mouth to speak—

Simon crunches his teeth into Hoyt's bottom lip like he's eating an apple.

Hoyt screams.

Simon rips back his head, and the great flap of Hoyt's lip comes with him, and he shakes his head, red droplets flying. He spits the meat onto the floor. Blood pours down; Simon's mouth and chin are smeared with it, his eyes burning red.

"DID YOU REALLY THINK YOU WERE LIKE ME?"

Simon, rampant.

"WE'RE NOT EVEN THE SAME FUCKING SPECIES."

Simon presses his hands on either side of Hoyt's face, leans in again, and Emma looks up desperately at the ceiling. Can't block out the screams.

Shivering, after a moment she sees Simon taking a knee beside her, his visage awful to behold and his eyes all aflame. *A firefly,* she thinks, *a firefly in the dark.*

"Dear Emma," he says. "You'll excuse me if I borrow this."

A sharp sliding pain that makes her gag, and Simon holds the scalpel in his hand, the scalpel that was in her arm.

"It's been a lovely evening, but it's time for the fin de partie." When he smiles, blood drips off his teeth.

He lifts his hand, strokes a finger down her cheek. Emma feels it like a crackle of lightning.

"You, I did not anticipate." His eyes travel over her face. "How interesting. Come and visit me again sometime, Emma. We'll have croissants."

Then Simon stands and follows Hoyt, who has crawled into the cage. The two of them are washed by the radiance of the moon shining through the barred windows.

"Before your interruption," Simon remarks, "we were discussing fairy tales. Do you remember the story of Rumpelstiltskin? When the queen found out his name, he thrust his foot into the ground and, in a passion, tore himself in two."

He gets no reply. Hoyt is beyond replying now.

"Well," Simon says, musing. "Let's see what we can manage...."

He steps in and turns Hoyt over, and Emma turns her head away.

CHAPTER FORTY-FOUR

I t doesn't take long to do the mop-up.

SWAT must have fixed the circuit breakers, because all the lights come on at once and there's the rattle of steel in the hall. Moments later, people flood into the room. Emma has almost managed to limp as far as the door by then, and one of the SWAT guys nearly bowls her over, but then everyone is way too busy rushing over to the ruckus in Simon's cell.

Emma sits herself on Pradeep's desk. She feels numb.

"Emma!"

Someone is hollering her name, but all she can do is sit there and look around at the chaos. Simon is being restrained by four SWAT team members, overseen by two more SWAT team members. Dr. Scott stands nearby, her hand over her mouth. Hoyt lies almost forgotten in the cell, the dark pool under his head and abdomen seeming to float the body, although Emma assumes that's a trick of the light.

After a moment, one of the SWAT guys asks if she needs to see the paramedic. Emma just laughs and laughs, and soon she realizes her laughs sound like sobs, so she exerts all her control, every last bit remaining to her, and makes herself stop. Then she slides down off the desk and heads for the door.

"Emma Lewis! Miss Lewis!"

She turns around, and it's Martino.

"Yes?"

"Miss Lewis, I . . ." He pauses then to take her in, eyes skating over her, his expression appalled and astonished at the same time. When she's about to ask if he called her for a particular reason, he finally speaks again. "Miss Lewis, I'm going to need to take a deposition from you about what happened here. You don't . . . you don't have to do it right away."

"That's . . ." She actually doesn't care anymore. "Okay. Whatever you need."

"Thank you." He tilts his head. "There's a SWAT team member giving emergency first aid to Mr. Bell and Miss Gutmunsson in the foyer. Do you want me to walk you up?"

"No," she says. "But thank you."

"Okay. If you're sure."

"I'm sure."

"Miss Lewis, I'm sorry." He steps closer. "Look, there won't be an official apology from the bureau, because they don't really do that. But I just wanted to tell you that me, personally? I'm sorry. Raymond's operation was fucked up from the start, and the unsub had the jump on us."

Emma lifts her chin. "That MT list Bell gave you. Do you still have it?"

"Yeah."

"Then you won't need to stretch far to ID that body in the cage over there."

"Ah, Jesus—" Martino grabs for the pocket on the inside of his jacket.

Emma turns away.

When she gets out into the great hall, she hears someone else calling her name, and at first she thinks it's Martino again, but then people in front of her are being pushed aside and Bell is there. His expression is so jagged, Emma almost takes a step back. He's got a better bandage around his chest but he still looks pale as hell, and his breaths are heaving.

"It's okay," Emma says, flopping a hand. "Everything is..."

She stops, because she doesn't know for sure if everything's okay. She looks up at Bell and he steps closer and cups her face in his hands. He wipes her cheeks with his thumbs and slowly, slowly, Emma sinks in until his arms wrap around and he is holding her. The warmth of him thaws some of the numbness inside, but Bell is solid; he keeps holding her while her shoulders shake.

And that's when she realizes that everything may not be okay, but everything is okay for now.

CHAPTER FORTY-FIVE

Ed Cooper's memorial service is at one in the afternoon at the St. John's Episcopal Church in Arlington. It's crowded in the church, and so humid from people's exhaled breath and body heat that the ushers open the rear doors.

Emma stands beside Bell near the back of the church during the service, hoping nobody will notice she's wearing a dress in navy, not black. The dress is an older one she originally packed when she was leaving for Quantico, and it has a matching bolero jacket with tight sleeves. She remembers she nearly took the dress and the jacket out of her suitcase, but her mother told her there might be a formal dinner, and that "you can't wear jeans to everything, Emma Anne."

Now she stands in her wrong-colored dress, watching Bell to ensure he doesn't fall over and listening to people tell commemorative stories about Cooper. At some point during the final eulogy by Cooper's brother, Emma excuses herself to step outside. Bell seems all right, and she needs some air.

She stands out in the green yard to the west of the church, near a big old oak tree, and takes off her scarf. After a while, with the filtered sun and the soft breeze on her face, she starts to feel improved. A little while after that, Bell comes out to see her, walking across the grass.

"Hey." He was discharged from the hospital only this morning. He's still moving stiffly from the bandages, and his eyes seem unfocused sometimes from the pain medication.

"Hey." She remembers the way he cupped her face last night, at the end of everything. The memory is very vivid, and she thinks it's maybe made them a little awkward around each other. It's strange to be awkward around Bell, and she tries to push the feeling aside.

"You okay?"

"Yeah. I just…" She stuffs her scarf in her pocket. "I'm not great with crowds."

"There's a lot of people in there, for sure." He glances back at the church, his hair blowing off his forehead. "It was a nice service."

Emma doesn't know what to say to that. She's been to too many funerals, and every one of them reminds her that death is empty and final, and that churches and memorials and gravestones are for the living.

"I'm driving back to Apple Creek," she blurts. "I mean, I'm leaving right after the service. I handed in my ID before I left Quantico."

"Emma, it's all right." Bell smiles softly. "I kind of figured you might do that."

"Oh. Okay. I didn't mean to, um…"

"You didn't. I'm not offended. I'm glad I get to say goodbye before you take off."

There's the Bell she knows. It makes her feel comfortable enough to step closer.

"Have you, uh..." She has trouble getting it out, because she's not sure she wants to know. "Have you heard any more news?"

"Raymond's not here, so I'm guessing he's dealing with the Office of Professional Responsibility investigation. Kristin is still in the hospital. They tell me she's gonna be okay. And Simon Gutmunsson...I don't know. I guess they're still arguing over what to do with him." Bell lifts his chin so the sun falls on his face, his eyelids shuttering. "I find I'm not much worried about any of that stuff right now."

"You must be looking forward to going home."

"It'll be good to see my sisters." He opens his eyes. "I'm not sure how I'm going to tell my mom I got a bullet hole in my dad's suit."

He grins, but it's thin, and he looks off down the street. For a moment, Emma wonders what would happen if she touched his face now, the same way he touched hers. The idea beckons, the moment stretches, and she steps in a little more.

"Will you be all right?"

He looks back, blinks at her. "I'll...I'll get better. What about you?"

Emma opens her mouth and nothing comes out for a full five seconds. Then a man walks over to them, and whatever Emma was going to do or say is swallowed up.

"Excuse me. Are you Mr. Bell and Miss Lewis?"

"We are," Bell says.

Emma just nods.

The man smiles with closed lips, but it's a reserved smile rather than a courtesy smile, and his eyes are kind. "I'm Special Agent Howard Carter. Ed Cooper was my friend and my colleague. Before he passed, he said I should try to get in touch with you. It's nice to finally meet you."

His handshake is firm and dry—a short, professional shake. He takes two envelopes out of the inside pocket of his jacket.

"Now, I know it's a little soon after St. Elizabeths—I'm aware that you're both recovering. But there's about to be some...rearrangements at the Quantico field office. I'm setting up a number of new units, specializing in different areas pertinent to Behavioral Science, and I'd like to continue the work that Agent Cooper started."

He hands them both envelopes.

Emma squeezes hers—it's heavy with papers. "Uh, Mr. Carter..."

"No. Please." He raises a hand. His palm is very pink against his black skin. "Don't give me an answer just yet. I'd really like you both to take a while to look over these documents. And I imagine you need to take a while just thinking about whether this is something you want."

The bureau has never before asked Emma about the things she wants. Carter has surprised her, which is hard to do these days.

"Anyway," Carter says, "that's the whole spiel. Thanks for hearing me out. There's a card in the envelope with my number on it, if you need to call."

"How long do we have to think it over?" Bell asks.

Carter is in the process of turning, but he turns back to answer. Now his smile is more relaxed. "Take your own sweet time, Mr. Bell. I believe you've both earned it."

He walks off.

Once he's given them some distance, Emma weighs the envelope in her hand. "Wow. Okay. That was...different. What do you think it means?"

Bell watches Carter make his way back up the church steps. "I think it means the bureau is trying to headhunt us. Again."

"What if we don't want to be headhunted?"

"Emma." Bell looks over at her. For a long moment, just the sound of the breeze in the leaves nearby. Then he tucks his envelope into his inside jacket pocket. "I don't know what you want to do with this. I think I know what I want to do. But whatever you decide, you know where I am. Any old time, any crazy situation..." He looks away, and grinning properly now, looks back. "I'm saying you can call me, Lewis. I'm here if you need."

He sticks his hand out. Emma shakes it. His hand is warmer than Carter's. Their fingers hold for just that little bit longer.

"Travel safe," she whispers. "Look after yourself, Travis."

"You too, Emma. Travel safe."

Bell smiles, bites his lip. Then he turns and walks back the way he came.

Emma watches him go. Then she turns, too, not toward the church, but back to face the view down the street.

The old oak hums nearby. Three paces take her up to it, and she puts her hand on the trunk to steady herself. Rough bark under her palm, and she's reminded of the trees near Quantico.

She tries not to think about Bell.

Do you think you're self-aware, Emma?

She doesn't want to hear Simon's voice now. She closes her eyes. Inhales and exhales deeply for a moment to stop the dizzy feeling.

Once she's sure she can move and breathe and think comfortably, Emma opens her eyes. Careful of her bandages, she takes off her jacket, slips off her formal shoes.

The envelope in her hand impedes her ability to carry everything, so she bends down and leans it against the base of the tree. She folds the jacket over her arm and picks up her shoes. She leaves the envelope where it is.

It's a short walk across the grass to the place where she parked the Rabbit. She unlocks the car and dumps her jacket and shoes on the back seat. Her running shoes are in the passenger footwell. She sits down on the edge of the passenger seat and pulls them on.

Emma Lewis, walking around the front of her car to get in behind the wheel, start the engine.

It's a six-and-a-half-hour drive back to Apple Creek.

AUTHOR'S NOTE

A lot of research goes into book-writing. I'm probably flagged on some government watchlist for weird internet searches and even weirder reading lists.

I'm grateful to the folks of *Trauma Fiction* and *Writer's Detective* FB groups for answering my various questions about debilitating injury, gory death, and law enforcement processes. Special thanks to my brother-in-law, Dr. Sebastian Corlette, for answering my bizarre queries about diethyl ether.

Many podcasts were listened to during the creation of *None Shall Sleep*. I'm particularly appreciative of the insight (and acknowledgment of the victims) of Laura Richards, Jim Clemente, and Lisa Zambetti, the hosts of *Real Crime Profile* on Wondery.

I'm a long-time fan of the work of John Douglas, whose book *Mindhunter* I first read in my twenties. While writing this book, I also read many of Douglas's other works, including *The Anatomy of Motive* and *Inside the Mind of BTK*. I'd also like to acknowledge the influence of Joe Penhall's Netflix series *Mindhunter*; Bryan Fuller's NBC series *Hannibal*; the work of Thomas Harris (especially *The Silence of the Lambs*, *Red Dragon*, and *Cari Mora*), Stephen King,

Barry Lyga, Leigh Bardugo, and Courtney Summers; and *The Psychopath Test* by Jon Ronson.

Including a list of author names would make a long index, but I consulted many open-source articles and academic papers related to forensic examination—ask me sometime about document analysis!—which I'd like to acknowledge.

I'd also like to thank personal contacts in the security services and within Sisters in Crime Australia, and initial contacts at the FBI. The FBI historical webpages are a great source of information, by the way, but I also read a number of articles by National Academy graduates and books on the history of the FBI, including *The Bureau* by Ronald Kessler.

ACKNOWLEDGMENTS

This is my ninth book, and it has been by far the easiest and the hardest one to write.

To Josh and Tracey Adams, my incredible agents. We got down to the wire with this one, but you held the line—thank you so, so much. Another massive thank-you to Caroline Walsh and Christabel McKinley, in the UK, for sharing this book outside the United States. My deepest gratitude, always, and long may the adventures continue!

To the extraordinary team at Little, Brown Books for Young Readers, all my thanks. I'm particularly grateful to my editor, Hannah Milton—for taking this journey with me, showing infinite wisdom, grace, and patience, and being as much of a *Mindhunter* fangirl as I am. Much appreciation to copyediting wizard Anna Dobbin and editorial assistant Ruqayyah Daud. Thank you to Janelle Barone, whose artistic work on the cover is an absolute knockout. Deep gratitude to the marketing and publicity team at LBYR, especially Siena Koncsol and Bill Grace, for getting this book into readers' hands. Many huge thank-yous to Hannah Koerner and the LBYR subrights team for their incredible hard work bringing this story to the world.

I'd like to acknowledge and give thanks to David Colón-Cabrera, who provided invaluable feedback around representation and encouraged the manuscript's improvement. I'd like to thank Shanese Mullins from LBYR for her excellent input.

I'd also like to thank Pam Gruber, who first championed this book.

Hugs and thanks also to Jodie Webster, Sophie Splatt, and Eva Mills at Allen & Unwin for your awesome support, always, and for everything you've done to bring Emma, Travis, Kristin, and Simon to readers in Australia.

Speaking of readers, this book would be nothing without you. High fives to my newsletter mates and to every supportive friend, reader, blogger, and booktuber who has connected with me online, especially on Twitter. You're awesome, and I thank you from the bottom of my heart. I pray you're never forced to listen to Simon recite Byronic poetry.

This book was first conceived on a winter writing retreat in 2018, when I said, "I want to write a YA serial killer thriller," and C. S. Pacat said, "That sounds amazing." During long evening phone calls and frenetic brainstorming sessions, she has been the colleague who has kept me focused, inspired, and (mostly) sane. This book would not have been written without her unstinting support and friendship, and I am forever grateful.

When I needed ideas and advice (OMG, so much advice) and time and quiet space to complete the book, Amie Kaufman gave me all those things and more. She is a gem. Amie, all the love to you and your fam.

I'm deeply grateful to Amanda for getting as excited about serial killers as me, and sharing resources, podcasts, and ideas. I'd also like to thank Jay Kristoff for his advice and Fist-Bumps of Encouragement, and for letting me borrow his wife's true-crime brain from time to time.

Everyone should have friends like Eliza Tiernan and Sarah Mayberry, who read the manuscript and declared it good and offered incredible insight. Thanks also to Liz Barr, who encouraged me to make Simon a real boy. Thank you to Kate Armstrong for explaining about Washington traffic, among other things. Thank you to Emma Viskic and Sulari Gentill for crime-fiction wisdom. I'm extra grateful to Jodi McAlister for adding to my store of knowledge about fairy princes.

I want to thank all the other members of the House of Progress, including Nicole, Lili, Peta, Ebony, Dave, Will, Kate, and Skye—I'd never have done this without your collective help. I'd also like to thank the women of the Vault, and I send lots of love to Fleur, Rachael, Nic, Gabrielle, Trin, and Bec. Thanks to other Australian writing compatriots, especially Angela, Kylie, Izzie, Alison, Nova, Simmone, Emily, Cate, Kelly, and Michael. I've probably left some people out, sorry—but friends, I see you, and I appreciate you every day.

I've been endlessly supported by Sisters in Crime Australia—special thanks to Carmel and Jacqui. All gratitude to friends from the Castlemaine community who understand what's going on when I'm wearing that glaze-eyed expression, especially Andy Johnston. Honorable mentions to Adele Walsh and Danielle Binks for YA enthusiasm. And I would like to thank Writers Victoria, for many years of assistance and for being generally excellent.

I've left the most important thanks for last—this book would not have been possible without the support and understanding of my family. Lots of love and hugs to Lucy, Bae, Millie, and Frankie.

Biggest love of all to my boys, Ben, Alex, Will, and Ned, who inspire me and encourage me every single day (even when I want to listen to that playlist of songs from 1982 *again*). And finally, it's Geoff who makes me omelets and reminds me to look after myself and picks up the slack and keeps me on the level. Love you so much, babe.

xxEllie

Christopher Tovo

ELLIE MARNEY

is an award-winning author of nine YA crime fiction titles, including the Every and Circus Hearts series and the novels *No Limits* and *White Night*. She has been behind the scenes at Westminster Public Mortuary in London and interviewed forensic autopsy specialists around the world in pursuit of just the right gory details—she may or may not know how to commit the perfect murder. Ellie has lived in Indonesia, India, and Singapore, and is now based in Australia with her partner and their four sons. Find out more at elliemarney.com.